THE GENERAL'S DAUGHTER

NELSON DEMILLE

THE GENERAL'S DAUGHTER

HarperCollins*Publishers*

HarperCollins*Publishers*
77–85 Fulham Palace Road,
Hammersmith, London W6 8JB

Published by HarperCollins*Publishers* 1993
9 8 7 6 5 4 3 2

A catalogue record for this book is
available from the British Library

ISBN 0 00 224051 3

Set in Times

Printed in Great Britain by
HarperCollins Manufacturing Glasgow

For Mom and Dad, Dennis
and Lillian, Lance and Joanie

Many thanks to my *consiglieri*,
Dave Westermann, Mike Tryon,
Len Ridini, Tom Eschmann, Steve Astor,
John Betts, and Nick Ellison.
Mille grazie.

What the dead had no speech for,
    when living,
They can tell you, being dead: the
    communication
Of the dead is tongued with fire beyond
    the language of the living.

T. S. Eliot
Four Quartets. ''Little Gidding''

THE GENERAL'S DAUGHTER

CHAPTER ONE

Is this seat taken?'' I asked the attractive young woman sitting by herself in the lounge.

She looked up from her newspaper but didn't reply.

I sat opposite her at the cocktail table and put down my beer. She went back to her paper and sipped on her drink, a bourbon and Coke. I inquired, ''Come here often?''

''Go away.''

''What's your sign?''

''No trespassing.''

''Don't I know you from somewhere?''

''No.''

''Yes. NATO Headquarters in Brussels. We met at a cocktail party.''

''Perhaps you're right,'' she conceded. ''You got drunk and threw up in the punch bowl.''

''Small world,'' I said. And indeed it was. Cynthia Sunhill, the woman sitting across from me now, was more than a casual acquaintance. In fact, we were once involved, as they say. Apparently she chose not to remember much of it. I said, ''*You* threw up. I told you bourbon and Coke wasn't good for your stomach.''

''*You* are not good for my stomach.''

1

You'd think by her attitude that I had walked out on her rather than vice versa.

We were sitting in the cocktail lounge of the Officers' Club at Fort Hadley, Georgia. It was the Happy Hour, and everyone there seemed happy, save for us two. I was dressed in a blue civilian suit, she in a nice pink knit dress that brought out her tan, her auburn hair, her hazel eyes, and other fondly remembered anatomy. I inquired, "Are you here on assignment?"

"I'm not at liberty to discuss that."

"Where are you staying?"

No reply.

"How long will you be here?"

She went back to her newspaper.

I asked, "Did you marry that guy you were seeing on the side?"

She put down the paper and looked at me. "I was seeing *you* on the side. I was *engaged* to him."

"That's right. Are you still engaged?"

"None of your business."

"It could be."

"Not in this lifetime," she informed me, and hid behind her paper again.

I didn't see an engagement ring or a wedding ring, but in our business that didn't mean much, as I'd learned in Brussels.

Cynthia Sunhill, by the way, was in her late twenties, and I'm in my early forties, so ours was not a May–November romance, but more May–September. Maybe August.

It lasted a year while we were both stationed in Europe, and her fiancé, a Special Forces major, was stationed in Panama. Military life is tough on relationships of all kinds, and the defense of Western civilization makes people horny.

Cynthia and I had separated a little over a year before this chance encounter, under circumstances that can best be described as messy. Apparently neither she nor I had gotten over it; I was still hurting and she was still pissed off. The betrayed fiancé looked a little annoyed, too, the last time I saw him in Brussels with a pistol in his hand.

THE GENERAL'S DAUGHTER

The O Club at Hadley is vaguely Spanish in architecture, perhaps Moorish, which may have been why *Casablanca* popped into my mind, and I quipped out of the side of my mouth, "Of all the gin joints in the world, she walks into mine."

Either she didn't get it or she wasn't in a smiling mood, because she continued to read her newspaper, the *Stars and Stripes*, which nobody reads, at least not in public. But Cynthia is a bit of a goody-goody, a dedicated, loyal, and enthusiastic soldier with none of the cynicism and world-weariness that most men display after a few years on this job. "Hearts filled with passion, jealousy, and hate," I prompted.

Cynthia said, "Go away, Paul."

"I'm sorry I ruined your life," I said sincerely.

"You couldn't even ruin my day."

"You broke my heart," I said with more sincerity.

"I'd like to break your neck," she replied with real enthusiasm.

I could see that I was rekindling something in her, but I don't think it was passion.

I remembered a poem I used to whisper to her in our more intimate moments, and I leaned toward her and said softly, " 'There hath none pleased mine eyes but Cynthia, none delighted mine ears but Cynthia, none possessed my heart but Cynthia. I have forsaken all other fortunes to follow Cynthia, and here I stand, ready to die if it pleases Cynthia.' "

"Good. Drop dead." She stood and left.

"Play it again, Sam." I finished my beer, stood, and walked back to the bar.

I sidled up to the long bar among men who had seen some of life; men with chests full of medals and Combat Infantry Badges, men with campaign ribbons from Korea, Vietnam, Grenada, Panama, and the Gulf. The guy to my right, a full colonel with gray hair, said, "War is hell, son, but hell hath no fury like a woman scorned."

"Amen."

"Saw the whole thing in the bar mirror," he informed me.

"Bar mirrors are interesting," I replied.

"Yup." In fact, he was studying me in the bar mirror now. Apropos of my civilian attire, he asked, "You retired?"

"Yes." But in fact, I was not.

He gave me his opinion of women in the military—"They squat to piss. Try doing that with sixty pounds of field gear"—then announced, "Gotta go drain the dragon," and ambled off to the men's room, where I presume he stood at the urinal.

I made my way out of the club into the hot August night and got into my Chevy Blazer. I drove through the main post, which is sort of like a downtown without zoning, encompassing everything from a PX and commissary to misplaced barracks and a deserted tank maintenance facility.

Fort Hadley is a small post in south Georgia, founded in 1917 to train infantry troops to be sent into the meat grinder on the Western Front. The area of the military reservation, however, is quite large— over 100,000 acres of mostly wooded terrain, suitable for war games, survival courses, guerrilla warfare training, and so on.

The Infantry School is phasing out now, and much of the post looks forlorn. But there is a Special Operations School here, the purpose of which seems somewhat vague, or perhaps, to be charitable, I could say experimental. As far as I can determine, the school is a mixture of psychological warfare, troop morale studies, isolation and deprivation studies, stress management courses, and other head and mind games. It sounds a bit sinister, but knowing the Army, whatever the original bright idea was, it has since become Drill and Ceremonies, and spit-shined boots.

To the north of Fort Hadley lies the medium-sized town of Midland, a typical Army town in some ways, populated with retired military personnel, civilian employees of the base, people who sell things to soldiers, as well as those who have nothing to do with the military and like it fine that way.

Midland was an English trading post as early as 1710, and before that it was an outpost of the Spanish colony of St. Augustine in Florida. Prior to that, it was an Indian town, the center of the Upatoi Nation. The Spanish burned the Indian town, the English burned the Spanish outpost, the French burned the English trading post, the British army burned and abandoned their fort there during the Revolution, and finally, the Yankees burned it in 1864. Looking at the place today, you wonder what all the fuss was about. Anyway, they've got a good volunteer fire department now.

I got on the interstate that skirts Fort Hadley and Midland and drove north, out into the open country toward a deserted trailer park. This was where I was temporarily staying, and I found the isolation convenient in terms of my job.

My job. I am an officer in the United States Army. My rank is unimportant, and in my line of work, it's also a secret. I am in the Criminal Investigation Division, the CID, and in the Army, which is very rank-conscious, the best rank to have is no rank. But, in fact, like most CID personnel, I am a warrant officer, a specialized rank that exists between noncommissioned officers and commissioned officers. This is a pretty good rank because you have most of the privileges of an officer but not much of the command responsibility, or the Mickey Mouse crap that goes along with it. Warrant officers are addressed as "Mister," and CID investigators often wear civilian clothing as I was that evening. There are times when I even have illusions that I'm a civilian.

There are, however, occasions when I do wear a uniform. On these occasions, the Department of the Army issues me orders with a new name, a rank appropriate to the case, and a uniform to match. I report for duty into a unit where my quarry is working, and I go about my assigned duties while gathering evidence for the judge advocate general.

When you're undercover, you have to be a jack-of-all-trades. I've been everything from a cook to a chemical warfare specialist—though in the Army that's not such a big difference. It's sort of difficult to get away with some of these roles, but I get by on my charm. It's all illusion anyway. So is my charm.

There are four warrant officer grades, and I'm topped out at grade four. All us fours are holding our breaths waiting for Congress to approve a five and six. Some of us have died of asphyxiation waiting.

Anyway, I'm part of a special CID team, a sort of elite unit, though I hesitate to use that word. What makes us special is that we're all long-time veterans with good arrest and conviction records. What also makes us special is that I have extraordinary powers to cut through Army red tape, which in the military is like having a magic mushroom in a Nintendo game. One of those extraordinary powers is the power to make an arrest of any military person any-where in the world, regardless of rank. I wouldn't push this and attempt to arrest one of the Joint Chiefs for speeding, but I always wanted to see how far I could go. I was about to find out.

My permanent duty station is at CID Headquarters in Falls Church, Virginia, but my cases take me all over the world. Travel, adventure, free time, mental and physical challenges, and bosses who leave me alone—what more could a man want? Oh, yes, women. There's some of that, too. Brussels wasn't the last time I had a woman, but it was the last time it mattered.

Unfortunately, there are some men who get their fun and chal-lenges in other ways. Sexual assault. Murder. That's what happened on that hot August night at Fort Hadley, Georgia. The victim was Captain Ann Campbell, daughter of Lieutenant General Joseph "Fighting Joe" Campbell. As if that weren't bad enough, she was young, beautiful, talented, bright, and a West Point graduate. She was the pride of Fort Hadley, the darling of the Army public rela-tions people, a poster girl for Army recruiters, a spokesperson for the new, nonsexist Army, a Gulf War veteran, and so forth and so on. Therefore, I wasn't particularly surprised when I heard that someone raped and murdered her. She had it coming. Right? Wrong.

But I didn't know any of that during the Happy Hour at the O Club. In fact, while I had been speaking to Cynthia, and talking man talk with that colonel at the bar, Captain Ann Campbell was still alive and was actually fifty feet away in the O Club dining room finishing a meal of salad, chicken, white wine, and coffee, as I learned during my subsequent investigation.

I arrived at the trailer park, set among the pine trees, and parked my Blazer some distance from my mobile home. I walked in the dark along a path of rotted planking. A few unoccupied trailers were scattered around the clearing, but mostly there were empty lots marked by cement blocks upon which there once sat about a hundred mobile homes.

There was still electric and telephone service available and a well that provided running water, which I made potable by adding Scotch whisky to it.

I unlocked the door of my trailer, stepped inside, and turned on the light, which revealed a kitchen/dining room/living room combination.

I thought of the trailer as a time capsule in which nothing had changed since about 1970. The furniture was sort of an avocado-green plastic, and the kitchen appliances were a kind of mustard color that I think used to be called harvest gold. The walls were paneled in a dark plywood, and the carpeting was a red and black plaid. If one were color-sensitive, this place could induce fits of depression and suicide.

I took off my jacket and tie, turned on the radio, got a beer from the refrigerator, and sat in the armchair that was bolted to the floor. There were three framed prints screwed to the walls, a bullfighter, a seascape, and a reproduction of Rembrandt's ''Aristotle Contemplating the Bust of Homer.'' I sipped my beer and contemplated Aristotle contemplating Homer's bust.

This particular trailer park, named Whispering Pines, if anyone cares, was developed by a few enterprising retired sergeants in the late sixties when it appeared that the war in Asia was going to last forever. Fort Hadley, an Infantry Training Center, was bursting with soldiers and their dependents back then, and I remember Whispering Pines when it was full of young married soldiers who were author- ized—actually encouraged—to live off post. There was an aboveground pool crammed with kids and young Army wives, and there was too much drinking, and too much boredom, and too little money, and the future was obscured by the fog of war.

The American dream was not supposed to look like this, and when the men went off to the war, too often other men came in the night to the bedroom at the back of the long, narrow trailers. In fact, I had lived here then and had gone off to war, and someone took my place in the bed and took my young wife. But that was a few wars ago, and so much has happened since, that the only lingering bitterness left is that the bastard also took my dog.

I read a few magazines, had a few more beers, thought of Cynthia, and didn't think of Cynthia.

Normally, I have a little more fun than this, but I had to be at the post armory at 0500 hours, a.k.a. five A.M.

CHAPTER TWO

The post armory. A cornucopia of American high-tech military goodies—things that go boom in the night.

I was on undercover assignment at the armory in the early morning hours near the time when Ann Campbell was murdered, which is why I caught the squeal, as my civilian counterparts would say. Some weeks earlier, I had assumed the duties and outward appearances of a slightly seedy supply sergeant named Franklin White, and with a real seedy supply sergeant named Dalbert Elkins, we were about to close a deal to sell a few hundred M-16 rifles, grenade launchers, and sundry other dangerous items from the armory to a group of Cuban freedom fighters who wanted to overthrow Mr. Fidel Castro, the Antichrist. In fact, the Hispanic gentlemen were Colombian drug dealers, but they wanted to make us feel better about the transaction. Anyway, I was sitting in the armory at 0600 hours, conversing with my coconspirator, Staff Sergeant Elkins. We were talking about what we were going to do with the $200,000 we would split. Sergeant Elkins was actually going to jail for the rest of his life, but he didn't know that, and men have to dream. It's my unpleasant duty to become their worst nightmare.

The phone rang, and I picked up the receiver before my new buddy could grab it. I said, "Post armory, Sergeant White speaking."

9

"Ah, there you are," said Colonel William Kent, the post provost marshal, Fort Hadley's top cop. "I'm glad I found you."

"I didn't know I was lost," I replied. Prior to my chance encounter with Cynthia, Colonel Kent was the only person on the post who knew who I was, and the only reason I could think of for him to be calling me was to tell me I was in imminent danger of being found out. I kept one eye on Sergeant Elkins and one on the door.

But as luck would have it, it wasn't as simple as that. Colonel Kent informed me, "There's been a homicide. A female captain. Maybe raped. Can you talk?"

"No."

"Can you meet me?"

"Maybe." Kent was a decent sort of guy, but like most MP types, he wasn't overly clever, and the CID made him nervous. I said, "I'm working, obviously."

"This is going to take priority, Mr. Brenner. It's a big one."

"So is this." I glanced at Sergeant Elkins, who was eyeing me carefully.

Kent said, "It was General Campbell's daughter."

"My goodness." I thought a moment. All my instincts said to avoid any cases that involved the rape and murder of a general's daughter. It was a lose-lose situation. My sense of duty, honor, and justice assured me that some other sucker in the special unit of the CID could handle it. Somebody whose career was down the toilet anyway. I thought of several candidates. But, duty and honor aside, my natural curiosity was aroused. I asked Colonel Kent, "Where can I meet you?"

"I'll meet you in the provost building parking lot and take you to the scene."

Being undercover, I shouldn't be anywhere near the provost marshal's office, but Kent is annoyingly dense. I said, "Not your place."

"Oh . . . how about the infantry barracks? The Third Battalion HQ. It's on the way."

Elkins, tense and paranoid already, was getting fidgety. I said to

10

Kent, "Okay, sweetheart. Ten minutes." I hung up and said to Sergeant Elkins, "My girlfriend. Needs some lovin'."

Elkins looked at his watch. "Kinda late . . . or early . . ."

"Not for this little gal."

Elkins smiled.

As per armory regulations, I was wearing a sidearm, and, satisfied that Elkins was cooled out, I unhooked the pistol belt and left it there as per post regulations. I didn't know then that I would need a weapon later. I said to Elkins, "Might be back."

"Yeah, okay. Give her one for me, boy."

"Sure thing."

I had left my Blazer back at the trailer park, and my POV— that's Army talk for privately owned vehicle, not point of view— was now a Ford pickup truck, issued to me for my current impersonation. It was complete with shotgun rack, dog hair on the upholstery, and a pair of hip waders in the back.

So off I went, through the main post. Within a few minutes I was into the area of the Infantry Training Brigade, long wooden World War II era barracks, mostly deserted now and looking dark and spooky. The cold war is over, and the Army, while not exactly withering away, is definitely downsizing, and the combat arms branches—the infantry, armor, and artillery, the reason for the Army's existence—are taking the biggest cuts. The CID, however, dealing as it does with crime, is a growth organization.

As a young private, I graduated Advanced Infantry Training School here at Fort Hadley many years ago, then went to Airborne School and Ranger School at Fort Benning, not far from here. So I'm an Airborne Ranger—the ultimate weapon, a killing machine, mean, lean, death from the skies, good to go, and so on. But I'm a little older now and the CID suits me fine.

Ultimately, even government institutions have to justify their existence, and the Army was doing a good job of finding a new role for itself in knocking around pissant countries who get out of line. But I've noticed a certain lack of esprit and purpose in the officers and men who had always felt that they were the only thing standing between the Russian hordes and their loved ones. It's sort of like a boxer, training for years for the title match, then finding out that the other contender just dropped dead. You're a little relieved, but there's also a letdown, a hollow place where your adrenaline pump used to be.

Anyway, it was that time of day that the Army calls first light, and the Georgia sky was turning pink, and the air was heavy with humidity, and you could figure out it was going to be a ninety-degree day. I could smell the wet Georgia clay, the pine trees, and the aroma of Army coffee wafting out of a nearby mess hall, or as we call it now, a dining facility.

I pulled off the road and onto the grassy field in front of the old Battalion Headquarters. Colonel Kent got out of his official olive-drab car, and I got out of my pickup truck.

Kent is about fifty, tall, medium build, with a pockmarked face and icy blue eyes. He's a bit stiff at times, not clever, as I said, but hardworking and efficient. He's the military equivalent of a chief of police, commanding all the uniformed military police at Fort Hadley. He's a stickler for rules and regulations, and, while not disliked, he's not anyone's best buddy.

Kent was all spiffy in his provost marshal's uniform with his white helmet, white pistol belt, and spit-shined boots. He said to me, "I have six MPs securing the scene. Nothing has been touched."

"That's a start." Kent and I have known each other about ten years, and we've developed a good working relationship, though in fact I only see him about once a year when a case brings me to Fort Hadley. Kent outranks me, but I can be familiar with him, actually give him a hard time, as long as I'm the investigating officer on the case. I've seen him testify at courts-martial, and he's everything a prosecutor could ask for in a cop: believable, logical, unemotional, and organized in his testimony. Yet, there's something about him that didn't play right, and I always had the feeling that the prosecutors were happy to get him off the stand. I think, maybe, he comes across as a little *too* stiff and unfeeling. When the Army has to court-martial one of its own, there is usually some sympathy, or at least concern, for the accused. But Kent is one of those cops who only sees black and white, and anyone who breaks the law at Fort Hadley has personally affronted Colonel Kent. I actually saw him smile once when a young recruit, who burned down a deserted barracks in a drunken stupor, got ten years for arson. But the law is the law, I suppose, and such a brittle personality as William Kent has found his niche in life. That's why I was a little surprised to discover that he was somewhat shaken by the events of that morning. I asked him, "Have you informed General Campbell?"

"No."

"Perhaps you'd better go to his house."

He nodded, not very enthusiastically. He looked awful, actually, and I deduced that he'd been to the scene himself. I informed Colonel Kent, "The general is going to have your ass for delaying notification."

He explained, "Well, I didn't have a positive identification until I saw the body myself. I mean, I couldn't go to his house and tell him that his daughter—"

"Who made the tentative identification?"

"A Sergeant St. John. He found the body."

"And he knew her?"

"They were on duty together."

"Well, that's a pretty positive identification. And you knew her?"

"Yes, of course. I made a positive identification."

"Not to mention dog tags and the name on her uniform."

"Well, that's all gone."

"Gone?"

"Yes . . . whoever did it took her uniform and dog tags . . ."

You get a sense for these things, or maybe you get a backlog of cases stored in your head, and when you hear the evidence and see the scene, you ask yourself, "What's wrong with this picture?" I asked Colonel Kent, "Underwear?"

"What? Oh . . . it's there . . ." He added, "Usually they take the underwear. Right? This is weird."

"Is Sergeant St. John a suspect?"

13

Colonel Kent shrugged. "That's your job."

"Well, with a name like St. John, we'll give him the benefit of the doubt for the moment." I looked around at the deserted barracks, the Battalion Headquarters, the mess hall, and the company assembly areas overgrown with weeds now, and in the gray light of dawn, I could imagine the young troops falling in for roll call. I can still remember being always tired, cold, and hungry before breakfast. I remember, too, being frightened, knowing that ninety percent of us standing there in formation were going to Vietnam, and knowing that the casualty rate among the frontline troops was high enough so that a Midland bookie wouldn't give you better than two-to-one odds that you'd make it back in the same shape you left. I said to Kent, "That was my company over there. Delta Company."

"I didn't know you were infantry."

"Long time ago. Before I became a copper. You?"

"Always an MP. But I saw some stuff in 'Nam. I was at the American Embassy when the Cong came over the walls that time. January '68." He added, "I killed one of them."

I nodded. "Sometimes I think the infantry was better. The bad guys were never one of your own. This crap is different."

"Bad guys are bad guys," Kent informed me. "The Army is the Army. Orders are orders."

"Yup." And therein lies the essence of military mentality. Ours is not to reason why, and there is no excuse for failure. This works pretty well in combat and most other military-type situations, but not in the CID. In the CID you must actually disobey orders, think for yourself, ignore the brass, and, above all, discover the truth. This does not always sit well in the military, which thinks of itself as a big family, where people still like to believe that "all the brothers are valiant, and all the sisters virtuous."

As though reading my thoughts, Colonel Kent said, "I know this could be a real messy case. But maybe not. Maybe it was committed by a civilian. Maybe it can be wrapped up right away."

"Oh, I'm sure it can, Bill. And you and I will get letters of commendation inserted into our permanent files, and General Campbell will invite us for cocktails.''

Kent looked very troubled. He said, ''Well, my ass is on the line here, frankly. This is my post, my beat. You can beg off if you want and they'll send another homicide guy. But you happen to be here and you happen to be special unit, and we've worked together before, and I'd like your name next to mine on the prelim report.''

''And you didn't even bring me a cup of coffee.''

He smiled grimly. ''Coffee? Hell, I need a drink.'' He added, ''You can get some rank out of this.''

''If you mean a reduction, you're probably right. If you mean a promotion, I'm topped out.''

''Sorry. I forgot. Bad system.''

I asked him, ''Are you up for a star?''

''Maybe.'' He looked a bit worried, as if the twinkling general's star that he'd seen in his dreams just blinked out.

I asked, ''Have you notified the local CID yet?''

''No.''

''Why in the world not?''

''Well . . . this is not going to be handled by them, anyway . . . I mean, Jesus, this is the post commander's daughter, and the CID commander here, Major Bowes, knew her, and so did everyone else here, so we need to show the general that we've gotten top talent from Falls Church—''

''The word you're looking for is scapegoat. But, okay, I'll tell my boss in Falls Church that this is best handled by a special investigator, but I don't know if I'm the guy who wants to do it.''

''Let's go see the body, then you can decide.''

As we started to walk to his car, we heard the post cannon boom—actually a recording of some long-scrapped artillery piece—and we stopped and faced the direction of the sound. From the loudspeakers mounted on the empty barracks came the recorded bugle sound of reveille, and we saluted, two solitary men standing in the predawn light, reacting to a lifetime of conditioning and centuries of military custom and ceremony.

15

The ancient bugle call, going back to the Crusades, echoed through the company streets and the alleyways between the barracks, and over the grassy assembly fields, and somewhere, the flags were being raised.

It's been years since I've been caught outdoors at reveille, but I sort of enjoy the pomp and ceremony once in a while, the communion with the living and the dead, the idea that there is something bigger and more important than I, and that I am part of it.

There is no civilian equivalent of this, unless watching *Good Morning America* has become a tradition, and though I'm on the periphery of Army life, I don't know if I'm ready yet to make the transition to civilian life. But that decision might already be in the making. Sometimes you sense when the last act has begun.

The final sounds of the bugle died away, and Kent and I continued toward his car. He remarked to me, "Another day begins at Fort Hadley, but one of its soldiers will not see it."

CHAPTER THREE

We headed south in Kent's car toward the far reaches of the military reservation.

Colonel Kent began: "Captain Ann Campbell and Sergeant Harold St. John were on duty at Post Headquarters. She was duty officer, he was duty sergeant."

"Did they know each other?"

Kent shrugged. "Maybe in passing. They don't work together. He's in the motor pool. She's an instructor at the Special Operations School. They just came down on orders and wound up together."

"What does she teach?"

"Psy-ops." He added, "She's got—she had a master's in psychology."

"Still has." There's always a question of tenses when referring to the recently dead. I asked Kent, "Do instructors usually pull that sort of duty?"

"No, not usually. But Ann Campbell put her name on several duty rosters she didn't have to be on." He added, "She tried to set an example. General's daughter."

"I see." The Army runs duty rosters for officers, noncommissioned officers, and enlisted men and women. These are completely random lists, ensuring that as nearly as possible everyone gets his or her chance at some sort of crap duty. There was a time when

17

female personnel were not on all lists, such as guard duty, but times change. What doesn't change is that young ladies walking around alone at night are at some risk. The hearts of evil men remain the same; the compulsion to stick it in the most available vagina supersedes Army regulations. I asked, ''And she was armed?''

''Sure. Had her sidearm.''

''Go on.''

''Well, at about 0100 hours, Campbell says to St. John that she is going to take the jeep and check the guard posts—''

''Why? Isn't that something the sergeant of the guard or the officer of the guard should do? The duty officer should stay with the phones.''

Kent replied, ''St. John said the officer of the guard was some young lieutenant, still pissing water from West Point. And Campbell, as I've indicated, is gung ho and she wants to go out there and check things for herself. She knew the sign and countersign, so off she goes.'' Kent turned onto Rifle Range Road. He continued, ''At about 0300 hours, St. John says he got a little concerned—''

''Why concerned?''

''I don't know . . . You know, it's a woman and—well, maybe he was annoyed because he thought she was goofing off somewhere and maybe he wanted to go to the latrine and didn't want to leave the phones.''

''How old is this guy?'' I asked.

''Fifty something. Married. Good record.''

''Where is he now?''

''Back at the provost building catching some cot time. I told him to stay put.''

We had passed rifle ranges one, two, three, and four, all of which lie to the right of the road, huge expanses of flat, open terrain, backed by a continuous earthen berm. I hadn't been out here in over twenty years, but I remembered the place.

Colonel Kent continued, ''So St. John calls the guardhouse, but Captain Campbell is not there. He asks the sergeant of the guard to call the guard posts and see if Campbell has come by. The sergeant of the guard calls back a while later and reports negative. So St. John asks the sergeant of the guard to send a responsible person to headquarters to watch the phones, and when one of the guards shows up, St. John gets in his POV and heads out. He starts checking the posts in order—NCO Club, Officers' Club, and so on—but not one of the guards has seen Captain Campbell. So, at about 0400 hours, he goes out toward the last guard post, which is an ammo storage shed, and on the way, at rifle range six, he sees her jeep . . . in fact, there it is.''

Up ahead, off to the right on the narrow road, was the humvee, which we old guys still refer to as a jeep, in which, presumably, Ann Campbell had driven to her rendezvous with death, if you will. Near the humvee was someone's POV—a red Mustang. I asked Kent, ''Where is the guard post and the guard?''

''The ammo shed is another klick up the road. The guard, a PFC Robbins, heard nothing, but saw headlights.''

''You questioned him?''

''Her. Mary Robbins.'' Kent smiled for the first time. ''PFC is a gender-neutral term, Paul.''

''Thank you. Where is PFC Robbins now?''

''On a cot in the provost building.''

''Crowded in there. But good thinking.''

Kent stopped the car near the humvee and the red Mustang. It was nearly light now, and I could see the six MPs—four men, two women—standing at various spots around the area. All of the rifle ranges had open bleacher seats off to the left side of the road facing the ranges, where the troops received classroom instruction before proceeding to the firing line. In the nearby bleachers to my left sat a woman in jeans and windbreaker, writing on a pad. Kent and I got out of the car, and he said to me, ''That is Ms. Sunhill. She's a woman.''

I knew that. I asked Kent, ''Why is she here?''

''I called her.''

''Why?''

''She's a rape counselor.''

19

"The victim doesn't need counseling. She's dead."

"Yes," Kent agreed, "but Ms. Sunhill is also a rape investigator."

"Is that a fact? What is she doing at Hadley?"

"That female nurse, Lieutenant Neely. You know about that?"

"Only what I read in the papers. Could there be a connection between these cases?"

"No. An arrest was made yesterday."

"What time yesterday?"

"About four P.M. Ms. Sunhill made the arrest and by five P.M. we had a confession."

I nodded. And at six P.M. Ms. Sunhill was having a drink in the O Club, quietly celebrating her success, and Ann Campbell, I was about to discover, was alive and having dinner there, and I was at the bar watching Cynthia and trying to get up the courage to say hello or make a strategic withdrawal.

Kent added, "Sunhill was supposed to go off to another assignment today. But she says she'll stay for this."

"How lucky we are."

"Yes, it's good to have a woman on these kinds of things. And she's good. I saw her work."

"Indeed." I noticed that the red Mustang, which was probably Cynthia's car, had Virginia license plates, like my own POV, suggesting that she was working out of Falls Church, as I was. But fate had not caused our paths to cross at the home office but had put us here under these circumstances. It was inevitable, anyway.

I looked out over the rifle range, on which sat a morning mist. In front of the berm stood pop-up targets, at different ranges, dozens of nasty-looking fiberboard men with rifles. These lifelike targets have replaced the old black silhouette targets, the point being, I suppose, that if you're being trained to kill men, then the targets should look you in the eye. However, from past experience, I can tell you that nothing prepares you for killing men except killing men. In any case, birds were perched on many of the mock men, which sort of ruined the effect, at least until the first platoon of the day fired.

When I went through infantry training, the firing ranges were bare of vegetation, great expanses of sterile soil unlike any battlefield condition you were likely to encounter, except perhaps the desert. Now, many firing ranges, like this one, were planted with various types of vegetation to partially obscure the fields of fire. About fifty meters opposite of where I was standing on the road there was a pop-up silhouette partially hidden by tall grass and evergreen bushes. Standing around this target and vegetation were two MPs, a man and a woman. At the base of the silhouette, I could make out something on the ground that didn't belong there.

Colonel Kent said, "This guy was a sick puppy." He added, as if I didn't get it, "I mean, he did it to her right there on the rifle range, with that pop-up guy sort of looking down at her."

If only the pop-up guy could talk. I turned and looked around the area. Some distance behind the bleachers and the fire control towers was a tree line in which I could see latrine sheds. I said to Colonel Kent, "Have you searched the area for any other possible victims?"

"No . . . well . . . we didn't want to disturb evidence."

"But someone else may also be dead, or alive and in need of assistance. Evidence is secondary to aiding victims. Says so in the manual."

"Right . . ." He looked around and called to an MP sergeant. "Get on the horn and have Lieutenant Fullham's platoon get down here with the dogs."

Before the sergeant could respond, a voice from the top of the bleachers said, "I already did that."

I looked up at Ms. Sunhill. "Thank you."

"You're welcome."

I wanted to ignore her, but I knew this wasn't going to be possible. I turned and walked onto the rifle range. Kent followed.

As we walked, Kent's stride got a bit shorter, and he fell behind. The two MPs there were at parade rest, pointedly looking away from the ground upon which lay Captain Ann Campbell.

I stopped a few feet from the body, which was lying on its back. She was naked, as Kent had indicated, except for a sports watch on her left wrist. A few feet from the body lay what we call a commercially purchased undergarment—her bra. As Kent had also said, her uniform was missing from the scene. Also missing were her boots, socks, helmet, pistol belt, holster, and sidearm. More interestingly, perhaps, was the fact that Ann Campbell was spread-eagled on her back, her wrists and ankles bound to tent pegs with cord. The pegs were a green vinyl plastic, and the cord was green nylon, both Army issue.

Ann Campbell was about thirty and well built, the sort of build you see on female aerobic instructors with well-defined leg and arm muscles and not an ounce of flab. Despite her present condition, I recognized her face from Army posters. She was quite attractive in a clean-cut way, and wore her blond hair in a simple shoulder-length style, perhaps a few inches beyond regulations, which was the least of her problems at the moment.

Around her neck was a long length of the same nylon cord that bound her wrists and ankles, and beneath this cord were her panties, which had been pulled over her head, one leg of the panties around her neck, so that the cord did not bite directly into her neck, but was cushioned by the panties. I knew what this meant, but I don't think anyone else did.

Cynthia came up beside me, but said nothing.

I knelt beside the body and noted that the skin appeared waxy and translucent, causing the powder blush on her cheeks to stand out sharply. Her fingernails and toenails, which had only a clear lacquer on them, had lost their pinkish color. Her face was un-bruised, unscratched, and without lacerations or bite marks, and so were the parts of her body that I could see. Aside from the obscene position of her body, there were no outward signs of rape, no semen around the genitals, thighs, or in the pubic hair, no signs of struggle in the surrounding area, no grass or soil marks on her skin, no blood, dirt, or skin under her nails, and her hair was mostly in place.

I leaned over and touched her face and neck, where rigor mortis usually sets in first. There was no rigor, and I felt her underarms, which were still warm. There was some livor mortis, or lividity, that had settled into her thighs and buttocks, and the lividity was a deep purple color, which would be consistent with asphyxia, which in turn was consistent with the rope around her neck. I pressed my finger against the purplish skin above where her buttocks met the ground, and the depressed spot blanched. When I took my finger away, the livid color returned, and I was reasonably certain that death had occurred within the last four hours.

One thing I learned a long time ago was that you never take a witness's statement as gospel truth. But so far, Sergeant St. John's chronology seemed to hold up.

I bent over further and looked into Ann Campbell's large blue eyes, which stared unblinking into the sun. The corneas were not yet cloudy, reinforcing my estimate of a recent death. I pulled at one of her eyelids and saw in the linings around the eye, small spotty hemorrhages, which is presumptive evidence of death by asphyxia. So far, what Kent had told me, and the scene that presented itself, seemed to comport with what I was discovering.

I loosened the rope around Ann Campbell's neck and examined the panties beneath the rope. The panties were not torn and were not soiled by the body or by any foreign substance. There were no dog tags under the panties, so these, too, were missing. Where the ligature, the rope, had circled the neck there was only a faint line of bruising, barely discernible if you weren't looking for it. Yet, death had come by strangulation, and the panties lessened the damage the rope would normally have done to the throat and neck.

I stood and walked around the body, noting that the soles of her feet were stained with grass and soil, meaning she had walked barefoot for at least a few steps. I leaned down and examined the bottom of her feet, discovering on her right foot a small tar or blacktop stain on the soft fleshy spot below her big toe. It would appear that she had actually been barefoot back on the road, which might mean she had taken off her clothes, or at least her boots and socks, near the humvee and was made to walk here, fifty meters away, barefoot or perhaps naked, though her bra and panties were near the body. I examined her bra and saw that the front clasp was intact, not bent or broken, and there were no signs of dirt or stress on the fabric.

23

All this time no one said a word, and you could hear the morning birds in the trees, and the sun had risen above the line of white pines beyond the berm, and long morning shadows spread across the firing ranges.

I addressed Colonel Kent. "Who was the first MP on the scene?"

Kent called over the female MP nearby, a young PFC, and said to her, "Give your report to this man."

The MP, whose name tag said Casey, looked at me and reported, "I received a radio call at 0452 hours advising me that a female body had been found at rifle range six, approximately fifty meters west of a humvee parked on the road. I was in the vicinity and I proceeded to this location and reached the scene at 0501 hours and saw the humvee. I parked and secured my vehicle, took my M-16, and proceeded onto the rifle range, where I located the body. I felt for a pulse, listened for a heartbeat, tried to detect breathing, and shined my flashlight into the victim's eyes, but they did not respond to the light. I determined that the victim was dead."

I asked her, "Then what did you do?"

"I returned to my vehicle and called for assistance."

"You followed the same path to and from the body?"

"Yes, sir."

"Did you touch anything except the body? The ropes, the tent pegs, the undergarments?"

"No, sir."

"Did you touch the victim's vehicle?"

"No, sir. I did not touch the evidence beyond determining that the victim was dead."

"Anything else you want to mention?"

"No, sir."

"Thank you."

PFC Casey saluted, turned, and resumed her position.

Kent, Cynthia, and I glanced at one another, as if trying to see what the others were thinking, or feeling. Truly, moments like this try the soul and become indelibly burned into the mind. I have never forgotten a death scene, and never want to.

I looked down at Ann Campbell's face for a full minute, knowing I would not see it again. This is important, I think, because it establishes a communion between the living and the dead, between the investigator and the victim. Somehow it helps—not her, but me.

We went back to the road and walked around the humvee that Ann Campbell had driven, then looked inside the driver's side window, which was open. Many military vehicles have no ignition keys, only a starter button switch, and the switch on the humvee was in the off position. On the front passenger seat was a black leather nonmilitary-issue handbag. Cynthia said to me, ''I would have gone through the bag, but I didn't want to do that without your permission.''

''We're off to a good start. Retrieve the handbag.''

She went around to the passenger side, and, using a handkerchief, opened the door, took out the bag with the handkerchief, then sat on the lower bench of the bleachers and began laying out the contents.

I got down on the road and slid under the humvee, but there was nothing unusual on the blacktop. I touched the exhaust system at various points and found it slightly warm in spots.

I stood, and Colonel Kent said to me, ''Any ideas?''

''Well, a few possible scenarios come to mind. But I have to wait until forensic gets finished. I assume you called them.''

''Of course. They're on their way from Gillem.''

''Good.'' Fort Gillem is outside Atlanta, about two hundred miles north of Hadley, and the CID lab there is a state-of-the-art operation that handles all of North America. The people who work there are good, and like me they go where they're needed. Major crimes are still relatively rare in the Army, so the lab can usually muster the resources it needs when a big one comes down. In this case, they'd probably show up with a caravan. I said to Colonel Kent, ''When they get here, tell them to be very curious about a black smudge on the sole of her right foot. I want to know what it is.''

Kent nodded, probably thinking to himself, *Typical CID bullshit*. And he might well have been right.

"Also, I want you to do a grid search. Let's say two hundred meters in each direction from the body, excluding an area fifty meters immediately around the body." This would mess up any footprints, but there were hundreds of bootprints in the area of the rifle range anyway, and the only ones I was interested in were those within fifty meters of the body. I said to Kent, "I want your people to gather up anything that isn't natural flora—cigarette butts, buttons, paper, bottles, and all that, and record the grid where they found it. All right?"

"No problem. But I think this guy got in and got out clean. Probably by vehicle, just like the victim."

"I think you're right, but we're creating files."

"We're covering our asses."

"Right. We go by the book." Which was safe and sometimes even effective. Bottom line on this one, though, I was going to have to get real creative, and I was going to piss off a lot of important people. That's the fun part.

I said to Kent, "I need Captain Campbell's personnel and medical files sealed and in your office before noon."

"Okay."

"And I need an office at your place, and a clerk."

"One desk or two?"

I glanced at Cynthia. "I guess two desks. But I'm not committing to this yet."

"Don't blow smoke up my ass, Paul. You in or not?"

"I'll see what they say at Falls Church. Okay, delay notifying the public information officer until about ten hundred hours. Send two guys to Captain Campbell's office and physically remove her desk, furniture, and all her personal possessions, and have everything locked up in your evidence room. And have Sergeant St. John and PFC Robbins remain in the provost marshal's office until I can see them. I don't want anyone speaking a word of this until they've spoken to me. And it is your unpleasant duty, Colonel, to pay an official call on General and Mrs. Campbell at their home. Go unannounced and with an appropriate chaplain and a medical officer in case anyone needs a sedative or something. They may not view the body at the scene. Okay?''

Kent nodded and let out a long breath. ''Jesus Christ . . .''

''Amen. Meanwhile, instruct your people not to say a word about what we found here, and give forensic a set of disqualifying fingerprints from PFC Casey, and disqualifying bootprints from everyone here at the scene, including yourself, of course.''

''Right.''

''Also, tape off the latrine sheds and don't let anyone use them. Also, the latrines are off limits to forensic until I have a chance to check them out.''

''Okay.''

I walked over to Cynthia, who was now putting everything back in the handbag, still using a handkerchief. ''Anything interesting?''

''No. Basic stuff. Wallet, money, keys, and everything appears intact. Here's a chit from the O Club. She had dinner last night. Salad, chicken, white wine, and coffee.'' She added, ''She was probably there in the dining room about the same time we were having a drink.''

Kent had joined us and he asked, ''You two had drinks together? You know each other?''

I replied, ''We had drinks separately. We are nodding acquaintances.'' I asked Cynthia, ''Campbell's address?''

''Off post, unfortunately. Victory Gardens on Victory Drive in Midland. Unit forty-five.'' She added, ''I think I know the place— a town-house complex.''

Kent said, ''I'll call Chief Yardley—that's the Midland police chief, and he'll get a court order and he can meet us there.''

''No. We'll keep this in the family, Bill.''

''You can't go search her off-post house without a civilian search warrant—''

Cynthia handed me the keys from Ann Campbell's bag and said, ''I'll drive.''

Kent protested, ''You can't go off post without civilian authority.''

I detached Ann Campbell's car keys from the key chain and gave them to Kent, along with the victim's handbag. "Find out where her car is and impound it."

As we walked toward Cynthia's Mustang, I said to Kent, "You should stay here to direct things. When you write your report, you can write that I said I was going to the Midland police. I'll take responsibility for my change of mind."

"Yardley is a tough, redneck son-of-a-bitch," Kent informed me. "He'll get your ass, Paul."

"He has to stand in line and wait his turn." To get Kent squared away so he didn't do anything stupid, I said, "Look, Bill, I have to have first look at Ann Campbell's place. I have to remove anything that might embarrass her, her family, the Army, or her military colleagues and friends. Right? Then we'll let Chief Yardley have his shot at the house. Okay?"

He seemed to process this correctly and nodded.

Cynthia got behind the wheel of her Mustang and I got in the passenger seat. I said to Kent, "I may call you from there. Think positive."

Cynthia threw the five-liter Mustang into first gear, made a U-turn, and we were off, zero to sixty in about six seconds, along the lonely Rifle Range Road.

I listened to the engine for a while and neither of us spoke, then Cynthia said, "I feel queasy."

"Pretty awful," I agreed.

"Disgusting." She glanced at me. "Are you used to it?"

"God, no." I added, "I don't see that many homicides and not many like this."

She nodded, then took a deep breath. "I think I can help you on this one. But I don't want it to be awkward."

"No problem," I said. "But we'll always have Brussels."

"Where?"

"Belgium. The capital." *Bitch.*

We sat in silence, then Cynthia asked, "Why?"

"Why is Brussels the capital? Or why will we always have it?"

"No, Paul, why was she *murdered*?"

28

"Oh . . . well, the possible motives in homicide cases," I replied, "are profit, revenge, jealousy, to conceal a crime, to avoid humiliation or disgrace, and homicidal mania. Says so in the manual."

"And what do you think?"

"Well, when rape precedes homicide, it usually comes down to revenge or jealousy or possibly to conceal the identity of the rapist. She may have known him, or she could have identified him afterward if he wasn't wearing a mask or disguise." I added, "On the other hand, this certainly looks like a lust murder, the work of a homicidal rapist—a person who gets his sexual release from the killing itself, and he may not even have penetrated her with his penis. That's what it looks like, but we don't know yet."

Cynthia nodded, but offered nothing.

I asked her, "What do *you* think?"

She let a few seconds go by, then replied, "Obviously premeditated. The perpetrator had a rape kit—the tent pegs, rope, and presumably something to drive the pegs into the ground. The perpetrator must have been armed in order to overcome the victim's own weapon."

"Go on."

"Well, the perpetrator got the drop on her, then made her toss away her weapon, then made her strip and walk out on the rifle range."

"Okay. I'm trying to picture how he managed to stake her out and still keep her under his control. I don't think she was the submissive type."

Cynthia replied, "Neither do I. But there may have been two of them. And I wouldn't make the assumption that the perpetrator or perpetrators was a *he* until we have some lab evidence."

"Okay." I was obviously having trouble with personal pronouns this morning. "Why weren't there any signs of struggle on her part, or brutalization on his—on the perpetrator's part?"

She shook her head. "Don't know. You usually get some brutalization . . . The ligature isn't what you'd call friendly, however."

"No," I replied, "but the guy didn't hate her."

29

"He didn't like her much, either."

"He may have. Look, Cynthia, you do this stuff for a living. Does this resemble any rape you've ever seen or heard about?"

She mulled that over, then said, "It has some of the elements of what we call an organized rape. The assailant planned a rape. But I don't know if the assailant knew her, or if the assailant was just cruising and she was a victim of opportunity."

"The assailant may have been in uniform," I suggested, "which was why she was not on her guard."

"Possible."

I looked out the open window, smelled the morning dews and damps among the thick pines, and felt the rising sun on my face. I rolled up the window and sat back, trying to picture what preceded what I had just seen, like running the film backward; Ann Campbell staked out on the ground, then standing naked, then walking from the jeep, and so on. A lot of it didn't compute.

Cynthia broke into my thoughts. "Paul, the uniform had her name tag on it, and so did her dog tags, obviously, and probably her helmet and boots had her name stenciled inside. So what do the missing items have in common? Her name. Correct?"

"Correct." Women bring different things to the party. And that's okay. Really.

She said, "So this guy is into . . . what? Trophies? Proof? Mementos and souvenirs? That's consistent with the personality and profile of an organized sex offender."

"But he left her underwear and handbag." I added, "Actually, what all the missing items have in common is that they are all her military issue, including her holster and sidearm, and they would not have her name on them. He left the *civilian* stuff behind, including her watch and her handbag, which has all sorts of things with her name on them. Correct?"

"Is this a contest?"

"No, Cynthia. It's a homicide investigation. We're brainstorming."

"Okay. Sorry. That's what partners are supposed to do in a homicide investigation."

"Right." *Partner?*

Cynthia stayed silent a moment, then said, "You know this stuff."

"I hope so."

"Okay, why did he take only her military issue?"

"Ancient warriors stripped the arms and armor from their dead enemies. They left the loincloths."

"That's why he took her military issue?"

"Maybe. Just a thought. Could be a red herring. Could be some other mental derangement that I'm not familiar with."

She glanced at me as she drove.

I added, "He may not have raped her. But he staked her out like that to draw attention to the sexual nature of his act, or possibly to dishonor her body, to reveal her nakedness to the world."

"Why?"

"Don't know yet."

"Maybe you do."

"I have to think about it. I'm starting to think he knew her." Actually, I *knew* he knew her. We rode in silence a while longer, then I said to Cynthia, "I don't know why it happened, but how does this sound for *how* it happened: Ann Campbell leaves Post Headquarters and goes directly to the rifle range, stopping a good distance from PFC Robbins's guard post. She has a preplanned rendezvous with a lover. They do this often. He plays the armed bandito and gets the drop on her, makes her strip, and they get into some kinky S&M and bondage thing." I glanced at Cynthia. "You know what I mean?"

"I know nothing about sexual perversions. That's your department."

"Well said."

She added, "Your scenario sounds like male fantasy. I mean, what woman would go through all that trouble to be staked out on the cold ground and call that fun?"

I could see this was going to be a long day, and I hadn't even had my breakfast yet. I said, "Do you know why her panties were under the rope around her neck?"

31

"No, why?"

"Check the homicide manual under sexual asphyxia."

"Okay."

"Also, did you notice that there seemed to be a blacktop stain on the sole of her right foot?"

"I didn't."

"If it came from the road, why was she barefoot on the road?"

"He made her strip in, or near, the jeep."

"Then why was her underwear on the rifle range?"

Cynthia replied, "She may have been forced to take off her clothes at, or in, the jeep, then she or the perpetrator carried them to where she was staked out."

"Why?"

"Part of the script, Paul. Sex offenders have incredibly involved fantasies that they perfect in their minds, things that have a strong sexual meaning for them but for no one else. Making a woman strip, then walk naked carrying her own clothes to a place where he intends to rape her may be his unique fantasy."

"So you know this stuff? I'm not in sole charge of perversions."

"I'm familiar with pathological sex acts and criminal deviations. I don't know much about consenting sexual perversions."

I let that one alone and pointed out, "The line between the two is a bit thin and indistinct on occasion."

"I don't believe that Ann Campbell was a consenting partner. Certainly, she didn't consent to being strangled to death."

"There are many possibilities," I mused, "and it's a good idea not to get married to any of them."

"We need forensic, we need the autopsy, and we need to question people."

We? I looked out at the landscape as we drove in silence. I tried to recall what I knew about Cynthia. She was originally from rural Iowa, a graduate of the state university, with a master's in criminology, which she received at some civilian university through the Army's Technological Enhancement Program. Like a lot of women, as well as minorities that I've known in the Army, the military offered more money, education, prestige, and career possibilities than they would have hoped for back on the farm, in the ghetto, or whatever disadvantaged background they came from. Cynthia, I seemed to recall, expressed positive views toward the Army—travel, excitement, security, recognition, and so on. Not bad for a farm girl. I said to her, "I've thought about you."

No reply.

"How are your parents?" I inquired, though I never met them.

"Fine. Yours?"

"Fine. Still waiting for me to get out, grow up, get hitched, and make them grandparents."

"Work on growing up first."

"Good advice." Cynthia can be sarcastic at times, but it's just a defense mechanism when she's nervous. People who've had a prior sexual relationship, if they're at all sensitive and human, respect the relationship that existed, and perhaps even feel some tenderness toward the ex-partner. But there's also that awkwardness, sitting side by side as we were, and neither of us, I think, knew the words or the tone of voice we should adopt. I said again, "I've thought about you. I want you to respond to that."

She responded, "I've thought about you, too," and we fell into a long silence as she drove, head and eyes straight ahead.

A word about Paul Brenner in the passenger seat. South Boston, Irish Catholic, still don't recognize a cow when I see one, high school graduate, working-class family. I didn't join the Army to get out of South Boston; the Army came looking for me because they'd gotten involved in a large ground war in Asia, and someone told them that the sons of working-class stiffs made good infantrymen.

Well, I must have been a good infantryman, because I survived a year over there. Since that time, I've taken college courses, compliments of the Army, as well as criminology courses and career courses. I'm sufficiently transformed so that I don't feel comfortable back in South Boston any longer, but neither do I feel comfortable at the colonel's house, watching how much I drink and making small talk with officers' wives who are either too ugly to talk to or too good-looking to stick to small talk.

So there we were, Cynthia Sunhill and Paul Brenner, from opposite ends of the North American continent, different worlds, lovers in Brussels, reuniting in the Deep South, having just had the common experience of looking at the naked body of a general's daughter. Can love and friendship flourish under those circumstances? I wasn't putting money on it.

She said, "I was sort of startled to see you last night. I'm sorry if I was rude."

"No ifs about it."

"Well, then, I apologize unequivocally. But I still don't like you."

I smiled. "But you'd like to have this case."

"Yes, so I'll be nice to you."

"You'll be nice to me because I'm your superior officer. If you're not nice, I'll send you packing."

"Cut the posturing, Paul. You're not sending me anywhere, and I'm not going anywhere." She added, "We've got a case to solve, and a personal relationship to straighten out."

"In that order."

"Yes, in that order."

CHAPTER FOUR

Victory Drive, formerly Pine Hollow Road, had been renamed during World War II in a frenzy of Orwellian name changing. It was once a two-lane country road heading south out of Midland, but by the time I saw it first in 1971, it was becoming a mixture of garden apartments and commercial garishness. Now, almost a quarter century later, there wasn't even a hint of Pine Hollow Road.

There is something uniquely ugly and depressing about commercial strips in the old South, great expanses of parking lots, motels, fast-food places, discount stores, car dealers, and what passes for nightclubs hereabouts. The old South, as I remember it, was perhaps not so prosperous, but it was picturesque with its tiny gas stations with the Coke cooler next to the fish-bait cooler, the sagging pine houses, the country stores, and the baled cotton bursting from sheds along the railroad sidings. These were the things that grew organically out of the soil, the lumber from the forests, the gravel roads from nearby quarries, and the people themselves a product of their environment. These new things seem artificial, transplanted. Convenience stores and shopping strips with mammoth plastic signs and no relationship to the land or the people, to history, or to local custom.

But, of course, the new South had embraced all of this, not

35

quickly, as we had done up North, but embraced it nonetheless. And in some strange way, the garish commercial strip was now more associated with the South than with anywhere else in the country. The carpetbaggers have finally taken over.

Within fifteen minutes of leaving the post, we arrived at Victory Gardens and parked the Mustang near unit forty-five.

Victory Gardens was actually a pleasant sort of place, comprised of about fifty attached town houses around a central courtyard, with landscaping and ample parking. There were no signs that said, "Officers Only," but the place had that air about it, and the rents probably approximated the off-post quarters' allowance for lieutenants and captains. Money aside, there are unwritten rules about where officers may live off post, and thus, Ann Campbell, daughter of a general and good soldier that she was, had not gone to the funky side of town, nor had she opted for the anonymity of a newer high-rise building, which, in this town, is somewhat synonymous with swinging singles. Yet, neither did she live in her parents' huge, government-issue house on post, which suggested that she had a life of her own, and I was about to discover something about that life.

Cynthia and I looked around. Though the Army workday starts early, there were still a few cars parked in front of the units. Most of them had the blue post bumper stickers signifying an officer's car, and some had the green bumper sticker of a civilian post employee. But mostly, the place looked as deserted as a barracks after morning mess call.

I was still wearing the battle dress uniform I'd had on in the armory, and Cynthia was, as I said, in jeans and windbreaker. As we approached the front door of unit forty-five along the row of red brick façades, I said to her, "Are you armed?"

She nodded.

"All right. You wait here. I'll go in through the back. If I flush somebody out the front, you stop them right here."

"Okay."

I made my way around the row of units and came to the back.

The rear yard was a common stretch of grass, but each unit had a patio separated from the next by a wooden fence for privacy. On Ann Campbell's patio was the standard barbecue grill and lawn furniture, including a lounge chair on which lay suntan oil and a travel magazine.

There were sliding glass doors facing onto the patio, and I was able to see through the vertical blinds into the dining area and part of the living room. There didn't appear to be anyone home. Certainly, Ann Campbell was not home, and I couldn't imagine a general's daughter having a live-in male lover, or even a female roommate, who would compromise her privacy. On the other hand, you never know who's inside a house, and when the subject is murder, you proceed with caution.

Where the patio met the back wall of the house was a basement window well, which meant these units had basements, which also meant a tricky descent down an exposed staircase. Maybe I'd send Ms. Gung Ho down there first. In any case, the window well was covered with a Plexiglas bubble that was bolted to the outside wall, so that no one could get out that way.

To the right of the sliding doors was a door that opened into the kitchen. There was a buzzer there, and I pushed it. I waited and rang again, then tried the doorknob, which is a good idea before breaking and entering.

I should have gone straight to the Midland city police, of course, as Colonel Kent suggested, and the police would have been happy to get a search warrant, and happier still to be included in the search of the victim's house. But I didn't want to bother them with this, so I found the house key on Ann Campbell's key chain and unlocked the door. I entered the kitchen, then closed the door behind me and relocked it.

On the far side of the kitchen was a solid-looking door that probably led to the basement. The door had a bolt, which I slid closed, so if someone was down there, he or she was locked in.

Having secured my rear, or perhaps having cut off my line of retreat, I moved unarmed and cautiously went through the house to the front door and opened it, letting Cynthia in. We stood there in the cool, air-conditioned foyer a moment, looked around, and listened. I motioned for Cynthia to draw her pistol, which she did, a .38 Smith & Wesson. That done, I shouted, ''Police! Stay where you are and call out!'' But there was no reply. I said to Cynthia, ''Stay here and be prepared to use that.''

''Why do you think I'm carrying the fucking thing?''

''Good point.'' *Bitch.* I walked first to the coat closet and pulled the door open, but no one was standing there with a tent peg in his hand. I moved from room to room on the ground floor, feeling a little silly, ninety-nine percent sure the house was empty, but remembering a case when it wasn't.

A staircase led from the foyer to the second floor, and staircases, as I indicated, are dangerous, especially if they squeak. Cynthia positioned herself at the base of the stairs, and I bounded up three steps at a time and flattened myself against the upstairs hallway wall. There were three doors coming off the upstairs hallway, one open, two closed. I repeated my order to stay put and call out, but again no answer.

Cynthia called up to me, and I looked down the stairs. She was halfway up and pitched the Smith & Wesson underhand. I caught it and motioned her to stay where she was. I flung open one of the closed doors, dropped into a firing stance, and shouted, ''Freeze!'' But my aggressiveness did not provoke a response. I peered into the unlit room and saw what appeared to be a spare bedroom, sparsely furnished. I closed the door, then repeated the procedure with the second closed door, which turned out to be a large linen closet. Despite all the acrobatics, I knew that if there was anyone up there with a gun who wanted to use it, I'd be dead by now. But you have to go through the drill. So I spun back against the hallway wall and glanced inside the door that had been open. I could see a large bedroom and another door that led to a bathroom. I motioned Cynthia to come up the stairs and handed her the Smith & Wesson. ''Cover me,'' I said, and entered the large master bedroom, keeping an eye on the sliding doors of the closet, and the open bathroom. I picked up a bottle of perfume from the dressing table and threw it in the bathroom, where it shattered. Recon by fire, as we used to say in the infantry, but again I did not provoke a response.

I gave the bedroom and bathroom a quick look, then rejoined Cynthia, who was in a crouched firing stance off to the side door, covering all the doors. I half expected, half wanted someone to be in this house so I could arrest him—or her—wrap the case, and get the hell back to Virginia. But that was not to be.

Cynthia looked into the large bedroom and commented, "She made her bed."

"Well, you know how those West Pointers are."

"I think it's sad. She was so neat and orderly. Now she's dead and everything will be a mess."

I glanced at Cynthia. "Well, let's begin in the kitchen."

CHAPTER FIVE

Indeed, there is something sad and eerie about intruding into a dead person's house, walking through rooms they will never see again, opening their cabinets, closets, and drawers, handling their possessions, reading their mail, and even listening to the messages on their answering machine. Clothes, books, videotapes, food, liquor, cosmetics, bills, medicine . . . a whole life suddenly ended away from home, and no one left behind, and a house filled with the things that sustain, define, and hopefully explain a life—room by room with no living guide to point out a favorite picture on the wall, to take you through a photo album, to offer you a drink, or tell you why the plants are dry and dying.

In the kitchen, Cynthia noticed the bolted door, and I informed her, "It leads to the basement. It's secure, so we'll check it out last."

She nodded.

The kitchen yielded very little except for the fact that Ann Campbell was for sure a neat-freak and ate the kind of healthful foods— yogurt, bean sprouts, bran muffins, and such—that make my stomach heave. The refrigerator and pantry also held many bottles of good wine and premium beer.

One cupboard was crammed with hard liquor and cordials, again all high-priced, even at post exchange prices. In fact, by the price tags still stuck on some of the bottles, the liquor did not come from the PX. I asked, "Why would she pay civilian prices for liquor?"

Cynthia, who is sensitive, replied, "Perhaps she didn't want to be seen in the PX liquor store. You know—single woman, general's daughter. Men don't worry about that."

I said, "But I can relate to that. I was once spotted in the commissary with a quart of milk and three containers of yogurt. I avoided the O Club for weeks."

No comment from Cynthia, but she did roll her eyes. Clearly, I was getting on her nerves.

It occurred to me that a junior male partner would not be so disrespectful. And neither would a new female partner. This familiarity obviously had something to do with us having once slept together. I had to process this.

"Let's see the other rooms," she said.

So we did. The downstairs powder room was immaculate, though the toilet seat was in the up position, and having just learned a thing or two from that colonel at the O Club, I concluded that a man had been here recently. In fact, Cynthia commented on it, adding, "At least he didn't drip like most of you old guys do."

We were really into this gender and generation thing now, and I had a few good zingers on the tip of my tongue, but the clock was ticking and the Midland police could show up any minute, which would lead to a more serious difference of opinion than that which was developing between Ms. Sunhill and me.

Anyway, we searched the living room and dining area, which were pristine, as though they were sanitized for public consumption. The decor was contemporary but, as with many career military people, there were mementos from all over the world—Japanese lacquers, Bavarian pewter, Italian glass, and so forth. The paintings on the walls would have been appropriate in a geometry classroom—cubes, circles, lines, ovals, and that type of thing, in mostly primary colors. They conveyed nothing, which was the point, I suppose. So far, I couldn't get a handle on Ann Campbell. I mean, I remember once searching the home of a murderer, and within ten minutes I had a grip on the guy. Sometimes it's a small thing like a record album collection, or paintings of cats on the walls, or dirty underwear on the floor. Sometimes it's the books on the shelves or the lack of them, a photo album, or, eureka, a diary. But here, in this place, so far, I felt I had mistakenly broken into the realtor's model unit.

The last room on the ground floor was a study lined with books, in which sat a desk, sofa, and armchair. There was also an entertainment console that held a TV and stereo equipment. On the desk was a telephone answering machine with a blinking light, but we left it alone for the moment.

We gave the study a thorough search, shaking out the books, looking in and under the desk drawers, and finally reading book titles and CD titles. Her taste in books ran to military publications, a few cookbooks, health and fitness books, no fiction or literature whatsoever. But there was a complete collection of Friedrich Nietzsche, and a large collection of titles on psychology, which reminded me that we were dealing with a person who not only was a psychologist but worked in a very arcane branch of this field, to wit: psychological warfare. This might develop into one of the most relevant aspects of this case, or the least relevant.

Heart and hormones aside, all crimes and criminal behavior begin in the mind, and the call to action comes from the mind, and the concealment of the crime completely occupies the mind afterward. So we eventually had to get into the minds of a lot of people, and that's where we would learn about the general's daughter, and learn why she was murdered. With a case like this, when you knew why, you could usually figure out who.

Cynthia was flipping through CDs and announced, "Elevator music, a few golden oldies, some Beatles and classical stuff, mostly Viennese guys."

"Like Sigmund Freud playing Strauss on the oboe?"

"Something like that."

I turned on the TV, expecting that it would be tuned to a fitness or news channel. But instead it was on the VCR channel. I rummaged through the videotape collection, which consisted of a few old black-

and-white classics, a few exercise tapes, and some hand-labeled tapes marked "Psy-Ops, Lecture Series."

I put one of them in the recorder and pushed the play button. "Take a look."

Cynthia turned around and we both watched as Captain Ann Campbell's image filled the screen, dressed in battle fatigues and standing at a rostrum. She was, indeed, a very good-looking woman, but beyond that she had bright and alert eyes that stared into the camera for a few seconds before she smiled and began, "Good morning, gentlemen. Today we are going to discuss the several ways in which psychological operations, or psy warfare, if you wish, can be used by the infantry commander in the field to decrease enemy morale and fighting effectiveness. The ultimate objective of these operations is to make your job as infantry commanders somewhat easier. Your mission—to make contact with and destroy the enemy—is a tough one, and you are aided by other branches of the Army, such as artillery, air, armor, and intelligence. However, a little-understood and too-little-used tool is available to you—psychological operations."

She went on, "The enemy's will to fight is perhaps the single most important element that you must calculate into your battle plans. His guns, his armor, his artillery, his training, his equipment, and indeed even his numbers are all secondary to his willingness to stand and fight." She looked out over her offscreen audience and let a moment pass before continuing. "No man wants to die. But many men can be motivated to risk their lives in defense of their countries, their families, and even an abstraction, or a philosophy. Democracy, religion, racial pride, individual honor, unit and interpersonal loyalty, the promise of plunder, and, yes, women . . . rape. These are among the historical motivators for frontline troops."

As she spoke, a slide projection screen behind her flashed images of ancient battle scenes taken from old prints and paintings. I recognized "The Rape of the Sabines," by Da Bologna, which is one of the few classical paintings I can name. Sometimes I wonder about myself.

Captain Campbell continued, "The objective of psychological

43

warfare is to chip away at these motivators, but not to tackle them head-on, as they are often too strong and too ingrained to be changed in any significant way through propaganda or psy-ops. The best we can hope to do is to plant some seeds of doubt. However, this does not crack morale and lead to mass desertions and surrender. It only lays the groundwork for stage two of psy-ops, which is, ultimately, to instill fear and panic into the enemy ranks. Fear and panic. Fear of death, fear of grotesque wounds, fear of fear. Panic—that least understood of all psychological states of mind. Panic—a deep abiding, free-floating anxiety, often without any reason or logical basis. Our ancestors used war drums, war pipes, bloodcurdling shouts, taunts, and even breast beating and primal screams to induce panic in the enemy camps.''

The image on the screen behind her now looked to be a depiction of a Roman army in full flight, being chased by a horde of fierce-looking barbarians.

She continued, ''In our pursuit of technical excellence and high-tech solutions to battlefield problems, we have forgotten the primal scream.'' Ann Campbell hit a button on the rostrum and a high-decibel, bloodcurdling scream filled the room. She smiled and said, ''That will loosen your sphincter.'' A few men in the classroom laughed, and the microphone picked up some guy saying, ''Sounds like my wife when she climaxes.'' More laughter, and Captain Campbell, reacting to the remark, laughed too, an almost bawdy laugh, completely out of character. She looked down a moment, as if at her notes, and when she looked up again, her expression had returned to business and the laughter died down.

I had the impression she was playing the crowd, getting them on her side the way most male Army instructors did with an off-color joke or an occasional personal comment. Clearly, she had reached out and touched the audience, had shared a moment of sexual complicity and revealed what was beneath the neat uniform. But only for a moment. I turned off the VCR. ''Interesting lecture.''

Cynthia said, ''Who would want to kill a woman like that? I mean, she was so *alive*. So vital and so self-assured . . .''

Which may be why someone wanted to kill her. We stood in silence a moment, sort of in respect, I suppose, as if Ann Campbell's presence and spirit were still in the room. In truth, I was quite taken with Ann Campbell. She was the type of woman you noticed, and once seen, was never forgotten. It wasn't only her looks that grabbed your attention, but her whole demeanor and bearing. Also, she had a good command voice, deep and distinct, yet feminine and sexy. Her accent was what I call Army brat—a product of ten or twenty duty stations around the world, with an occasional southern pronunciation taking you by surprise. All in all, this was a woman who could command the respect and attention of men, or drive them to distraction.

As for how women related to her, Cynthia seemed impressed, but I suspected that some women might find her threatening, especially if their husbands or boyfriends had any proximity to Ann Campbell. How Ann Campbell related to other women was, as yet, a mystery. Finally, to break the silence, I said, "Let's finish this business."

We went back to our search of the study. Cynthia and I both went through a photo album we found on the shelf. The photos appeared to be entirely *en famille:* General and Mrs. Campbell, a young man who was probably the son, shots of Daddy and Ann in mufti, uncle and aunt types, West Point, picnics, Christmas, Thanksgiving, ad nauseam, and I had the impression her mother put the album together for her daughter. This was documentary proof positive that the Campbells were the happiest, most loving, best adjusted, most socially integrated family this side of the Father, Son, and the Holy Spirit, with Mary taking most of the snapshots. "Pablum," I said. "But it *does* tell one something, does it not?"

"What?" asked Cynthia.

"They probably all hate one another."

"You're being cynical," she said. "And jealous," she added, "because we don't have families like this."

I closed the album. "We'll soon find out what's behind their cheesy smiles."

At this point, the enormity of what we were doing seemed to hit

Cynthia and she said, "Paul . . . we have to question General Campbell . . . Mrs. Campbell . . ."

I replied, "Murder is unpleasant enough. When it's rape and murder and it doesn't appear random, and the victim's father is a national hero, then the idiots who are going to examine the victim's life had better know what they're getting into. Understand?"

She contemplated this a moment and informed me, "I really want this case. I feel . . . you know . . . some affinity for her. I didn't know her, but I know life wasn't easy for her in this man's Army."

"Spare me, Cynthia."

"Well, really, Paul, how would you know?"

"Try being a white man these days."

"Give me a break."

"Now I remember what we used to fight about."

"Neutral corners."

We walked to opposite sides of the room, though not the corners, and continued our search. I looked at the framed things on the wall—Ann Campbell's West Point diploma, her Army commission, training certificates, commendations, and a few other Department of the Army and Department of Defense certificates, including one that recognized her contribution to Operation Desert Storm, though the nature of the contribution was not specified. I cleared my throat and said to Ms. Sunhill, "Did you ever hear about Operation Bonkers during Desert Storm?"

She replied, "Not that I recall."

"Well, some smart cookie in psy-ops had this idea of dropping hard-core porno photos on the Iraqi positions. Most of those poor bastards had not seen a woman in months or years, so this psy-ops sadist wants to bury them in photos of hot, pink flesh, which will drive them bonkers. The idea goes all the way up to the joint command, and it's a definite winner, a go, until the Saudis hear about it and go ballistic. You know, they're a little tight and not as enlightened as we are about bare tits and ass. So the thing was squashed, but the word was that the idea was brilliant and could have shortened the ground war from four days to fifteen minutes." I smiled.

Cynthia replied frostily, "It's disgusting."

"Actually, I agree in theory. But if it saved one life, it might have been justified."

"The means do not justify the ends. What's the point?"

"Well, what if the idea of the porno bombardment had come from a woman instead of some male pig?"

"You mean Captain Campbell?"

"Certainly that idea came out of the Special Operations School here. Let's check it out."

Cynthia went into one of her contemplative moods, then looked at me. "Did *you* know her?"

"I knew *of* her."

"What did you know *of* her?"

"What most everyone else knew, Cynthia. She was perfect in every way, made in the USA, pasteurized and homogenized by the Public Information Office, and delivered fresh to your doorstep, creamy white and good for you."

"And you don't believe that?"

"No, I don't. But if we discover that I'm wrong, then I'm in the wrong business and I'll resign."

"You may wind up doing that anyway."

"Most probably." I added, "Please consider how she died, how bizarre it was, and how unlikely it would be for a stranger to have gotten the drop on a soldier who was alert, bright, armed, and ready to shoot."

She nodded, then said as if to herself, "I have considered what you are suggesting. It's not uncommon for a female officer to lead two lives—public rectitude and private . . . whatever. But I've also seen women, rape victims, married and single, who led exemplary private lives and who wound up as victims by pure chance. I've also seen women who lived on the jagged edge, but whose rape had not a thing to do with their promiscuity or the crazies they hung out with. Again, it was pure chance."

"That's a possibility, and I don't discount it."

"And don't be judgmental, Paul."

"I'm not. I'm no saint. How about you?"

"You know better than to ask." She walked over to where I was

47

standing and put her hand on my shoulder, which sort of took me by surprise. She said, ''Can we do this? I mean together? Are we going to screw this up?''

''No. We're going to solve it.''

Cynthia poked her finger in my stomach, sort of like I needed a punctuation mark for that sentence. She turned and walked back to Ann Campbell's desk.

I turned my attention back to the wall and noticed now a framed commendation from the American Red Cross in appreciation for her work on a blood donor drive, another commendation from a local hospital thanking her for her work with seriously ill children, and a teaching certificate from a literacy volunteer organization. Where did this woman find the time to do all that, plus her regular job, plus volunteering for extra duty, plus the mandatory social side of Army life, plus have a private life? Could it be, I wondered, that this extraordinarily beautiful woman *had* no private life? Could I be so far off base that I wasn't even in the ballpark?

Cynthia announced, ''Here's her address book.''

''That reminds me. Did you get my Christmas card? Where are you living these days?''

''Look, Paul, I'm sure your buddies at headquarters have snooped through my file for you and told you everything about me in the past year.''

''I wouldn't do that, Cynthia. It's not ethical or professional.''

She glanced at me. ''Sorry.'' She put the address book in her handbag, went over to the telephone answering machine, and pushed the play button.

A voice said, ''Ann, this is Colonel Fowler. You were supposed to stop by the general's house this morning after you got off duty.'' The colonel sounded brusque. He continued, ''Mrs. Campbell prepared breakfast for you. Well, you're probably sleeping now. Please call the general when you get up, or call Mrs. Campbell.'' He hung up.

I said, ''Maybe she killed herself. I would.''

Cynthia commented, ''It certainly couldn't be easy being a general's daughter. Who is Colonel Fowler?''

"I think he's the post adjutant." I asked Cynthia, "How did that message sound to you?"

"Official. The tone suggested some familiarity, but no particular warmth. As if he was just doing his duty by calling his boss's forgetful daughter, whom he outranks, but who is nevertheless the boss's daughter. How did it sound to you?"

I thought a moment and replied, "It sounded made up."

"Oh . . . like a cover call?"

I pushed the play button again, and we listened. I said, "Maybe I'm starting to imagine things."

"Maybe not."

I picked up the phone and dialed the provost marshal's office. Colonel Kent was in and I got him on the line. "We are still at the deceased's house," I informed him. "Have you spoken to the general yet?"

"No . . . I haven't . . . I'm waiting for the chaplain . . ."

"Bill, this thing will be all over post in a matter of hours. Inform the deceased's family. And no form letters or telegrams."

"Look, Paul, I'm up to my ass in alligators with this thing, and I called the post chaplain and he's on his way here—"

"Fine. Did you get her office moved?"

"Yes. I put everything in an unused hangar at Jordan Field."

"Good. Now get a bunch of trucks out here with a platoon of MPs who don't mind hard work and know how to keep their mouths shut, and empty her house. I mean everything, Colonel—furniture, carpeting, right down to the light bulbs, toilet seats, refrigerator, and food. Take photos here, and put everything in that hangar in some semblance of the order that it's found. Okay?"

"Are you crazy?"

"Absolutely. And be sure the men wear gloves and get forensic to print everything that they'd normally print."

"Why do you want to move the whole house?"

"Bill, we have no jurisdiction here, and I'm not trusting the town police to play fair. So when the Midland police get here, the only thing they can impound is the wallpaper. Trust me on this. The scene of the crime was a U.S. military reservation. So this is all perfectly legal.''

''No, it's not.''

''We do this my way, or I'm out of here, Colonel.''

There was a long pause, followed by a grunt that sounded like ''Okay.''

''And send an officer down to Dixie Bell in town and have Ann Campbell's number forwarded to a number on post. In fact, get it forwarded to a line in that hangar. Plug her answering machine in and put in a new incoming message tape. Hold on to the old tape. It's got a message on it. Mark it as evidence.''

''Who do you think is going to call after the headlines are splashed all over the state?''

''You never know. Did forensic get there yet?''

''Yes. They're at the scene. So is the body.''

''And Sergeant St. John and PFC Robbins?''

''They're still sleeping. I put them in separate cells. Unlocked. Do you want me to read them their rights?''

''No, they're not suspects. But you can hold them as material witnesses until I get around to them.''

''Soldiers have *some* rights,'' Kent informed me. ''And St. John has a wife, and Robbins's CO probably thinks she went AWOL.''

''Then make some calls on their behalf. Meantime, they're incommunicado. How about Captain Campbell's medical and personnel files?''

''Got them right here.''

''What are we forgetting, Bill?''

''The Constitution.''

''Don't sweat the small stuff.''

''You know, Paul, I have to work with Chief Yardley. You guys are in and out. Yardley and I get along all right, considering the problems—''

''I said I'll take the rap.''

''You'd damn well better.'' He asked, ''Did you find anything interesting there?''

''Not yet. Did you?''

"The grid search hasn't turned up much beyond a few pieces of litter."

"Did the dogs find anything?"

"No more victims." He added, "The handlers let them sniff inside the jeep, and the dogs beelined right to the body. Then the dogs went back to the humvee, across the road, past the bleachers, and right out to the latrines in the trees. Then they lost the scent and doubled back to the humvee." He continued, "We can't know if the dogs picked up this guy's scent or just her scent. But somebody, maybe the victim and the perpetrator together, or one or the other, did go out to the latrines." He hesitated, then said, "I have the feeling that the murderer had his own vehicle, and since we see no tire marks in the soil anywhere, the guy never left the road. So he was parked there on the road before or after she stopped. They both dismount, he gets the drop on her and takes her out to the range and does it. He then goes back to the road . . ."

"Carrying her clothes."

"Yes. And he puts the clothes in his vehicle, then . . ."

"Goes to the latrine, washes up, combs his hair, then goes back to his vehicle and drives away."

Kent said, "That's the way it could have happened. But that's just a theory."

"I have a theory that we're going to need another hangar to hold the theories. Okay, about six trucks should do it. And send a sensitive female officer to supervise. And send someone from community affairs who can cool out the neighbors while the MPs empty the place. See you later." I hung up.

Cynthia said, "You have a quick and analytical mind, Paul."

"Thank you."

"If you had a little compassion and heart, you'd be a better person."

"I don't want to be a better person." I added, "Hey, wasn't I a good guy in Brussels? Didn't I buy you Belgian chocolates?"

She didn't reply immediately, then said, "Yes, you did. Well, should we go upstairs before upstairs winds up at Jordan Field?"

"Good idea."

CHAPTER SIX

The master suite, as I indicated, was neat and clean, except for the shattered perfume bottle on the bathroom floor that now stunk up the place. The furniture was functional modern, sort of Scandinavian, I suppose, with no soft touches, nothing to suggest that it was madam's boudoir. It occurred to me that I wouldn't want to make love in this room. The carpet, too, was unsuited for a bedroom, being a tight woven Berber that left no footprints. Something, however, did stand out: twenty bottles of perfume, which Cynthia said were very expensive, and the civilian clothes in the closet, which she said were equally overpriced. A second, smaller closet—what would have been "his" closet if she had a husband or live-in—was filled with neat Army uniforms for the summer season, including greens, battle dress, combat boots, and all the necessary accessories. More interesting, in the far corner of the closet was an M-16 rifle with a full magazine and a round in the chamber, locked and loaded, ready to rock and roll. I said, "This is a military issue—fully automatic."

"Unauthorized off post," Cynthia observed.

"My goodness." We rummaged around a while longer, and I was going through Ann Campbell's underwear drawer when Cynthia said, "You already looked in there, Paul. Don't get strange on me."

"I'm looking for her West Point ring," I replied with annoyance. "It wasn't on her finger, and it's not in her jewelry box."

"It was taken off her finger. I saw the tan line."

I pushed the drawer shut. "Keep me informed," I said.

"You too," she snapped.

The bathroom was standing tall as they say in the Army: West Point, white-glove immaculate. Even the sink basin had been wiped as per regulations, and there wasn't a hair on the floor, certainly no pubic hair of a swarthy stranger.

We opened the medicine cabinet, which held the usual assortment of cosmetics, feminine products, and such. There were no prescription medicines, no men's shaving stuff, only one toothbrush, and nothing stronger than aspirin. "What," I asked my female partner, "do you deduce from this?"

"Well, she wasn't a hypochondriac, she didn't have dry or oily skin, she didn't dye her hair, and she keeps her method of birth control somewhere else."

I said, "Maybe she required her men to use a condom." I added, "You may have heard that condoms are in fashion again because of disease. These days you have to boil people before you sleep with them."

Cynthia ignored that and said, "Or she was chaste."

"I never thought of that. Is that possible?"

"You never know, Paul. You just never know."

"Or could she have been . . . how do we say it these days? Gay? A lesbian? What's the politically correct term?"

"Do you care?"

"For my report. I mean, I don't want to get into trouble with the feminist thought police."

"Take a break, Paul."

We exited the bathroom and Cynthia said, "Let's see the other bedroom."

We passed through the upstairs hallway into the small room. At this point, I didn't expect to encounter anyone, but Cynthia drew her pistol and covered me while I peeked under the double bed.

Aside from the bed, the room held only a dresser and a night table and lamp. An open door led to a small bathroom, which looked as if it were never used. Clearly, the entire room was never used, but Ann Campbell maintained it as a guest room.

Cynthia pulled back the bedspread, revealing a bare mattress. She said, "No one sleeps here."

"Apparently not." I pulled open the dresser drawers. Empty.

Cynthia motioned toward a set of large double doors on the far wall. I stood to the side and flung one of them open. A light inside went on automatically, and it sort of startled me, and Cynthia, too, because she crouched and aimed. After a second or two, she stood and approached what turned out to be a large walk-in cedar closet. We both went inside the closet. It smelled good, like a cheap cologne I once had that kept moths and women away. There were two long poles on either side from which hung bagged civilian clothes for every climate on earth, and more Army uniforms, ranging from her old West Point uniforms, to desert battle dress, to arctic wear, to Army whites, blue mess and evening mess uniforms for social functions, and sundry other rarely worn uniforms, plus her West Point saber. The overhead shelf had matching headgear, and on the floor was matching footwear.

I said, "This was one squared-away soldier. Equally prepared for a military ball or the next war in the jungle."

"Doesn't your uniform closet look like this?"

"My uniform closet looks like the third day of a close-out sale." Actually, it looked worse than that. I have a tidy mind, but that's as far as it goes. Captain Campbell, on the other hand, seemed clean, tidy, and organized in every external way. Perhaps, then, her mind was pure chaos. Perhaps not. This woman was elusive.

We exited the closet and the guest room.

On the way down the stairs, I said to Cynthia, "Before I was in the CID, I couldn't see a clue if it bit me in the ass."

"And now?"

"And now I see everything as a clue. The lack of clues is a clue."

"Is that so? I haven't progressed to that level yet. Sounds Zen."

"I think of it as Sherlockian. You know, the dog that did not bark in the night." We went into the kitchen. "Why did the dog not bark?"

"It was dead."

It's hard adjusting to a new partner. I don't like the young, sycophantic guys who hang on your every word. But I don't like smart-asses, either. I'm at that age and rank where I get respect and earn respect, but I'm still open to an occasional piece of reality.

Cynthia and I contemplated the bolted basement door. I said, not apropos of the door, but of life, "My wife left clues all over the place."

She didn't reply.

"But I never saw the clues."

"Sure you did."

"Well . . . in retrospect I did. But when you're young, you're pretty dense. You're full of yourself, you don't read other people well, you haven't been lied to and cheated too much, and you lack the cynicism and suspicion that makes for a good detective."

"A good detective, Paul, has to separate his or her professional life from his or her personal life. I wouldn't want a man who snooped on me."

"Obviously not, considering your past."

"Fuck off."

Score one for Paul. I threw back the bolt on the door. "Your turn."

"Okay. I wish you had your pistol." She handed me her Smith & Wesson and opened the basement door.

"Maybe I should go and get that M-16 upstairs," I offered.

"Never rely on a weapon you just found and never tested. Says so in the manual. Just call out, then cover me."

I shouted down the stairs, "Police! Come to the staircase with your hands on your head!" This is the military version of hands-up and makes a little more sense if you think about it. Well, no one came to the base of the stairs, so Cynthia had to go down. She said in a quiet voice, "Leave the lights off. I'll break to the right. Wait five seconds."

"You wait one second." I looked around for something to throw down the stairs and spotted a toaster oven, but Cynthia was off and running, down the cellar stairs in long leaps, barely hitting the steps on her way down. I saw her shoulder-roll to the right and lost sight of her. I followed, breaking to the left, and wound up in a firing crouch, peering into the darkness. We waited in silence for a full ten seconds, then I shouted, "Ed, John, cover us!" I wished there were an Ed and John around, but as Captain Campbell might have said, "Create phantom battalions in the minds of the enemy."

By now, I figured that if anyone was down there, they weren't lying in ambush, but were cowering. Right?

Anyway, Cynthia, who was obviously impatient with my caution, bounded back up the stairs and hit the light switches. Fluorescent bulbs flickered all over the large open basement, then burst into that stark white light that I associated with unpleasant places.

Cynthia came back down the stairs and we surveyed the basement. It was a standard layout of washer and dryer, workbench, storage, heating, air-conditioning, and so on. The floor and walls were bare concrete, and the ceiling was bare beams, electric, and plumbing.

We examined the workbench and the dark corners, but it was uninteresting in the extreme except that Ann Campbell possessed a lot of sporting equipment. In fact, the entire wall to the right of the workbench was pegboard, from floor to ceiling, from which protruded those wire holders in every size and shape, and hanging from the wire holders were skis, tennis rackets, squash rackets, a baseball bat, scuba gear, and so forth. Very organized. Also, fixed to the pegboard with screws was a recruiting poster, about six feet from top to bottom, showing none other than Captain Ann Campbell, a head-to-foot shot of her in battle dress uniform, wearing full field gear, with an M-16 rifle slung under her right arm, a radiotelephone cradled against her ear, while she juggled a field map and checked her watch. Her face was smeared with camouflage greasepaint, but only a eunuch would fail to see the subtle sexuality in this photo. The caption on top of the poster said, *Time to Synchronize Your Life*. On the bottom, it said, *See Your Army Recruiter Today*. What it didn't say was, "Meet people of the opposite sex in close proximity, sleep with them out in the woods, bathe with them in streams, and engage in other intimate outdoorsy things where no one has any privacy."

Well, maybe I was projecting my own sexual reveries into the photo, but I think the civilian advertising types who put the poster together were a little bit aware of what my dirty mind saw. I nodded toward the poster and said to Cynthia, "What do you think?"

She shrugged, "Good poster."

"Do you see the subliminal sexual message?"

"No. Point to it."

"Well . . . it's subliminal. How can I point to it?"

"Tell me about it."

I had the feeling I was being baited, so I said, "Woman with a gun. Gun is penis object, penis substitute. Map and watch represent a subconscious desire to have sex, but on her terms, timewise and locationwise. She's talking to a man on the radiophone, giving him her grid coordinates and telling him he has fifteen minutes to find her."

Cynthia glanced at her own watch and informed me, "I think it's time to go, Paul."

"Right."

We started back up the stairs, but then I glanced back into the basement and said, "We're missing some floor space."

As if on cue, we both turned and beelined for the pegboard wall, the only wall that did not show the bare concrete foundation wall. I knocked on the pegboard, pushed on the four-by-eight-foot panels, but they seemed solid enough, nailed firmly in place to a stud frame, which I could see through the small peg holes. I found a long, pointed awl on the workbench and slid it through one of the peg holes, and after about two inches it struck a solid object. I pushed farther, and the point of the awl penetrated into something soft, something that was not a concrete foundation wall. I said to Cynthia, "This is a false wall. There's no foundation behind it."

She didn't reply, and I looked to my left where Cynthia was standing facing the recruiting poster. She grasped the wooden frame of the poster with her fingertips, pulled, and the poster swung out on blind hinges, revealing a dark open space. I moved quickly beside her and we stood there, backlighted by the bright fluorescents of the basement.

After a few seconds, during which time we were not perforated with bullet holes, my eyes adjusted to the darkness of the space before us, and I could begin to make out some objects in the room that appeared to be furniture. I could also make out the glow of a digital clock across the room, and I estimated that the room was fifteen feet deep and probably about forty or fifty feet long, the length of the town house itself from front to rear.

I handed Cynthia her .38 and felt along the inside wall for a light switch, commenting, "This is where the Campbells probably keep their demented, drooling relative." I found the switch and flipped it, turning on a table lamp, which revealed a completely finished and furnished room. I moved forward cautiously, and out of the corner of my eye, I saw Cynthia in a firing crouch, her .38 sweeping the room.

I kneeled and peeked under the bed, then stood and moved around, checking the closet, then a small bathroom off to the right, while Cynthia covered me.

Cynthia and I stood across from each other, and I said, "Well, here it is."

And, indeed, there it was. There was a double bed, a nightstand on which sat the lighted lamp, a chest of drawers, a long table on which sat a stereo system, a television, a VCR, and a camcorder with a tripod for home movies, and everything sat on a deep white plush carpet, which wasn't as clean as the other carpets. The walls were finished in a light-colored wood paneling. To the far left of the room was a rolling hospital-type gurney, suitable for massages or whatever. I noticed now a mirror mounted on the ceiling over the bed, and the open closet revealed some lacy and transparent numbers that would make a clerk in Victoria's Secret blush. In addition, there was a nice, neat nurse's uniform, which I didn't think she wore down at the hospital, a black leather skirt and vest, a sort of whorish red-sequined dress, and, interestingly, a standard battle dress uniform of the type she would have been wearing on duty when she was killed.

Cynthia, Ms. Goody Two-Shoes, was looking around the room, and she seemed somewhat unhappy, as though Ann Campbell had posthumously disappointed her. "Good Lord . . ."

I said, "How she died does indeed appear linked to how she lived. But we will not jump to conclusions."

The bathroom, too, was not so clean as the other two, and the medicine cabinet held a diaphragm, condoms, contraceptive sponges, spermicidal jelly, and so on: enough birth control devices to cause a drop in the population of the Indian subcontinent. I asked, "Aren't you supposed to just use one method?"

Cynthia replied, "Depends on your mood."

"I see." Along with the contraceptive devices were mouthwash, different-colored toothbrushes, toothpaste, and six Fleet enemas. I didn't think anyone who ate bean sprouts would have a problem with constipation. "My goodness," I said, picking up a premeasured douche bottle whose flavor was strawberry; not my very favorite.

Cynthia left the bathroom, and I peeked into the shower. That, too, was sort of grungy, and the washcloth was still damp. Interesting.

I rejoined Cynthia in the bedroom, where she was examining the contents of the night table drawer: K-Y Jelly, mineral oil, sex manuals, one regular-sized vibrator, batteries included, and one rubber charlie of heroic proportions.

Fixed high up on the false wall that partitioned this bedroom from the basement workshop was a set of leather manacles, and lying on the floor below was a leather strap, a birch switch, and incongruously, or perhaps not, a long ostrich feather. My mind involuntarily

59

took off into a flight of fancy that I think brought a red blush to my cheeks. "I wonder," I mused, "what those things are for?"

Cynthia made no comment, but seemed transfixed by the manacles.

I pulled back the bed sheets, and the bottom sheet looked a bit lived in. Here was enough pubic hair, body hair, peter tracks, and undoubtedly other dermatological refuse to keep the lab busy for a week.

I noticed Cynthia staring down at the sheet and wondered what was going through her mind. I resisted the urge to say, "I told you so," because, in fact, on one level, I almost hoped we would find nothing, for, as I've indicated, I had already developed a soft spot in my heart for Ann Campbell. And, while I'm not judgmental in regard to sexual behavior, I could imagine that many people would be. I said, "You know, I'm actually relieved to see she wasn't the sexless, androgynous poster girl the Army made her out to be."

Cynthia glanced at me and sort of nodded.

I said, "A shrink would have a field day with this apparent split personality. But you know, we all lead two or more lives." On the other hand, we don't usually outfit a whole room for our alter ego. I added, "Actually, she *was* a shrink, wasn't she?"

And so we moved to the TV, and I popped a random tape into the VCR and turned it on.

The screen brightened, and there was Ann Campbell, dressed in her red-sequined dress, with high heels and jewelry, standing in this very room. An off-camera tape or disc was playing "The Stripper," and she began taking it all off. A male voice, presumably the cameraman, joked, "Do you do this at the general's dinner parties?"

Ann Campbell smiled and wiggled her hips at the camera. She was down to her panties and a rather nice French bra now, and was unclasping it when I reached out and shut off the tape, feeling very self-righteous about that.

I examined the other tapes and saw they were all hand-labeled, with rather pithy titles like "Fucking with J.," "Strip search for B.," "Gyno Exam—R," and "Anal with J.S."

Cynthia said, "I think we've seen enough for now."

"Almost enough." I opened the top dresser drawer and discovered a pile of Polaroid photos, and thinking I'd hit pay dirt, I flipped through them, looking for her friends, but every photo was of only her in various poses ranging from nearly artistic and erotic to obscene gynecological shots. "Where're the guys?"

"Behind the camera."

"There's got to be . . ." Then, in another stack of photos, I found a shot of a well-built naked man holding a belt, but wearing a black leather hood. Then another shot of a guy on top of her, possibly taken with a time delay or by a third person, then a photo of a naked gent, manacled to the wall, his back to the camera. In fact, all the men—and there were at least twelve different bodies— were either turned away from the camera or wearing the leather discipline hood. Obviously, these guys didn't want any face photos left here, and similarly, they probably had no face shots of Ann Campbell in their possession. Most people are a little careful of photos like these, and when the people have a lot to lose, they are very careful. Love and trust are okay, but I had the feeling this was more lust and "What's your name again?" I mean, if she had a real boyfriend, a man she liked and admired, she wouldn't bring him here, obviously.

Cynthia was going through the photos also, but handling them as though they carried a sexually transmittable disease. There were a few more shots of men, close-ups of genitals, ranging from much ado about nothing to as you like it to the taming of the shrew. I observed, "All white guys, all circumcised, mostly brown hair, a few blonds. Can we use these in a lineup?"

"It would be an interesting lineup," Cynthia conceded. She threw the photos back in the drawer. "Maybe we shouldn't let the MPs see this room."

"Indeed not. I hope they don't find it."

"Let's go."

"Just a minute." I opened the bottom three drawers, finding more sexual paraphernalia, toys for twats as they're known in the

61

trade, along with panties, garter belts, a cat-o'-nine tails, a leather jockstrap, and a few things that I confess I couldn't figure out. I was actually a bit embarrassed rummaging through this stuff in full view of Ms. Sunhill, and she was probably wondering about me by now, because she said, "What else do you have to see?"

"Rope."

"Rope? Oh . . ."

And there it was: a length of nylon cord, curled up in the bottom drawer. I took it out and examined it.

Cynthia said, "Is it the same?"

"Possibly. This looks like the rope at the scene—standard Army-green tent cord, but there's about six million miles of it out there. Still, it is suggestive." I looked at the bed, which was an old four-poster, suitable for bondage. I don't know a great deal about sexual deviations except for what I've read in the CID manual, but I do know that bondage is a risky thing. I mean, a big healthy woman like Ann Campbell could probably defend herself if something got out of hand. But if you're spread-eagled on the bed or the ground with your wrists and ankles tied to something, you'd better know the guy real well, or something bad could happen. Actually, it did.

I turned out the lights and we left the bedroom. Cynthia swung the framed recruiting poster closed. I found a tube of wood glue on the workbench, opened the hinged poster a crack, and ran a bead of glue along the wood frame. That would help a little, but once you figured out that some floor space was missing, you'd figure out the rest of it, and if you didn't realize some space was missing, the poster looked like it belonged there. I said to Cynthia, "Fooled me for a minute. How smart are MPs?"

"It's more a matter of spatial perception than brains. And if they don't find it, the police might when they get here." She added, "Someone might want that poster. I think we either have to let the MPs empty the room for the CID lab, or we cooperate with the civilian police before they padlock this place."

"I think we do neither. We take a chance. That room is our secret. Okay?"

She nodded. "Okay, Paul. Maybe your instincts are good on this."

We went up the basement stairs, turned off the lights, and closed the door.

In the front foyer, Cynthia said to me, "I guess your instincts were right about Ann Campbell."

"Well, I thought we'd be lucky if we found a diary and a few steamy love notes. I didn't expect a secret door that led into a room decorated for Madame Bovary by the Marquis de Sade." I added, "I guess we all need our space. The world would actually be a better place if we all had a fantasy room in which to act out."

"Depends on the script, Paul."

"Indeed."

We left by the front door, got into Cynthia's Mustang, and headed back up Victory Drive, passing a convoy of Army trucks heading the other way as we approached the post.

As Cynthia drove, I stared out the side window, deep in thought. *Weird*, I thought. *Weird*. Weird things, right on the other side of a gung-ho recruiting poster. And that was to become metaphor for this case: shiny brass, pressed uniforms, military order and honor, a slew of people above reproach, but if you went a little deeper, opened the right door, you would find a profound corruption as rank as Ann Campbell's bed.

CHAPTER SEVEN

As Cynthia drove, she divided her attention between the road and Ann Campbell's address book, mostly at the expense of the road. I said, "Give me that."

She threw it on my lap in a gesture that was definitely meant to be aggressive.

I flipped through the address book, a thick leather-bound and well-worn book of good quality, written in a neat hand. Every space was filled with names and addresses, a good number of them crossed out and reentered with a new address as people changed duty stations, homes, wives, husbands, units, countries, and from alive to dead. In fact, I saw two entries marked KIA. It was a typical address book of a career soldier, spanning the years and the world, and, while I knew it was probably her desktop official address book and not the little black book that we hadn't yet found, I was still fairly certain that someone in this book knew something. If I had two years, I could question all of them. Clearly, I had to give the book to headquarters in Falls Church, Virginia, where my immediate superior, Colonel Karl Gustav Hellmann, would parcel it out all over the world, generating a stack of transcribed interviews taller than the great Teutonic pain-in-the-ass himself. Maybe he'd decide to read them and stay off my case.

A word about my boss. Karl Hellmann was actually born a

German citizen close to an American military installation near Frankfurt, and, like many hungry children whose families were devastated by the war, he had made himself a sort of mascot for the American troops and eventually joined the U.S. military to support his family. There were a good number of these galvanized German Yankees in the U.S. military years ago, and many of them became officers, and some are still around. On the whole, they make excellent officers, and the Army is lucky to have them. The people who have to work for them are not so lucky. But enough whining. Karl is efficient, dedicated, loyal, and correct in both senses of the word. The only mistake I ever knew him to make was when he decided I liked him. Wrong, Karl. But I do respect him, and I would trust him with my life. In fact, I have.

Obviously, this case needed a breakthrough, a shortcut by which we could get to the end quickly, before careers and reputations were flushed down the toilet. Soldiers are encouraged to kill in the proper setting, but killing within the service is definitely a slap in the face to good order and discipline. It raises too many questions about that thin line between the bloodcurdling, screaming bayonet charge—"What's the spirit of the bayonet? *To kill! To kill!*"—and peacetime garrison duty. A good soldier will always be respectful of rank, gender, and age. Says so in the *Soldier's Handbook*.

The best I could hope for in this case was that the murder was committed by a slimeball civilian with a previous arrest record going back ten years. The worst I could imagine was . . . well, early indications pointed to it, whatever it was.

Cynthia said, apropos of the address book, "She had lots of friends and acquaintances."

"Don't you?"

"Not in this job."

"True." In fact, we were a bit out of the mainstream of Army life, and so our colleagues and good buddies are fewer in number. Cops tend to be cliquish all over the world, and when you're a military cop on continuing TDY—temporary duty—you don't make many friends, and relationships with the opposite sex tend to be short and strained, somewhat like temporary duty itself.

Midland is officially six miles from Fort Hadley, but as I said, the town has grown southward along Victory Drive, great strips of neon commerce, garden apartments, and car dealers, so that the main gate resembles the Brandenburg Gate, separating chaotic private enterprise and tackiness from spartan sterility. The beer cans stop at the gate.

Cynthia's Mustang, which I had noted sported a visitor's parking sticker, was waived through the gate by an MP, and within a few minutes we were in the center of the main post, where traffic and parking are only slightly better than in downtown Midland.

She pulled up to the provost marshal's office, an older brick building that was one of the first permanent structures built when Fort Hadley was Camp Hadley back around World War I. Military bases, like towns, start with a reason for being, followed by places to live, a jail, a hospital, and a church, not necessarily in that order.

We expected to be expected, but it took us a while, dressed as we were—a male sergeant and a female civilian—to get into his majesty's office. I was not happy with Kent's performance and lack of forethought so far. When I went through Leadership School, they taught us that lack of prior planning makes for a piss-poor performance. Now they say don't be reactive, be proactive. But I have the advantage of having been taught in the old school, so I know what they're talking about. I said to Kent, in his office, "Do you have a grip on this case, Colonel?"

"Frankly, no."

Kent is also from the old school, and I respect that. I asked, "Why not?"

"Because you're running it your way, with my support services and logistics."

"Then you run it."

"Don't try to browbeat me, Paul."

And so we parried and thrusted for a minute or two in a petty but classical argument between uniformed honest cop and sneaky undercover guy.

Cynthia listened patiently for a minute, then said, "Colonel Kent, Mr. Brenner, there is a dead woman lying out on the rifle range. She was murdered and possibly raped. Her murderer is at large."

That about summed it up, and Kent and I hung our heads and shook hands, figuratively speaking. Actually, we just grumbled.

Kent said to me, "I'm going to General Campbell's office in about five minutes with the chaplain and a medical officer. Also, the victim's off-post phone number is being forwarded to Jordan Field, and the forensic people are still at the scene. Here are Captain Campbell's medical and personnel files. The dental file is with the coroner, who also wants her medical file, so I need it back."

"Photocopy it," I suggested. "You have my authorization."

We were almost at it again, but Ms. Sunhill, ever the peacemaker, interjected, "I'll copy the fucking file."

This sort of stopped the fun, and we got back to business. Kent showed us into an interrogation room—now called the interview room in newspeak—and asked us, "Who do you want to see first?"

"Sergeant St. John," I replied. Rank has its privileges.

Sergeant Harold St. John was shown into the room, and I indicated a chair across a small table at which Cynthia and I sat. I said to St. John, "This is Ms. Sunhill and I am Mr. Brenner."

He glanced at my name tag, which said White, and my stripes, which said staff sergeant, and he didn't get it at first, then he got it and said, "Oh . . . CID."

"Whatever." I continued, "You are not a suspect in the case that we are investigating, so I will not read you your rights under Article 31 of the Uniform Code of Military Justice. You are therefore under orders to answer my questions fully and truthfully. Of course, your voluntary cooperation would be preferable to a direct order. If, during the course of this interview, you say something that I or Ms. Sunhill believes would make you a suspect, we will read you your rights, and you have the right to remain silent at that point." Not fucking likely, Harry. "Do you understand?"

"Yes, sir."

"Good." We chatted about nothing important for five minutes while I sized him up. St. John was a balding man of about fifty-five, with a brownish complexion that I thought could be explained by caffeine, nicotine, and bourbon. His life and career in the motor pool had probably predisposed him to look at the world as a continuing maintenance problem whose solution lay somewhere in the *Maintenance Handbook*. It may not have occurred to him that some people needed more than an oil change and a tune-up to get them right.

Cynthia was jotting a few notes as St. John and I spoke, and in the middle of my small talk, he blurted out, "Look, sir, I know I was the last person to see her alive, and I know that means something, but if I killed her, I wasn't going to go report I found her dead. Right?"

Sounded reasonable, except for the verb tenses and syntax. I said to him, "The last person to see her alive was the person who murdered her. The person who murdered her was also the first person to see her dead. You were the second person to see her dead. Right?"

"Yeah . . . yes, sir . . . What I meant—"

"Sergeant, if you would be good enough not to think ahead of the questions, I would really like that. Okay?"

"Yes, sir."

Ms. Compassion said, "Sergeant, I know this has been very trying for you, and what you discovered must have been fairly traumatic, even for a veteran—have you been in a theater of war?"

"Yes, ma'am. 'Nam. Saw lots of dead, but never nothing like that."

"Yes, so when you discovered the body, you couldn't believe what you were seeing. Correct?"

He nodded enthusiastically. "I couldn't, you know, believe my eyes. I didn't even think it was her. You know, I didn't recognize her at first, because . . . I never . . . never saw her that way . . . Jesus Christ, I never saw anybody that way. You know, there was a good moon last night, and I see the humvee, and I get out of my car, and off a ways I see . . . you know—this thing lying there on the rifle range, and I get a little closer and a little closer, and then I know what it is and go right up to her and see if she's dead or alive."

"Did you kneel beside the body?"

"Hell, no, ma'am. I just beat feet the hell out of there, got into my car, and tore ass right over to the provost marshal."

"Are you certain she was dead?"

"I know dead when I see dead."

"You'd left headquarters at what time?"

"About 0400 hours."

"What time did you find the body?" Cynthia asked.

"Well, must have been about twenty, thirty minutes later."

"And you stopped at the other guard posts?"

"Some of them. Nobody saw her come by. Then I get to thinking she headed off toward the last post first. So I skipped some posts and went right out there."

"Did you ever think she was malingering somewhere?"

"No."

"Think again, Sergeant."

"Well . . . she wasn't the type. But maybe I thought about it. I do remember thinking she could have got lost out on the reservation. That ain't hard to do at night."

"Did you think she could have had an accident?"

"I thought about it, ma'am."

"So when you found her, you weren't actually taken by complete surprise?"

"Maybe not." He fished around for his cigarettes and asked me, "Okay to smoke?"

"Sure. Don't exhale."

He smiled and lit up, puffed away, and apologized to Ms. Sunhill for fouling the air. Maybe what I don't miss about the old Army is twenty-five-cent-a-pack cigarettes, and the blue haze that hung over everything except the ammo dumps and fuel storage areas.

I let him get his fix, then asked, "Did the word 'rape' ever cross your mind as you were driving around looking for her?"

He nodded.

"I didn't know her," I said. "Was she good-looking?"

He glanced at Cynthia, then looked at me. "Real good-looking."

"What we call rape bait?"

69

He didn't want to touch that one, but he replied, "She never flaunted it. Real cool customer. If a guy had anything on his mind, he'd get it out of there real quick. Everything I heard about her said she was a fine woman. General's daughter."

Harry was going to learn otherwise in the coming days and weeks, but it was interesting that the conventional wisdom seemed to be that Ann Campbell was a lady.

St. John added gratuitously, "Some of these women, like the nurses, you know, they should be a little more . . . you know?"

I could actually feel Cynthia heating up beside me. If I had any real balls, I would have told him that the CID women were worse. But I survived 'Nam, and I wasn't going to push my luck. Back to business. I asked, "After you discovered the body, why didn't you go on to the next guard post, where PFC Robbins was, and use her telephone?"

"Never thought to do that."

"And never thought to post Robbins at the scene of the crime?"

"No, sir. I was really shook."

"What made you go out and look for Captain Campbell in the first place?"

"She was gone a long time, and I didn't know where she was at."

She was supposed to be behind the preposition, but I let that slide and asked, "Do you make it a habit to check up on superior officers?"

"No, sir. But I had the feeling something was wrong."

Ah-ha. "Why?"

"Well . . . she was . . . kind of . . . like jumpy all night . . ."

Cynthia's turn. "Will you describe her behavior for me?"

"Yeah . . . well, like I said—jumpy. Kind of like out of it. Worried, maybe."

"Did you know her prior to that night?"

"Yeah . . . not real well. But like everybody knew her. General's daughter. She did that recruiting commercial on TV."

I asked him, "Did you ever speak to her before that night?"

"No, sir."

"Did you ever see her on post?"

"Yes, sir."

"Off post?"

"No, sir."

"So you really can't compare her normal behavior with the behavior of that evening?"

"No, sir, but I know what worried looks like." He added, in probably a rare moment of insight, "I could tell she was a cool customer, like the way she did her job that night, real cool and efficient, but every once in a while, she'd get quiet and I could see she had something on her mind."

"Did you comment to her about that?"

"Hell, no. She woulda snapped my fucking head off." He smiled sheepishly at Cynthia, revealing two decades of victimization by Army dentists. "Sorry, ma'am."

"Speak freely," said Ms. Sunhill with a winning smile that indicated good dental hygiene and civilian dentists.

And, actually, Cynthia was right. Half these old Army types couldn't express themselves without swearing, jargon, foreign words from some duty station or another, and a little regional southern dialect, even if they weren't from around here.

Cynthia asked him, "Did she make or receive any phone calls during the night?"

Good question, but I already knew the answer before St. John said, "She never made one while I was in the room. But maybe the times I was out. She got a call, though, and asked me to leave the room."

"What time was that?"

"Oh, about . . . about ten minutes before she left to check the guard."

I asked, "Did you eavesdrop?"

He shook his head emphatically. "No, sir!"

"Okay, tell me, Sergeant, how close did you get to the body?"

"Well . . . a few feet."

71

"I don't understand how you could determine she was dead."

"Well . . . I just figured she was dead . . . Her eyes were open . . . I called out to her . . ."

"Were you armed?"

"No, sir."

"Aren't you supposed to be armed for duty?"

"I guess I forgot to bring it along."

"So you saw the body, figured she was dead, and hightailed it."

"Yes, sir . . . I guess I shoulda checked closer."

"Sergeant, a naked woman is lying at your feet, a superior officer at that, someone you knew, and you didn't even bend over to see if she was alive or dead."

Cynthia gave me a tap under the table.

Having become the bad cop, it was time for me to leave the witness with the good cop. I stood and said, "You two continue. I may be back." I left the room and went to the holding cells, where PFC Robbins was lying on a cot, dressed in BDUs, barefoot. She was reading the post newspaper, a weekly effort of the Public Information Office, dealing mostly with manufacturing good news. I wondered how they were going to sanitize the rape and murder of the post commander's daughter: *Unidentified Woman Not Communicating on Rifle Range.*

I opened the unlocked cell and entered. PFC Robbins eyed me a moment, then put the newspaper down and sat up against the wall.

I said, "Good morning. My name is Mr. Brenner from the CID. I'd like to ask you some questions about last night."

She looked me over and informed me, "Your name tag says White."

"My aunt's uniform." I sat on a plastic chair. "You are not a suspect in this case," I began, and went through my rap. She seemed unimpressed.

I began my inconsequential chatter, and I received one-word replies. I took stock of PFC Robbins. She was about twenty, short blond hair, neat appearance, and alert eyes considering her long night and day, and all in all not bad-looking. Her accent was Deep South, not very far from here, I guessed, and her socioeconomic status prior to taking the oath was way down there. Now she was equal to every PFC in the Army, superior to the new recruits, and probably on the way up.

I asked the first question of consequence. "Did you see Captain Campbell that evening?"

"She came around the guardhouse about 2200 hours. Spoke to the officer of the guard."

"You recognized her as Captain Campbell?"

"Everyone knows Captain Campbell."

"Did you see her at any time after that?"

"No."

"She never came to your post?"

"No."

"What time were you posted at the ammunition shed?"

"At 0100 hours. To be relieved at 0530 hours."

"And between the time you were posted and the time the MPs came for you, did anyone else pass your post?"

"No."

"Did you hear anything unusual?"

"Yes."

"What?"

"Screech owl. Not many around these parts."

"I see." *Yo, Cynthia. Switch.* "Did you see anything unusual?"

"Saw the headlights."

"What headlights?"

"Probably the humvee she came up in."

"What time?"

"At 0217 hours."

"Describe what you saw."

"Saw the headlights. They stopped about a klick away, went out."

"Did they go out right after they stopped, or later?"

"Right after. Saw the headlights bouncing, stop, out."

"What did you think about that?"

"Thought somebody was headin' my way."

"But they stopped."

73

"Yup. Didn't know what to think then."

"Did you think to report it?"

"Sure did. Picked up the phone and called it in."

"Who did you call?"

"Sergeant Hayes. Sergeant of the guard."

"What did he say?"

"He said there's nothing to steal way out there except where I was at the ammo shed. Said to remain at my post."

"And you replied?"

"Told him it didn't look right."

"And he said?"

"Said there was a latrine about there. Somebody might be using it. Said it could be an officer snooping around and to keep alert." She hesitated, then added, "He said people go out there to fuck on nice summer nights. That's his words."

"Goes without saying."

"I don't like cussin'."

"Me neither." I regarded this young woman a moment. She was artless and ingenuous, to say the least: the best type of witness when coupled with some powers of observation, which she obviously had, by training or by nature. But apparently, I did not fit into her narrow frame of reference, so she wasn't offering anything free. I said, "Look, Private, you know what happened to Captain Campbell?"

She nodded.

"I have been assigned to find the murderer."

"Heard she got raped, too."

"Possibly. So I need you to talk to me, to tell me things I'm not asking. Tell me your . . . your feelings, your impressions."

Her face showed a little emotion, she bit her lower lip, and a tear ran from her right eye. She said, "I should've gone to see what was going on. I could've stopped it. That stupid Sergeant Hayes . . ." She cried quietly for a minute or two, during which time I sat looking at my boots. Finally, I said, "Your standing orders were to remain at your post until properly relieved. You obeyed your orders."

She got control of herself and said, "Yeah, but anybody with a lick of common sense and a rifle would've gone over to see what was going on. And then, when the headlights never came on again, I just stood there like a fool, and I was afraid to call in again. Then when I saw the other headlights comin' and they stopped, and then they turned around real quick and whoever it was goes barrelin' back up the road like a shot, then I knew somethin' bad happened."

"What time was that?"

"At 0425 hours."

Which would tally with the time St. John said he found the body. I asked her, "And you saw no headlights between the ones at 0217 and 0425?"

"No. But I saw some after that. 'Bout 0500. That was the MP who found the body. 'Bout fifteen minutes later, another MP came by and told me what happened."

"Could you hear any of these vehicles from that distance?"

"No."

"Hear the doors slam?"

"Could've if the wind was with me. I was upwind."

"Do you hunt?"

"I do."

"For what?"

"Possum, squirrels, rabbit."

"Bird?"

"No. I like the looks of them."

I stood. "Thank you. You've been very helpful."

"Don't think so."

"I do." I went toward the cell door, then turned back. "If I let you go back to your barracks, do I have your word that you won't say anything about this to anyone?"

"Who'm I givin' my word to?"

"An officer in the United States Army."

"You got sergeant stripes, and me and you don't know your name."

"Where's home?"

75

"Lee County, Alabama."

"You have a one-week administrative leave. Give your CO a phone number."

I went back to the interrogation room, where I found Cynthia, alone, her head in her hands, reading her notes or thinking.

We compared interviews and concluded that the time of death was somewhere between 0217 and 0425 hours. We speculated that the killer or killers were either in the humvee with Ann Campbell or already at the scene. If the killer had used his own vehicle, he had not used his headlights or had parked some distance from where PFC Robbins was posted. At that point, I leaned toward the theory that Ann Campbell had picked him or them up and driven him or them to the scene, but I did not discount the possibility of a prearranged rendezvous at the scene of the murder. A random and fateful encounter seemed less likely, considering her headlights went out immediately after the humvee stopped, because if Ann Campbell had been waylaid, there should have been some time lapse between the stopping of the vehicle and the extinguishing of the lights. Cynthia asked, "If this was a secret rendezvous or a tryst, why did she use her headlights at all?"

"Probably so as not to attract undue attention. She had legitimate business out there, but if she'd been spotted by a passing MP patrol without her headlights on, she'd be stopped and questioned."

"That's true. But PFC Robbins was alerted by the lights, so why didn't Campbell check Robbins's post first, assure her, then go back to her rendezvous?"

"Good question."

"And why rendezvous within a kilometer of a guard post anyway? There are about a hundred thousand acres of military reservation out there."

"Right, but there's that latrine with running water, and, according to Robbins, who got it from her sergeant, people go out there to fuck. Presumably, they might want to wash up afterward."

"Well, it's still possible that she was waylaid by a psycho who didn't realize how close he was to a guard post."

"Possible, but the visible evidence suggests otherwise."

"And why would she do it on a night she was on duty?" Cynthia added.

"Part of the kick. The woman was into kicks and kink."

"She was also into doing her duty while on duty. The other stuff was her other life."

I nodded. "Good point." I asked her, "Do you think St. John is hiding anything?"

"Well, he wasn't hiding his opinions. But basically, he told us all he knew. How about Robbins?"

"She told me more than she knew she knew. Not bad-looking, either. Clean country girl from 'Bama."

"If she's a PFC, she's young enough to be your great-grand-daughter."

"Probably a virgin."

"Then she can run faster than her uncles and brothers."

"My, aren't we in a rare mood."

She rubbed her temples. "Sorry, but you bug me."

"Well, why don't you go get some lunch, and I'll go call Karl Gustav before he hears about this from someone else and has me shot."

"Okay." She stood. "Keep me on this case, Paul."

"That's Herr Hellmann's decision."

She poked me in the gut again. "It's *your* decision. You tell him you want me."

"What if I don't?"

"But you do."

I walked her outside to her car, and she got in. I said, "I enjoyed working with you these last six hours and twenty-two minutes."

She smiled. "Thank you. I enjoyed about fourteen minutes of it myself. Where should I meet you, and when?"

"Back here at 1400 hours."

She pulled out of the lot, and I watched the red Mustang blend into midday post traffic.

I went back into the provost marshal's office and found out where my requisitioned office was. Kent had me in a windowless room with two desks, two chairs, one file cabinet, and enough room left over for a trash can.

I sat at one of the desks and glanced through the leather address book, then threw it aside and tried to think it all out—not the case itself, but the politics of the case, the interpersonal relationships, and my best course of action regarding protecting my ass. Then I thought about the case itself.

Before I called Hellmann, I had to get my facts straight and keep my theories and opinions to myself. Karl deals in facts but will consider personal assessments if they can somehow be used against a suspect. Karl is not a political animal, and the underlying problems with this case would not impress him. In the area of personnel management, he assumes that everyone would work well together if he ordered it. Last year in Brussels, I had asked him not to assign me to any case or any continent on or in which Ms. Cynthia Sunhill worked. I explained that we'd had a personal falling-out. He didn't know what that meant, but he gave me a firm assurance that he might possibly consider thinking about it.

And so I picked up the phone and called Falls Church, taking some satisfaction in the knowledge that I could ruin Karl's day.

CHAPTER EIGHT

T he Oberführer was in, and his clerk-typist, Diane, put me through. "Hello, Karl."

"Hello, Paul," he replied with a hint of a German accent.

The pleasantries aside, I informed him, "There's been a murder here."

"Yes?"

"General Campbell's daughter, Captain Ann Campbell."

Silence.

I continued, "Possibly raped, definitely sexually abused."

"On post?"

"Yes. At one of the rifle ranges."

"When?"

I replied, "This morning between 0217 and 0425 hours," which completed the who, what, where, and when questions.

He asked the why question. "Motive?"

"Don't know."

"Suspects?"

"None."

"Circumstances?"

"She was duty officer and went out to check the guard posts."
I filled in the details and added my involvement through Colonel Kent, my meeting up with Cynthia Sunhill, and our examination of

the scene and of the victim's off-post residence. I didn't mention the recreation room in the basement, knowing that this conversation might be recorded and that, strictly speaking, it wasn't privileged information. Why put Karl in an awkward position?

He stayed silent a moment, then said, "I want you to go back to the scene after the body has been removed and, using the same tent pegs, you will stake Ms. Sunhill to the ground."

"Excuse me?"

"I see no reason why a healthy woman could not pull the stakes out."

"Well, I can. The stakes were angled away from the body, Karl, and she wouldn't have the leverage, and presumably there was someone there with a rope around her neck, and I think—my assumption is that it was a game at first—"

"Perhaps, perhaps not. But at some point she knew it was not a game. We know from past experience what strength a woman can summon when her life is in danger. She may have been drugged or sedated. Be sure toxology looks for sedatives. Meanwhile, you and Ms. Sunhill will attempt to re-create the crime from beginning to end."

"You're talking about a simulation, I hope."

"Of course. Don't rape or strangle her."

"You're getting soft, Karl. Well, I'll relay your suggestion."

"It is not a suggestion. It is an order. Now tell me in more detail what you found in Captain Campbell's house."

I told him, and he made no comment about my failure to notify the civilian authorities. So I asked him, "For the record, do you have any problems with my entering her house and removing the contents?"

"For the record, you notified her next of kin, who agreed to or even suggested that course of action. Learn to cover your own ass, Paul. I'm not always available for that job. Now you have five seconds for homicidal reverie."

I took the five seconds, painting a delightful mental image of me with my hands around Karl's neck, his tongue sticking out, his eyes bulging . . .

"Are you back?"

"Another second" . . . his skin turning blue, and finally . . . "I'm back."

"Good. Do you want FBI assistance?"

"No."

"Do you want another investigator from this office, or from our detachment at Hadley?"

"Let's back up. I don't even want this case."

"Why not?"

"I already have an unfinished case here."

"Finish it."

"Karl, do you understand that this murder is very sensitive . . . very . . ."

"Did you have any personal involvement with the victim?"

"No."

"Fax me a preliminary report to be on my desk by 1700 hours today. Diane will assign a case number. Anything further?"

"Well, yes. There's the media, the official statement from the Department of the Army, the Judge Advocate General's Office, the Justice Department, the general's own personal statement and that of his wife, the general continuing his duties here, the—"

"Just investigate the murder."

"That's what I want to hear."

"You've heard it. Anything further?"

"Yes. I want Ms. Sunhill removed from the case."

"I didn't assign her to the case. Why is she on the case?"

"For the same reason I'm on the case. We were here. We're not connected to the power structure or personalities here. Kent asked us to help him until you officially assign a team."

"You're officially assigned. Why don't you want her on the case?"

"We don't like each other."

"You never worked together. So what is the basis of that dislike?"

"We had a personal falling-out. I have no knowledge of her professional abilities."

"She's quite competent."

"She has no homicide experience."

"You have very little rape experience. Now, here we have a rape homicide, and you two will make an excellent team."

"Karl, I thought we discussed this once. You promised not to assign us to the same duty station at the same time. Why was she here?"

"I never made such a promise. The needs of the Army come first."

"Fine. The needs of the Army would best be served if you reassigned her today. Her case here is finished."

"Yes, I have her report."

"So?"

"Hold on."

He put me on hold. Karl was being particularly insensitive and difficult, which I know is his way of telling me he has every confidence in my ability to handle a tough assignment. Still, it would have been nice to hear a word or two acknowledging that I'd caught a bad squeal. *Yes, Paul, this will be very sensitive, very difficult, and potentially harmful to your career. But I'm behind you all the way.* Maybe even a few words about the victim and her family. *Tragic, yes, tragic. Such a young, beautiful, and intelligent woman. Her parents must be devastated.* I mean, get human, Karl.

"Paul?"

"Yes?"

"That was Ms. Sunhill on the line."

I thought it might be. I said, "She has no business going over my head—"

"I reprimanded her, of course."

"Good. You see why I don't—"

"I told her you don't wish to work with her, and she claims that you are discriminating against her because of her sex, her age, and her religion."

"*What?* I don't even *know* her religion."

"It's on her dog tags."

"Karl, are you jerking me around?"

"This is a serious charge against you."

"I'm telling you, it's *personal*. We don't get along."

"You got along very well in Brussels, from what I've been told."

Fuck you, Karl. "Look, do you want me to spell it out?"

"No, I've already had it spelled out for me by someone in Brussels last year and by Ms. Sunhill a minute ago. I trust my officers to behave properly in their personal lives, and, while I don't require that you be celibate, I do require that you be discreet, and that you don't compromise yourself, the Army, or your assignment."

"I never did."

"Well, if Ms. Sunhill's fiancé had put a bullet through your head, you would have left *me* with the mess."

"That would have been my last thought as my brain exploded."

"Good. So you are a professional, and you will establish a professional relationship with Ms. Sunhill. End of discussion."

"Yes, sir." I asked him, "Is she married?"

"What difference does it make to you?"

"There *are* personal considerations."

"Neither you nor she has a personal life until you conclude this case. Anything further?"

"Did you tell Ms. Sunhill about your rather odd experiment?"

"That's your job." Karl Gustav hung up, and I sat a moment, considering my options, which boiled down to resigning or pushing on. Actually, I had my twenty years in, and I could put in my papers anytime, get out with half pay, and get a life.

There are different ways to end an Army career. Most men and women spend the last year or so in a safe assignment and fade away into oblivion. Some officers stay too long, fail to make the next grade, and are asked to leave quietly. A fortunate few go out in a blaze of glory. And then there are those who go for that last moment of glory and crash in flames. Timing is everything.

Career considerations aside, I knew that if I pulled out, this case would haunt me forever. The hook was in, and, in fact, I don't know what I would have said or done if Karl had tried to take me off the case. But Karl was a contrary and counter-suggestible son-of-a-bitch, so when I said I didn't want the case, I had the case, and when I said I didn't want Cynthia, I had Cynthia. Karl is not as smart as he thinks.

On the desk in my new office were Captain Ann Campbell's personnel and medical files, and I flipped through the former. These files contain a soldier's entire Army career, and they can be informative and interesting. Chronologically, Ann Campbell entered West Point some twelve years before, graduated in the top ten percent of her class, was given the traditional thirty-day graduation leave, and was assigned, at her request, to the Military Intelligence Officer Course at Fort Huachuca, Arizona. From there, she went to graduate school at Georgetown and received her master's in psychology. Her next step was to apply for what we call a functional area, which in this case was psychological operations. She completed the required course at the John F. Kennedy Special Warfare School at Fort Bragg, then joined the 4th Psychological Operations Group, also at Bragg. From there, she went to Germany, then back to Bragg. Then the Gulf, the Pentagon, and finally Fort Hadley.

Her officer efficiency reports, at first glance, looked exceptional, but I didn't expect otherwise. I found her Army test battery of scores and noted that her IQ put her into the genius category, the top two percent of the general population. My professional experience has been that an inordinate number of two-percenters wind up on my desk as suspects, usually in homicide cases. Geniuses don't seem to have much tolerance for people who annoy them, or hinder them, and they tend to think they are not subject to the same rules of behavior as the mass of humanity. They are often unhappy and impatient people, and they can also be sociopaths, and sometimes psychopaths who see themselves as judge and jury and, now and then, as executioner, which is when they come to my attention.

But here I had not a suspect, but a victim who was a two-percenter, which could be a meaningless fact in this case. But my instinct was telling me that Ann Campbell was a perpetrator of something before she became a victim of that something.

I opened the medical file and went directly to the back, where psychological information, if any, is usually placed. And here I found the old psychological evaluation report, which is required for entry into West Point. The reporting psychiatrist wrote:

This is a highly motivated, bright, and well-adjusted person. Based on a two-hour interview and the attached testing results, I found no authoritarian traits in her personality, no delusional disorders, mood disorders, anxiety disorders, personality disorders, or sexual disorders.

The report went on to say that there were no apparent psychological problems that would prevent her from fulfilling her duties and obligations at the United States Military Academy. Ann Campbell was a normal eighteen-year-old American girl, whatever that meant in the latter part of the twentieth century. All well and good.

But there were a few more pages in the psychological section, a short report dated in what would have been the fall semester of her third year at West Point. Ann Campbell had been ordered to see a staff psychiatrist, though who had ordered this, and why, was not stated. The psychiatrist, a Dr. Wells, had written:

Cadet Campbell has been recommended for therapy and/or evaluation. Cadet Campbell claims "There is nothing wrong with me." She is uncooperative, but not to the extent that I can forward a delinquency report on her to her commanding officer. In four interviews, each lasting approximately two hours, she repeatedly stated that she was just fatigued, stressed by the physical and academic program, anxious about her performance and grades, and generally overworked. While this is a common complaint of first- and second-year cadets, I have rarely seen this degree of mental and physical stress and fatigue in third-year students. I suggested that something else was causing her stress and feelings of anxiety, perhaps a love interest or problems at home. She assured me that everything was fine at home and that she had no love interest here at the academy or anywhere.

I observed a young woman who was clearly underweight, obviously distracted, and, in general terms, troubled and depressed. She cried several times during the interviews, but always got her emotions under control and apologized for crying.

At times, she seemed on the verge of revealing more than common cadet complaints, but always drew back. She did say once, however, "It doesn't matter if I go to class or not, it doesn't matter what I do here. They're going to graduate me anyway." I asked if she thought that was true because she was General Campbell's daughter, and she replied, "No, they're going to graduate me because I did them a favor."

When I asked what she meant by that, and who "they" were, she replied, "The old boys." Subsequent questions elicited no response.

I believe we were on the threshold of a breakthrough, but her subsequent appointments, originally ordered by her commander, were canceled without explanation by a higher authority whose name I never learned.

My belief is that Cadet Campbell is in need of further evaluation and therapy, voluntary or involuntary. Lacking that, I recommend a psychiatric board of inquiry to determine if Cadet Campbell should be given a psychiatric separation from the academy. I further recommend a complete medical examination and evaluation.

I digested this brief report, wondering, of course, how a well-adjusted eighteen-year-old had turned into a depressed twenty-year-old. The rigors of West Point could easily explain that, but obviously Dr. Wells wasn't buying it, and neither was I.

I leafed through the file, intending at some early date to read it from cover to cover. As I was about to close the folder, an errant scrap of paper caught my eye and I read the handwritten words:

Whoever fights monsters should see to it that in the process he does not become a monster. And when you look long into the abyss, the abyss also looks into you.—Nietzsche.

What that quote was doing there, I don't know, but it was appropriate in the file of a psy-ops officer and would have been appropriate in the file of a CID man as well.

CHAPTER NINE

I did not need to be, nor did I want to be, Sergeant Franklin White any longer, especially since Sergeant White had to salute every snot-nosed lieutenant he passed. So I made the half-mile walk to the Infantry Training Brigade and retrieved my pick-up truck, then headed out to Whispering Pines to change into civvies.

I drove past the post armory, but didn't see Sergeant Elkin's POV parked in the lot. I had this unsettling thought that Elkins was going to consummate the deal behind my back and take off for parts unknown, leaving me to explain how I let a few hundred M-16s and grenade launchers get into the hands of Colombian banditos.

But first things first. I left post and got onto the highway. The drive to Whispering Pines took about twenty minutes, during which time I reconstructed the events of the morning from the time the phone rang in the armory. I do this because my employer, the United States Army, is big on chronology and facts. But in a murder investigation, what you see and when you saw it is not the whole game, because by the nature of the act of murder, the crucial things happened before you got there. There is sort of a spirit world that coexists with the world of empirical observation, and you have to get in touch with that world through the detective's equivalent of the séance. You don't use a crystal ball, though I'd like one that worked—but you do clear your mind and listen to what isn't said and see things that aren't there.

That aside, Karl needed a written report, so I drafted one in my mind: *Further to our phone conversation, the general's daughter was a whore, but what a magnificent whore. I can't get her out of my mind. If I had been obsessively in love with her and found out she was fucking for everyone, I would have killed her myself. Nevertheless, will find son-of-a-bitch who did it and see that he faces a firing squad. Thanks for the case. (Signed) Brenner.*

That might need a little work. But it's important, I think, to admit to yourself the truth of how you feel about things. Everyone else is going to lie, posture, and dissemble.

Regarding that, I thought about Cynthia. In truth, I couldn't get the woman out of my mind. I kept seeing her face and hearing her voice, and I was right then missing her. This is presumptive evidence of a strong emotional attachment, perhaps a sexual obsession, and, God forbid, love. This was worrisome, not only because I wasn't ready for this but because I wasn't sure how she felt. Also, there was the murder. When you get handed a murder, you have to give it everything you've got, and if you don't have much left to give, you have to draw on psychic energy that you've been saving for other things. Eventually, of course, there's nothing left to borrow, and people like Cynthia, young and filled with a sense of duty and enthusiasm, call you cold, callous, and cynical. I deny this, of course, knowing I'm capable of emotions and feelings, of love and warmth. I was sort of like that in Brussels last year, and look at what it got me. Anyway, murder deserves one's undivided attention.

I looked out the windshield as I approached Whispering Pines Trailer Park. Up ahead, on the left, I saw a county road crew making a blacktop repair, and I recalled two and a half decades ago when I saw my first Georgia chain gang. I don't think they use chain gangs on the roads anymore, and I hope they don't. But I recall the sight vividly, the prisoners, filthy and bowed, their ankles connected by chains, and the guards in sweaty tan uniforms, carrying rifles and shotguns. I couldn't believe at first what I was seeing. Paul

Brenner, late of South Boston, simply could not comprehend that men were chained together, working like slaves in the blistering sun, right here in America. I actually felt my stomach tighten as though someone had punched me.

But that Paul Brenner no longer existed. The world had become softer, and I'd become harder. Somewhere on the time line, the world and I had been harmonious for a year or two, then went our separate ways again. Maybe my problem was that my worlds changed too much: Georgia today, Brussels last year, Pago Pago next week. I needed to stop in one place for a while, I needed to know a woman for more than a night, a week, or a month.

I passed between two stripped pine trees to which had been nailed a hand-painted sign overhead that once read "Whispering Pines." I parked the pickup truck near the owner's mobile home and began the trek to my aluminum abode. I think I liked rural southern poverty better when it was housed in wooden shacks with a rocking chair and a jug of corn squeezings on the front porch.

I did a walk around the trailer, checking for open windows, footprints, and other signs that someone had been there. I came around to the entrance and inspected the strand of sticky filament I'd placed across the door and the frame. It's not that I'd seen too many movies where the detective goes into his house and gets clubbed over the head. But I spent five years in the infantry, one of them in 'Nam, and about ten years in Europe and Asia dealing with everyone from drug traffickers, to arms smugglers, to just plain murderers, and I know why I'm alive, and I know how to stay that way. In other words, if you have your head up your ass, four of your five senses aren't working.

I entered the mobile home and left the door open as I checked to see that I was the only one there. I seemed to be alone, and the premises seemed to be the way I'd left them.

I walked to the back bedroom. This was the room I used for my office where my pistols were kept, along with my notes, reports, codebooks, and other tools of the trade. I had put a hasp and padlock on this bedroom door so no one, including the owner of the trailer park, could get into it, and I'd also put epoxy glue in the sliders of the only window. I unlocked the padlock and went inside.

The bedroom furniture came with the place, but I'd signed out a camp desk and chair from the post quartermaster, and on the desk I saw that the light on the telephone answering machine was blinking. I hit the message button, and a prerecorded male voice with a nasal problem announced, "You have one message." Then another male voice said, "Mr. Brenner, this is Colonel Fowler, the post adjutant. General Campbell wishes to see you. Report to his home, ASAP. Good day."

Rather curt. All I could deduce from that was that Colonel Kent had finally got around to informing the deceased's next of kin and had volunteered the information that this Brenner guy from Falls Church was the investigating officer and had given Colonel Fowler my phone number. Thanks, Kent.

I had no time for General or Mrs. Campbell at the moment, so I erased the message from the tape and from my mind.

I went to the dresser and took my 9mm Glock automatic with holster, then exited the spare bedroom, closing the padlock behind me.

I entered the master bedroom, changed into a blue tropical wool suit, adjusted the holster, went into the kitchen, popped a cold beer, then exited the trailer. I left the pickup truck where it was and got into the Blazer. Thus transformed, I was outwardly prepared to deal with rape and murder, though somewhere along the line I had to log some cot time.

I took a few pulls on the beer as I drove. This state has a law about open alcoholic beverage containers which the locals say means, if you open it, you have to finish it before you throw it out the window.

I detoured into a depressing suburb of small ranch houses called Indian Springs. There were no Indians around, but there were plenty of cowboys, judging from the souped-up vehicles in the driveways. I pulled into the driveway of a modest home and hit the horn a few times. This is in lieu of getting out and ringing the bell, and is perfectly acceptable hereabouts. A wide woman came to the door, saw me, and waved, then disappeared. A few minutes later, Sergeant Dalbert Elkins ambled out of the house. One of the good things about pulling night duty is that you get the next day off, and Elkins was obviously enjoying the day, dressed in shorts, T-shirt, and sandals, a beer in each hand. I said to him, ''Get in. We got to see a guy on post.''

''Aw, sheet.''

''Come on. I'll get you back here, ASAP.''

He yelled back into the house, ''Gotta go!'' Then he climbed into the passenger seat and handed me one of the beers.

I took it, backed out of the driveway, and drove off. Sergeant Elkins had four questions for me: Where'd you get this Blazer? Where'd you get that suit? How was the pussy? Who we gotta see?

I replied that the Blazer was borrowed, the suit came from Hong Kong, the other thing was A-one, and we had to see a guy in jail.

''In *jail*?''

''A good buddy. They got him locked in the provost office. I got to see him before they take him to the stockade.''

''Why? What for?''

''They got him for DWI. I got to drive his car out to his place. His old lady's nine months pregnant and she needs the wheels. They live out by you. You follow me back in the Blazer.''

Sergeant Elkins nodded as if he'd done this before. He said, ''Hey, tell me about the pussy.''

So, wanting him to be happy, I went into my good ol' boy rap. ''Well, I got me a little slopehead 'bout as tall as a pint of piss, and I just pick her up by the ears and stick her on my dick, then slap her upside the head and spin her 'round my cock like the block on a shithouse door.''

Elkins roared with laughter. Actually, that wasn't bad. You'd never know I was from Boston. God, I'm good.

We made small talk and sipped beer. As we drove onto the post, we lowered the beer cans as we passed the MPs, then tucked them away under the seats. I pulled up to the provost marshal's office and we got out and went inside.

92

The duty sergeant stood and I put my CID badge case up to his face and kept walking. Sergeant Elkins either didn't notice or it happened too fast for him. We walked down a corridor to the holding cells. I found a nice empty one in the corner with an open door, and I nudged Sergeant Elkins inside. He seemed confused and a little anxious. He asked, "Where's your buddy . . . ?"

"You're my buddy." I closed the cell door and it locked. I spoke to my buddy through the bars. "You are under arrest." I held up my badge case. "The charge is conspiracy to sell military property of the United States without proper authority, and frauds against the United States." I added, "Plus, you weren't wearing your seat belt."

"Oh, Jesus . . . oh, Lord . . ."

The expression on a man's face when you announce that he's under arrest is very interesting and revealing, and you have to judge your next statement by his reaction. Elkins looked like he'd just seen St. Peter giving him a thumbs-down. I informed him, "I'm going to give you a break, Dalbert. You're going to handwrite and sign a full confession, then you're going to cooperate with the government in nailing the guys we've been talking to. You do that, and I'll guarantee you no jail time. You get a dishonorable discharge and forfeiture of all rank, pay, allowances, and retirement benefits. Otherwise, it's life in Leavenworth, good buddy. Deal?"

He started to cry. I know I'm getting soft because there was a time I wouldn't have even offered such a great deal, and if a suspect started to cry, I'd slap him around until he shut up. But I'm trying to become more sensitive to the needs and wants of criminals, and I tried not to think of what those two hundred M-16s and grenade launchers could do to cops and innocent people. Not to mention the fact that Staff Sergeant Elkins had broken a sacred trust. I said to Elkins, "Deal?"

He nodded.

"Smart move, Dalbert." I fished around in my pocket and found the rights card. "Here. Read this and sign it." I handed him the card and a pen. He wiped his tears as he read his rights as an accused. I said, "Sign the damn thing, Dalbert."

He signed and handed me the card and the pen. Karl was going to fly into a monumental fit when I told him I'd turned Elkins into a government witness. Karl's philosophy is that everyone should go to jail, and no one should be able to cut a deal. Court-martial boards didn't like to hear about deals. Okay, but I had to shortcut this case to get on to the case that had the potential to harm me. Karl said to finish it. It was finished.

An MP lieutenant approached and asked me to explain and identify myself. I showed him my CID identification and said to him, ''Get this man some paper and pen for a confession, then take him to the post CID and turn him over to them for further interrogation.''

Staff Sergeant Elkins was sitting on the cot now, looking very forlorn in his shorts, T-shirt, and sandals. I've seen too many men like that through steel bars. I wonder how I look to them from the other side of the bars.

I left the holding cells and found my assigned office. I flipped through Ann Campbell's address book, which held about a hundred names, mine not included. She used no stars or hearts or anything like that to denote a romantic interest or a rating system, but as I said, there was probably another list of names and phone numbers somewhere, possibly in her basement rec room, or perhaps buried in her personal computer.

I scribbled out a rather perfunctory and annoyingly terse report for Karl—not the one I'd made up in my mind, but one that neither the judge advocate general nor the attorney for the defense could criticize later. There wasn't a document in the country that was safe anymore, and the Confidential classification might as well say, ''Widest Possible Distribution.''

The report completed, I hit the intercom button on the telephone and said, ''Have a clerk report to me.''

Army clerks are sort of like civilian secretaries, except that many of them are men, though I'm seeing more female clerks these days. In either case, like their civilian counterparts, they can make or break a boss or an office. The one who reported to me was a female, dressed in the green B uniform, which is basically a green skirt and blouse, suitable for hot offices. She reported well enough, with a crisp salute and a good voice. "Specialist Baker, sir."

I stood, though this is not required of me, and extended my hand. "I am Warrant Officer Brenner, CID. I am working on the Campbell case. Do you know all of that?"

"Yes, sir."

I regarded Specialist Baker a moment. She was about twenty-one, looked alert enough, not beautiful, but sort of bright-eyed and perky. Maybe cute. I asked her, "Do you want to be detailed to this case?"

"I work for Captain Redding in Traffic Enforcement."

"Yes or no?"

"Yes, sir."

"Fine. You will report only to me and to Ms. Sunhill, who is also on this case, and you will speak to no one else. Everything you see and hear is highly confidential."

"I understand."

"Good. Type this report, photocopy this address book, send the copies to this fax number in Falls Church, and leave the originals on my desk."

"Yes, sir."

"Put a sign on this door that says, 'Private, authorized personnel only.' You, me, and Ms. Sunhill are the only authorized personnel."

"Yes, sir."

In the military, where honesty, honor, and obedience are still held in high regard, you theoretically don't need locks on doors, but I'm seeing more locks these days. Nevertheless, being from the old school, I didn't order one. However, I did tell Specialist Baker, "You will empty the wastebaskets every evening and put the contents through a shredder."

"Yes, sir."

"Any questions?"

"Who will speak to Captain Redding?"

"I will speak to Colonel Kent about that. Any further questions?"

95

"No, sir."

"Dismissed."

She took the address book and my handwritten report, saluted, turned, and left.

It's not easy being a traveling pain-in-the-ass. Anyone can be a pain-in-the-ass on the home court, but it takes a unique individual to come into an environment whose pecking order, nuances, and personalities have already been shaped and fit into place. Yet, if you don't get the upper hand on the first day, you'll never get it, and they'll mess you around until you become worse than useless.

Power, I've learned, is derived in many legitimate ways. But if the institution has not fully empowered you, but has given you a job that is very important and really sucks, then you have to take the power you need to get it done. I think the Army expects that, expects you to demonstrate initiative, as they constantly tell you. But you have to be careful, because this only works if you're getting the job done. If you're not getting the job done, then they get you. Worse, when the job is successfully completed, they pat you on the head like an exhausted sled dog, then eat you, which is why I never stay around for cocktails when a case is completed. Karl says I hide under his desk for a week, which is not true, but I have been known to take a few weeks in Switzerland.

It was 1400 hours and Warrant Officer Sunhill had not made an appearance yet, so I left the provost building to get my vehicle and discovered my partner parked at the front door, sleeping behind the wheel, the Grateful Dead on the CD player, which may have been appropriate.

I got in and slammed the door, waking her up. "Sleeping?" I asked.

"No, resting my eyes."

She always used to say that, and we exchanged quick smiles of recognition. I said, "Rifle range six, please."

CHAPTER TEN

Cynthia shifted into high gear as we cleared the main post and broke out into the wooded reservation. She said, "Nice suit."

"Thank you." The Grateful Dead was singing "A Touch of Grey." I shut off the CD player.

"Did you have lunch?" she inquired.

"No."

"Did you do anything useful?" she asked.

"Probably not."

"Are you annoyed about something?"

"Yes."

"Karl can be annoying."

"If you call him again regarding this case, I'll have you up on charges."

"Yes, sir."

We drove in silence awhile, then she said, "I need your phone number and address."

I gave them to her and she said, "I'm staying in the visiting officers' quarters." She added, "Why don't you move in? I mean, into the VOQ. It's more convenient."

"I like Whispering Pines Trailer Park."

"Trailer parks in the woods are spooky."

"Not for real men."

"Oh, do you have one living with you?" She thought this was funny and laughed at her own joke, then covered her mouth in a theatrical gesture and said, "Oops, sorry, I should be trying to get on your good side."

"Don't waste your time."

Cynthia is not a manipulator, but she has been known to manipulate. A fine distinction, but an important one. She's basically ingenuous and honest, and if she likes the way a man looks or acts, she tells him. I've told her to be a little less sincere, that some men take this as a come-on. But she doesn't get it, and this is a woman who handles rape cases.

I said to her, "We have a clerk-typist, a Specialist Baker."

"Male or female?"

"I don't notice these things. And by the way, what religion are you?"

She smiled and pulled her dog tags out of her shirt, and read them as she drove. "Let's see . . . AB . . . American Baptist? No, that's my blood type . . . Here it is. Presbyterian."

"I'm not amused."

"I'm sorry about that. Karl knew it was a joke."

"Karl can't identify a joke unless people around him are laughing."

"Come on, Paul. You don't take any of this sensitivity stuff seriously anyway. If I may give you a suggestion—be careful. You don't have to talk newspeak or confess to your prejudices, but don't make fun of the new stuff, either. There's no upside to that, professionally speaking."

"Are you a commissar?"

"No, I'm your partner." She poked my arm. "Don't get old on me."

"Okay." Obviously, Cynthia was in a somewhat less confrontational mode. Either something good had happened to her in her two-hour absence, or she had rethought or remembered things about Paul Brenner that weren't all bad. To get back to business, I inquired, "Did you look up 'sexual asphyxia'?"

"Of course. It's totally weird."

"Sex is weird if you think about it."

"Maybe for you."

"Tell me about sexual asphyxia."

"All right . . . it's basically having a tightened cord around your neck during sexual arousal. Usually men do it to themselves while masturbating. Autoerotic. But women have been known to practice autoerotic asphyxia, too. Sometimes heterosexual and homosexual partners do it to each other during sex. It's usually consensual, but not always, and sometimes it leads to a fatality, either accidental or on purpose. That's when it becomes a police matter."

"Correct. Have you ever seen it in practice?"

"No. Have you?"

"Have you ever done it?"

"No, Paul. Have you?"

"No, but I have seen it once. A guy rigged up something to hang himself while he masturbated, looking at a porno video. He didn't mean to die, but the stool he was standing on slipped away and he hanged himself for real. An autoerotic fatality. The MPs thought it was suicide, of course. But when the victim is naked, and there is erotic paraphernalia around, then you can be pretty sure it was an accident. Try explaining that to the family."

"I can imagine." She shook her head and said, "I'm not sure how that's fun. Didn't say in the manual."

"Well, it's in other manuals. Here's how it's fun: When you get a disruption of blood supply and oxygen to the brain, certain sensations are heightened, partly as a result of diminished ego controls. A temporary lack of oxygen causes giddiness, light-headedness, and even exhilaration. It's a high without drugs or alcohol. In this state, many people experience a more intense sexual arousal and feeling." I added, "I've heard that when you come, you *really* come, but if you misjudge, then you've come and gone. You're history."

"That's not fun."

"No. Also, only part of the kick is physiological. The other thing is the ritualistic behavior that accompanies most acts of sexual

99

asphyxia—the nakedness or the wearing of unusual clothes, the sexual paraphernalia and erotic materials, the fantasy, the setting, and ultimately the danger.''

''Who invented this one?''

''Undoubtedly, it was discovered accidentally. Maybe there're pictures of it in Egyptian pyramids. Human beings are ceaselessly ingenious when it comes to self-gratification.''

She stayed silent while she drove, then glanced at me, and finally asked, ''And you think something like this happened to Ann Campbell?''

''Well . . . the panties around her neck were put there so as not to leave a telltale rope mark. That's very specific for sexual asphyxia when it is not meant to lead to death.'' I added, ''That is one way to interpret the scene that presented itself to us, but let's examine the forensic evidence.''

''Where were her clothes?''

''She may have dropped them off somewhere.''

''Why?''

''It's part of the danger and the fantasy. As you mentioned earlier, we have no way of knowing what was sexually significant to her, or what elaborate constructs she had developed in her mind. Think, if you will, of your own secret garden of delights, and try to imagine how those scenarios would be viewed by another person.'' To fill the awkward silence, I added, ''This type of personality is ultimately only satisfied with his or her own elaborate fantasies, with or without a partner. I'm beginning to think that what we saw on rifle range six was produced, directed, and scripted by Ann Campbell, not by her partner or assailant.''

Cynthia said nothing, so I continued, ''Most likely, it was a consensual act that included sexual asphyxia in which her partner strangled her to death by accident, or on purpose, in a moment of anger. An assailant, a stranger, who was bent on rape and murder would not have put the panties around her neck to minimize tissue damage.''

''No, but as we discussed, consider that perhaps the partner did

100

not kill her in a moment of anger. Consider that the partner *intended* to kill her, and she *thought* it was a game.''

''That's another possibility.''

Cynthia said, ''I keep thinking about that room in the basement. There may have been men who wanted her dead out of jealousy or revenge, or she may have been blackmailing someone.''

''Right. She was a homicide victim waiting to happen. But we need more information. You'll write all of that in your case book. Okay?''

Again she nodded but said nothing. Clearly, Cynthia, who dealt with garden-variety rapes that did not lead to murder, was somewhat overwhelmed by these new facets of human depravity and sexual diversity. Yet, I was sure she had seen women brutalized by men, but she must have compartmentalized those crimes or categorized them in some fashion that she could deal with. She didn't seem to hate all men—in fact, she liked men—but I could see how she could, or would, one day begin to hate. I asked Cynthia, ''The Neely case. Who was the guy?''

''Oh . . . some young trainee at the Infantry School. He fell in love with this nurse and followed her out to her car one night as she left the hospital. He made a full confession and will make a full apology, then plead guilty and take five to ten.''

I nodded. It was not Army policy, but it was becoming more common to have the convicted or confessed criminal apologize to the victim or the family, and also to his or her own commanding officer. This sounded more Japanese than English common law to me, but I suppose it's okay. Ironically, General Campbell had instituted this policy here at Fort Hadley. I said, ''Good God, I wouldn't want to be the guy who had to apologize to the general for raping and murdering his daughter.''

''It would be hard to find just the right words,'' Cynthia agreed. She added, ''Are we back to rape and murder?''

''Perhaps. But it could have been murder and rape. Do you want to discuss necrophilia?''

''No. Enough.''

"Amen." Up ahead, I could see the outline of a huge green open-sided tent, like a pavilion that you see at lawn parties. The forensic people pitch these over an outdoor crime scene to protect the evidence from the elements.

Cynthia said, "I appreciate the confidence in me that you've expressed to Karl."

I didn't recall that conversation with Karl, so I let that pass and said, "Karl wants us to reconstruct the crime. Complete with tent pegs, ropes, and so forth. You're Ann Campbell."

She thought about this a moment, then said, "All right . . . I've done that before . . ."

"Good. I'm looking forward to it."

We had arrived at the scene, and Cynthia pulled over behind a forensic unit van. She said, "Are we going to see the body again?"

"No." By now the body was bloating, and there would be a faint odor about it, and, as irrational and unprofessional as this sounds, I wanted to remember Ann Campbell as she was.

CHAPTER ELEVEN

There were about a dozen vans and cars on the narrow road, belonging to the CID forensic lab and the local MPs.

Cynthia and I walked on a trail of green tarpaulin toward the open pavilion.

It was a typically hot Georgia afternoon, with an occasional soft breeze that carried the resinous scent of pines through the humid air.

Death does not cause a halt in military activities, and the rifle ranges to our left and right were being used despite the problem at rifle range six. I could hear the far-off fusillades of M-16s, sharp, staccato bursts of fire, and, as always, that sound stirred unpleasant memories. But those memories did put things into perspective. I mean, this case was unpleasant, but jungle combat was way down there on the list of unpleasant activities. Things could be worse. I was alive, and a young woman, fifty meters away, wasn't.

In and around the pavilion were at least thirty men and women, all engaged in the business of forensic work.

Forensic science is based largely on the theory of transfer and exchange. It is an article of faith with forensic people that the perpetrator will take away traces of the scene and of the victim, and will leave traces of himself at the scene or on the victim. This is especially true with sexual assault, which by its nature puts the perpetrator and victim in close juxtaposition.

There are, however, cases where the perpetrator is extremely bright and savvy, and has no intention of giving the forensic lab so much as a pubic hair or a drop of semen or saliva, or even a whiff of after-shave lotion. Based on what I'd seen earlier, this seemed like it could be one of those cases. And if it turned out that it was, then I had to rely solely on old-fashioned interrogation, intuition, and legwork. But even if I found the perpetrator, a conviction without a shred of forensic evidence was unlikely.

I stopped before I got to the pavilion, and a short, bald man separated himself from the crowd around the body and came toward us. I recognized Chief Warrant Officer Cal Seiver, who was probably the OIC—the officer in charge—of the entire team. Seiver is basically a good guy, a professional with an uncanny sense of what piece of thread or what speck of dust is important. But, like many technical types, he lives and breathes minutiae and can't see the forest for the trees. This is good, though, because the forest is my job, and the trees are his. I don't like forensic types who play detective.

Cal was looking a bit pale as he always does when he sees a body. We shook hands and I introduced him to Cynthia, but they knew each other. He said, "The entire fucking world walked around this body, Paul."

We go through this every time. I replied, "Nobody knows how to levitate yet."

"Yeah, well, you people stomped on everything."

"Any nonmilitary footwear?"

"Yeah. Running shoes." He looked at Cynthia's shoes. "Did you—"

"Yes," she replied. "I'll give you my footprints. Any other footprints aside from boots?"

"Yeah. I picked up a partial bare footprint, probably the deceased's, but everything else is boots, boots, boots. Some soles make different marks, you know, uneven wear, cuts in the leather, different brands of heels—"

"I think you told me that once," I reminded him.

"Yeah. We've got to take disqualifying sole prints from every-body, but I have to tell you, the area probably had dozens of prints already, and this range is covered with scrub brush and grass."

"I see that."

"I hate outdoor crime scenes." He pulled out a handkerchief, took off his BDU cap, and mopped his sweaty pate.

I informed him, "New memo from the Pentagon, Cal. You are not short and bald—you are a vertically challenged man of scalp."

He looked at Cynthia. "You got to work with this guy?"

"He's trying to bug me, not you. I just gave him a lecture on sensitivity."

"Yeah? Don't waste your time."

"Precisely," agreed Cynthia. "Did you get the stuff I sent you on the Neely case?"

"Yeah. We did a DNA match on the semen we had from her vagina, and the stuff you sent over yesterday from the confessed rapist. Same stuff, so you got a true confession. Congratulations."

I added my congratulations and inquired of Cal, "Any traces of semen on this victim?"

"I ran an ultraviolet light over her, and there're no traces of semen. We took vaginal, oral, and anal swabs, and we'll know about that in a half hour or so." He added, "The latent-prints people have already done the body, the humvee, her handbag, the tent pegs, and ropes. The photographers are nearly done, and I have the serology people in the vans now with the blood, saliva, and orifice samples. The chemistry people are vacuuming trace evidence from the body, but I have to tell you, I don't even see a stray hair on the body, and what lint there is probably came from her own underwear and clothes. I also brought along a team from the tool marks lab, and they're examining the tent pegs and rope, but it's standard-issue stuff and the pegs are old and used, and so is the rope. So, to answer all your questions, we don't have a physical clue for you yet."

Cal tends to be negative. Then later, he tells you that after hours of hard and brilliant lab work, he's got something. The secret to becoming a legend is to make the job look harder than it is. I do

105

that once in a while myself. Cynthia doesn't get it yet. I asked Cal, "Have you removed the tent pegs?"

"Just the one near the left ankle to get at an anal sample, and to determine if there's any dirt on the peg that's different from the dirt it's stuck in now. But it seems like all red Georgia clay."

"I want you to determine if either of the tent pegs near the wrists could have been pulled out by the victim if she were free to do so. Also, see if either of the knots on the wrists is a slipknot. Also, I would like you to tell me if you think she had or could have had either end of the ligature in her hands."

"Now?"

"Please."

Cal turned and walked away.

Cynthia said to me, "If none of those things are true or possible, then we can rule out an autoerotic fatality. Correct?"

"Correct."

"Then we look for a perpetrator."

"A perpetrator or an accomplice. It still looks like it started out as fun." I added, "That is not for public dissemination."

"Obviously." She said, "I don't mind seeing the body again. I know what we're looking for." She followed the tarpaulin trail to the pavilion and disappeared into the crowd as she knelt beside the body. I turned and walked back to the road and stood beside the humvee. I looked up the road toward the guard post where PFC Robbins had stood, but I could not see the ammo shed from a kilometer away. I turned and looked down the road toward the direction we had come from and saw that the road made a right-hand bend, so that if a vehicle stopped about a hundred meters away, at rifle range five, its headlights might not be seen from where Robbins had been standing. There was something about the times of the headlights that bugged me, and I had to consider the possibility that the first headlights that Robbins saw were not necessarily those of Ann Campbell's humvee—because if they were, what was Ann Campbell doing between the time she left Post Headquarters at 0100 hours and the time Robbins saw the first headlights at 0217 hours?

Cynthia and Cal approached, and Cal informed me, ''The tent pegs are solid in the clay. A guy with surgical gloves almost got a hernia pulling them out. The knots have been classified as granny knots, and you can barely untie them even using a mechanical aid. As for the ligature, the ends do reach her hands, but if you're asking for my opinion, I don't think she could have pulled them herself. You looking for an autoerotic accident?''

''Just a thought. Between us.''

''Yeah. But it looks like she had company last night, though we haven't found any traces of her company yet.''

''Where was the bare footprint?''

''About halfway between the road and the body. About there.'' He pointed to where one of his people was taking a casting of a print.

I nodded. ''How was the rope cut?''

Cal replied, ''Compression cut. Like an ax or cleaver, maybe on a wooden surface. Probably not done here—the tool mark guys checked the bleacher seats for cuts. Most likely, the lengths were precut and brought here.'' He added, ''Like a rape kit,'' but resisted the temptation to say words like ''premeditated'' or ''organized rapist.'' I like people who stick to their area of expertise. In fact, what looked like part of a rape kit was more likely bondage parapher- nalia from the victim's own storehouse of equipment. But it was best if everyone kept thinking rape.

Cal said to me, ''You wanted to know about the black smudge on her right foot.''

''Yes.''

''Ninety-nine percent sure it's blacktop. Know for sure in about an hour. I'll match the smudge to the road here, but it won't be conclusive.''

''Okay.''

He asked me, ''How'd you pull this case?''

''I begged for it.''

He laughed, then said, ''I wouldn't want to be in your boots.''

''Me neither, if you found my bootprints in the humvee.''

He smiled, and it seemed he was enjoying my company, so I

107

reminded him, "If you botch anything, you should think about where you can live on half pay. A lot of guys go to Mexico."

"Hey, if I botch anything, I can cover my ass. If you botch anything, your ass is grass, and Colonel Hellmann is the lawn mower."

Which was an unpleasant truth. I informed him, "The victim's office, household goods, and personal effects are in a hangar at Jordan Field, so when you're through here, go there."

"I know. We'll be done here by dark, then we'll do an all-nighter at the hangar."

"Was Colonel Kent here?"

"Just for a few minutes."

"What did he want?"

"Same as you, without the wisecracks." He added, "Wants you to see the general. Did you get that message?"

"No. All right, Cal, I'm at the provost marshal's office. All reports and inquiries go to me or Cynthia directly, sealed and marked 'Confidential.' Or you can call or drop by. My clerk is Specialist Baker. Don't discuss this case with anyone, not even the post provost marshal. If he asks you anything, refer him to me or Cynthia. And instruct your people to do the same. Okay?"

Cal nodded, then asked, "Not even Colonel Kent?"

"Not even the general."

He shrugged. "Okay."

"Let's go look at the latrines, then your people can process the premises."

"Okay."

As we walked, Cynthia asked Cal, "When can you release the body to the coroner for autopsy?"

Cal scratched his bald head. "Well . . . I guess in about three hours."

She said, "Why don't you call the post hospital and get the coroner out here so he can examine the body in place? Then tell him we would appreciate an autopsy ASAP, even if he has to work late, and we'd like a preliminary coroner's report sometime tonight.

108

Tell him the general would appreciate it, too, and that the general and Mrs. Campbell would like to get on with the funeral arrangements.''

Cal nodded. "Okay."

Cynthia seemed to be getting the hang of it. Obviously, I was teaching by example.

The three of us made our way past the bleachers, over an open stretch of thick grass that left no footprints, and into the tree line where two latrine sheds stood. Kent had cordoned off the area, and we stepped over the yellow crime scene tape. The older shed was marked ''Male Personnel,'' and the newer one ''Female Personnel.'' The word ''personnel'' may seem superfluous, but Army regulations prohibit brevity and common sense. We entered the latrine shed for male personnel, and I turned on the lights using my handkerchief.

The floor was concrete, the walls wooden, and there were screens where the wall met the ceiling. There were three sinks, three stalls, and three urinals, all fairly clean. I assumed that if a unit had fired the previous day, they would have finished no later than 1700 hours, and they would have assigned a latrine clean-up detail. In fact, the wastebaskets were empty and there was nothing floating in the commodes, and all the seats were in the upright position.

Cynthia drew my attention to one of the sinks. There were water spots and a small hair in the basin. I said to Cal, ''Here's something.''

He walked over and bent over the bowl. ''Human, Caucasian, head.'' He looked closer. ''Fell out, maybe cut, but not pulled out. No root. Not much of a sample, but I may be able to get you a blood type, maybe the sex, but without the root I can't get you a genetic marker.''

''How about the owner's name?''

Cal was not amused. He surveyed the latrine and said, ''I'll give this next priority after we finish out there.''

''Open the sink traps, too.''

''Do I need to be told that?''

"I guess not."

We went into the female latrine, which was as clean as its male counterpart. There were six stalls, and here, also, the toilet seats were all up, which was an Army regulation, despite the fact that women had to put them down. I said to Cal, "I want you to tell me if Captain Campbell used this latrine."

He replied, "If nothing else, we may be able to find a trace of perspiration or body oil on the toilet seat, or skin cells in the sink trap. I'll do my best."

"And don't forget fingerprints on and around the light switch."

"Do you forget to breathe?"

"Once in a while."

"I don't forget anything."

"Good." We looked around, but there was no visible evidence that could be connected to the victim, to the crime scene, or to a perpetrator. But if you believe in the theory of transference and exchange, the place could be crawling with evidence.

We went out into the sunlight and walked back toward the road. I said to Cal, "Don't get insulted, but I have to remind you to establish a proper chain of custody with the evidence, and label and document everything as if you were going to be cross-examined by a savage defense attorney who was only getting paid for a not-guilty verdict. Okay?"

"Don't worry about it. Meantime, you get a suspect, and we'll scrape his skin, and take his blood, and pull his hair, and get him to pop off inside a rubber like Cynthia here did with this guy the other day."

"I hope there's something here to compare to a suspect."

"There's always something. Where are her clothes, by the way?"

"Gone. She was wearing BDUs."

"So's everybody else. If I find BDU fibers, it means nothing."

"No, it doesn't."

"Forensic's not easy when everybody's wearing the same clothes and boots."

"True enough. Did you get disqualifying footprints from all the MPs on the scene?"

110

"Yeah."

"Including Colonel Kent?"

"Yup."

We got back to the road and stopped. Cynthia said, "Remember, Cal, the only pressure on you is from us. Nobody else counts."

"I hear you." He glanced back toward the body and offered, "She was very pretty. We have one of those recruiting posters of her in the lab." He looked at Cynthia and me, and said, "Hey, good luck."

Cynthia replied, "You, too."

Cal Seiver turned and ambled off toward the body.

Cynthia and I got in her car and she asked, "Where to?"

"Jordan Field."

CHAPTER TWELVE

S peed, speed, speed. The older the case, the colder the trail. The colder the trail, the harder the case.

Transference and exchange. Officially, this relates to forensic evidence, bits and pieces of physical matter. But for the homicide investigator, it can relate to something almost metaphysical. By using offender profiles and analyses of violent crimes, you begin to know the murderer without having met him. By using victimology analysis and psychological autopsy, you begin to know more about the victim than what people are telling you. Eventually, you may guess at the relationship between the victim and the murderer and deduce that they knew each other, as is most often the case. Going on the theory that there was an emotional and psychological transfer and exchange between the deceased and the murderer, you can start narrowing the suspect list. On the other hand, I'd welcome a DNA marker and a fingerprint from Cal Seiver.

We headed north in the direction of the main post, but turned left at a sign that said, "Jordan Field." I informed Cynthia, "Based on Cal's findings with the tent pegs and rope, I don't think you have to be staked out."

She replied, "Karl is the typical armchair detective."

"True." Among Karl's other annoying traits was his bad habit of coming up with bright ideas. He'd sit there in Falls Church and read lab reports, witnesses' statements, and look at photos, then formulate theories and avenues of investigation. The men and women in the field love this. Karl fancies himself as some sort of European savant, and the fact that he's batting zero doesn't seem to bother him.

But Karl is a good commander. He runs a tight operation, kisses no ass, and stands up for his people. In this particular case, Colonel Karl Gustav Hellmann would undoubtedly be called to the Pentagon to report. Standing, perhaps, in the chief of staff's office before the secretary of the Army, the head of the FBI, the judge advocate general, and other assorted brass and steely-eyed presidential flunkies, he would announce, "My best man, Chief Warrant Officer Paul Brenner, is on the case, and he tells me he needs no outside assistance, and he assures me he can successfully conclude this case within a matter of days. An arrest is imminent." Right, Karl. Probably mine.

Cynthia glanced toward me. "You look a little pale."

"Just tired."

We approached Jordan Field, an Army installation that is part of Fort Hadley. Most of Hadley is an open post, and people come and go as they please, but Jordan Field is a security area, and we were stopped at the gate by an MP. The MP looked at Cynthia's ID and asked, "Are you working on the murder case, ma'am?"

"Yes," she replied. "This is my father."

The MP smiled. "Hangar three, ma'am."

Cynthia put the car in gear and we proceeded toward hangar three. Jordan Field was originally built by the now-defunct Army Air Corps in the 1930s and looks like a set for a World War II movie. It was too small to be taken over by the new Air Force after the war, but it is much bigger than the Army needs for its limited air arm, and, as a troop staging area, it is redundant and superfluous. In fact, if this whole military complex, including Hadley and Jordan, belonged to General Motors, half of it would be moved to Mexico and the other half closed. But the Army issues no P&L statements, and the end product, national defense, is somewhat of an abstract, like peace of mind, and therefore priceless. In reality, however, Hadley and Jordan are no more than government work projects for the local economy. What the war booms created, the peace dividend would maintain.

Sitting on the tarmac were two Huey helicopters and three Army artillery spotter planes. We proceeded to hangar three, in front of which was parked Kent's staff car, and a blue and white Ford with police markings. In fact, a gold shield on the door of the police car was emblazoned with the words "Midland Police Chief."

Cynthia said, "That will be Chief Yardley's car. I worked with him once. Have you?"

"No, and I don't intend to start now."

We walked into the cavernous hangar, where I noticed, first, a white BMW 325 convertible, which I assumed was Ann Campbell's car. At the far end of the hangar were Ann Campbell's household effects, arranged, I assumed, in some sort of room-by-room order, with the ripped-up carpeting laid out according to the floor plan of the town house. As I got closer, I noticed her office furniture, as well. As we got even closer, I saw a long table covered with Polaroid photos of her house and office. There were a few MPs on the fringes of the layout, and there was Colonel Kent, and there was a man wearing a cowboy hat who looked like he could have been, and probably was, Police Chief Yardley. The man was big, bursting out of his tan poplin suit, and his face was red, leading me to wonder if he was sunburned, had high blood pressure, or was monumentally pissed-off.

Yardley and Kent were conversing and glancing toward Cynthia and me as we approached. Yardley finally turned and came toward me as I came toward him. He greeted me with these words: "You got a shitload of explaining to do, son."

I thought not, and informed him, "If you've touched anything or come in contact with anything, I will need prints from you, and fibers from your clothing."

Yardley stopped a foot from me and sort of stared for a long time, then laughed. "You son-of-a-bitch." He turned to Kent. "You hear that?"

114

Kent forced a smile, but he was not happy.

I continued, "Please keep in mind that you are on a military reservation and that I have the sole responsibility for this case."

Kent, a bit belatedly, said, "Chief Yardley, may I introduce Mr. Brenner and Ms. Sunhill."

"You may," replied Yardley, "but I'm not real delighted."

Yardley, you may have guessed, had a rural Georgia accent that grates on my nerves in the best of circumstances. I can only imagine how my South Boston accent sounded to him.

Yardley turned to Cynthia, and, all southern charm now, he touched his cowboy hat. "I believe we've met, ma'am."

I mean, was this guy out of central casting, or what? I asked Yardley, "Can you tell me what your official business is here?"

Again he smiled. I seemed to amuse him. He said, "Well, now, my official business is to ask you how all this stuff got here."

Remembering Karl's nearly intelligent advice and wanting this guy gone, I replied, "The deceased's family asked that I take charge of these items and transport them here."

He mulled that over a moment, then said, "Good thinkin', son. You skunked me."

"Thank you." Actually, I liked this guy. I'm partial to assholes.

Yardley said, "Tell you what—you give me and the county lab access to this stuff, and we'll call it even."

"I'll consider that after the CID lab is finished with it."

"Don't mess with me, son."

"I wouldn't dream of it."

"Good. Hey, how's this sound—you let us in on this matter, and I'll give you access to the deceased's house, which we got all locked up and guarded now."

"I don't care about the house." Except the basement. The guy had an ace he didn't know about.

"Okay, I got some official files on the deceased."

The deal was getting better, but I said, "I'll subpoena your files if I have to."

Yardley turned to Kent. "This is a horse trader." He turned back to me. "I got things up here"—he tapped his head, which sounded hollow—"things that you can't subpoena."

"You knew the deceased?"

"Hell, yeah, boy. How 'bout you?"

"I didn't have the pleasure." Double entendre, perhaps.

"I know the old man, too. Hey, tell you what," said Chief Yardley, using that annoying expression, "you come on down to my office and we'll jawbone this one."

Recalling how I had suckered poor Dalbert Elkins inside a cell, I replied, "If we do speak, we'll do it in the provost marshal's office."

The mention of Kent's title seemed to arouse him and he said, "We will all cooperate in the sharing of files, leads, and forensic reports."

Cynthia spoke for the first time. "Chief, I understand your feeling that we've acted improperly, but don't take that personally, or view it as a professional insult. If the victim had been almost anyone else, we would have asked you to join us at the house and conferred with you regarding the best way to proceed."

Yardley was pursing his lips, as though he were contemplating this statement or was forming the word "bullshit."

Cynthia continued, "We get just as upset when a soldier is arrested in town for some minor infraction that a local boy would get away with."

Unless the local boy was black, of course. Don't say it, Brenner.

"So," Cynthia continued with sweet reason, "we will sit down at a mutually convenient time tomorrow and formulate a good working relationship." And so on and so forth.

Yardley nodded, but his mind was elsewhere. Finally, he replied, "Makes sense to me." He said to Kent, "Thanks, Colonel. Call me at home tonight." He turned to me and slapped me on the shoulder. "You skunked me, boy. I owe you one." He strode away, across the long floor of the hangar, looking like a man who would be back.

After he exited the small personnel door, Kent said, "I told you he would be ripped."

116

I replied, "Who cares?"

Kent replied, "I don't want to get into a pissing match with this guy. The fact is, he can be very helpful. Half the military personnel live off post on his turf, and ninety percent of the civilian workers on post live in Midland. When we get a list of suspects, we'll need Yardley."

"Maybe. But I think every suspect will wind up on government land at some point. If not, we'll kidnap them."

Kent shook his head, which seemed to stir his brain, and he asked, "Hey, did you see the general yet?"

"No. Am I supposed to?"

"He wants to see you, ASAP. He's home."

"All right." The bereaved have many things on their minds, but talking to the investigating officer is not usually one of them. But a general, I suppose, is another species of human being, and General Campbell, perhaps, had a need to make things happen, to show he was still in command. I said to Kent, "I just saw Cal Seiver, the forensic OIC. You met him?"

"Yes," replied Kent. "He seems to have things under control. Has he come up with anything?"

"Not yet."

"Have you?"

"I have a preliminary list of possible suspects."

Kent looked almost startled. "Already? Who?"

"Well, you, for one."

"What? What the hell are you talking about, Brenner?"

"My suspects are everyone who had contact with the crime scene and/or the victim's town house. Forensic will pick up traces, footprints, and fingerprints of those people, and I have no way of knowing if those traces were left before, during, or after the crime." I added, "The preliminary suspects, then, are Sergeant St. John, PFC Casey, who responded to the call, you, any other MPs who were at the scene, Cynthia, and me. These are not likely suspects, but I have to deal with the forensic evidence."

Kent said, "Then you'd better start getting alibis."

"Okay. What's yours?"

"All right . . . I was home in bed when I got a call from my duty sergeant."

"You live on post, correct?"

"Correct."

"What time did you get home?"

"At about midnight. I had dinner in town, then went to the office, worked late, then went home."

"Your wife can verify that?"

"Well . . . no, she's visiting her parents in Ohio."

"Ah."

"Oh, fuck off, Paul. Just fuck off."

"Hey, take it easy, Colonel."

"You know, you think you're funny, but you're not. There's nothing funny about making a joke about murder and murder suspects."

I looked at him and saw he was truly agitated.

He continued, "There's going to be enough of that crap as it is. Enough rumors, whispering, finger-pointing, and suspicion. We don't need you here making it worse."

"All right," I said, "I apologize. But I assumed that three law officers could speak their minds. Nothing we say is leaving this hangar, Bill, and if we speculate, or even make a few idiotic remarks, we understand that it's between us. Okay?"

But he didn't look mollified, and he snapped at me, "Where were *you* last night?"

I said, "Home alone in my trailer until about 0430 hours. Got to the post armory around 0500 hours. No witnesses."

"A likely story," snorted Kent, who seemed inordinately happy that I had no alibi. He turned to Cynthia, "And you?"

"I got to the VOQ about 1900 hours and wrote my report on the Neely case until about midnight, then went to bed, alone, and was awakened by an MP knocking on my door at about 0530 hours."

I commented, "I've never heard three weaker alibis in my life. But, okay, we'll let them stand for now. The point is, this post is like a small town, and the deceased's circle of friends, family, and acquaintances includes the top echelons of this community." I said to Kent, "You wanted somebody on this case who was an outsider. Correct?"

"That's right. But don't push it, Paul."

"Why did you have an MP summon Ms. Sunhill?"

"Same reason I called you. Out-of-town talent."

It occurred to me that out-of-town talent was another way of saying, "We want two investigators who don't have a clue about the dirt that everyone here knows about." I asked Kent, "How well did you know Ann Campbell?"

He hesitated a moment, then chose the words "Fairly well."

"Would you expound?"

Clearly, Colonel Kent, who outranked me and was himself a cop, was not pleased. But he was a professional and therefore knew what was required of him. He forced a smile and said, "Should we read each other our rights?"

I smiled in return. This was awkward, but necessary.

He cleared his throat and said, "Captain Campbell was stationed here about two years ago. I was here at the time and so were General and Mrs. Campbell. The Campbells invited me to their home with a few other officers to meet their daughter. Our work areas were not related in the usual sense, but as a psychologist she was interested in criminal behavior, and I was interested in the criminal mind. It's not unusual for a law enforcement officer and a psychologist to have common interests."

"So you became friends?"

"Sort of."

"Lunch?"

"Sometimes."

"Dinner? Drinks?"

"Once in a while."

"Alone?"

"Once or twice."

"But you didn't seem to know where she lived."

"I knew she lived off post. But I've never been to her house."

119

"Has she been to yours?"

"Yes. A number of times. For social functions."

"Does your wife like her?"

"No."

"Why not?"

"You figure it out, Brenner."

"Okay. I figured it out." Cynthia had the good sense to not join in my interrogation of a high-ranking officer, so I turned to her. "Any questions for Colonel Kent?"

Cynthia replied, "Just the obvious one." She looked at Kent.

He said, "I was never intimate with her. If I had been, I would have told you from minute one."

"One hopes so," I said. I asked him, "Did she have a steady boyfriend?"

"Not that I know of."

"Did she have any known enemies?"

He thought about that, then replied, "Some women didn't like her. I think they felt threatened. Some men didn't like her. They felt . . ."

"Inadequate?" Cynthia prompted.

"Yes. Something like that. Or maybe she was a little cool with some of the younger, unmarried officers who had the hots for her. But as for real enemies, I don't know of any." He hesitated, then added, "Considering how she died, I think it was a lust murder. I mean, there are women who you might have healthy sexual or romantic fantasies about, but Ann Campbell, I think, provoked rape fantasies in some men. I think somebody just went for it. After the rape, the guy knew he was in a world of serious trouble. Maybe Ann taunted him, for all we know. I wouldn't put it past her. The guy thought about life in Leavenworth and strangled her." Kent looked at me and Cynthia. "A lot of guys are pulled around by the one-eyed, heat-seeking monster, and it leads them right to hell. I've seen too much of that on this job. So have you."

True enough. But in this case, I was focusing more on the thing that the monster was seeking. I asked Kent, "Well, do you know if she dated? Was she sexually active?"

120

"I don't know if she was sexually active. I only know one unmarried officer who dated her—Lieutenant Elby, one of the general's aides—but she never discussed her private life with me, and her behavior never came to my attention professionally. On the other hand, you have to wonder what she did for fun."

"What do you think she did for fun?"

"What I would do in her situation. Keep my professional life here separate from my social life in the civilian community."

"What kind of files does Yardley have on her?"

"Well . . . I guess he means when she was arrested in Midland about a year ago. Before she was even booked, Yardley called me and I went downtown and picked her up."

"So she did come to your attention professionally."

"Sort of. This was unofficial. Yardley said there would be no file, no record of the arrest."

"Obviously he lied. What was she arrested for?"

"Yardley said it was for disturbing the peace."

"In what way did Ann Campbell disturb the peace of Midland?"

"She had an altercation with some guy on the street."

"Any details?"

"No. Yardley wouldn't say. Just said to get her home."

"So you took her home."

"No, I told you I don't know where she lives, Brenner. Don't try that shit with me. In fact, I took her back to post. That was at about 2300 hours. She was cold sober, by the way. So I took her for a drink at the O Club. She never told me what happened, and I didn't ask. I called her a taxi and she left about midnight."

"You don't know the name of the man involved, or the arresting officer?"

"No. But I'm sure Yardley does. Ask him"—Kent smiled—"now that you have his full cooperation. Any other questions?"

Cynthia said to him, "How did you feel when you were informed that she was dead?"

"Stunned."

"Sad?"

"Of course. And sad for General and Mrs. Campbell. And

121

damned angry, and a little upset knowing it happened on my beat. I liked her, but we weren't so close that I took it very badly. I'm more upset professionally.''

I commented, ''I appreciate your honesty.''

''You're going to appreciate it more when you start hearing the bullshit.''

''No doubt.'' I asked him, ''Any questions for me?''

He smiled. ''What did you say the traveling time was between post and Whispering Pines?''

''Half an hour. Less in the early morning hours.''

He nodded, then surveyed the furniture and household goods in the hangar. ''Look all right to you?''

''It's okay. Good job. But get some portable partitions up, hang the pictures, and hang the clothes on poles where the closets were.'' I asked him, ''Did they get the stuff out of the basement?'' I glanced at Cynthia.

Kent replied, ''Yes. Over there, still in boxes. We'll get some tables and shelves to simulate the basement area.'' He thought a moment, then commented, ''I would have thought there would be . . . something more here. Did you happen to notice, for instance, that there were no . . . personal items?''

''You mean like birth control items? Letters from men, photos of boyfriends, sexual aids and erotica?''

''Well, I don't know if single women keep sexual aids . . . and I didn't look closely for letters and such . . . I guess I meant birth control pills or devices.''

''Did you touch anything, Bill?''

''No.'' He pulled a pair of surgical gloves out of his trouser pockets. ''But I may have touched something bare-handed when I was supervising the unloading. Yardley touched a few things, too, by accident.''

''Or on purpose.''

Kent nodded. ''Or on purpose. Add another suspect to the list.''

''I already have.'' I walked over to where Ann Campbell's office furniture had been placed. It was the sort of spartan stuff that the

Army likes to buy on the one hand, while they lobby Congress for three-million-dollar tanks on the other.

The office consisted of a steel desk, a swivel chair, two folding chairs, a bookshelf, two upright file cabinets, and a computer station. The books on the shelves were all standard texts on psychology, plus military publications on the same subject, as well as on psychological operations, POW studies, and other related subjects.

I opened a file drawer and read the folder tabs, which seemed to refer to lecture notes. The next drawer was marked "Confidential," so I opened it and saw that the folders were not named, but numbered. I drew out one of the folders and scanned the papers inside. The pages appeared to be a transcribed interview with a person identified only by the initials "R.J." The interviewer was identified as "Q," for question or questioner. It looked like a typical format for a psychological interview or session, but the person being interviewed, according to page one, was a convicted sex offender. The questions were things like "How did you pick your victim?" and "What did she say to you when you told her she had to perform oral sex on you?" I closed the file. This was pretty standard stuff in a police or prison psychologist's office, but I didn't see how it related to psychological warfare. Obviously, this was a private interest of Ann Campbell's.

I closed the drawer and went to her computer station. I don't even know how to turn these things on, but I said to Kent, "There is a woman in Falls Church, Grace Dixon, who squeezes the brains of personal computers. I'll get her down here, and I don't want anyone else messing with this thing."

Cynthia had gone into the transplanted study and was looking at the answering machine. "There's a call here."

Kent nodded. "Came in about noon, a few minutes after the phone company got the call-forwarding in place."

Cynthia pushed the play button and a male voice said, "Ann, this is Charles. I tried you earlier, but your phone was out of order. I knew you wouldn't be at work this morning, but I want you to know that a group of MPs were here and they've removed your entire office. They wouldn't tell me anything about it. Please call me, or meet me at the O Club for lunch or something. This is very strange. I'd call the police, but they are the police.'' He chuckled, but it was forced. He continued, ''I hope this is nothing serious. Call me.''

I asked Kent, ''Who is that?''

''Colonel Charles Moore. Ann's boss at the school.''

''What do you know about him?''

''Well, he's a shrink, too, of course. Ph.D. type. An odd duck. Sort of on the fringes. That whole school is on the fringe. Sometimes I think they should put a fence around it, with guard towers.''

Cynthia asked Kent, ''Were they friends?''

Kent nodded. ''They seemed to be close. He was sort of her mentor, which doesn't say a lot for her judgment. Excuse me.''

I said to him, ''We don't have to speak only well of the dead in a homicide investigation.''

''Yes, but that was out of line.'' Kent rubbed his eyes. ''I'm just a little . . . tired.''

Cynthia observed, ''It's been a stressful day for you. I don't suppose it was pleasant informing the Campbells of their daughter's death.''

''No. I called their home and got Mrs. Campbell. I asked her to call the general and requested that they meet me at their home.'' He added, ''She knew something had happened. I showed up with the head chaplain, Major Eames, and a medical officer, Captain Swick. When they saw us . . . I mean, how many times have we seen or been part of a notification detail? But when it's a combat death, you can say the right things. When it's murder, then . . . there's not much to say.''

Cynthia asked, ''How did they take it?''

''Bravely. That's what you'd expect of a professional soldier and his wife. I only had to stay a few minutes, then I left them with the chaplain.''

I asked, ''Were you at all explicit?''

''No. I just told them that Ann had been found on the rifle range, dead, apparently murdered.''

"And he said?"

"He said . . . 'She died while doing her duty.' " Kent paused, then added, "I suppose that is comforting."

"You didn't go into details about her condition, the possible rape?"

"No . . . He did ask how she died, and I said she was apparently strangled."

"And he said?"

"Nothing."

"And you gave him my name and phone number?"

"Yes. Well, he asked if the CID was doing everything possible. I told him I'd taken advantage of your presence here, and Ms. Sunhill's presence, and that I'd requested that you take the case."

"And he said?"

"He said he wanted Major Bowes, the CID commander here, to take the case, and that you and Ms. Sunhill were relieved of your responsibility."

"And you said?"

"I didn't want to get into it with him, but he understands that this is one thing that he has no control of on this post."

"Indeed not."

Cynthia asked, "And how did Mrs. Campbell take it?"

Kent replied, "She was stoic, but about to fall apart. Appearances are important with general officers and their ladies, and they're both from the old school."

"All right, Bill. Forensic will be here after dark, and they'll stay through the night. Tell your people here that no one else is allowed in, except us."

"Right." He added, "Don't forget—the general would like to see you at his home, soonest."

"Why?"

"Probably to get the details of his daughter's death, and to ask you to brief Major Bowes, and to ask you to step aside."

"Sounds good to me. I can do that over the phone."

"Actually, I got a call from the Pentagon. The judge advocate general agrees with your boss that you and Ms. Sunhill, as outside parties and being more experienced than the local CID people at Hadley, are best equipped to handle this. That's the final word. You can pass that on to General Campbell when you see him. And I suggest you do so now.''

''I'd rather speak to Charles Moore now.''

''Make an exception, Paul. Do the politics first.''

I looked at Cynthia and she nodded. I shrugged. ''Okay. General and Mrs. Campbell.''

Kent walked with us across the hangar. He said, ''You know, it's ironic . . . Ann had a favorite expression, a sort of personal motto that she got from . . . some philosopher . . . Nietzsche. The expression was, 'What does not destroy us, makes us stronger.' '' He added, ''Now she's destroyed.''

CHAPTER THIRTEEN

We headed toward the general's quarters on main post. Cynthia said, "I'm starting to see a picture of a tortured, unhappy young woman."

"Adjust your rearview mirror."

"Cut it out, Paul."

"Sorry."

I must have drifted off because the next thing I remember is Cynthia poking me. "Did you hear what I said?"

"Yes. Cut it out."

"I said, I think Colonel Kent knows more than he's telling."

I sat up and yawned. "One gets that impression. Can we stop for coffee someplace?"

"No. Tell me, is Kent really a suspect?"

"Well . . . in a theoretical sense. I didn't like it that his wife was out of town and he had no corroboration for his alibi. Most married men, in the early morning hours, are in bed with their wives. When the wives are out of town, and something like this happens, you have to wonder if it was his bad luck or something else."

"And Chief Yardley?"

"He's not as stupid as he sounds, is he?"

"No," confirmed Cynthia, "he is not. I worked a rape case with

127

him about a year ago when I returned from Europe. The suspect was a soldier, but the victim was a Midland girl, so I had the pleasure of meeting Chief Yardley.''

''He knows his business?''

''He's been at it a long time. As he pointed out to me then, officers and soldiers come and go from Hadley, but he's been a Midland cop for thirty years, and he knows the territory, on and off post. He's actually very charming when he wants to be, and he's extremely cunning.''

''He also leaves his fingerprints in places where he suspects they might already be.''

''So did Kent. So did we.''

''Right. But I know I didn't kill Ann Campbell. How about you?''

''I was sleeping,'' Cynthia said coolly.

''Alone. Bad luck. You should have invited me up to your room. We'd both have an alibi.''

''I'd rather be a murder suspect.''

The road was long, straight, and narrow, a black slash between towering pines, and heat waves shimmered off the hot tar. ''Does it get this hot in Iowa?''

''Yes,'' she replied, ''but it's drier.''

''Did you ever think about going home?''

''Sometimes. How about you?''

''I get back fairly often. But there's less there each time. South Boston is changing.''

''Iowa stays the same. But I've changed.''

''You're young enough to get out and start a civilian career.''

''I like what I do,'' she replied.

''Do it in Iowa. Join the county police force. They'd love to have your experience.''

''The last felon in the county was found dead of boredom ten years ago. There are ten men on the county police force. They'd want me to make coffee and screw for them.''

''Well, at least you make good coffee.''

"Fuck off, Paul."

Score another zinger for me. As I said, it's hard to hit on just the right tone and tint when speaking to someone you've seen naked, had sexual intercourse with, lain in bed with, and talked through the night with. You can't be stiff and cold, as if it never happened, yet you can't be too familiar because it's not happening anymore. You watch your language and watch your hands. You don't pinch the other person's cheek, or pat their butt, though you may want to. But neither do you avoid a handshake, and I guess you can put your hand on the other person's shoulder, or poke your finger in their stomach as Cynthia did to me. There really ought to be a manual for this kind of thing, or, lacking that, a law that says that ex-lovers may not come within a hundred yards of each other. Unless, of course, they're trying to get it on again. I said to her, "I always had the feeling that we left things up in the air."

She replied, "I always had the feeling that you chose to avoid a confrontation with my . . . my fiancé and walked away." She added, "I wasn't worth the trouble."

"That's ridiculous. The man threatened to kill me. Discretion is the better part of valor."

"Maybe. But sometimes you have to fight for what you want. If you want it. Weren't you decorated for valor?"

I was getting a little annoyed now, of course, having my manhood questioned. I said, with some anger, "I received a Bronze Star for valor, Ms. Sunhill, for charging up a fucking hill that I didn't particularly need or want. But I'll be damned if I'm going to put on a show for your amusement." I added, "Anyway, I don't recall getting any encouragement from you."

She replied, "I wasn't quite sure which of you I wanted, so I thought I'd just go with whoever was left alive."

I looked at her, and she gave me a glance, and I saw she was smiling. I said, "You're not funny, Cynthia."

"Sorry." She patted my knee. "I love it when you get angry."

I didn't reply, and we rode in silence.

We entered the outskirts of the main post, and I saw the cluster of old concrete buildings with the sign that said, "U.S. Army Training School—Psy-Ops—Authorized Personnel Only."

Cynthia commented, "Can we hit that place after we see the general?"

I looked at my watch. "We'll try." Speed, speed. Beyond the problems of cold trails, I had the feeling that the more time everyone in Washington and Fort Hadley had to think, the more likely they'd start screwing me up. Within seventy-two hours, this base would be knee-deep in FBI guys and CID brass trying to score points, not to mention the media, who, even now, were probably in Atlanta trying to figure out how to get here from there.

Cynthia asked me, "What are we going to do about the stuff in her basement?"

"I don't know. Maybe we won't need it. That's what I'm counting on. Let it sit for a few days."

"What if Yardley finds that room?"

"Then it's his problem what to do with the information. We saw enough to get the idea."

"The clue to her killer may be in that room."

I stared out the side window and watched the post go by. After a minute, I said, "Here's what's in that room—enough compromising evidence to ruin careers and lives, including her parents' lives, not to mention the deceased's posthumous reputation. I don't know that we need anything more from that room."

"Is this Paul Brenner speaking?"

"It's Paul Brenner the career Army officer speaking. Not Paul Brenner the cop."

"Okay. I understand that. That's good."

"Sure." I added, "I'd do the same for you."

"Thanks. But I have nothing to hide."

"Are you married?"

"None of your business."

"Right."

We arrived at the general's official residence, called Beaumont, a huge brick plantation house complete with white columns. The house was set in a few acres of treed grounds on the eastern edge of the main post, an oasis of magnolias, stately oaks, flower beds and such, surrounded by a desert of military simplicity.

Beaumont is an antebellum relic, the former home of the Beaumont clan, who still exist in the county. Beaumont House escaped Sherman's March to the Sea, being not in the direct path of the march, but it had been looted and vandalized by Yankee stragglers. The locals will tell you that all the women in the house had been raped, but, in fact, the local guidebook says the Beaumonts fled a few steps ahead of the Yankees.

The house was expropriated by the Union occupation forces for use as a headquarters, then at some point returned to the rightful owners, then, in 1916, sold along with the plantation acreage to the federal government, who designated it Camp Hadley. So, ironically, it is again Army property, and the cotton fields around the house have become the main post, while the remainder of the 100,000 wooded acres is the training area.

It's hard to gauge how much of history impacts on the local population, but in these parts, I suspect the impact is greater than a kid from South Boston or an Iowa farm girl can fully understand. I deal with this as best I can and calculate it into my thinking. But in the end, when someone like me meets someone like Yardley, there is very little meeting of minds and souls.

We got out of the car and Cynthia said, "My knees are shaking."

"Walk around the gardens. I'll take care of this."

"I'll be all right."

We climbed the steps to the columned porch and I rang the bell. A handsome young man in uniform answered. He was a lieutenant, and his name tag said Elby. I announced, "Warrant Officers Brenner and Sunhill to see General and Mrs. Campbell at the general's request."

"Oh, yes." He looked over Cynthia's informal attire, then stepped aside, and we entered. Elby said, "I'm the general's personal aide. Colonel Fowler, the general's adjutant, wishes to speak to you."

131

"I'm here at the general's request to see the general."

"I know, Mr. Brenner. Please see Colonel Fowler first."

Cynthia and I followed him into the large foyer decorated in the style and period of the house, but I suspected that this wasn't original Beaumont stuff, but bits and pieces collected from the down-and-out minor gentry since the Army bought the place. Lieutenant Elby showed us into a small front room, a sort of official waiting room for callers with lots of seating and little else. The life of a plantation owner was, I'm certain, different from the life of a modern-day general, but what they had in common was callers, and lots of them. Tradesmen went around back, gentry were shown directly to the big sitting room, and callers on official business got as far as this room, until a decision could be made regarding their status.

Elby took his leave, and Cynthia and I remained standing. She said, "That was the young man who Colonel Kent said dated Ann Campbell. He's quite good-looking."

"He looks like a wimp and a bed wetter."

Changing the subject, she asked me, "Did you ever want to be a general?"

"I'm just trying to hang on to my little warrant officer bar."

She tried to smile, but was clearly nervous. I wasn't exactly at ease, either. To break the tension, I fell back on an old Army expression. "Remember, a general puts his pants on one leg at a time, just like you do."

"I usually sit on the bed and pull my pants on both legs at once."

"Well, you know what I mean."

"Maybe we can just speak to the adjutant and leave."

"The general will be very courteous. They all are."

"I'm more nervous about meeting his wife. Maybe I should have changed."

Why do I try to figure these people out?

Cynthia said, "This will hurt his career, won't it?"

"Depends on the outcome. If we never find the killer, and no one ever finds that room, and if there's not too much dirt dragged up, he'll be all right. He gets the sympathy vote. But if it gets very messy, he'll resign."

"And that's the end of his political ambitions."

"I'm not sure he has any political ambitions."

"The papers say he does."

"That's not my problem." But, in fact, it could be. General Joseph Ian Campbell had been mentioned as a possible vice-presidential choice, and was also mentioned as a potential candidate for senator from his native state of Michigan, or as a candidate for governor of that state. Plus, his name had come up to succeed the present Army chief of staff, which meant a fourth star, or another possibility was an appointment as the president's top military advisor.

This embarrassment of riches was a direct result of General Campbell's service in the Persian Gulf War, prior to which no one had ever heard of him. As the memory of the war faded, however, so was his name fading from public consciousness. This was either a clever plan on the part of Joseph Campbell, or he honestly didn't want any part of the nonsense.

How and why Fighting Joe Campbell got assigned to this backwater that the Army called Fort Hades and the GIs called Fort Hardly, was one of those mysteries of the Pentagon that only the connivers and plotters there could explain. But I had the sudden thought that the power brokers in the Pentagon knew that General Campbell had a loose cannon rolling around the ramparts, and the loose cannon was named Ann. Was that possible?

A tall man entered, wearing the Army-green dress uniform, type A with colonel's eagles, the insignia of the Adjutant General Corps, and a name tag that said Fowler. He introduced himself as General Campbell's adjutant. In the service, when in uniform, it is redundant to introduce yourself by name and rank, but people appreciate a short job description so they can ascertain if they have to work with you or ever see you again.

We shook hands all around, and Colonel Fowler said, "Indeed, the general wishes to see you, but I want to speak to you first. Won't you have a seat?"

We all sat, and I regarded Colonel Fowler. He was a black man, and I could imagine the generations of former slaveowners who lived here spinning in their graves. Anyway, Fowler was extremely well groomed, well spoken, and carried himself with good military bearing. He seemed like the perfect adjutant, a job which is sort of like a combination of a personnel officer, senior advisor, a receiver and communicator of the general's orders, and so forth. An adjutant is not like the deputy commander, who, like the vice-president of the United States, has no real job.

Fowler had long legs, which may seem irrelevant, but an adjutant has to do the adjutants' walk, which means long strides between the general and his subordinates to relay orders and bring back reports. You're not supposed to run, so you have to develop the adjutants' walk, especially on a big parade ground where short stubby legs hold up the whole show. Anyway, Fowler was every inch the officer and the gentleman. Unlike some white officers who can get a little sloppy, like myself, the black officer, like the female officer, has something to prove. Interestingly, blacks and women still use the standards of the white officer as their ideal, though, in fact, that ideal and those standards were and are myths. But it keeps everybody on their toes, so it's fine. The Army is fifty percent illusion, anyway.

Colonel Fowler said, "You may smoke if you wish. A drink?"

"No, sir," I said.

Fowler tapped the arms of his chair for a few beats, then began. "This is certainly a tragedy for the general and Mrs. Campbell. We don't want it to become a tragedy for the Army."

"Yes, sir." The less said, the better, of course. He wanted to talk.

He continued, "Captain Campbell's death, occurring as it did on post—on this very post where her father is commander—and occurring in the manner it did, will certainly cause a sensation."

"Yes, sir."

"I don't think I have to tell either of you not to speak to the press."

"Of course not."

Fowler looked at Cynthia. "I understand you made an arrest in that other rape case. Do you think there's a connection here? Could there be two of them? Or could you have gotten the wrong man in the other case?''

''No on all counts, Colonel.''

''But it *is* possible. Will you look into that?''

''No, Colonel. These are two different cases.''

Clearly, the general's staff had met and some bright boy brought this up as a possibility, or as wishful thinking, or as the official story; i.e., there was a gang of young trainees running around, laying the pipe to unsuspecting female officers. I said to Colonel Fowler, ''It doesn't wash.''

He sort of shrugged and turned his attention back to me. ''Well, do you have any suspects?''

''No, sir.''

''Any leads?''

''Not at the moment.''

''But you must have a theory or two, Mr. Brenner.''

''I do, Colonel. But they are *only* theories, and all of them would upset you.''

He leaned forward in his chair, obviously not pleased. ''I'm only upset that a female officer has been raped and murdered and that the culprit is at large. Not much else about this case is going to upset me.''

Wanna bet? I said, ''I've been told that the general wishes to relieve me and Ms. Sunhill from this case.''

''I believe that was his early reaction. But he's spoken to some people in Washington, and he's rethinking this. That's why he wants to meet you and Ms. Sunhill.''

''I see. Sort of a job interview.''

''Perhaps.'' He added, ''Unless you don't want this case. If you don't, it will not reflect negatively in your records. In fact, a letter of commendation will be inserted into your files in recognition of your initial work on this case. And you would both be offered thirty days of administrative leave, to begin immediately.'' He looked from me to Cynthia, then back to me. ''Then there will be no reason to see the general, and you may both leave now.''

Not a bad deal if you thought about it. The idea was not to think about it. I replied, "My commanding officer, Colonel Hellmann, has assigned me and Ms. Sunhill to this case, and we have accepted the assignment. This is a closed issue, Colonel."

He nodded. I couldn't quite get a handle on Fowler. Behind the stiff façade of the adjutant was a very facile operator. He had to be in order to survive this job, which by almost any military standards sucked. But you'd never become a general until you'd served on a general's staff, and clearly, Colonel Fowler was only a hop, skip, and a jump away from his first Silver Star.

Fowler seemed deep in thought, and there was a silence in the room. I, having said my piece, now had to wait for his reply. Higher-ranking officers had this unsettling habit of letting long silences pass, and the unwise junior officer would sometimes charge into the breach with an afterthought, then get clobbered with an icy stare or a reprimand. It was sort of like a trap play in football, or in war, and, although I didn't know Colonel Fowler very well, I knew the type too well. The man was testing me, testing my nerve and resolve, perhaps to see if he was dealing with an overly enthusiastic asshole or someone as shrewd as himself. Cynthia, to her credit, let the silence drag on, too.

Finally, he said to me, "I know why Ms. Sunhill is here at Fort Hadley. But what brings a special unit CID investigator to our little outpost?"

"I was on undercover assignment. One of your armory NCOs was about to go into business for himself. You ought to tighten security at the armory, and you should know that I've saved you some embarrassment." I added, "I'm sure the provost briefed you."

"In fact, he did. Some weeks ago when you got here."

"So you knew I was here."

"Yes, but not *why* you were here."

"Why do you suppose Colonel Kent asked me to take this case in light of the fact that no one else here wants me to take it?"

He thought a moment, then replied, "To be honest with you, Colonel Kent is not fond of the local CID commander, Major

Bowes. In any case, your people at Falls Church would have put you on it immediately. Colonel Kent did what he thought was best for everyone.''

''Including Colonel Kent. What is the problem between Colonel Kent and Major Bowes?''

He shrugged. ''Probably just jurisdictional. Turf.''

''Not personal?''

''I don't know. Ask them.''

''I will.'' In the meantime, I asked Colonel Fowler, ''Did you know Captain Campbell personally?''

He looked at me a moment, then replied, ''Yes. In fact, the general has asked me to give the eulogy at her funeral.''

''I see. Were you with General Campbell prior to this assignment?''

''Yes, I've been with General Campbell since he was an armored division commander in Germany. We served together in the Gulf, then here.''

''Did he request this assignment?''

''I don't think that's relevant.''

''I assume you knew Ann Campbell before Fort Hadley?''

''Yes.''

''Could you give me an idea of the nature of your relationship?'' How was that for smooth?

Fowler leaned forward in his chair and looked me in the eyes. ''Excuse me, Mr. Brenner. Is this an interrogation?''

''Yes, sir.''

''Well, I'll be damned.''

''I hope not, Colonel.''

He laughed, then stood. ''Well, you both come to my office tomorrow and you can fire away. Call for an appointment. Follow me, please.''

We followed Colonel Fowler back into the central foyer, then toward the rear of the mansion, where we came to a closed door. Colonel Fowler said to us, ''No need to salute, quick condolences, you'll be asked to take a seat. Mrs. Campbell will not be present.

She's under sedation. Please keep this short. Five minutes.'' He knocked on the door, opened it, and stepped inside, announcing us as Warrant Officers Brenner and Sunhill of the CID. Sounded like a TV series.

Cynthia and I followed and found ourselves in a sort of den of highly polished wood, leather, and brass. The room was dark, the drapes drawn, and the only light came from a green-shaded desk lamp. Behind the desk stood Lieutenant General Joseph Campbell, in a dress-green uniform with a chest full of medals. The first thing you noticed about him was that he was huge, not only tall but big-boned, like the Scottish clan chiefs from which he must have descended, and on this occasion I also noticed the unmistakable smell of Scotch whisky in the room.

General Campbell extended his hand to Cynthia, who took it and said to him, ''My deepest condolences, sir.''

''Thank you.''

I took his hand, which was huge, passed on my condolences, and added, ''I'm very sorry to have to bother you at a time like this,'' as though this meeting had been my idea.

''Not at all.'' He sat and said, ''Please be seated.''

We sat in leather chairs facing his desk. I regarded his face in the shaded light. He had a full head of blondish-gray hair, bright blue eyes, craggy features, and a good jaw with a cleft chin. A handsome man, but aside from the eyes, Ann Campbell's beauty must have come from her mother.

With a general, one never speaks until spoken to, but the general wasn't speaking. He stared off, between Cynthia and me, at some point behind us. He nodded, I suppose to Fowler, and I heard the door close behind us, as Colonel Fowler departed.

General Campbell now looked at Cynthia, then at me, and addressed us both in a quiet voice, which I knew, from radio and television, was not his normal speaking voice. He said, ''I take it that you two wish to remain on this assignment.''

We both nodded and said, ''Yes, sir.''

He looked at me. ''Can I convince you that everyone would be better served if you turn this matter over to Major Bowes here at Fort Hadley?''

"I'm sorry, General," I responded. "This matter transcends Fort Hadley and transcends your personal grief. None of us can change that.''

General Campbell nodded. "Then I will give you my full cooperation and promise you the cooperation of everyone here.''

"Thank you, sir.''

"Do you have any idea who could have done this?''

"No, sir." *Do you?*

"Do I have both your assurances that you will work quickly and that you will work with us to minimize the sensational aspects of this incident and that you will do more good than harm here?''

I replied, "I assure you that our only objective is to make an arrest as soon as possible.''

Cynthia added, "We have taken steps, General, from the very beginning to minimize outside involvement. We have transported the entire contents of Captain Campbell's home to this post. Chief of Police Yardley seems upset about that, and I suspect he will contact you in that regard. If you would be so kind as to tell him you authorized this before it happened, we would be very appreciative. Regarding minimizing sensationalism and harm to the post and the Army, a word from you to Chief Yardley would go a long way in achieving that goal.''

General Campbell looked at Cynthia for a few long seconds. Undoubtedly, he could not look at a young, attractive woman of that age without thinking of his daughter. *What* he was thinking of his daughter is what I didn't know. He said to Cynthia, "Consider it done.''

"Thank you, General.''

I said, "It is my understanding, General, that you were supposed to see your daughter this morning after she got off duty.''

He replied, "Yes . . . we were to have breakfast. When she didn't arrive, I called Colonel Fowler at headquarters, but he said she wasn't there. I believe he called her home.''

"About what time was that, sir?''

"I'm not certain. She was due at my house at 0700. I probably called headquarters at about 0730."

I didn't pursue this but said to him, "General, we appreciate your offer of full cooperation and will take you up on it. At your first available opportunity, I'd like to conduct a more detailed interview with you, and with Mrs. Campbell. Perhaps tomorrow."

"I'm afraid we have to make funeral arrangements tomorrow and attend to other personal business. The day after the funeral may be convenient."

"Thank you." I added, "The family often has information that, without realizing it, can be critical in resolving a case."

"I understand." He thought a moment, then asked, "Do you think . . . was this someone she may have known?"

"It's quite possible," I replied, and our eyes met.

He kept good eye contact and said to me, "I have that feeling, too."

I asked him, "Has anyone, aside from Colonel Kent, spoken to you about the circumstances of your daughter's death?"

"No. Well, Colonel Fowler did. He briefed me."

"About the possible rape, and how she was found?"

"That's correct."

There was a long silence, and I knew from past experience with general officers that he was not waiting for me to speak, but that the interview was over. I said, "Is there anything we can do for you at this time?"

"No . . . just find the son-of-a-bitch." He stood and pressed a button on his desk, then said, "Thank you for your time."

Cynthia and I stood, and I said, "Thank you, General." I shook his hand. "And, again, my deepest sympathy to you and your family."

He took Cynthia's hand, and perhaps it was my imagination, but he seemed to hold it a long time and he looked into her eyes. Then he said, "I know you'll do your very best. My daughter would have liked you. She liked self-assured women."

"Thank you, General," Cynthia replied. "You have my promise I'll do my best, and again, my deepest condolences."

The door behind us opened, and Colonel Fowler escorted us out, through the central hallway and toward the front door. He said to me, "I understand that you have special arrest powers. But I'm going to ask that before you arrest anyone, you notify me."

"Why?"

"Because," he replied a bit sharply, "we don't like our personnel being arrested by outside people without our knowing about it."

"It happens fairly often," I informed him. "In fact, as you may know, I just threw the armory sergeant in jail a few hours ago. But if you wish, I'll notify you."

"Thank you, Mr. Brenner." He added, "As always, there are three ways of doing things—the right way, the wrong way, and the Army way. I have the feeling you're trying to do it the right way, which is the wrong way, Mr. Brenner."

"I know that, Colonel."

He looked at Cynthia and said, "If you change your mind about thirty days' free leave, let me know. If you don't, please keep in touch with me. Mr. Brenner appears to be the type of man who gets so immersed in his work that he could forget the protocols."

"Yes, sir," Cynthia replied. "And please try to get us an early appointment with General and Mrs. Campbell. We'll need at least an hour. Also, please call us at the provost marshal's office if you think of anything significant."

He opened the door and we stepped outside. Before he closed it, I turned and said to him, "By the way, we heard your message to Captain Campbell on her answering machine."

"Oh, yes. It seems a bit silly now."

"What time did you make that call, Colonel?"

"About 0800 hours. The General and Mrs. Campbell expected their daughter at about 0700 hours."

"Where did you make the call from, sir?"

"I was at work—at Post Headquarters."

"Did you look around Post Headquarters to see if Captain Campbell was delayed on duty?"

"No . . . I just assumed she forgot and went home." He added, "It wouldn't be the first time."

"I see. Did you look to see if her car was in the headquarters' parking lot?"

"No . . . I suppose I should have."

I asked him, "Who briefed you regarding the details of Captain Campbell's death?"

"I spoke to the provost marshal."

"And he told you how she was found?"

"That's correct."

"So you and General Campbell know that she was tied, strangled, and sexually assaulted?"

"Yes. Is there something else we should know?"

"No, sir." I asked him, "Where can I contact you during off-duty hours?"

"I live in officer housing on post. Bethany Hill. Do you know where that is?"

"I believe so. South of here, on the way to the rifle ranges."

"That's right. My phone number is in the post directory."

"Thank you, Colonel."

"Good day, Mr. Brenner, Ms. Sunhill."

He closed the door, and Cynthia and I walked toward her car. She asked me, "What did you think of Colonel Fowler?"

"Not as much as Colonel Fowler thinks of himself."

"He actually has an imposing presence. Some of it is just spit-shined staff pompousness, but I suspect he's as cool, smooth, and efficient as he looks."

"That doesn't do us any good. His loyalty is to the general, and only the general. His fate and the general's are intertwined, and his Silver Star rises only when the general's career is on course."

"In other words, he'll lie to protect the general."

"In a heartbeat. In fact, he lied about his call to Ann Campbell's house. We were there before 0800, and the message was already on her answering machine."

Cynthia nodded. "I know. There's something not right about that call."

"Add a suspect," I said.

CHAPTER FOURTEEN

Cynthia asked, "Psy-Ops School?"

It was five-fifty P.M. on my civilian watch, and a new Happy Hour was about to begin. "No, drop me off at the O Club."

We headed out toward the Officers' Club, which is set on a hill, away from the activities of the post, but close enough to be convenient.

Cynthia inquired, "How are we doing so far?"

"Do you mean personally or professionally?"

"Both."

"Well, professionally, I'm doing a hell of a job. How about you?"

"I'm asking *you*."

"So far, so good. You're a pro. I'm impressed."

"Thank you. And personally?"

"Personally, I enjoy your company."

"And I enjoy yours."

After a few seconds of pregnant silence, she changed the subject and asked me, "How did General Campbell seem to you?"

I thought a moment. It's important to gauge the reaction of friends, family, and coworkers to the news of a death as soon after the death as possible. I've solved more than one homicide case just by determining who didn't act right and following up on that. I said to Cynthia, "He did not have that look of total desolation and inconsolable grief that a parent has on learning of the death of a child. On the other hand, he is who he is."

She asked, "But who *is* he?"

"A soldier, a hero, a leader. The higher up the power ladder you go, the more distant the individual becomes."

"Maybe." She stayed silent a moment, then said, "Taking into account how Ann Campbell died . . . I mean, how she was found . . . I certainly don't think her father was the killer."

"We don't know that she died where she was found, or if she died with her clothes on or off. Things are not always as they seem. With a clever killer, you only see what the killer wants you to see."

"Still, Paul, I can't believe he would strangle his own daughter."

"It's not common, but it's not unheard of, either." I added, "If she were my daughter, and I knew about her sexual antics, I might be enraged."

"But you wouldn't fly into a homicidal rage with your own daughter."

"No, I wouldn't. But you never know. I'm just identifying motives."

We pulled up to the Officers' Club, which, as I said, is a Spanish-style stucco building. This was apparently a popular style in the 1920s when this club and other permanent structures were built after Camp Hadley became Fort Hadley. The war to end all wars had been won, but somewhere in the back of a bunch of collective minds must have been the thought that there was a need for a large standing Army for the next war to end all wars, and I had the pessimistic thought that the current reduction in force was just a temporary state of affairs.

I opened the car door and said to Cynthia, "You're not dressed for the club or I'd invite you to dinner."

"Well . . . I'll change, if you'd like. Unless you'd rather dine alone."

"I'll meet you in the grill." I got out of the car and she drove off.

I went into the club as retreat was being sounded over the PA system. I found the secretary's office, showed my CID badge, and commandeered the telephone and post directory. Colonel Charles Moore had no post housing listing, so I called the Psy-Ops School. It was a little after six, but the nice thing about the Army is that there's usually somebody on duty somewhere. We never sleep. A duty sergeant answered and connected me to Colonel Charles Moore's office. "Psy-Ops, Colonel Moore speaking."

"Colonel Moore, this is Warrant Officer Brenner. I'm with the Army Times."

"Oh . . ."

"Regarding the death of Captain Campbell."

"Yes . . . oh, God, how awful . . . just tragic."

"Yes, sir. Could I trouble you for a few words?"

"Of course. Well . . . I was Captain Campbell's commanding officer—"

"Yes, sir. I know that. Colonel, would it be convenient for you to meet me at the O Club now? I won't keep you more than ten minutes." Unless you interest me, Colonel.

"Well . . ."

"I have a deadline in about two hours, and I'd like to get at least a few words from her commanding officer."

"Of course. Where—?"

"The grill. I'm wearing a blue civilian suit. Thank you, Colonel." I hung up. Most Americans know that they don't have to speak to the police if they choose not to, but somehow they think that they have an obligation to speak to the press. Be that as it may, I'd spent the better part of the day as Paul Brenner, CID, and the need to be deceitful was more than I could bear.

I pulled the Midland telephone directory toward me and located a Charles Moore in the same garden apartment complex where Ann Campbell had lived. In and of itself, this was not unusual, though Victory Gardens was not where a colonel would normally choose to live. But maybe he had debts, or maybe, as a shrink, he didn't care if he bumped into lieutenants and captains in the parking lot. Or maybe he wanted to be near Ann Campbell.

I jotted down his address and phone number, then called the VOQ and reached Cynthia just as she got into her room. "Colonel Moore is meeting us. We're from the Army Times. Also, see if you can get me a room there. I can't go back to Whispering Pines with Chief Yardley on the prowl. Stop at the PX and pick me up a toothbrush, razor, and all that. Also, jockey shorts, medium, and socks. Maybe a fresh shirt, too, size fifteen collar, and be sure to bring walking shoes for yourself for later when we go out to the rifle range, and a flashlight. Okay? Cynthia? Hello?"

Bad connection, I guess. I hung up and went downstairs to the grill room, which is not as formal as the main dining room, and where you can get immediate sustenance. I ordered a beer from the bar and dined on potato chips and bar nuts while I listened to the conversations around me. The subject was Ann Campbell, and the tone of the conversation was cautious and muted. This was, after all, the Officers' Club. The subject in the Midland bars would be the same, but there would be more opinions expressed.

I saw a middle-aged man in dress greens with colonel's eagles enter the grill, and he scanned the big open basement room. I watched him for a full minute, noting that no one waved or said hello to him. Obviously, Colonel Moore was not well known or perhaps not well liked. I stood and approached him. He saw me and smiled tentatively. "Mr. Brenner?"

"Yes, sir." We shook hands. Colonel Moore's uniform was wrinkled and badly tailored, the true sign of an officer in one of the specialized branches. "Thank you for coming," I said. Colonel Moore was about fifty, had black curly hair that was a bit too long, and an air about him that suggested a civilian shrink called to active duty the day before. Army doctors, Army lawyers, Army shrinks, and Army dentists always intrigue me. I can never determine if they're on the run from a malpractice suit or if they're simply dedicated patriots. I led him to a table in the far corner, and we sat. "Drink?"

"Yes."

I signaled a waitress, and Colonel Moore ordered a glass of cream sherry. We were off to a bad start already.

146

Moore stared at me as though trying to guess my mental disorder. Not wanting to disappoint him, I volunteered, "Sounds like she got nailed by a psycho. Maybe a serial murderer."

True to his profession, he turned the statement back on me and asked, "Why do you say that?"

"Just a wild guess."

He informed me, "There have been no similar rapes and murders in this area."

"Similar to what?"

"To what happened to Captain Campbell."

Exactly what happened to Captain Campbell should not have been general knowledge at this point, but the Army thrives on rumor and hearsay. So, what Colonel Moore knew and Colonel Fowler knew and General Campbell knew, and when they knew it and how they knew it, was anyone's guess at this point in the day. I asked, "What *did* happen to her?"

He replied, "She was raped and murdered, of course. Out on the rifle range."

I took out my notebook and sipped on my beer. "I just got called in from D.C., and I don't have much information. I heard she was found naked, tied up."

He considered his response, then said, "You'd better check with the MPs on that."

"Right. How long were you her commanding officer?"

"Since she got here at Fort Hadley, about two years ago."

"So you knew her fairly well?"

"Yes. It's a small school. There are only about twenty officers and thirty enlisted men and women assigned."

"I see. How did you feel when you heard the news?"

He said to me, "I'm in total shock over this. I still can't believe this happened." And so forth. He actually looked all right to me despite the total shock. I work with psychologists and psychiatrists now and then, and I know they tend toward inappropriate behavior while saying appropriate things. Also, I believe that certain professions attract certain types of personalities. This is especially true in the military. Infantry officers, for instance, tend to be somewhat

147

aloof, a bit arrogant, and self-assured. CID people are deceitful, sarcastic, and extremely bright. Your average shrink has chosen a life that is involved with troubled minds, and it might be a cliché, but a lot of them have gone around the bend themselves. In the case of Charles Moore, psychological warfare specialist, who tried to make healthy enemy minds into troubled enemy minds, you had the equivalent of a physician cultivating typhus germs for the biological warfare people.

So, anyway, as we spoke, Charles Moore seemed to me not completely well. He seemed distant for short periods of time, then he'd stare at me at inappropriate times as though trying to read something in my face or read my mind. The guy actually made me uneasy, and that takes a lot of doing. Besides being slightly weird, his eyes were a bit sinister—very dark, very deep, and very penetrating. Also, his voice had that slow, deep, pseudo-soothing tone that they must teach at shrink school.

I asked him, "Did you know Captain Campbell prior to this assignment?"

"Yes. I first met her about six years ago when she attended the functional area school at Fort Bragg. I was her instructor."

"She had just completed her master's in psychology at Georgetown."

He looked at me the way people look at you when you say something they didn't think you knew. He replied, "Yes, I believe so."

"And were you together at Bragg while she was with the Psy-Ops Group?"

"I was at the school—she was working at her trade with the Fourth Psy-Ops."

"Then what?"

"Germany. We were there at about the same time. Then we returned to the JFK School at Bragg, and we both instructed for a while, then we were assigned on the same orders to the Gulf, then to the Pentagon, briefly, and two years ago we came here to Fort Hadley. Is all this necessary?"

"What do you do at Fort Hadley, Colonel?"

"That's confidential."

"Ah." I nodded as I scribbled. It is not common for two people to share so many assignments, even in a specialized area like psychological operations. I know married military couples who have not been so lucky. Take poor Cynthia, for example, who, though not married to that Special Forces guy at the time, was engaged to him, and there she was in Brussels while he was in the Canal Zone. I said to Colonel Moore, "You had a good professional relationship."

"Yes. Captain Campbell was extremely motivated, bright, articulate, and trustworthy."

That sounded like what he put on her officer evaluation report every six months. Clearly, they were a team. I asked him, "Was she sort of your protégé?"

He stared at me as though my use of one French word might lead to or suggest another French word like, perhaps, *paramour*, or some other dirty foreign word. He replied, "She was my subordinate."

"Right." I wrote that down under the heading *Bullshit*. I found that I was annoyed that this geek had been around the world with Ann Campbell and had shared so many years with her. How's that for nuts? I had half a mind to say to him, "Look here, Moore, you shouldn't even be on the same planet with this goddess. I'm the one who could have made her happy. You're a sick little freak." Instead, I said to him, "And do you know her father?"

"Yes. But not well."

"Had you met him prior to Fort Hadley?"

"Yes. Now and then. We saw him a few times in the Gulf."

"We?"

"Ann and I."

"Ah." I wrote that down.

I asked him a few more questions, but clearly neither of us was getting anything interesting out of this. What I wanted from this meeting was to get an impression of him before he knew whom he was talking to. Once they know you're a cop, they go into an act.

149

On the other hand, *Army Times* reporters can't ask questions like "Did you have a sexual relationship with her?" But cops can, so I asked him, "Did you have a sexual relationship with her?"

He stood. "What the hell kind of question is that? I'm going to have you up on charges."

I held up my badge case. "CID, Colonel. Have a seat."

He stared at the badge a second, then at me, and those eyes shot red death rays at me, *zip, zip,* like in a bad horror flick.

I said again, "Sit down, Colonel."

He looked furtively around the half-filled room, sort of like he was wondering if he was surrounded or something. Finally, he sat.

There are colonels, and then there are colonels. Theoretically, the rank transcends the man or woman wearing it, and you pay respect to the rank, if not the person. In reality, this is not so. Colonel Fowler, for instance, had the power and the authority, and you had to be careful with him. Colonel Moore was not connected to any power structure that I knew about. I said to him, "I am investigating the murder of Captain Campbell. You are not a suspect in this case, and I am not going to read you your rights. Therefore, you will answer my questions truthfully and fully. Okay?"

"You have no right to pass yourself off as—"

"Let me worry about my split personality. Okay? First question—"

"I refuse to speak to you without an attorney present."

"I think you've seen too many civilian movies. You have no right to an attorney and no right to remain silent unless you are a suspect. If you refuse to cooperate voluntarily, then I *will* consider you a suspect and read you your rights and take you down to the provost marshal's office and announce that I have a suspect who requires an attorney. You are in what is called a military bind. So?"

He thought a moment, then said, "I have absolutely nothing to hide, and I resent your having put me in a defensive position like this."

"Right. First question. When was the last time you saw Captain Campbell?"

He cleared his throat and adjusted his attitude, then replied, "I last saw her yesterday at about 1630 hours in my office. She said she was going to go to the club to get something to eat, then report for duty."

"Why did she volunteer for duty officer last night?"

"I have no idea."

"Did she call you from Post Headquarters during the evening, or did you call her?"

"Well . . . let me think . . ."

"All phone calls on post can be traced, and there is a duty officer's log." In fact, intra-post calls could not be traced, and Captain Campbell would not have logged any incoming or outgoing calls of a personal nature.

Moore replied, "Yes, I did call her . . ."

"What time?"

"About 2300 hours."

"Why so late?"

"Well, we had some work to discuss for the next day, and I knew things would be quiet by that hour."

"Where were you calling from?"

"From my home."

"Where is that?"

"Off post. Victory Drive."

"Isn't that where the deceased lived?"

"Yes."

"Have you ever been to her house?"

"Of course. Many times."

I tried to imagine what this guy looked like naked with his back to the camera, or with a leather mask on. I wondered if the forensic lab had an official pecker checker, some man (or woman) who could compare a blow-up photo of a pecker with this guy's equipment. Anyway, I asked him, "Were you ever sexually involved with her?"

"No. But you can be sure you'll hear rumors. Rumors have followed us wherever—"

151

"Are you married?"

"I was. Divorced about seven years ago."

"Do you date?"

"Occasionally."

"Did you find Ann Campbell attractive?"

"Well . . . I admired her mind."

"Did you ever notice her body?"

"I don't like this line of questioning."

"Neither do I. Did you find her sexually attractive?"

"I was her superior officer, I am almost twenty years older than she, she is a general's daughter. I never once said anything to her that could be construed as sexual harassment."

"I'm not investigating a charge of sexual harassment, Colonel. I'm investigating a rape and murder." I said to him, "Then why were there rumors?"

"Because people have dirty minds. Even Army officers." He smiled. "Like yourself."

On that note, I ordered two more drinks; another sherry to loosen him up, a beer to calm my impulse to deck him.

Cynthia arrived, wearing black pants and a white blouse. I introduced her to Colonel Moore, then said to her, "We're not with the Army Times anymore. We're CID. I was asking Colonel Moore if he was ever sexually involved with the deceased, and he assures me he wasn't. We're in a confrontational mode at the moment."

Cynthia smiled and said to Moore, "Mr. Brenner is extremely tense and tired." She sat and we all chatted for a few minutes as I brought Cynthia up to date. Cynthia ordered a bourbon and Coke and a club sandwich for herself and a cheeseburger for me. She knows I like cheeseburgers. Colonel Moore declined to dine with us, explaining that he was still too upset to eat. Cynthia asked him, "As her friend, did you know anyone who she might have been involved with?"

"You mean sexually?"

"I believe that's the subject on the table," she replied.

"Well . . . let me think . . . She was seeing a young man . . . a civilian. She rarely dated soldiers."

"Who was the civilian?" Cynthia asked.

"A fellow named Wes Yardley."

"Yardley? Chief of Police Yardley?"

"No, no. Wes Yardley, one of Burt Yardley's sons."

Cynthia glanced at me, then asked Moore, "How long were they seeing each other?"

"On and off since she arrived here. They had a stormy relationship. In fact, without pointing fingers, there's a man you should speak to."

"Why?"

"*Why?* Well, it's obvious. They were *involved*. They fought like cats and dogs."

"About what?"

"About . . . well, she mentioned to me that he treated her badly."

This sort of took me by surprise. I said to Moore, "*He* treated *her* badly?"

"Yes. He wouldn't call, he went out with other women, he saw her when it suited him."

This wasn't computing. If I was in love with Ann Campbell, why wasn't every other man following her around like a puppy dog? I said to Moore, "Why would she put up with that? I mean, she was . . . desirable, attractive . . ." Incredibly beautiful, sexy, and she had a body you could die for. Or kill for.

Moore smiled, almost knowingly, I thought. This guy made me uncomfortable. He said, "There is a type of personality—I'll put this in layman's terms: Ann Campbell liked the bad boys. Whoever showed her the slightest bit of attention, she considered weak and contemptible. That included most men. She was drawn to men who treated her badly, almost abusive men. Wes Yardley is such a man. He's a Midland policeman like his father, he is a local playboy and has many women friends, he's good-looking, I suppose, and has some of the charm of a southern gentleman and all of the macho posturing of a good ol' boy. Rogue or scoundrel might be good words to describe him."

I was still having trouble with this, and I said, "And Ann Campbell was involved with him for two years?"

"On and off."

Cynthia said, "She discussed all of this with you?"

"Yes."

"Professionally?"

He nodded at her astuteness. "Yes, I was her therapist."

I was not as astute, perhaps because my mind was unsettled. I was extremely disappointed in Ann Campbell. The playroom and the photos didn't upset me, perhaps because I knew that these men were just objects and she used them as such. But the idea of a boyfriend, a lover, someone who abused her, a relative of Burt Yardley at that, really pissed me off.

Cynthia said to Moore, "You know just about everything there is to know about her."

"I believe so."

"Then we'll ask you to help us with the psychological autopsy."

"*Help* you? You couldn't even scratch the surface, Ms. Sunhill."

I composed myself and said to him, "I'll need all your notes and transcripts of all your sessions with her."

"I never took a single note. That was our arrangement."

Cynthia said, "But you will *assist* us?"

"Why? She's dead."

Cynthia replied, "Sometimes a psychological autopsy helps us develop a psychological profile of the killer. I assume you know that."

"I've heard of it. I know very little about criminal psychology. If you want my opinion, it's mostly nonsense, anyway. We're all criminally insane, but most of us have good control mechanisms, internal and external. Remove the controls and you have a killer. I've seen well-adjusted men in Vietnam kill babies."

No one spoke for a while, and we just sat there with our own thoughts.

Finally, Cynthia said, "But we expect you, as her confidant, to tell us everything you know about her, her friends, her enemies, her mind."

"I suppose I have no choice."

"No, you don't," Cynthia assured him. "But we'd like your cooperation to be voluntary, if not enthusiastic. You do want to see her killer brought to justice."

"I'd like to see her killer found because I'm curious about who it may be. As for justice, I'm fairly certain that the killer thought he was administering justice."

Cynthia asked, "What do you mean by that?"

"I mean, when a woman like Ann Campbell is raped and murdered almost under her father's nose, you can be certain that someone had it in for her, her father, or both, and probably for a good reason. At least good in his own mind." He stood. "This is very upsetting for me. I feel a strong sense of loss. I'm going to miss her company. So if you'll excuse me . . .."

Cynthia and I stood also. He was a colonel, after all. I said, "I'd like to speak to you tomorrow. Please keep your day loose, Colonel. You interest me."

He left and we sat down.

The food came and I picked at my cheeseburger. Cynthia said, "Are you all right?"

"Yes."

"I think Ann Campbell's choice of lovers has upset you. You kind of went into a funk when he said that."

I looked at her. "They say never get emotionally involved with witnesses, suspects, or victims. But sometimes you can't help it."

"I always get emotionally involved with rape victims. But they're alive and hurting. Ann Campbell is dead."

I didn't respond to that.

Cynthia continued, "I hate to say this, but I know the type. She probably took sadistic delight in mentally torturing men who couldn't keep their eyes or minds off her good looks, then she masochistically gave herself to a man who she knew was going to treat her like dirt. Most likely, on some dim level, Wes Yardley knew his part and played it well. Most probably, she was sexually jealous of his other women, and, most probably, he was indifferent to her threats to find another boyfriend. They had a good relationship within the unhealthy world they created. Wes Yardley is probably the least likely suspect.''

''How do you know all that?''

''Well . . . I haven't been there myself, but I know lots of women who have. I see too many of them.''

''Really?''

''Really. You know men like that, too.''

''Probably.''

''You're showing classical symptoms of fatigue. You're getting dull and stupid. Go get some sleep and I'll wake you later.''

''I'm fine. Did you get me a room?''

''Yes.'' She opened her purse. ''Here's the key. The stuff you asked for is in my car, which is open.''

''Thanks. How much do I owe you?''

''I'll put it on my expense account. Karl will get a laugh out of the men's underwear.'' She added, ''You can walk to the VOQ from here, unless you want to borrow my car.''

''Neither. Let's go to the provost marshal's office.'' I stood.

''You could use a little freshening up, Paul.''

''You mean I stink?''

''Even a cool guy like you sweats in Georgia in August.''

''All right. Put this stuff on my tab.''

''Thanks.''

''Wake me at 2100.''

''Sure.''

I walked a few paces from the table, then came back and said, ''If she didn't have anything to do with the officers on post, and she was crazy over this Midland cop, who were those guys in the photos?''

Cynthia looked up from her sandwich. ''Go to bed, Paul.''

CHAPTER FIFTEEN

The phone in my room rang at 2100 hours, waking me out of a restless sleep. The voice said, "I'll be downstairs."

"Give me ten minutes." I hung up, went into the bathroom, and washed my face. The visiting officers' quarters at Fort Hadley is a two-story structure of tan brick that vaguely resembles a civilian motor inn. It's okay, and the rooms are clean, but, in typical military fashion, there's no air-conditioning, and there's a common bathroom between every two rooms just in case you get the idea that the Army is getting soft on its junior officers. When you use the bathroom, you're supposed to bolt the door that leads to the other room, then remember to unbolt it when you leave so the person next door can get in. This rarely works out right.

I brushed my teeth with the recently purchased items, then went into the bedroom and unwrapped my new shirt, wondering how I was going to get my stuff from Whispering Pines to here without running into the local fuzz. This was not the first time I'd become persona non grata in town, and it wouldn't be the last. Usually, we can straighten things out so I can drive away after I'm finished with a case. But once, at Fort Bliss, Texas, I had to be helicoptered out and didn't see my car for a few weeks, until someone was detailed to drive it to Falls Church. I put in for the nineteen cents a mile, but Karl turned it down on a technicality.

Anyway, the jockey shorts were small, not medium. Women can be petty. I got dressed, complete with Glock 9mm accessories, and went out into the hall, where I saw Cynthia coming out of the next room. I asked her, "Is that your room?"

"No, I'm cleaning it for a total stranger."

"Couldn't you get me a room down the hall or something?"

"Actually, this place is full of summer reservists doing their two weeks. I had to pull my CID routine to get you *any* room." She added, "I don't mind sharing a bathroom with you."

We got outside and into her Mustang. She said, "Rifle range six?"

"Right." She was still wearing the black pants and white blouse, but had put on running shoes and a white sweater. The flashlight I asked her to bring was on the console between the seats. I asked her, "Are you carrying?"

"Yes. Why? Are you expecting trouble?"

"A criminal always returns to the scene of the crime."

"Nonsense."

The sun had set, a full moon was rising, and I hoped that the conditions at this hour were close enough to those of the early morning hours out on the rifle ranges to get a sense of what may have happened, and to give me inspiration.

We drove past the post movie theater, where a crowd was letting out, then past the NCO Club, where the drinks are better than in the Officers' Club, the food is cheaper, and the women are friendlier.

Cynthia said, "I went to the provost marshal's office and saw Colonel Kent."

"Good initiative. Anything new?"

"A few things. First, he wants you to go easy on Colonel Moore. Apparently, Moore complained about your aggressive behavior."

"I wonder who Kent complains to."

"Here's more good news. You had a message from Karl, and I took the liberty of calling him at home. He's royally pissed-off about someone called Dalbert Elkins, who he says you transformed from a criminal into a government witness with immunity."

158

"I hope someone does the same for me someday. Anything else?"

"Yes. Karl, round two. He has to report to the judge advocate general at the Pentagon tomorrow, and he'd like a more comprehensive report than the one you filed earlier today."

"Well, he can wing it. I'm busy."

"I typed out a report and faxed it to his home."

"Thank you. What did the report say?"

"There's a copy of it on your desk. Do you trust me or not?"

"Of course. It's just that if this case goes bad, you may be safe if you don't have your name on things."

"Right. I signed your name to it."

"What?"

"Just kidding. Let me worry about my career."

"Fine. Anything from forensic?"

"Yes. The hospital sent a preliminary protocol to the provost marshal's office. Death occurred no earlier than midnight and no later than 0400 hours."

"I know that." The autopsy report, known for some unexplained reason as the protocol, generally picked up where forensic left off, though there was some overlap, which is fine. The more ghouls, the better.

"Also, death was definitely a result of asphyxia. There were internal traumas discovered in her neck and throat, and she'd bitten her tongue. All consistent with strangulation."

I've seen autopsies, and, as you can imagine, they are not pleasant things to watch. Being murdered and naked is undignified enough, but being sliced up and examined by a team of strangers is the ultimate violation. "What else?" I asked.

"Lividity and rigor were consistent with the position of the body as it was found, so it appears that death occurred there, and there was no movement of the body from another location. Also, there were no other wounds aside from the ligature around her neck, no other trauma to exposed tissue or to bones, brain, vagina, anus, mouth, and so forth."

I nodded, but made no response. "What else?"

159

Cynthia gave me a rundown of stomach contents, bladder and intestine contents, conditions of the internal organs, and anatomical findings. I'm glad I hadn't finished that cheeseburger, because my stomach was getting jumpy. Cynthia said, "There *was* some erosion of the cervix, which could be consistent with an abortion, a prior disease, or perhaps insertions of large objects."

"Okay . . . is that it?"

"That's it for now. The coroner hasn't done microscopic examinations of tissue and fluids yet, or toxology, which they want to do independent of the forensic lab." Cynthia added, "She didn't keep any secrets from them, did she?"

"Only one."

"Right. Also, there were some preliminary notes from Cal. They finished the serology tests and found no drugs or poisons in the blood, just a trace of alcohol. They found saliva at the corners of her mouth, running downward, consistent with the position of her body. They found perspiration in various places, and they found dried tears running downward from the eyes, again consistent with the position of the body. All three liquids have been identified as belonging to the victim."

"Tears?"

"Yes," Cynthia said. "Lots of tears. She'd been crying."

"I missed that . . ."

"That's all right. They didn't."

"Right . . . but tears are not consistent with the lack of wounds, and not necessarily consistent with a strangulation."

"No," Cynthia agreed, "but it is consistent with being tied up by a madman and being told you're going to die." She added, "What is not consistent with this is your theory that she was a voluntary participant. So maybe you have to change your theory."

"I'm fine-tuning my theory." I thought a moment, then said, "You're a woman. What made her cry?"

"I don't know, Paul. I wasn't there."

"But we have to get ourselves there. This was not a woman who would cry easily."

160

Cynthia nodded. "I agree with that. So whatever made her cry was perhaps an emotional trauma."

"Right. Someone she knew made her cry without even touching her."

"Perhaps. But she may have made herself cry. We don't know at this point."

"Right." Forensic evidence is objective. That is, dried tears were present in large quantities. The tears belonged to the victim. They flowed from the eyes toward the ears, indicating that they flowed when the body was in a supine position. End of statement. Exit Cal Seiver, enter Paul Brenner. The tears indicated *crying*. Therefore, *who* made her cry? *What* made her cry? *Why* did she cry? *When* did she cry? Is this important to know? Somehow, I thought it was.

Cynthia said, "Trace fibers were from her own underwear and from BDUs that are probably her own but could be from another person. There were no other fibers found. Also, the only hair found on and around the body was her own."

"How about the hair in the latrine sink?"

"That was not hers. It was black, undyed, from a Caucasian, came from the head, probably fell out, not pulled or cut, and from the shaft they determined that it was blood type O. There were no roots, so no genetic markers, and the sex can't be determined conclusively, but Cal's guess, based on the length and the lack of any dye, conditioner, styling preparations, and so forth, is that it belonged to a man. It was characterized as curly, not straight or wavy."

"I just met a guy with that kind of hair."

"Yes. We should get a strand of Colonel Moore's hair for microscopic comparison."

"Right. What else?"

"Well, there was no semen found on her skin or in any of her orifices. Also, there was no trace of any type of lubrication in her vagina or anus that would suggest a penetration by a foreign object, or by a lubricated condom, for instance."

I nodded. "No sexual intercourse took place."

161

"It could have taken place if a man dressed in the same BDUs she wore got on top of her, leaving no body hair, saliva, or perspiration of his own. Using a condom without lubrication, or using no condom, he penetrated her but did not ejaculate. That could have happened."

"But it didn't. No sexual intercourse took place. Transference and exchange has got to occur to some extent. Even a microscopic extent."

"I tend to agree. But we can't rule out some sort of genital stimulation. If the rope around her neck was to induce sexual asphyxiation, as you suggested, then it follows that genital stimulation was supposed to take place."

"That would be logical. But I've given up on logic in this case. Okay, how about fingerprints?"

"None on her body. They couldn't lift any complete or distinct prints from the nylon rope, but they got several from the tent pegs."

"Are they good enough to run through the FBI?"

"No, but they're good enough to match to known prints. In fact, some of the prints were Ann Campbell's. Some were not and may belong to the other person."

"I hope so."

Cynthia said, "So she handled the tent pegs, which means she was forced to assist the perpetrator, or she voluntarily assisted the perpetrator, as in a consensual act of sexual fantasy or whatever."

"I lean toward the latter."

"I would, too, except what made her cry?"

"Happiness. Ecstasy." I pointed out, "Crying is an empirically observable event. The cause of the crying is open to different interpretations." I added, "Some people do cry after orgasm."

"I've heard. So anyway, we know a lot more than we did at sunrise, but in some ways we know a lot less. Some of this stuff is not fitting together in the normal way."

"That's an understatement. Any fingerprints from the humvee?"

"Lots. They were still working on that and on the latrines. Cal took the humvee and the lower bleacher seats to the hangar. He's set up shop there."

162

"Good." I thought a moment, then said, "I've only had two homicide cases that I've solved to my satisfaction where I've failed to get a conviction. And those two involved bright people who took care not to leave any forensic evidence behind. I don't want this to be one of those cases."

"Well, Paul, as they say, long before there was scientific evidence, there were confessions. Often the perpetrator needs to confess and is just waiting for us to ask him to do so."

"That's what they said during the Inquisition, the Salem witch trials, and the Moscow show trials. I'd like to see some evidence."

We drove through the outskirts of the main post, neither of us saying much. I rolled down my window, letting in the cool night air. "Do you like Georgia?"

She glanced at me. "I never had a permanent duty station here. Just here and gone. But I like it. How about you?"

"Brings back memories."

We left the main post, and Cynthia found Rifle Range Road without too much difficulty. The moon was still below the trees, and it was dark except for our headlights on the road. You could hear crickets, tree frogs, locusts, and all sorts of other nocturnal things that make weird sounds, and the smell of the pines was overwhelming, reminding me of Whispering Pines many years ago: sitting outside at night on lawn chairs, drinking beer with the other young soldiers and their wives, listening to Jimi Hendrix, Janis Joplin, or whomever, waiting for the mimeographed papers that began, "You are hereby ordered to report . . ."

Cynthia asked, "What did you think of Colonel Moore?"

"Probably the same as you. He's an odd duck."

"Yes, but I think he's a key to *why* Ann Campbell was killed."

"Quite possibly." I asked her, "Do you consider him a suspect?"

"For the record, no. We have to keep him talking. But between us, I can see him as a suspect."

"Especially if that was his hair in the sink," I pointed out.

"What would be his motive?" Cynthia asked.

"Well, it wasn't classical sexual jealousy."

"Do you believe that he never slept with her, or even proposi-tioned her?"

"Yes. That shows how sick he is."

"That's an interesting observation. The more I deal with men, the more I learn."

"Good for you. What do *you* think his motive could be?"

"Well, I agree with you that Colonel Moore is somewhat asexual. But she may have threatened to break off their platonic or therapeutic relationship, and he couldn't handle it."

"Then why kill her that way?" I asked.

"How do I know? We're dealing with two shrinks here."

"Right. But I'll bet Moore knows why. Moore knows how she got there on the ground, even if he didn't kill her himself. For all we know, he told her it was good therapy to have sex with strangers in open places. I've heard of that kind of thing."

Cynthia nodded. "You're getting close to something."

"Just another theory to store in the hangar."

After a moment of quiet, I said to her, apropos of nothing except my whole life, "Did you marry Major what's-his-name with the gun?"

She replied, not enthusiastically, I thought, "Yes, I did."

"Well, congratulations. I'm extremely happy for you, Cynthia, and wish you all the best that life has to offer."

"I've filed for divorce."

"Good."

We rode in silence awhile, then she said, "I felt guilty after Brussels, so I accepted his proposal. Actually, I guess I was engaged to be married to him, so we got married. But . . . he never let me forget that he didn't trust me anymore. Your name came up once or twice."

"Am *I* supposed to feel guilty? I don't."

"You shouldn't. He turned out to be a possessive manipulator, anyway."

"You didn't see that?"

"No. The best thing about some long-distance relationships is that they're long-distance. It's very romantic. Living together is another matter."

"I'm sure you bent over backward to please."

"If that's sarcasm, you're wrong. I did bend over backward. But every time I had to go off on assignment, he got very nasty, and every time I came back from assignment, he interrogated me. I don't like being interrogated."

"No one does."

"I never fooled around on him."

"Well, once."

"You know what I mean. So anyway, I got to thinking that military life and married life don't go together. He wanted me to resign. I said no. He got violent, and I had to pull my gun on him."

"My goodness. You're lucky he didn't have that automatic he pulled on me."

"Well, he did, but I'd taken the firing pin out months before. Look, it's all so tawdry, and I feel embarrassed even talking about it. But I think I owe you at least that explanation of my life between Brussels and now."

"Thank you. Does he have the firing pin back in the gun?"

She laughed. "He's all right. He accepted it gracefully. He's tired of ripping himself apart with jealousy. He's back on a good career track, and he has a girlfriend."

"Where is this happy psychopath stationed?"

"He's at the Ranger School at Benning."

"That's commuting distance to here."

"He doesn't even know where I am now. Are you worried?"

"No. I just need to know what I'm dealing with. Basic intelligence gathering."

"What are you dealing with?"

"The past, the present, and the future. Same old stuff."

"Can we be friends without being lovers?"

"Of course. I'll ask Colonel Moore where he got himself neutered."

"You're so basic." She thought a moment, then said, "I don't want another jealous crazy."

"Let's talk about this tomorrow, or next week."

"Fine."

After a minute or two, I asked, "Are you seeing anyone else?"

"Is it next week already?"

"I just don't want to get shot. You know?"

"No, I'm not seeing anyone."

"Good. Because I don't want to get shot."

She said, "Paul, shut up or *I'll* shoot you. God, you bug me."

"Don't shoot."

She laughed. "Stop it."

We rode the last mile in silence, then I said, "Pull over here and kill the lights and the engine."

The sky was a clear moonlit blue, and the temperature had dropped, but it was still comfortable despite the humidity. It was a nice evening, the kind of night made for romantic trysts out in the countryside. I listened to the nightbirds and the breeze in the pines. I said, "Not only have I thought about you, but I've missed you."

"I know. Me, too."

I nodded. "So what did we do wrong? Why did we go our own ways?"

She shrugged. "Maybe we just blew it." She added, "I wanted you to . . . well, but that's past."

"What did you want me to do?"

"I wanted you not to accept my decision to break it off. I wanted you to take me away from him."

"That's not my style, Cynthia. You made a decision. I respected it."

"Oh, God, Paul, you're such a goddamned sharp detective, aren't you? You can read a killer's heart at a hundred yards, and spot a liar in the blink of an eye. But you don't know how to read yourself, and you damned sure don't know much about women."

So I sat there, like the idiot I am, realizing she was right, and at a loss for words, knowing what I felt in my heart, but unable to express it or unwilling actually to commit my feelings to words. I wanted to say, "Cynthia, I love you, I've always loved you. I will continue to love you. Run away with me." But I couldn't, so I said, slowly and deliberately, "I know what you're saying, I agree with you, I'm working on it, and we'll work it out."

She took my hand and held it awhile, then said, "Poor Paul. Do I make you nervous?"

"Yes."

"You don't like that feeling, do you?"

"No."

She squeezed my hand. "But I see some improvement since last year in Brussels."

"I'm trying."

"You're trying my patience."

"We're going to be okay."

"Good." She leaned over and kissed me lightly, then released my hand. "What now?"

"Well, let's get to work." I opened my door.

"This is not rifle range six," she pointed out.

"No, this is five."

"Why are we getting out here?"

"Take the flashlight." I got out of the car and she followed.

CHAPTER SIXTEEN

We stood a few feet apart listening for a while, adjusting to the darkness and the nuances of the night, the way we were taught in school.

Finally I said, "I have this nagging thought that the headlights that PFC Robbins saw at 0217 hours were not from Ann Campbell's humvee. That, indeed, as you suggested, she drove to rifle range six without her headlights. She knew where the guard was posted, of course, and didn't want to attract attention. She turned off her lights about here and went the rest of the way in the dark, which is no problem with this moonlight. She had come directly here to meet someone after she left Sergeant St. John at headquarters at 0100 hours. That's why no other guard post saw her. Logical?"

"If you're assuming that this was a preplanned rendezvous, then, yes, it's logical so far."

"Let's assume that. She could have gotten here as early as 0115 hours."

"Possible."

"Okay," I said, trying to think this out, "the person she was supposed to meet probably got here first."

"Why?"

"Because she told him to. She knew she could be held up by something at headquarters. She calls this person from Post Headquarters and says, 'Be there no later than half past midnight. Wait for me.' ''

''Okay.''

''So this person she was supposed to meet may have had no business or reason to be out here, and he may have been driving a POV. So as not to attract attention from the guard post, which he also knows is up the road, he goes as far as here, range five, and turns off the road to the left.'' We walked off the road into a graveled parking area.

I said to Cynthia, ''This graveled field also serves ranges four and six. The troop carriers stop here, leave off the men for all three ranges, turn around and leave, and the men walk to their assigned ranges. I remember that from my days here.''

''Except they don't use muskets anymore.''

''Right. So the guy who was supposed to meet her here knows to pull off on the gravel so as not to leave tire marks. Follow me.'' We walked across the gravel, which was crisscrossed with the impressions of dozens of tires, none of them distinct enough in the crushed stone to be worth photographing or trying to get a cast of. But as we got past the bleachers of rifle range five, the gravel thinned, and with the flashlight we could make out tire marks where no truck or car should have been. The tire marks continued toward a stand of scrub pine, then stopped. I said, ''Any vehicle parked here would not be seen from the road, but he did leave his tire marks.''

''Paul, this is incredible. These could be the tire marks of the perpetrator.''

''These are probably the tire marks of the person who met her here. The person did not want his vehicle seen by a passing MP patrol or by the guard truck that would have come by this way at about 0100 hours to relieve the guard at the ammo shed a kilometer up the road, and to post PFC Robbins at that shed. This person was already here before that time and parked here, then walked on the back trail to rifle range six and went into the latrine to wait. While there, he may have used the latrine and may have washed his

169

face and hands, leaving water spots and a hair behind. Logical so far?''

''So far.''

''Let's walk.'' We found the back trail, made from small logs laid side by side to form an all-weather road or path, what the Army calls a corduroy surface. This surface left no footprints. We followed it for about a hundred meters through the brush until it came out into the area behind the latrines of rifle range six. ''Okay, the guy waits here, in or around the latrines. The first thing he sees is the guard truck going up the road to the ammo shed, then, a while later, the truck returns after having relieved the original guard and posting Robbins. The truck does not go all the way to main post, where it may have met Ann Campbell coming the other way. It turns off toward Jordan Field to post and relieve guards at the hangars, which takes a while. I recall that from when I was stationed here. So Ann Campbell probably did not cross the path of the guard truck and proceeded directly to range six. She extinguished her headlights at some point and parked the humvee where we found it on the road. Okay?''

''So far. But it's all speculation.''

''Right. That's what reenactment mostly is. You're here to find holes, not tell me I'm making it up.''

''All right. Go on.''

''Okay. The person waiting here near the latrines sees her stop her humvee on the road, and he walks across this open area—'' I began to walk toward the road, and Cynthia followed. ''He approaches Ann Campbell, who is in or near her humvee, and tells her that the guard truck has come and gone, as it should have by this time, and there's nothing to worry about now, except perhaps a random MP patrol. But that's not likely out here. This road dead-ends at range ten, and there will be no through traffic. The only other people who might come by are the officer of the guard or the sergeant of the guard, but they would not come out this way so soon after the changing of the guard, and, most likely, they wouldn't bother at all. The only other person who would conceivably come out here is the post duty officer, and on this night, the duty officer is Captain Ann Campbell. Follow?''

"Up to a point. Why would she pull up here? Why not hide her vehicle if she was here for a sexual rendezvous? In fact, why the hell was she on the rifle range, so close to the road?''

"I'm not sure. Except that whatever she did, she did it the way she wanted to do it. None of this was random, and everything was planned, including apparently volunteering for duty officer on a moonlit night. Therefore, she had a reason for leaving her vehicle right here, and a reason for picking that spot, fifty meters from the road.''

"Okay . . . we'll let that slide.''

"So, to continue, I have no idea what transpired between her and the person she met, but at some point here on the road, she took off her pistol, then all her clothes except her bra and panties. She had a blacktop smudge on her foot. She and this person walked on the well-trod path between the firing lanes. Her clothes and pistol were probably back in the jeep. She, or the other person, is carrying tent pegs, precut rope, and a small sledgehammer. They pick their spot at the base of that pop-up target over there.'' We both looked out onto the range. The pavilion was still pitched, and the tarpaulins were still laid out to form a trail to the spot where the body had lain. I asked Cynthia, "How does this sound so far?''

"It has its own internal logic. But I don't get it.''

"Neither do I. But it's pretty much what happened.'' I said, "Let's walk.'' We followed the tarpaulin trail and stopped under the pavilion. Cynthia shined her flashlight on the spot where Ann Campbell had lain, revealing an outline of the spread-eagled body made with white chalk powder. Yellow marker flags stuck out of the holes where the tent pegs had been.

Cynthia said, "Shouldn't there be MPs here?''

"There should be. Kent slipped up.'' I looked out over the moonlit rifle range where about fifty lifelike targets stood like a platoon of infantry advancing through the brush. I said to Cynthia, "Obviously, this had some symbolism for Ann Campbell—armed

171

men coming to gang-rape her, or watching her as she was tied naked on the ground—or who knows what she was trying to create or express?''

Cynthia said, ''All right, they're standing here. Ann Campbell in her bra and panties, this man carrying the rape kit or sexual paraphernalia if she's a willing accomplice. He's not armed, and she's going along with this.''

''Right. So together they bind one end of each rope around her wrists and ankles. Probably at this point, she removes her bra and panties and puts the panties around her neck, since we found no trace of soil on them.''

''Why did she wear the bra?''

''I can't say for sure, but she may have just left it on without thinking, then threw it on the ground where we found it. They've planned this, but they're understandably a little nervous. Okay?''

''Okay. I'm nervous just talking about it.''

''So they pick their spot at the base of this pop-up target, she lies down here, spreads her arms and legs, and he pounds the four tent pegs into the ground.''

''Doesn't this make noise?''

''The pegs were polyvinyl. Also, he may have used a handkerchief to muffle the sound. The wind is blowing from the direction of the guard post a kilometer away, and PFC Robbins couldn't even hear a car door slam.''

''All right,'' Cynthia said. ''The tent pegs are in, and he ties her ankles and wrists to the pegs.''

''Correct. Then he wraps the long rope around her neck, over the panties.''

''So she's now as we found her.''

''Yes,'' I said, ''she is now as we found her, except, at this point, she was still alive.''

Cynthia had one hand in the pocket of her pants now and was staring at the ground where her flashlight beam ended, obviously deep in thought. Finally, she said, ''He knelt near her and applied tension to the rope, inducing sexual asphyxia. Maybe, using his

fingers, or an object, he stimulates her. She had an orgasm . . .''
Cynthia added, ''He would have masturbated at some point though
we found no semen on her, and he may have taken photos, which
is common after going through all this trouble. I've had cases where
an audiotape was made, and one where a videotape was made . . .''
She paused a moment, then continued, ''All right . . . she's done,
he's done, she wants to be untied. At this point, he snaps for some
reason and strangles her to death, or he'd planned to do that all
along, or he may have honestly strangled her by accident during the
act.'' She looked at me. ''That's it, isn't it?''

''Yes. I think so.''

''But there's more to it,'' Cynthia reminded me. ''Her clothes,
dog tags, her West Point ring, and her pistol are missing.''

''I know. That's a problem.'' I said, ''We're back to souvenirs.''

''Yes, they do take souvenirs. But you know, if I had just killed a
general's daughter out on the rifle range, on purpose or by accident, I
don't think I'd put her clothes in my car and drive around with the
evidence that would put me in front of a firing squad.''

''Not likely, is it? And remember, she had her watch on. Why?''

''I don't know,'' Cynthia replied. ''That may be insignificant.''

''It may be. Let's walk.'' We retraced our steps along the tarpaulin path and came back to the road where Ann Campbell's humvee
had been parked. ''All right,'' I said, ''he comes back here to the
vehicle. He takes her BDUs, her helmet, dog tags, socks, boots,
and so forth, but leaves her handbag on the passenger seat of the
vehicle.''

''He may have forgotten the handbag. Men often do. I've seen
that before.''

I turned toward the latrines. ''Carrying those items, he crosses
the grassy area, passes the bleachers, passes the latrines, and finds
the corduroy trail. He would not walk on the road.''

''No.''

''Okay, if they'd started at about 0115 hours, it is now about
0215 hours, give or take a few minutes. It can't be later because
PFC Robbins saw headlights at 0217 hours.''

173

"And you're sure they were not Ann Campbell's headlights?"

"I'm making the strong assumption she got here earlier, and she drove up without headlights. So this vehicle comes by, sees her parked humvee, stops, turns off the lights, and gets out of his or her vehicle. That is what Robbins saw at 0217 hours."

"And he or she can see Ann Campbell from the road. Right?"

"Sergeant St. John did. The moon was nearly full. Anyone who saw the parked humvee would look around. Fifty meters away, this person sees something on the rifle range. It's almost a human instinct to recognize another human form, especially a naked one. We've both heard similar stories—someone walking in the woods sees something lying on the ground, and so on."

"All right. So what does that person do?"

"That person goes up to her and sees that she's dead, goes back to his or her vehicle, makes a U-turn, and gets the hell out of there."

"Without turning his or her headlights back on."

"Apparently. PFC Robbins was transfixed by the headlights and kept watching, but never saw them go on again. The next lights she saw were Sergeant St. John's at 0425 hours."

"Why would this person not turn their headlights back on when they were leaving? Why turn them off to begin with? It's damned spooky out here, Paul. I'd leave my lights on if I got out of my car. And who is this new person you've introduced, and why didn't this person make a report?"

"The only answer I can come up with is that Ann Campbell had not gone through all this trouble for one tryst. Her fantasy may have been multiple rapes. She may have had several appointments."

"That's very weird." She added, "But possible."

I said, "Let's follow the path that Ann Campbell's assistant or assailant took back." We retraced our steps and intersected the corduroy path in the bush behind the rifle ranges, then turned left onto it and headed back to rifle range five. I said, "Here, in these bushes, will probably be a plastic bag containing her clothes."

Cynthia looked at me. "Are you psychic, too?"

"The area search turned up nothing, and neither did the dogs, so

174

the clothes will be in a plastic, odorproof bag, probably a trash bag, and they will be farther away than the search. When we get closer to rifle range five, you'll turn that flashlight into the bush. We may have to come back tomorrow—"

Cynthia stopped. "Wait."

"What?"

"The latrine sheds."

"Damn it! You're right."

So back we went to the latrine sheds. A line of steel-mesh trash pails sat between the two sheds, and I turned one of them over and jumped onto the roof of the shed for male personnel. There was nothing on the flat, pitched roof, but as I scrambled to my feet, I saw on the next latrine roof a brown plastic trash bag shining in the moonlight. I took a running start, jumped onto the adjoining shed, and kicked the bag off, following it to the ground. Somewhere in midair, I remembered my paratrooper training, flexed my knees into a shoulder roll, and bounded up on my feet.

Cynthia asked, "Are you all right?"

"I'm fine. Get a handkerchief."

She took a handkerchief from her pocket, knelt, and untwisted the wire tie, then carefully pulled open the mouth of the bag and shined her flashlight into it. Inside, we could see a jumble of clothing, a pair of boots, and a white sock. Carefully, with her hand wrapped in the handkerchief, Cynthia moved the things around, uncovering the pistol belt and holster with the automatic still in it, then finally the dog tags, which she held up and read in the beam of her flashlight. "Campbell, Ann Louise." She let the dog tags drop back into the bag and stood. She looked up at the top of the latrine shed. "One of the older tricks in the book. But why did this guy care about hiding her clothes?"

I thought a moment. "It seems that the clothes were supposed to be recovered later."

"By whom? The perpetrator? A third party?"

"Don't know. But I like the idea of a third party."

A pair of headlights lit up the road, then I heard the engine of a

175

vehicle, then saw it, an olive-drab staff car that stopped. The engine remained running, and the headlights stayed on. I felt for my pistol and so did Cynthia.

The driver's door opened, and the interior lights revealed the figure of Bill Kent as he got out drawing his pistol and looking toward our flashlight. He slammed his door and issued a challenge. "Identify yourselves."

I called back, "Brenner and Sunhill, Colonel." A little formal, but you don't fool around when being challenged by an armed man.

We stayed motionless until he said, "I'm coming to you."

"Understand." We both stood until he got closer, then saw him holster his pistol, and heard him say, "Recognize."

All a little silly, too, except that every once in a while, a guy gets plugged messing around with challenges and such. Kent asked us, "What are you doing here?"

I replied, "This is the scene of the crime, Bill, and detectives and criminals always return to it. What are *you* doing here?"

"I resent the implication, wise guy. I'm here for the same reason you are—to try to get a feeling for the scene at night."

"Let me be the detective, Colonel. I expected to see MPs posted here."

"I suppose I should have posted a few. But I have patrols going by."

"I haven't seen any. Can you get a couple of people here?"

"All right." He asked Cynthia, "Why is your car way back there?"

She replied, "We wanted to walk in the moonlight."

He looked like he was going to ask why, but then noticed the bag. "What is that?"

"That is," Cynthia replied, "the missing items."

"What items?"

"Her clothing."

I watched Kent as he took this in. He seemed almost indifferent, I thought. He asked, "Where'd you find them?"

"On top of the female latrine shed. Your guys missed it."

"I guess they did." He asked, "Why do you think her clothes were up there?"

"Who knows?"

"Are you through here?"

"For now."

"What's next?"

I replied, "We'll meet you at Jordan Field in about an hour."

"Okay." He added, "Colonel Moore is very upset with you."

"Then he should file formal charges instead of crying on your shoulder. Do you know the guy?"

"Only through Ann." He looked at his watch. "One hour."

"Right."

We parted, he backed toward his car on the road, we along the corduroy trail, me carrying the plastic trash bag.

Cynthia said to me, "You don't trust him, do you?"

"I did . . . I've known Bill Kent for over ten years. But now . . . I don't know. I don't think he's a suspect, but there's no doubt in my mind that he, like just about everybody here, is hiding something."

"I know. I get that feeling, too. It's like we've arrived in a small town and everybody knows everybody's dirty secrets, and we know there are skeletons in the closet, but we can't find the closets."

"That's about it."

We reached the car, and I put the bag in the trunk.

Cynthia and I got in, and she started the engine, then brushed something from my shoulder. "Anything broken, soldier? Can I take you to the hospital?"

"No, but I need my head examined. Psychological Operations School."

CHAPTER SEVENTEEN

We arrived at the Psy-Ops School at about 2300 hours, and Cynthia parked near the school headquarters. The school was made up of a cluster of about thirty concrete buildings, all of which were a uniquely depressing slate gray, the color of suicide, of Seattle.

There was not much grass, few trees, and the inadequate exterior lighting would be unacceptable in a civilian setting, but in the Army, muggings and lawsuits were not yet a problem.

Most of the buildings were dark, except for two that looked like living quarters, and in the nearby headquarters building, a single ground floor window was lit.

As we walked toward the headquarters, Cynthia asked me, ''What exactly goes on here?''

''This is a subcommand of the JFK Special Warfare School at Bragg. In reality, it's not a school at all, but that's the cover.''

''Cover for what?''

''It's a research facility. They don't teach, they learn.''

''What do they learn?''

''I think they learn what makes people tick, then they find out how to make them stop ticking without putting a bullet in them.'' I added, ''Most of it is experimental.''

''Sounds spooky.''

"I'm with you. Bullets and high explosives work every time. Screw panic and free-floating anxiety."

A humvee turned the corner up ahead and came toward us. It stopped and an MP dismounted from the passenger side while the driver stayed in the vehicle, pointing his headlights at us. The MP, a corporal named Stroud, saluted, which is customary, then asked us, "Do you have business here?"

I replied, "Yes. CID." I held up my identification, which he examined with a flashlight, then examined Cynthia's and turned out his light. "Who do you have business with, sir?"

"The duty sergeant. Why don't you escort us, Corporal?"

"Yes, sir." He walked with us to the headquarters and asked, "The Campbell murder?"

"I'm afraid so."

"Damned shame."

"Did you know her?" Cynthia asked.

"Yes, ma'am. Not well, but I'd see her here at night sometimes. Lots of what they do here, they do at night." He added, "Nice lady. Got any leads?"

I replied, "Not yet."

"Glad to see you're working all night on this."

We all entered the headquarters building, where a staff sergeant was sitting in an office located to the right of the small lobby. He saw us and stood as we entered. After the preliminaries, I said to the duty sergeant, whose name was Corman, "Sergeant, I'd like to see Colonel Moore's office."

Sergeant Corman scratched his head and glanced at Corporal Stroud, then replied, "Can't do that, sir."

"Sure you can. Let's go."

He stood his ground. "I really can't without proper authorization. This is a restricted area."

In the Army, you don't actually need probable cause or a search warrant, and if you did, the warrant wouldn't be issued by a military judge because they have no power outside a court-martial. What I needed was someone in the chain of command. I asked Sergeant

179

Corman, "Does Colonel Moore keep a personal locker in his office?"

He hesitated, then replied, "Yes, sir."

"Good. Go and get me his hairbrush or comb."

"Sir?"

"He needs to comb his hair. We'll stay here and cover the phone."

"Sir, this is a restricted area. I must ask you to leave."

I said, "May I use your phone?"

"Yes, sir."

"Privately."

"I can't leave—"

"MP Corporal Stroud will stay here. Thank you."

He hesitated, then walked out of the office. I said to Stroud, "Whatever you hear is confidential."

"Yes, sir."

I looked up Colonel Fowler's Bethany Hill phone number in the post directory, and Fowler answered on the third ring. I said, "Colonel, this is Mr. Brenner. I'm sorry to bother you at this hour." Actually I wasn't. "But I need you to authorize me to remove something from Colonel Moore's office."

"Where the hell are you, Brenner?" He sounded as if he might have been sleeping.

I replied, "At the Psy-Ops School, Colonel."

"At this hour?"

"I must have lost track of the time."

"What do you have to remove from Colonel Moore's office?"

"Actually, I'd like to remove the entire office to Jordan Field."

He replied, "I can't authorize that. That school is run from Fort Bragg, and it's a restricted area. Colonel Moore's office is full of classified documents. But I'll call Bragg in the morning and see what I can do."

I didn't mention that I already had Ann Campbell's office at Jordan Field. This is what happens when you ask permission to do anything in the Army. The answer is always no, then you negotiate. I said, "Well, then, Colonel, give me permission to seal the office."

"Seal the office? What the hell's going on?"

"A murder investigation."

"Don't be flippant with me, Mr. Brenner."

"Yes, sir."

"I'll call Bragg in the morning. That's all I can do."

"That's not enough, Colonel."

"You know, Mr. Brenner, I appreciate your hard work and initiative, but you can't be charging around like a bull, wreaking havoc wherever you go. There's only one murderer out there, and you should give some thought to the feelings of the remainder of the people on this post. And while you're doing that, you may want to keep in mind Army regulations, customs, protocols, and courtesy. Do you follow me, Mr. Brenner?"

"Yes, sir. What I actually need at the moment is a sample of Colonel Moore's hair to match up with a strand found at the scene of the murder. You could call Colonel Moore at home, sir, and have him report to the forensic lab at Jordan Field for a plucking, or we can get a sample of his hair from his comb or brush here, which I would prefer, as time is short. Also, I'd rather that Colonel Moore did not know he was a suspect at the moment." I noticed Corporal Stroud's eyes widen.

There was a long silence, then Colonel Fowler said, "All right, I'll let you take his brush or comb, but if anything else in his office is touched, I'll have you charged."

"Yes, sir. Will you instruct the duty sergeant?"

"Put him on."

"Yes, sir." I motioned to Stroud, who went out and got Sergeant Corman. I said to Corman, "Colonel Fowler, the post adjutant, wishes to speak to you."

He took the phone without enthusiasm, and his end of the conversation went something like "Yes, sir. Yes, sir. Yes, sir. Yes, sir." He hung up and said to me, "If you'll cover the phones, I'll go look for his brush or comb."

"Fine. Wrap it in a handkerchief."

He took a set of keys and left the office. I heard his footsteps retreating down the hallway.

181

I said to Corporal Stroud, "We'll be outside. Wait here and collect the evidence."

"Yes, sir."

Corporal Stroud seemed happy to be of help in the case. Cynthia and I went outside and stood in the headlights of the MP vehicle.

Cynthia said to me, "This place is tight."

"If you were conducting experiments in brainwashing, interrogation techniques, morale destruction, and producing fear and panic, you might not want outsiders snooping around."

"That's what she was involved in, wasn't it?"

"I believe so." I added, "They have cell blocks here where they keep volunteers for their experiments, and they have an entire mock POW camp out on the reservation."

"How do you know all this?"

"I worked on a case with a psychologist about a year ago who had once been stationed here. He applied for a transfer."

"I guess this place could get to you."

"Yes. You know, I found a piece of paper in Ann Campbell's personnel file—another Nietzsche quote. It said, 'Whoever fights monsters should see to it that in the process he does not become a monster. And when you look long into the abyss, the abyss also looks into you.' "

"How in the world did that get in there?"

"Don't know, but I think I understand what it means."

"Yes . . . I think we both do." She said, "Sometimes I want to do something else for a living. I'm getting tired of vaginal swabs and DNA testing of sperm, and taking statements from rapists and rape victims."

"Right. I think ten years is the limit. I've had almost twenty. This is my last case."

"Do you say that every time?"

"Yes."

Corporal Stroud came out of the headquarters building holding something in his hand, and as he got closer, we could see him smiling. He called out, "He found it."

We met him on the sidewalk, and he handed me a hairbrush wrapped in an olive-drab handkerchief.

I said to him, "You know about chain of custody. I need a statement from you describing how and where we found this, when, who, and so forth."

"Yes, sir."

"Signed, sealed, marked 'Brenner,' and in the provost marshal's office before 0600 hours."

"Yes, sir."

Cynthia asked him, "Would you know what kind of vehicle Colonel Moore drives?"

He thought a moment. "Let's see . . . old car . . . kind of beat-up . . . gray sedan . . . what the hell is that? Right, a big Ford Fairlane, about '85 or '86."

"You've been very helpful." She added, "This is all strictly confidential."

Corporal Stroud nodded and offered, "Anything else you want to know about Colonel Moore, ask me, and if I don't know, I'll find out."

"Thank you," I said. Clearly, there were those who would like to see Colonel Moore on death row in Leavenworth.

We exchanged salutes and went back to our respective vehicles.

Cynthia put the Mustang in gear. "Jordan Field?"

"Right."

We left the main post again and drove out onto the military reservation. The 100,000 acres of government property computed to something like 150 square miles of mostly uninhabited land. There are, however, backcountry people, poachers, hunters, and trappers who trespassed frequently. Also, from the days that preceded Camp Hadley, there are ghost towns, old cemeteries, country churches, abandoned quarries and logging camps, as well as ramshackle structures from what used to be the Beaumont Plantation. It was a unique environment, sort of frozen in time when the government exercised its right of eminent domain to meet the national emergency of the great war to end all wars.

As I said, I took my infantry basic training and advanced infantry training here, and I still remember the terrain: an inhospitable and eerily quiet landscape of wooded hills, lakes and ponds, swamps and marshes, and a species of hanging moss that gave off a phosphorescent glow at night that caused visual disorientation.

The training itself was a grueling program whose objective was to turn normally fucked-up American kids into efficient, motivated, and loyal combat-ready soldiers with a healthy desire to kill. The whole process took only four months, though they were long, intensive months. With a little leave time thrown in, you could enter the Army in June, after high school, as I did, and find yourself in the jungle with an M-16 rifle before Christmas, as I also did, with new clothes and a different head. Amazing.

Cynthia said, apropos of my silence, "Are you solving the case?"

"No, I was reminiscing. I took my infantry training here."

"Was that World War II or Korea?"

"You're engaging in unacceptable ageism. Watch yourself."

"Yes, sir."

I said, "Have you ever penetrated into the wilds of this reservation?"

"No. Rifle range six is as far as I've gone."

"That's only scratching the surface. If you take this road coming up to the left here—General Pershing Road—it leads to the major training sites. There are artillery and mortar practice ranges and areas for special training exercises, like things called 'The Rifle Company in the Attack,' and 'Armor and Infantry Joint Operations,' 'The Ambush,' 'The Night Patrol,' and so on."

"No picnic areas?"

"Not that I recall. There's also an old ranger camp in there, a mock European town for urban warfare, and a mock Vietnamese village where I got killed about six times."

"You must have learned your lesson."

"Apparently. There's also a mock POW camp, which the Psy-Ops School has taken over. That's still active, and it's a restricted area."

184

"I see." She thought a moment, then said, "So, with all that space out there, a hundred thousand acres, tell me why Ann Campbell picked a spot on an active rifle range, fifty meters from the road, with guard trucks, MPs, and a guard post a kilometer away."

"Well, I thought about that, and three things come to mind. First, the obvious thing is that she was just going about her duties and got jumped. *She* didn't pick the spot. *He* did. That's what everybody here thinks, but we're not buying that."

"No, we're not. So if *she* picked the spot, she picked a spot that her partner could find easily, because unless you were a good ranger or something, you could miss a rendezvous out in the deep woods."

"That's correct. That was my second thought. The guy was not comfortable or familiar with the woods at night." I said, "Here's your turn for Jordan Field."

"I see it." She made the right onto the airfield road and asked me, "Your third thought?"

"Well, Ann Campbell picked what amounted to a nearly public place *because* it presented an element of danger. Part of the kick, and maybe, just maybe, an element of 'let's see what I can get away with on Daddy's property.' " I looked at Cynthia, who was nodding.

Cynthia said, "You may have something there, Paul. Pushing it in Daddy's face."

"Yes. But that's supposing that Ann and Daddy seriously did not like each other," I pointed out.

"You suggested that when we were searching her house."

"Right. But I don't know why I thought that. It's just that I thought it can't be easy to be the child of a powerful man, to live in his shadow. It's a common syndrome."

"Yes . . . I don't have one piece of information that says that's so in this case, so why do I think it *is* so?"

"Because the lack of something said is as revealing as what *is* said. More so. Did anyone *say* the general and his daughter were inseparable, close, loving, or even good friends?"

"Well, the general did say his daughter would have liked me."

"I don't care what the *general* said. No one else said anything like that—not Kent, not Fowler, not Moore, not Yardley, and not even General Campbell himself, if you think about it. So now we should find out what General and Captain Campbell thought of each other."

Again she nodded, and said, "I have this feeling that there's not much more left in the clue bag, and we'd better start putting it all together before we get booted or pushed aside by the FBI."

"You got that right. I give this case two or three more days. After that we start running into well-entrenched defenses. As it says in the tank commander's manual, our immediate advantage is shock, mobility, and firepower. We've got to hit them hardest where they're softest, and fastest where they're slowest."

"And get there firstest with the mostest."

"Precisely."

We pulled up to the MP booth at Jordan Field, showed our ID, and were waved through.

Cynthia parked her car among the vans and trucks of the forensic lab, and I took the plastic bag of clothing out of the trunk, using a handkerchief, while Cynthia carried the hairbrush. Cynthia said, "If she took her own clothes off, he held the bag, so there may not be any of the other person's prints on her holster, boots, belt buckle, or anywhere. Except perhaps the bag itself."

"We'll soon find out."

We walked toward the hangar, and she said, "You're pretty sharp, Brenner. I'm starting to admire you."

"But do you like me?"

"No."

"Do you love me?"

"I don't know."

"You said you did in Brussels."

"I did, in Brussels. We'll talk about it next week, or maybe later tonight."

CHAPTER EIGHTEEN

Hangar three was bathed in bright overhead lighting and busy with the activities of Fort Gillem's transplanted forensic units. Colonel Kent had not yet arrived, which was fine for the moment.

I presented the plastic trash bag and the hairbrush to Cal Seiver, who needed no explanation. He gave the bag and the brush to a fingerprint technician and instructed him to pass it on to the trace evidence section after the prints had been lifted.

With that bag of clothing, hangar three now contained all the known artifacts of Captain Ann Campbell, excluding the mortal remains of the victim herself, but including her automobile, her office, and home. In addition, I saw that we also had in the hangar the humvee she had used that night. As we got toward the rear of the hangar, I saw the recently developed photos of the crime scene, all of which were pinned to rolling bulletin boards, plus sketch maps and diagrams of the crime scene, a rising stack of laboratory reports, the protocol complete with color photos of the cadaver, which I did not look at, plaster casts of footprints, cellophane bags of evidence, forensic laboratory equipment, and about thirty personnel, male and female.

In one corner of the hangar were about two dozen cots, and in another corner was a coffee bar. The Army, of course, has almost unlimited resources and personnel, and there's no overtime pay to worry about, and probably no other major crime at the moment that would divert any resources. Sometimes even I am in awe of the force that is assembled and set in motion with a few words, sort of like when Roosevelt said to Eisenhower, "Assemble a force for the invasion of Europe." Simple, direct, and to the point. This is the Army at its best. It's at its worst when politicians try to play soldier and soldiers start to play politics. That can happen in criminal investigations, as well as in war, which is why I knew my time to act freely could be counted in days and hours.

Cal Seiver showed me a copy of the *Midland Dispatch,* the local daily, whose headline announced, GENERAL'S DAUGHTER FOUND DEAD AT FORT.

Cynthia and I read the article, the thrust of which was that Captain Ann Campbell had been found naked, bound, strangled, and possibly raped, out on a rifle range. The story was about half accurate, and the only direct quote from Fort Hadley came from a Captain Hillary Barnes, a public information officer, who stated that she had no official comment except that the apparent homicide was being investigated by the Army Criminal Investigation Division.

There was, however, a quote from the Midland chief of police, Burt Yardley, who said, "I've offered my assistance to Colonel Kent, provost marshal at Fort Hadley, and we are in close contact."

He failed to mention the problem of the purloined house or that he wanted my ass delivered to him on a silver platter, but after our next meeting, he might start whining to the press about me.

Cal asked Cynthia, "Are those the running shoes you wore at the scene?"

"Yes. Do you want just the shoes or my feet in them?"

"Just the shoes, please."

Cynthia sat on a folding chair, pulled off her running shoes, and handed them to Cal. He said to me, "Where are the boots you were wearing at the scene?"

"In my off-post quarters. I forgot to bring them."

"Can I have them one of these days?"

"Sure. One of these days. I'm sort of confined to the post for a while."

"Again? Jesus, Brenner, every time I work on a case with you that involves the civilian police, you piss them off."

"Not every time. Okay, Cal, I'd like you to send a team out to rifle range five to get casts of some tire marks." I told him where they would be found, and he started to amble off to take care of it. I said, "One more thing. When they're finished there, have them go to Victory Gardens on Victory Drive and take casts of a set of tires on a Ford Fairlane, probably gray, 1985 or '86, with an officers' bumper sticker. I don't have a license plate number for you, but look around unit thirty-nine."

He regarded me a moment and replied, "If the car belongs to a soldier, we can wait until the car shows up on post."

"I want it tonight."

"Come on, Brenner, I can't collect evidence outside government property without permission from the locals, and you already blew that."

"Right. Don't use an Army vehicle. Unit forty-five, the victim's residence, is probably being secured by the Midland police, but the cop on duty will most likely be inside. Tell your guys to be careful and be quick."

"It can wait until the car gets on post."

"Okay." I put my hand on his shoulder. "I understand. I just hope those tires don't disappear from that car by morning. Gosh, I hope the whole car doesn't disappear tonight. But that's all right. Wait until morning."

"Okay, Victory Gardens. You're pushing your luck, hotshot." He walked off toward a group of people who were labeling plaster footprints and making notations on a sketch map of the crime scene. Cal handed them Cynthia's running shoes and spoke to them, pre-sumably about their midnight mission, because he kept jerking his thumb toward me, and the techs were glaring at me.

I got a cup of coffee for myself and brought one to Cynthia, who was leafing through lab reports. She took the coffee and said,

189

"Thanks. Look at this." She showed me a report from the footprint people. "They found a print of a smooth-soled shoe, size seven, possibly a woman's civilian shoe. That's not usual on a rifle range, is it?"

"No, it's not."

"What does that suggest?"

I scanned the report, which speculated that the footprint was recent. I said, "Interesting. But it could have been made a few days ago, for all we know. It hasn't rained here in about a week."

"Right. But it's something to think about."

We flipped through reports from the various forensic units for about fifteen minutes, then Cal called over to us from one of his makeshift lab areas, and we joined him at a table where a female technician was peering through a microscope. Cal said, "You may have hit pay dirt with that hairbrush. Where'd it come from?"

I patted his bald head. "Not from you."

The technician laughed as she buried her face in the microscope.

Cal was not amused and said to Cynthia, "Since you're the one with the brains on this team, why don't you look in that microscope?"

The technician moved aside, and Cynthia sat at the table. The technician, a Specialist Lubbick, said, "The hair on the right was recovered from the sink basin in the male latrine at rifle range six. The hair on the left was taken from the hairbrush."

Cynthia looked into the microscope as Specialist Lubbick continued, "I actually examined twenty hairs taken from the brush to satisfy myself that the brush hairs all belonged to the same individual. My opinion is that they do, and that statistically and logically, there should be no other individual's hair on that brush, though I'll examine every one of them for my report."

I wanted to say, "Get to the point," but you have to let technical types do it their way or they get sulky.

Specialist Lubbick continued, "Hairs have what we call class characteristics. That means they can't be matched absolutely to a given sample. They can be used to exclude a suspect, but not to identify a suspect in a court of law, unless both samples submitted

190

have roots so that we can get the sex of an individual and a genetic marker.''

Cal said to her, ''I think they know that.''

''Yes, sir. Anyway, the sample found in the latrine has no roots, but from the shaft, I've determined that the individual had blood type O, and that the individual whose hair was on the brush also had blood type O. Also, both samples are Caucasian, are visually similar in texture, color, lack of artificial treatment, and general condition of health.''

Cynthia looked up from the microscope. ''Yup. They look similar.''

Specialist Lubbick concluded, ''My opinion is that they're from the same individual, though the sample from the sink basin is too small to perform other tests such as spectro-analysis that might yield more similarities. Any further tests will alter or destroy this single strand taken from the latrine.'' She added, ''Some of the hairs from the brush *do* have roots, and in about an hour I can tell you the sex of that individual and get a DNA marker for you.''

I nodded. ''Understand.''

Cynthia stood and said to Lubbick, ''Please mark and bag this and attach a report.''

''Yes, ma'am.''

''Thanks.''

Seiver asked me, ''Is this enough for an arrest?''

''No, but it's enough to start looking at a guy real close.''

''What guy?''

I took him off to the side, away from the technicians, and said, ''A guy named Colonel Charles Moore whose tire tracks you are going to compare. Moore's office is also at the Psy-Ops School. He was the victim's boss. I'm trying to get his office sealed until we can get authorization to bring it here.''

Cynthia joined us and said, ''In the meantime, Cal, match the fingerprints found on Colonel Moore's hairbrush to the fingerprints found on the humvee, and also to any fingerprints found on the trash bag and the articles found inside the bag.''

''Right.'' He thought a moment, then said, ''But a match doesn't conclusively place this Colonel Moore at the scene if Moore and the victim knew each other. He has a believable reason why his fingerprints could be on, let's say, her holster, or on the humvee.''

I replied, ''I know, but he would have a harder time explaining why his prints are on the trash bag, or why his tire marks are out on range five.''

Cal nodded. ''Still, you need to place him there at the time of the murder.''

''Right. So I want you to compare the fingerprints on the hairbrush to the partial prints you found on the tent pegs. If we have his tire marks and enough fingerprints that match, then the rope around *his* fucking neck gets much tighter. Okay?''

Cal nodded. ''Okay. You're the detective. I'd vote guilty, but you never know these days.'' He turned and walked toward the fingerprint unit.

Cynthia said to me, ''If we interrogate Moore and present him with the evidence, there's a good chance he will tell us he did it.''

''Right, or he will tell us he didn't. Then we wind up in front of a court-martial board, all holding our breaths while they decide if a colonel in the United States Army strangled General Campbell's daughter, or if Warrant Officers Brenner and Sunhill got the wrong guy, missed the right guy, totally dishonored themselves and the Army, and blew it big-time.''

Cynthia thought a moment and asked me, ''If all the forensic evidence points to Moore, do *you* have any reasonable doubts?''

''Do you?''

''Reasonable doubts, yes. I just can't see Ann Campbell doing whatever she was doing out there with that guy, and I can't see him strangling her. He looks like the kind of sicko who'd put poison in your coffee, but he's not a hands-on killer.''

''That's what's bothering me. But you never know . . . she may have asked him to do it. Pleaded with him to kill her. I had one like that once. And for all we know, Moore could have been flying on mind-altering drugs. Something he got from work.''

''That's possible.''

192

I looked over Cynthia's shoulder. "Meanwhile, here comes the law."

Colonel Kent was making the long walk across the hangar, and we met him halfway. He asked, "Anything new here?"

I replied, "We're close to something, Bill. I'm waiting for fingerprints and tire tracks."

His eyes widened. "No kidding? Who?"

"Colonel Moore."

He seemed to think about that, then nodded. "It fits."

"How does it fit, Bill?"

"Well . . . they had a close relationship, he would have the opportunity, and I wouldn't put it past him. He's weird. I just don't know what his motive would be."

"Me neither." I asked Kent, "Tell me about Captain and General Campbell."

"What about them?"

"Were they close?"

He looked me right in the eye and said, "They were not."

"Go on."

"Well . . . perhaps we can discuss that another time."

"Perhaps we can discuss it in Falls Church."

"Hey, don't threaten me."

"Look, Colonel, I'm the investigating officer in a homicide case. You may feel that you're under some social and professional restraints, but you're not. Your duty is to answer my questions."

Kent did not seem happy, but at the same time, he seemed relieved to be told in no uncertain terms that he had to unburden himself. He walked off toward the center of the hangar, and we followed him. He said, "Okay. General Campbell disapproved of his daughter's choice of military occupation specialty, her choice of men, her decision to live off post, her associations with people like Charles Moore, and probably a half dozen other things that I'm not privy to."

Cynthia asked, "Wasn't he proud of her?"

"I don't think so."

"The Army was proud of her," Cynthia pointed out.

193

Kent replied, "The Army had about as much choice in the matter as General Campbell did. Ann Campbell had one hand on her father's balls and the other on the Army's balls, to be quite blunt."

Cynthia asked him, "What does that mean?"

"That means that, as a woman, a general's daughter, a West Pointer, and a nearly public figure, she got away with a lot. She wangled her way into that recruiting stuff before her father knew what was happening, and all of a sudden she's got the power of public notoriety, doing radio and TV, and addressing colleges and women's groups, pushing an Army career for women and all that. Everyone loved her. But she didn't give a damn about the Army. She just wanted to become untouchable."

Cynthia asked him, "Why?"

"Well, as much as the general disapproved of her, she hated his guts ten times more. She did everything she could to personally embarrass him, and there wasn't much he could do to her without screwing up his own career."

"My goodness," I said, "that's interesting information. You must have forgotten to tell us that as you were agonizing over how to break the news to the general."

Kent glanced around him, then said in a soft voice, "That's between us. Officially, they loved each other." He hesitated, then said, "To tell you the truth, General Campbell may have disapproved of this or that, but he didn't hate her." He added, "Look, this is all hearsay, but I'm passing it on to you in confidence, so you know what the hell is going on here. You didn't hear it from me, but you can follow up on it."

I nodded, "Thanks, Bill. Anything else?"

"No."

But of course there was. "Who," I asked, "were these men that the general disapproved of, aside from Colonel Moore?"

"I don't know."

"Was Wes Yardley one of them?"

He looked at me a long time, then nodded. "I think so."

"Was Wes Yardley the man she had an altercation with in Midland?"

194

"Possibly."

"Why did she want to embarrass her father?"

"I don't know."

"Why did she hate his guts?"

"If you find out, let me know. But whatever the reason was, it was one hell of a big one."

"What was her relationship with her mother?"

Kent replied, "Strained. Mrs. Campbell was torn between being the general's lady and being the mother of a very independent woman."

"In other words," I said, "Mrs. Campbell is a doormat, and Ann Campbell tried to raise her consciousness."

"Something like that. But it was a little more complex."

"How so?"

"You should speak with Mrs. Campbell."

"I intend to." I said to him, "Tell me again that you never went to Ann Campbell's house, so I can explain in my report why your fingerprints were found on a bottle of her liquor."

"I told you, Brenner, I touched a few of the things."

"The liquor was sealed in a box by your MPs and not opened until about an hour ago."

"You can't pull that crap with me, Paul. I'm a cop, too. If you have evidence, let's talk to Seiver and he can show it to me."

"Look, Bill, let's clear the air here so we can get onto more important things, like Colonel Moore. Here's the question, and remember that you have a duty to answer truthfully, and if that doesn't impress you, remember that I may discover the truth myself. Okay? Here's the big question—were you fucking her?"

"Yes."

No one spoke for a few long seconds, and I noticed that Kent seemed rather at ease with his confession. I didn't remind him that he had said he would have told me that from minute one, because it was better if we all made believe this was minute one and that previous statements contained no lies.

Finally, Cynthia said, "Is that one of the ways that Ann Campbell tried to embarrass her father?"

Kent nodded. "Yeah . . . I never took it for anything more than that. The general knows—she made sure he did. But my wife doesn't, obviously. That's why I held back on that."

My goodness, I thought, the things people will tell you at midnight, under stress, trying to put their lives in order because another life just ended, and trying to save whatever they can of their career and marriage. Obviously, Colonel William Kent needed our help. I said to him, "We'll try to leave that out of the report."

He nodded. "Thanks. But with Ann gone, the general has a clear field to settle some scores. I'll be given the opportunity to resign for the good of the service. I might be able to save my marriage."

Cynthia said, "We'll do what we can."

"Appreciate it."

I asked him, "What other scores would the general like to settle?"

Kent smiled grimly. "Christ, she fucked for the general's entire male staff."

"*What?*"

"Everybody. Well, at least most of them. Everyone from that young lieutenant, Elby, his aide-de-camp, right up the chain through most of his immediate staff, plus the staff judge advocate, and people like me in key positions."

"My God . . ." said Cynthia, "are you serious?"

"I'm afraid I am."

"But why?"

"I told you. She hated her father."

"Well," Cynthia said, "she didn't think much of herself, either."

"No, she didn't. And if I'm any indication, then the men who slept with her didn't think much of themselves afterward." He added, "It wasn't easy to turn that down." He looked at me and tried to smile. "Can you relate to that, Mr. Brenner?"

I felt a bit uncomfortable with the question, but answered truthfully. "Yes, I understand. But I'm not married, and I don't work for General Campbell."

He smiled wider. "Then you wouldn't have been one of her candidates, so you'd never be put to the test."

"Well . . ."

He added, "If you had no power, you got no pussy."

Cynthia interjected, "And she told you—told everyone—who she slept with?"

"I assume she did. I think that was part of the program, to spread corruption, mistrust, fear, anxiety, and so forth. But I think she lied sometimes about who she'd serviced."

"So, for instance," I asked, "you can't say for sure if she had slept with the post chaplain, Major Eames, or the post adjutant, Colonel Fowler?"

"Not for sure. She claimed she'd seduced both of those two, for example, but I think at least Colonel Fowler was not taken in by her. Fowler once told me that he knew all about this and that I was part of the problem. I think he meant that he wasn't. He was the only one the general trusted completely, and probably for that reason."

I nodded. I could see Fowler telling Ann Campbell something like "Don't try that with me, young lady. I don't need you."

Cynthia said to Kent, "This is bizarre . . . I mean, it's sick."

Kent nodded. "Well, regarding that, Ann once told me she was conducting a field experiment in psychological warfare, and the enemy was Daddy." He laughed, but it was not a happy laugh. He said, "She *hated* him. I mean from the bottom of her guts and with all her heart. She couldn't destroy him, but she was doing a hell of a job hurting him."

Again, no one spoke for some time, then Cynthia said, as if to herself, "But *why*?"

"She never told me," Kent replied. "I don't think she ever told anyone. She knew, he knew, and maybe Mrs. Campbell knew. This was not a real happy family."

"And maybe," I said, "Charles Moore knew."

"No doubt about it. But maybe *we* will never know. I'll tell you one thing I believe. Moore was the force behind this. Moore told

197

her how she could get back at her father for whatever it was he did to her.''

Which, I thought, was probably true. But that didn't establish a motive for him to kill her. Quite the opposite. She was his protégé, his shield against the general's wrath, his most successful experiment. The bastard deserved to die, but he should die for the right reason. I asked Kent, ''And where did your trysts with the general's daughter take place?''

He replied, ''Here and there. Mostly motels out on the highway, but she wasn't shy about doing it right here on post, in her office, my office.''

''And at her place?''

''Once in a while. I guess I misled you about that. But she liked to keep her place off limits.''

Either he didn't know about the room in the basement, or he didn't know I knew, and if he was in any of those photos, he wasn't going to volunteer that information.

Kent said to us, ''So if Moore is the killer, you've wrapped it up without too much damage to the Army and to the people here at Hadley. But if Moore is *not* the killer, and you're looking for new suspects, then you're going to have to start questioning a lot of men here on this post, Paul. I've come clean, and you should make them come clean, too. As you say, this is homicide, and to hell with careers, reputations, and good order and discipline.'' He added, ''Jesus, can you see the newspapers? Think about that story. An entire general staff and most of the senior officers on an Army post corrupted and compromised by a single female officer. That will set things back a few decades.'' He added, ''I hope Moore is the guy, and that's as far as it has to go.''

I replied, ''If you're hinting that Colonel Moore is the best man to hang, though perhaps not the right man, then I have to remind you of our oath.''

''I'm just telling you both that you should not dig where you don't have to dig. And if Moore is the guy, don't let him try to take everyone with him. If he committed murder, then everyone else's adulteries and actions unbecoming an officer are not relevant, and are not mitigating circumstances for his crime. That's the law. Let's take one court-martial at a time.''

Kent turned out to be not as dull as I'd remembered him. It's amazing how sharp a man can get when he's looking at dishonor, disgrace, divorce, and perhaps a board of official inquiry into his behavior. The Army still prosecutes for wrongful diddling, and Colonel Kent definitely diddled wrong. Sometimes I'm awed at the power of raw sex, at how much people are willing to risk—their honor, their fortunes, even their lives—for an hour between two thighs. On the other hand, if the thighs belonged to Ann Campbell . . . but that's a moot issue.

I said to Kent, "Indeed, I appreciate your honesty, Colonel. When one man comes forth and tells the truth, others will do the same.''

"Maybe," Kent replied, "but I would appreciate it if you kept my name out of it.''

"I will, but it doesn't matter in the long run.''

"No, it doesn't. I'm finished." He shrugged. "I knew that two years ago when I first got involved with her.'' He added, almost light-heartedly, "She must have kept some sort of service schedule, because just when I thought I could make myself believe I'd never slept with her, she'd stop by my office and ask me to have drinks with her.''

Cynthia inquired, "Didn't you ever think to say no?''

Kent smiled at Cynthia. "Did you ever ask a man to have sex with you, and the guy said no?''

Cynthia seemed a bit put off by that and replied, "I don't ask men.''

"Well," Kent advised her, "try it. Pick any married man and ask him to have sex with you.''

"The subject," said Cynthia, very coolly, "is not me, Colonel.''

"All right, I apologize. But to answer your question, Ann Campbell would not take no for an answer. I'm not saying she blackmailed anyone. She never did, but there was an element of coercion sometimes. Also, she expected expensive gifts—perfume, clothes, airline tickets, and so forth. And here's the crazy thing—she really didn't care about the gifts. She just wanted me, and I guess everyone else, to feel the pinch once in a while, to part with more than a little time. It was sort of a control thing with her.'' He added, ''I remember once she asked me to bring her a bottle of some expensive perfume. Can't remember what it was, but it set me back about four hundred dollars, and I had to cover that at home with a loan from the credit union, and eat lunch in the damned mess hall for a month.'' He laughed at the thought, then said, ''My God, I'm glad it's all over.''

''Well, but it's not,'' I reminded him.

''It is for me.''

''I hope so, Bill.'' I asked him, ''Did she ever ask you to compromise your duties?''

He hesitated, then replied, ''Just small things. Traffic tickets for friends, a speeding citation for her once. Nothing major.''

''I beg to differ, Colonel.''

He nodded. ''I have no excuses for my conduct.''

That's exactly what he was going to say in front of a board of inquiry, and that was the best and only thing he could say. I wondered how she compromised the other men, besides sexually. A favor here, a special consideration there, and who knew what else she wanted and got? In my twenty years in the service, including fifteen in the Criminal Investigation Division, I had never seen or heard of such rampant corruption on an Army base.

Cynthia asked Kent, ''And the general could neither stop her nor get rid of her?''

''No. Not without exposing himself as an ineffective and negligent commander. By the time he realized his recruiting poster daughter had screwed and compromised everyone around him, it was too late for official action. The only way he could have righted things was to inform his superiors in the Pentagon of everything, ask for everyone's resignation here, then offer his own resignation.'' Kent added, ''He couldn't have gone too wrong if he just shot himself.''

''Or killed her,'' Cynthia suggested.

200

Again, Kent shrugged. "Maybe. But not the way she was killed."

"Well," I said, "if we didn't already have a prime suspect, you'd be one of many, Colonel."

"Right. But I didn't get burned as badly as some of the others. Some of them were actually in love with her, obsessed, and maybe homicidally jealous. Like that young kid, Elby. He used to mope for weeks when she ignored him. Interrogate Moore, and if you think he didn't kill her, then ask him for *his* list of suspects. That bastard knew everything about her, and if he tells you it is privileged information, let me know and I'll put a pistol in his mouth and tell him he can take the information to the grave with him."

"I might be a little more subtle." I informed him, "I'm trying to get Moore's office padlocked until I can get clearance to bring it here."

"You should just put the damn cuffs on him." Kent looked at me and said, "Anyway, you see why I didn't want the local CID guys in on this."

"I guess I do now. Were any of them involved with her?"

He pondered a moment, then replied, "The CID commander, Major Bowes."

"Are you certain of that?"

"Ask him. He's one of your people."

"Do you and Bowes get along?"

"We try."

"What's the problem?"

"We have jurisdictional problems. Why do you ask?"

"Jurisdictional meaning criminal activity, or meaning something else?"

He looked at me, then replied, "Well . . . Major Bowes had become possessive."

"He didn't like to share."

Kent nodded. "A few of her boyfriends got that way. That was when she dumped them." He added, "Married men are real pigs."

He thought a moment, then said, "Don't trust anyone on this post, Paul."

"Including you?"

"Including me." Kent looked at his watch. "Is that it? Did you want to see me for something in particular?"

"Well, whatever it was, it's not real important now."

"Right. I'm going home. You can reach me there until 0700, then I'll be in my office. Where can I find you tonight if something comes up?"

Cynthia replied, "We're both in the VOQ."

"All right. Well, my wife's probably been trying to call me from Ohio. She'll start thinking I'm having an affair. Good evening." He turned and left, making the long walk with a lot less spring in his step than when he'd entered.

Cynthia commented, "I can't *believe* this. Did he just tell us that Ann Campbell slept with most of the senior officers on post?"

"Yes, he did. Now we know who those men were in her photos."

She nodded. "And now we know why this place seemed so strange."

"Right. The suspect list just got real long."

So, I thought, Colonel Kent, Mr. Clean, Mr. Law and Order, broke nearly every damned rule in the book. This brittle, stuffy man had a libido, and it led him right to the dark side of the moon. I said to Cynthia, "Would Bill Kent commit murder to safeguard his reputation?"

Cynthia replied, "It's conceivable. But I think he was indicating that his secret was public knowledge, and his career was just waiting for General Campbell to have a chance to ax it."

I nodded. "Well, if not to avoid disgrace and humiliation, as it says in the manual, then how about jealousy?"

She thought a moment, then said, "Kent is also indicating that his relationship with Ann Campbell was just sport for him. A little lust, but no emotional involvement. I can believe that." She saw that I wanted more from her, and she pondered a moment, then added, "On the other hand, the motive he assigned to Major

Bowes—possessiveness and, by extension, jealousy may not be true and may actually be what Bill Kent himself felt. Remember, this guy's a cop, and he read the same manual we did. He knows how we think.''

"Precisely. Yet, I find it hard to think of that guy as passionate, jealous, or emotionally involved with any woman."

"I know. But it's the cool ones who burn hot at the center. I've seen his type before, Paul. Authoritarian, control freaks, conservative, and obsessed with rules and regulations. It's a mechanism they use because they're frightened of their own passions, and they know what lurks beneath the neat suit or uniform. In reality, they have no natural checks and balances on their behavior, and when they spin out of control, they're capable of anything."

I nodded. "But maybe we're getting too psychobabbly."

She shrugged. "Maybe. But let's keep an eye on Colonel Kent. He's got a different agenda than we do."

CHAPTER NINETEEN

Cal Seiver said he was finished with Ann Campbell's study, or what was once her study, so I sat on her sofa and played another videotape of her psy-ops lecture series. Around me, the men and women of the forensic laboratory went about their occupation of examining the microscopic particles of a person's existence, the type of stuff that other people called dirt—hairs, fibers, dust, fingerprints, smudges, and stains.

In and of themselves, hairs, fibers, prints, and all that were innocuous, but if, for instance, a set of fingerprints was lifted from a liquor bottle in Ann Campbell's cupboard, and if the prints turned out to belong to, say, Colonel George Fowler, then the possibilities were two: he gave the bottle to her and she took it home, or he was in her home. But if Fowler's prints were found, say, on the mirror of her bathroom, that would be presumptive evidence that he was actually in the bathroom. In fact, however, the latent-fingerprint section, using prints on file, had not yet matched any known prints to the ones they'd found, except mine, Cynthia's, Ann Campbell's, and Colonel Kent's—which could be explained two ways. Eventually, they would match prints to Chief Yardley, and again, Yardley, being one of the polluters of the stored evidence, had an explanation. They'd find Moore's prints, too, but as her boss and neighbor, that was meaningless. And since we had no further access to things like

Ann Campbell's bathroom mirror or her shower, those kinds of prints, which were very suggestive, were not going to be found by us, but by Chief Yardley, who would have the whole house dusted by now. And any prints he didn't like, such as his son's, would disappear.

Knowing who had been in her house might eventually lead to her killer in a conventional, plodding type of homicide investigation, and knowing who was in her basement boudoir would give me a list of men who suddenly had a lot to lose unless they cooperated fully. But that room remained sealed for now, and that might be a false, though very scenic trail to follow.

Knowing who was at the crime scene was more to the point, and we were close to establishing that Colonel Charles Moore was there, though when he was there and what he was doing there needed clarification.

Colonel William Kent. Now, there was a man who suddenly had a career problem, not to mention the little chat he'd eventually have to have with Mrs. Kent. Thank God I don't have those kinds of problems.

Kent had made what amounted to a confession of sexual misbehavior, dereliction of duty, and actions unbecoming an officer, to name just three charges that the JAG office could come up with. People often do this in a murder investigation, like making a small sacrifice on the altar of the goddess of Justice, hoping that the goddess will accept it and go someplace else to find a human blood sacrifice.

Cynthia's estimation of Kent was interesting because literally no one would think that William Kent was a passionate, possessive, or jealous man. But in some instinctive way, she saw or sensed something that I never did. What we knew now was that Kent had had sexual relations with Ann Campbell. And I don't believe Kent is into sport-fucking. Ergo, Kent was in love with her and killed her out of jealousy. But I didn't know that, and there were too many suppositions on the way to that ergo.

One of the side benefits of having forensic lab people all over the place is that you can lie to suspects about this or that, though it doesn't say so in the manual. I had to know, or suspect, of course, that a person was here or there or did this or that before trying to bully and deceive that person. And sometimes you get your head handed to you, the way Kent did to me. Still, I think I smoked him out with the accusation.

My mind returned to the television screen and I focused on Ann Campbell. She stood in front of me, speaking directly to me, and we made good eye contact. She wore the light summer green B uniform with a short-sleeve blouse and a skirt, and now and then she'd walk away from the lectern and stand at the edge of the stage in the lecture hall, speaking as she moved around, very much at ease in her gestures, body language, and facial expressions.

For all her reported coolness, she seemed accessible during her lecture. She smiled, looked directly at a questioner in the audience, and laughed at her own occasional joke and at amusing comments from the hundred or so men in the lecture hall. She had this sexy habit of throwing back her head and brushing her long blond hair away from her face. Now and then, she'd bite her lip in thought or look wide-eyed as a combat veteran told an interesting anecdote, then she'd ask intelligent questions of her own. This was no programmed android droning on behind the lectern like so many Army and academic lecturers, as I'm sure Colonel Moore was. This was a woman with an inquiring mind, a good sense of when to talk and when to listen, and an exuberance for her slightly offbeat subject. Now and then, the camera would scan the audience and you could see a lot of alert men out there who clearly enjoyed what they were hearing as much as what they were seeing.

Ann Campbell was talking about psychological operations directed at specific individuals, and I tuned in to what she was saying. "We've spoken about psy-ops directed toward enemy combat soldiers, toward support personnel, and toward the civilian population as a whole. Now I'd like to speak about psychological operations directed toward individuals, specifically enemy military commanders and political leaders."

Cynthia sat down beside me with a fresh cup of coffee and a plate of donuts. She asked me, ''Good movie?''

''Yes.''

''Can we turn this off?''

''No.''

''Paul, why don't you go get some sleep?''

''Quiet.''

Cynthia stood and walked away. Ann Campbell continued, ''And the last time we used this tool effectively was in World War II against the Nazi political and military leaders. We had the advantage of knowing something about them, about their personal histories, their superstitions, their sexual preferences, their beliefs in the oc-cult or in omens, and so forth. And what we didn't know, we found out through various intelligence-gathering sources. Thus, we had a biographical and psychological profile of many of these men, and we were able to target them individually, and we were able to exploit their weaknesses, undermine their strengths, and introduce false and deceptive elements into their decision-making process. In short, the goal was to weaken their self-confidence, lower their sclf-esteem, and demoralize them through the process of what is sometimes called mind-fucking. Excuse me.''

She waited until the laughter and applause died down, then con-tinued, ''We'll call it mind-fudging, because we're on tape today. Okay, how do you fudge up someone's mind who is a thousand miles away, deep in the heart of enemy territory? Well, in much the same way you do it with your wife, girlfriend, boss, or pain-in-the-neck neighbor. First, you have to be aware that this is something you want to do, and have to do. Then you have to know the other person's mind—what worries that person, what annoys that person, what frightens that person. You can't manipulate until you know how all thc levers, switches, and buttons work. Finally, you have to be in contact with that person. Contact is made on several levels—personal contact, surrogate contact through a third party, written contact in the form of documents, newspapers, letters, air-dropped leaflets—don't do that with your wife or boss—radio contact in the

207

form of propaganda transmissions, or planted and managed news stories, and so on.''

She expounded on this awhile, then said, ''In regard to surrogate or personal contact, this is the most effective and ancient of all contacts with the enemy leader. This sort of contact is an interactive contact, and, though difficult to achieve, it pays off handsomely. One type of personal contact with the enemy that we in the United States Army do not officially condone, or use, is sexual contact—Mata Hari, Delilah, and other famous seductresses, sex sirens, and seducers.''

She continued, ''If women ever become field commanders, we'll need guys like you to sneak into their tents at night.''

A little laughter, and you could hear someone say something about putting a flag over the face of some old battle-ax lady general and screwing her for Old Glory.

Then someone asked, ''If you get that close to an enemy leader, why not kill him?''

Ann Campbell replied, ''Why not, indeed? Aside from moral and legal considerations is the fact that a compromised, frightened, or totally bonkers leader, such as a Hitler or Hussein, is like you having ten more infantry divisions at the front. The damage that an ineffective leader can do to his own military operation is incalculable. We in the military have to relearn what we knew in the past—what all armies in the field knew throughout history, which is this: the troops are already filled with doubt and homesickness and with irrational battlefield superstitions and fear. You have to do the same to the generals.''

Fade to black. I stood and shut off the TV. It all seemed very clever, very logical, and very effective as she presented it in a classroom situation. Obviously, too, she'd had at least one field experiment in progress, as Kent had suggested. If I could believe Kent, Ann Campbell was waging a planned, deliberate, and totally vicious campaign against her enemy, her father. But what if he deserved it? What did Moore say about her killer? That whoever it was thought he was justified. Likewise, perhaps, Ann Campbell thought that what she was doing to her father was justified. Therefore, he'd done something to her, and whatever it was, it had set her on a course of revenge and, ultimately, self-destruction. One thing that came to mind that would make a daughter do that to her father, and to herself, was sexual abuse and incest.

That was what the shrinks would tell me when I asked, and that fit every psychological case history I'd ever heard about. But if it was true, the only person who would confirm it was dead. The general *could* confirm it, but even Paul Brenner wasn't going to touch that one. However, I could make discreet inquiries, and maybe, just maybe, Mrs. Campbell could be delicately questioned on the subject of her daughter's relationship with her father. What the hell, I had my twenty years in.

On the other hand, as Kent suggested, why dig up muck that had nothing to do with the homicide at hand? But who's to know what muck you needed and what muck you didn't?

So, did the general kill his daughter to stop her fury, or to shut her up? Or did Mrs. Campbell do it for the same reasons? And what was Colonel Moore's role in this? Indeed, the more muck I raked up, the more the ladies and gentlemen of Fort Hadley got splattered.

Cynthia came up to me and forced a piece of donut in my mouth. Obviously, we were on the verge of something more intimate than sharing a car, a bathroom, and a donut. But to tell you the truth, at my age, at two in the morning, Private Woody wasn't going to stand tall. Cynthia said, ''Maybe the JAG Office will give you those videotapes when the case is closed.''

''Maybe I'd rather have the tapes in her basement.''

''Don't be disgusting, Paul.'' She continued on the subject, as women will do, ''It's not healthy, you know.''

I refused to respond.

''When I was a teenager, I fell in love with James Dean. I'd watch *Rebel Without a Cause* and *Giant* on late night TV, and cry myself to sleep.''

''What an astonishing admission of necrophilia. What's the point?''

"Forget it. Here's the good news. The tire tracks on rifle range five were made by Colonel Moore's car, or what we're pretty sure is his car. The prints on Moore's hairbrush, which we assume were made by Moore, match two prints on the tent peg, at least six prints on the humvee, and one in the male latrine; also in the latrine, in the sink trap, was another hair that matched Moore's hair. Also, all the fingerprints on the trash bag are Moore's and Ann Campbell's, and ditto the prints on her boots, holster, and helmet, suggesting that they both handled those items. So your reconstruction of the crime, the movements and actions of Ann Campbell and Colonel Moore, seem to comport with the physical evidence. Congratulations."

"Thank you."

"So does this guy hang?"

"I think they shoot officers. I'll check before I speak to Colonel Moore."

"Case closed?"

"I'll check that with Colonel Moore."

"If he doesn't confess, will you go to the judge advocate general with what we've got?"

"I don't know. It's not an airtight case yet."

"No," Cynthia agreed, "it's not. We have your theory of the wrong times of the headlights, for one thing. We can put Moore at the scene of the crime, but we can't put the rope in his hands at the time of death. Also, we don't know his motive."

"Right. And without motive, you've got a tough job with a jury." I added, "There's also the possibility it was an accident."

"Yes, that's what he's going to say if he says anything."

"Right. He'll have a dozen of his shrink buddies explain to the court-martial board about sexual asphyxia, and how it was a consensual act, and how he misjudged her physical state while she was having an orgasm and he was stimulating her. And the officers on the court-martial board will be completely grossed-out and fascinated. Eventually, they'll have reasonable doubt, and they'll have to agree that the physical evidence does not support an act of violent and forcible rape. They'll believe it was a good time gone bad. And

I don't think they can even find for manslaughter. You have two consenting adults engaging in kinky sex, and one of them inadvertently causes the death of the other. The charge is reckless endangerment, if even that."

Cynthia commented, "Sex crimes are tough. There're all sorts of other things involved."

I nodded, recalling a CID case, not my own, where a guy was into high-colonic enemas, and the woman administering them gave him one too many, and the guy's intestine burst, leading to death by hemorrhaging and infection. The crew at Falls Church and the boys in the JAG Office had a good time with that one, but in the end decided not to prosecute. The woman, a young lieutenant, was asked to resign, and the man, an older sergeant major with a chest full of medals, was given a military funeral with honors. All for the good of the service.

Sex. Ninety percent of the human sex drive comes from the mind, and when the mind is wrong, the sex is wrong. But if you have consent, you don't have rape, and if it was or could have been an accident, you don't have murder. You have someone in need of serious counseling.

Cynthia asked me, "So? Do we make an arrest?"

I shook my head.

She said, "I think that's the right decision at this point."

I picked up the telephone and dialed Colonel Fowler's number. A sleepy woman answered. I identified myself, and Fowler got on the line. "Yes, Mr. Brenner?" He sounded a little annoyed.

I said, "Colonel, I've decided I don't want Colonel Moore's office padlocked or the contents confiscated at this time. I wanted you to know."

"Now I know."

"You asked me to let you know about arrests, and I've had second thoughts about placing him under arrest."

"I didn't know you intended to arrest him, Mr. Brenner, but if you rethink it again, will you please wake me up later so I can keep score?"

"Of course." This was fun. I liked a man with a dry sense of humor. I said to him, "I called to ask you not to mention this to anyone. It could jeopardize the case."

"I understand. But I will report this to the general."

"I suppose you have no choice."

"None whatsoever." He cleared his throat. "Do you have any other suspects?"

"Not at the moment. But I have some good leads."

"That's encouraging. Anything further?"

"I'm starting to turn up evidence that Captain Campbell . . . how shall I put this . . . ? That Captain Campbell had an active social life."

Dead silence.

So I continued, "It was inevitable that this would come out. I don't know if this relates to her murder, but I'll do my best to keep this in perspective and to minimize the damage to the fort and the Army if this information should become public, and so on."

"Why don't we meet at, say, 0700 hours at my house for coffee?"

"Well, I don't want to disturb you at home at that hour."

"Mr. Brenner, you are borderline insubordinate and definitely pissing me off. Be here at 0700 hours sharp."

"Yes, sir." The phone went dead. I said to Cynthia, "I'll have to speak to the Signal Corps people about the phone service at Fort Hadley."

"What did he say?"

"Colonel Fowler asks that we join him for coffee, 0700, his house."

She looked at her watch. "Well, we can get a little sleep. Ready?"

I looked around. Most of the hangar was in darkness now, and most of the cots were filled with sleeping men and women, though a few diehards were still at it, bent over typewriters, test tubes, and microscopes. "Okay, half a day today."

As we walked through the hangar, I asked Cynthia, "Did they find her West Point ring in that bag of clothes?"

"No, they didn't."

"And it hasn't turned up in her household possessions yet?"

"No, I asked Cal about it."

"Odd."

"She may have lost it," Cynthia said. "Maybe it's being cleaned."

"Maybe."

Cynthia said to me, "Paul, if we had found her on that rifle range alive, and she was right here with us now, what would you say to her?"

"What would *you* say to her? You're the rape counselor."

"I'm asking *you*."

"Okay. I'd say to her that whatever happened in the past should be dealt with in a healthy way, not a destructive way. That she needed good counseling, not bad counseling, that she should try to find a spiritual answer to her pain, that she should try to forgive the person or persons who . . . mistreated her and took advantage of her. I'd tell her she was an important and worthwhile human being with a lot to live for, and that people would care about her in a good way if she started caring about herself. That's what I'd say to her."

Cynthia nodded. "Yes, that's what someone should have said to her. Maybe someone did. But something bad happened to her, and what we see and hear is her response to that. This type of behavior in a bright, educated, attractive, and professionally successful woman is often the result of . . . some past trauma."

"Such as?"

We left the hangar and walked out into the cool evening. The moon had set and you could see a billion stars in the clear Georgia sky. I looked out across the huge dark expanse of Jordan Field, recalling when it was lit every night, and remembering a particular flight that used to come in after midnight two or three times a week. I said to Cynthia, "I unloaded bodies from Vietnam here."

She didn't respond.

I said, "If they don't bury her here in Midland, this is where everyone will gather after church to see her off. Tomorrow or the next day, I guess."

"Will we be here?"

"I plan to be."

We went to her car and she said to me, "In answer to your question . . . I think her father is the key to her behavior. You know, a domineering figure, pushed her into the military, tried to control her life, a weak mother, extended absences, lots of moving around the world, total dependence on and deference to his career. She rebels in the only way she knows how. It's all pretty much textbook stuff."

We got in the car and I said, "Right. But there are a million well-adjusted daughters out there with the same backgrounds."

"I know. But it's how you handle it."

"I'm thinking about a more . . . abnormal relationship with her father that would explain her hate."

We headed toward the gates of the airfield. She said, "I know what you're saying, and I thought that, too. But if you think rape and murder are hard to prove, try proving incest. I wouldn't touch that if I were you, Paul. That one could hurt you."

"Right. My first case as a CID officer was a barracks theft. Look how far I've come. Next step, the abyss."

CHAPTER TWENTY

Cynthia parked at the VOQ, and we took the outside staircase up to the second floor and found our rooms. "Well," she said, "good night."

"Well," I replied, "I'm bursting with energy, second wind, too wound up to sleep, adrenaline pumping, and all that. How about a little TV and a drink?"

"I don't think so."

"We'd be better off not sleeping at this point. You'll feel worse when you have to get up. We'll just relax, shower, change, and off to Colonel Fowler's."

"Well, maybe . . . but . . ."

"Come on in." I opened my door, and she followed me inside. She picked up the phone and called the charge-of-quarters person and left a wake-up call for 0530 hours. She said to me, "Just in case we pass out."

"Good idea," I said. "Well, as it turns out, I can't offer you a drink, and I don't see a TV here. How about charades?"

"Paul . . ."

"Yes?"

"I can't do this."

"Then how about rock, scissors, and paper? Do you know how to play that? It's easy—"

"I can't stay here. This has been an upsetting day for me. This wouldn't be right. It wouldn't be any good, anyway." And so on.

I said, "I understand. Go get some sleep. I'll call you when I get the wake-up call."

"Okay. Sorry. I'll leave the bathroom doors unbolted."

"Fine. See you in a few hours."

"Good night." She went toward the bathroom door, turned and came back, kissed me lightly on the lips, started to cry, then disappeared into the bathroom. I heard the water running, then heard the other door open to her room, then silence.

I undressed and hung my clothes and got into bed. I must have passed out within seconds, then the next thing I remember is the phone ringing. I answered it, expecting to hear a wake-up call, or hear Cynthia's voice asking me to come to her room. But, no, it was the deep, bass voice of Colonel Fowler. "Brenner?"

"Yes, sir."

"Sleeping?"

"No, sir."

"Good. Do you take milk?"

"Excuse me?"

"I don't have any milk or cream, Brenner."

"That's okay—"

"I wanted to let you know."

"Thank you, Colonel."

I thought I heard a laugh before the phone went dead. My watch said it was nearly five A.M., so I got up, stumbled into the bathroom, turned on the shower, and got under it. What a day. Half of it didn't even seem real. I was firing on two cylinders and my tank was on empty. But I needed about forty-eight more hours at this pace, then I'd be out of here in a blaze of glory, or I'd crash in flames.

Personal and career considerations aside, there was something very wrong here at Fort Hadley, a festering sore, and it needed to be lanced and washed clean. That much I knew I could do.

Through the rippled glass and steam on the shower door, I saw a figure standing in the entrance to Cynthia's room. "Okay if I come in?"

216

"Sure."

She was wearing something white, probably a nightshirt, and disappeared into the stall where the toilet was. A few minutes later she reappeared and went to the sink, her back to me. She washed her face and called out over the noise of the shower, "How do you feel?"

"Fine. How about you?"

"Not bad. Did I hear your phone ring?"

"Yes. Colonel Fowler. Just a harassment call."

She laughed. "You deserve it." She began brushing her teeth.

My phone rang again, and I said, "That's the CQ. Can you get it?"

She rinsed her mouth. "Sure." She went into my room and came back a few seconds later. "It's five-thirty." She went back to the sink, gargled, then asked me, "Are you taking one of your marathon showers?"

"Yes. Do you want to save time?"

Silence. Maybe that was too subtle. "Cynthia?"

She turned away from the sink, and I heard her say to herself, "Oh, what the hell."

I saw her pull off her nightshirt, and she opened the shower door and stepped inside. "Do my back."

So I did. Then I did her front. We embraced and kissed, and the water ran over us, and our bodies pressed closer together. The body remembers an old lover, I think, and a flood of good memories came back to me, and it was as if we were in Brussels again. Woody remembered, too, and rose happily, like an old hound dog whose master walks in the door after a year's absence. Ruff, ruff!

"Paul . . . it's all right . . . go ahead."

"Yes, it's all right. It's good. Here or in bed?"

"Here. Now."

But, as luck would have it, the phone rang again, and she said, "You'd better get that."

"Damn it!" We separated, and Cynthia hung the washcloth on my hook and laughed.

I threw the washcloth aside and said, "Don't go anywhere." I got out of the shower, grabbed a towel on my way, and picked up the phone on my nightstand. "Brenner here."

"Well, now, you're a hell of a hard man to find."

"Who's this?"

"It ain't your mommy, son."

"Oh . . ."

Chief Yardley informed me, "Bill Kent just told me you decided to stay on post. Why don't you come on home to your trailer?"

"What?"

"I spent the whole damn day tryin' to figure where you were at, and I get here and you're AWOL, boy. Come on home."

"What the hell—are you in my trailer?"

"Sure thing, Paul. But you ain't."

"Hey, Chief, do you practice that cracker accent, or what?"

"Sure 'nuf, boy." He laughed. "Hey, tell you what—I'm cleanin' this place out for you. No use payin' rent someplace you ain't gonna see again."

"You have no right—"

"Hold that thought awhile, son. We might get back to that. Meantime, come on down to my office and gather up your stuff."

"Chief, there is government property in there—"

"Yeah, I saw that. Had to bust a lock. Got a gun here, some official-lookin' papers, some weird book fulla codes or somethin' . . . what else we got here? Pair of cuffs, some uniforms and ID from a guy named White . . . you sleepin' with some guy?"

Cynthia came into the room wrapped in a bath towel and sat on the bed. I said to Yardley, "Okay, you skunked me."

"Let's see . . . box of rubbers, prissy little bikini shorts . . . that yours or your boyfriend's?"

"Chief—"

"Tell you what, son—you come on over to the station and pick this here stuff up. I'll be waitin' on ya."

"You deliver the government property to the provost office. I'll meet you there at noon."

"Let me think on that awhile."

"You do that. And bring Wes with you. I'd like to talk to him."

Silence, followed by, "You can talk to him at my office."

"I'll just wait to see him at the funeral service here. I assume he'll attend."

"I reckon he will. But we don't conduct business at funerals around here."

"You should. That's where everybody shows up after a murder."

"I'll tell you what—I'll let you talk to him because I want to see the son-of-a-bitch who done this in the pokey. But I'm lettin' you know now, my boy was on duty when it happened, and his partner will verify that, and we got tapes of his radio calls all night."

"I'm sure of that. Meanwhile, you can have access to the hangar as of now. I want to send my lab people to Captain Campbell's house."

"Yeah? What for? Y'all took every damn thing. My boys had to bring their own damn toilet paper."

"I'll see you and Wes at noon. Bring my stuff and the government's stuff."

"Don't hold your breath, son."

He hung up, and I stood, wrapping the towel around me. Cynthia asked, "Burt Yardley?"

"Sure 'nuf."

"What did he want?"

"My ass, mostly. The SOB cleaned out my trailer." I laughed. "I like this guy. Too many wimps around these days. This guy is a genuine, hard-ass old prick."

"That'll be you next year."

"I hope so." I looked at my watch on the nightstand. "It's ten after six. Do we have time?"

She stood. "I have to dry my hair, get dressed, do my face—"

"All right. Rain check?"

"Sure." She walked to the bathroom door, then turned and asked me, "Are you seeing anyone?"

"Yes. Colonel Fowler at seven, then Moore about eight—"

219

"I forgot, you don't like that expression. Are you romantically involved with anyone?"

"No, I'm kind of between meaningful relationships at the moment. Truth is, no one since you."

"Good. Keeps it simple."

"Right. Except for Major what's-his-name. Your husband?"

"I'm very clear about that now."

"That's encouraging. We don't want a repeat of Brussels, do we?"

She laughed. "Sorry. Why do I find that funny?"

"Because you weren't looking down the muzzle of the gun."

"No, but you didn't have to listen to him for the next year. But, okay, Paul, I owe you for that. I'll pay off tonight, then we'll see where it goes."

"Looking forward to it."

"Me, too." She hesitated, then said, "You're too obsessed with . . . this case. You need a release."

"You're a sensitive and nurturing partner."

She disappeared into the bathroom, and I found yesterday's shorts and yesterday's socks. I got dressed, thinking, as I went through the motions, that life is a series of complications, some small, like where to get clean underwear, some a little bigger, like the one who just left the room. How you handle life depends a lot on how you handle plan B, or if you have a plan B.

Anyway, as I checked to see if my Glock had a firing pin and ammunition, I considered that the time had come for me to settle down a bit, and that what I didn't need anymore was a little light sport-fucking now and then.

Right. Whatever happened tonight with Cynthia would be the real thing. Something good had to come out of this mess.

CHAPTER TWENTY-ONE

Bethany Hill is Fort Hadley's Shaker Heights, though considerably smaller and not as well manicured. There are about thirty solid brick colonial-style homes set in an area of some sixty acres of oaks, beech, maple, and other high-ranking trees, while the lowly southern pine is specifically absent. All of the houses go back to the 1920s and '30s, when officers were gentlemen, were expected to live on post, and there weren't so many of them.

Times change, and the officer population has swelled beyond the Army's needs and its ability to give each one a house, a horse, and a manservant. But the top dogs on post still get the houses on the hill if they want them, and Colonel Fowler probably felt that living on post was good politics. Mrs. Fowler may have also preferred Fort Hadley. Not that Midland is a bastion of Old South attitudes toward blacks; it is not, having been influenced by decades of close proximity to the fort. But Bethany Hill, sometimes called the colonels' ghetto, was probably more comfortable in social terms than a similar neighborhood in town.

Bethany Hill's only disadvantage was its proximity to the rifle ranges, range number one being about five miles south of the hill. I could imagine that during a night firing exercise, with the wind from the south, you could hear the gunfire. But for some of the old infantry types, it was probably as soothing as a lullaby.

Cynthia was wearing a green silk blouse and a tan skirt, and, presumably, clean undergarments. I said to her, "You look very nice this morning."

"Thank you. How long do I have to see that blue suit?"

"Think of it as the duty uniform of the week." I added, "Your makeup didn't cover the dark circles under your eyes, which are also bloodshot and puffy."

"I'll look fine with a good night's sleep. You need a more recent birthday."

"Are you a little grumpy this morning?"

"Yes. Sorry." She put her hand on my knee. "These aren't the best circumstances for us to renew our friendship."

"No. But we got real close there."

We found the house, a good-sized brick structure with standard green door, green trim, and green shutters. A Ford station wagon and Jeep Cherokee were parked in the driveway. American-made vehicles are not de rigueur for high-ranking officers, but it's not a bad idea, either.

We parked on the street, got out of Cynthia's Mustang, and proceeded up the front walk. It was still cool on the hill at 0700 hours, but the hot sun was slanting in at a low angle under the trees, and it felt like another one of those days in the making.

I said to Cynthia, "Colonels with enough time in grade and time in service to be a general, such as Colonels Fowler and Kent, are extremely sensitive to career-limiting problems."

Cynthia replied, "Every problem is an opportunity."

I said, "Sometimes every problem is a problem. Kent, for instance, is finished." It was exactly 0700 hours and I knocked on the green door.

An attractive black woman, wearing a nice aqua summer dress, opened the door and forced a smile. Before I could announce ourselves, which is customary, she said, "Oh . . . Ms. Sunhill and Mr. Brenner. Correct?"

"Yes, ma'am." I was willing to forgive her for recognizing the younger and obviously lower-ranking warrant officer first. Civilians, even colonels' wives, sometimes got it wrong, and to be honest, rank among warrant officers is like virginity among prostitutes: there ain't none.

We stood there awkwardly a moment, then she showed us in and escorted us down the center hall.

Cynthia said to her, "This is a beautiful home."

She replied, "Thank you."

Cynthia asked her, "Did you know Captain Campbell well?"

"Oh . . . no . . . not well."

Which was a rather odd reply. I mean, how could General Campbell's adjutant's wife not know General Campbell's daughter? Clearly, Mrs. Fowler was distracted, forgetting all sorts of little social courtesies that should be second nature to a colonel's wife. I asked her, "Have you seen Mrs. Campbell since the tragedy?"

"Mrs. Campbell? No . . . I've been . . . too upset . . ."

Not as upset as the victim's mother, however, and that was a sympathy call that should have been made by now.

I was about to ask another question, but we reached our destination, a screened porch in the rear of the house where Colonel Fowler was speaking on the telephone. He was already dressed in his green A uniform, his shirt buttoned and his tie snug, though his jacket was draped over a chair. He motioned us into two wicker chairs opposite him at a small table, and we sat.

The military is perhaps the last American bastion of fixed and clearly defined social customs, rank, responsibilities, and required courtesies, and in case you needed guidance, there's an entire six-hundred-page book for officers, explaining what your life is and should be about. So when things seem a little askew, you start wondering.

Mrs. Fowler excused herself and disappeared. Colonel Fowler was listening on the phone, then said, "I understand, sir. I'll tell them." He hung up and looked at us. "Good morning."

"Good morning, Colonel."

"Coffee?"

"Please."

He poured two cups of coffee and indicated the sugar. He began without preamble, "I've encountered very little discrimination in the Army, and I can speak for other minorities when I say that the Army is, indeed, a place where race and religion are not a factor in advancement or in any other area of Army life. There may be racial problems among the enlisted personnel, but there is no systemic racial discrimination.''

I wasn't sure where this was going, so I put sugar in my coffee.

Colonel Fowler looked at Cynthia. ''Have you experienced any discrimination based on your sex?''

Cynthia hesitated, then replied, ''Perhaps . . . yes, on a few occasions.''

''Have you ever been harassed because of your gender?''

''Yes.''

''Have you been the subject of rumors, innuendos, or lies?''

''Maybe . . . once that I know of.''

Colonel Fowler nodded. ''So you see that I as a black man have had fewer problems than you as a white woman.''

Cynthia replied, ''I know that the Army is less accepting of females than of males. But so is the rest of the world. What is the point, Colonel?''

''The point, Ms. Sunhill, is that Captain Ann Campbell had a very difficult time here at Hadley. If she had been the general's son, for instance, and had fought in the Gulf, Panama, or Grenada, she would have been idolized by the troops as so many sons of great warriors have been throughout history. Instead, the rumor going around is that she fucked for everyone on post. Excuse my language.''

I offered, ''And if Captain Campbell had been the son of a fighting general who came home covered with glory and fucked all the female personnel on post, he'd never have to buy another drink in the O Club.''

Colonel Fowler looked at me. ''Precisely. We have that odd double standard for men and women that we would not tolerate if it were racial. So if you have some hard information concerning Captain Campbell's sexual conduct, I'd like to hear it, though I don't care if it's true or not.''

I replied, "I'm not at liberty to reveal my sources at this time. My only interest in Captain Campbell's sexual conduct is how or if it relates to her murder. I have no prurient interest in her sex life as an entertaining sidelight to her rape and strangulation out there on the rifle range." Actually, of course, she wasn't raped, but I wasn't giving out free copies of the autopsy.

Colonel Fowler said, "I'm sure that's true, Mr. Brenner, and I didn't mean to question your professional ethics. But you'd damned well better keep that connection in mind and not let your investigation become a witch-hunt."

"Look, Colonel, I appreciate your distress, and the distress of the deceased's family. But we're not talking about rumor and innuendo, as you suggested. We're talking about hard facts that I have. Ann Campbell had not only an active sex life, which in her position in this man's Army is not solely her business, but she led a potentially dangerous sex life. We can argue about double standards all morning, but when I hear that a general's daughter slept with half the senior married officers on post, I think of suspects, not tabloid headlines. The words 'slut' and 'whore' don't pop into my detective's mind. But the words 'blackmail' and 'motive' do. Do I make myself clear, sir?"

Colonel Fowler must have thought so, because he was nodding, or perhaps he was agreeing with some thought in his head. He said to me, "If you make an arrest, do I have your assurances that only the minimal amount of this information appears in your report?"

I had half a mind to tell him about Ann Campbell's hidden store of sexual delights and how I had already compromised myself to minimize the damage. I said, "The evidence in Captain Campbell's house could have and should have been shared with Chief Yardley. But Ms. Sunhill and I took a precautionary move to ensure that anything in the house of an unmarried, attractive female officer that would be embarrassing to her family or the Army did not wind up as a public amusement. Actions speak louder than words, and that's the only assurance I can give you."

Again, he nodded, then said quite unexpectedly, "I'm very

pleased with both of you. I've checked you both out, and you come to us with the highest recommendations. It's our privilege to have you assigned to this case.''

I lifted my feet because the bullshit was getting higher, but I replied, ''That's very good of you to say that.''

He poured us more coffee and said, ''So you have a prime suspect. Colonel Moore.''

''That's correct.''

''Why is he a suspect?''

''Because,'' I replied, ''there is forensic evidence that he was at the scene of the crime.''

''I see . . . but no evidence that he actually murdered her?''

''No. It's possible that he was there earlier or later than the time of the crime.''

''But you have no evidence that anyone *else* was there.''

''No conclusive evidence.''

''Then doesn't that leave him as the most likely suspect?''

''As of now.''

''If he doesn't confess, will you charge him?''

''I can only recommend in a case like this. The final decision as to charges will undoubtedly be made in Washington.''

''It seems to me that your report and recommendation will be the deciding factor.''

''It should be the only factor, considering that no one else has a clue to what happened.'' I added, ''I must tell you, sir, that these rumors linking Ann Campbell to certain officers on post may or may not include people such as the staff judge advocate, and others who may not be as objective or impartial as they should be in this matter. I hate to be the one to sow seeds of mistrust, but I'm only advising you of what I've heard.''

''Heard from whom?''

''I can't say. But it came from a good source, and I suspect you know how widespread this problem is. I don't think you can clean your own house here, Colonel. Your broom is dirty. But perhaps Ms. Sunhill and I can.''

He nodded. "Well, on that subject, I was speaking to General Campbell when you arrived. There's been a new development."

Uh-oh. I don't like new developments. "Yes?"

"The Justice Department, in a meeting with your superior, Colonel Hellmann, and the Army judge advocate general and other interested parties, has decided to assign the FBI to this case."

Oh, shit. I said to Colonel Fowler, "Well, then, the damage control is out of my hands. You and everyone else who wears a green uniform should know that."

"Yes. Some people are upset. Not everyone in the Pentagon knows how much damage control is necessary, so they caved in to these demands without a good fight. But they did get a compromise."

Neither Cynthia nor I bothered to ask what it was, but Colonel Fowler informed us, "You two are to remain on the case until noon tomorrow. If, after that time, you haven't made an arrest and recommended charges, you will be relieved of your investigative duties. Though you will remain available to the FBI for consultation."

"I see."

"A task force is assembling right now in Atlanta consisting of FBI personnel, a team from the Judge Advocate General's Office, the Attorney General's Office, and senior officers from your own CID in Falls Church."

"Well, I hope the SOBs all have to stay in the VOQ."

Colonel Fowler forced a smile. "We don't want this, of course, and I suspect you don't, either. But if you think about it, it was inevitable."

Cynthia said, "Colonel, Army captains are not murdered every day, but this sounds like overkill, and sounds more like PR than good police science."

"That point was raised. The reality, however, is that it *was* a female, she was *raped*, and it *was* General Campbell's daughter." He added, "There is equal justice for all, but some people get more of it."

I said, "I realize you have nothing to do with this decision, Colonel, but you ought to discuss this with General Campbell and see if he can get this decision reversed or at least modified."

"I did. That's how we got the compromise. As of about 2300 hours last night, you and Ms. Sunhill were relieved. General Campbell and Colonel Hellmann bought you some time. They thought you were very close to an arrest. So perhaps if you have good evidence and strong suspicions regarding Colonel Moore, you'll make that arrest. You have our permission to do so if you feel you need that."

I thought a moment. Colonel Moore seemed to be the most popular candidate for scapegoat. And why not? Evidence aside, he was a loony who did weird work in secret, and his uniform was sloppy, and General Campbell disliked his relationship with Ann Campbell according to Kent, and he had no significant awards or medals, and he was not a popular officer. Even an MP corporal couldn't wait to rat him out. This guy was walking into a noose with his face buried in a book of Nietzsche nuttiness. I said to Colonel Fowler, "Well, if I have about thirty hours, I'll take it."

Fowler seemed a little disappointed. He inquired, "What's keeping you from acting on the evidence you have?"

"There's not enough of it, Colonel."

"There seems to be."

"Did Colonel Kent tell you that?"

"Yes . . . and you indicated that the forensic evidence put Colonel Moore at the scene of the crime."

"Right. But it's a matter of times, motive, and ultimately the nature of the act itself. I have probable cause to believe Colonel Moore was somehow involved with what happened out there, but I can't say he acted alone, or even with malice, or indeed that he can be charged with murder in the first degree. I feel that I have to perfect a case against him, rather than just arrest him and throw the case onto the court."

"I see. Do you think he would confess?"

"You never know until you ask."

"When will you ask?"

"I usually ask when the suspect and I are both ready for that kind of conversation. In this case, I may wait until the clock runs out."

"All right. Do you need the assistance of the post CID?"

"I've been informed that Major Bowes was also a lover of the deceased."

"That's hearsay."

"That's right. But if I—no, Colonel, if *you* ask him on his honor as an officer, he will probably tell you the truth. In any case, since we may never know for sure, and since it's come up, he has to disqualify himself from this case. And I don't want to deal with the people under his command, either."

"I'm sensitive to that, Mr. Brenner, but a vague accusation— even a confession of sexual involvement with the victim—does not automatically disqualify Major Bowes from the investigation."

"I think it does. And I think it puts him on the B or C list of suspects until I hear his alibi or lack of same. And on that subject, Colonel, if you're finished, may I begin my interview with you?"

Colonel Fowler poured himself another cup of coffee with a rock-steady hand. The sun was higher now and the screened porch was a little darker. My stomach was gurgling with coffee and not much else, and my mind was not as alert as it should have been. I glanced at Cynthia and thought she looked better than I felt, but this high-noon deadline meant having to choose between sleep, sex, food, and work. Plan B.

Colonel Fowler asked, "Can I offer you breakfast?"

"No, thank you, Colonel."

He looked at me and said, "Fire away."

I opened fire. "Were you sexually involved with Ann Campbell?"

"No."

"Do you know anyone who was?"

"Colonel Kent has told you he was. I won't mention any other names since to do so seems to put them on your suspect list."

"Okay, let's go right to the list—do you know of anyone who might have had a motive for killing her?"

"No, I don't."

229

"Did you know that General Campbell's junior aide, Lieutenant Elby, was infatuated with her?"

"Yes, I did. That's not uncommon, nor was it unwise of him to pay attention to his commanding officer's daughter. They were both single, attractive, and officers. Marriages actually evolve from these situations." Colonel Fowler added, "I give the young man credit for balls."

"Amen. But did she return his attentions?"

Colonel Fowler thought a moment, then replied, "She never returned any man's attentions. She initiated all the attention, and ended it when it pleased her."

"That's a rather startling statement from you, Colonel."

"Oh, please, Mr. Brenner, you know all of this by now. I'm not trying to protect her reputation from you two. The woman was a . . . God, I wish I could come up with the right word . . . more than a seductress, not a tease—she delivered—not a common slut . . ." He looked at Cynthia. "Give me a word."

Cynthia replied, "I don't think we have a word for what she was, except perhaps avenger."

"Avenger?"

Cynthia said, "She wasn't the victim of rumor, as you first tried to suggest, and she wasn't promiscuous in the conventional sense, and neither was she clinically a nymphomaniac. She was, in fact, using her charms and her body to exact a revenge, Colonel, and you know it."

Colonel Fowler did not seem pleased with this evaluation. I suspected that Colonel Kent had given him only an edited briefing of what he'd told us and failed to include the fact that Ann Campbell's sexual behavior had a specific purpose, and that the purpose was to make Daddy look like a horse's ass. Colonel Fowler said to Cynthia, "She did hate the Army."

Cynthia replied, "She hated her father."

Fowler seemed, for the first time, uncomfortable. The man was a cool customer, and his armor was tried and tested, and so was his sword, but Cynthia just informed him that his rear was exposed.

Fowler said, "The general truly loved his daughter. Please believe that. But she had developed an obsessive and unreasonable hate for him. In fact, I spoke to an outside psychologist about it, and though he couldn't analyze the dynamics from afar, he did suggest that the daughter might be suffering from a borderline personality disorder."

Cynthia commented, "From what I've heard so far, it doesn't sound so borderline."

"Well, who the hell knows what these people mean? I couldn't follow all he was saying, but it comes down to the fact that the children of powerful men who try to follow in the father's footsteps become frustrated, then go through a period of questioning their own worth, then eventually to preserve their ego they find something they can do well, something very different from their father's world, where they will not be in direct competition with him, but something that society considers important. Thus, according to this psychologist, many of them wind up in social work, or as teachers, even nurses or some other nurturing profession." Colonel Fowler added, "Including psychology."

I remarked, "Psychological warfare is not exactly a nurturing profession."

"No, which is where this analysis diverts from the norm. This psychologist told me that when the son or daughter remains in the father's world, it's often because they want to harm the father. They can't compete, they won't or can't go off on their own, so they stay close to the source of their anger and engage in what amounts to guerrilla warfare, ranging from petty annoyances to major sabotage."

He thought a moment, then added, "They do this because it is the only way they can avenge—yes, as you said, Ms. Sunhill—avenge themselves over these imagined injustices or whatever. In Captain Campbell's case, she was in a unique position to do this. Her father couldn't fire her, and she had developed a power base of her own. Many sons and daughters who have these feelings against their father, according to this psychologist, engage in promiscuous behavior, drunkenness, gambling, and other antisocial acts that they

231

know will embarrass the authority figure in his world. Captain Campbell, perhaps as a result of her knowledge in the field of psychology, took it a step further, and apparently sought to seduce the men around her father.''

Colonel Fowler leaned across the table and said to us, ''I hope you understand that Ann's behavior was irrational, and that it had nothing to do with her father's behavior toward her. We all have imagined enemies, and when it's a parent, no amount of parental love or caring can overcome that anger in the child's mind. This was a very disturbed woman who needed help, and she wasn't getting it. In fact, that son-of-a-bitch Moore was fueling the flames of her anger for his own sick purposes. I believe he wanted to see how far he could push and control the dynamics of this situation.''

No one spoke for a full minute, then Cynthia inquired, ''Why wasn't some drastic action taken by the general? Isn't this the man who led an armored task force to the Euphrates River?''

Colonel Fowler replied, ''*That* was easy. Handling Ann Campbell was not so easy. Actually, the general considered such action about a year ago. But according to the professional advice I was getting, had the general intervened by having Colonel Moore transferred, for instance, or having Ann ordered into therapy, which he could do as a commander, the situation may have gotten worse. So the general listened to this advice and let the situation take its own course.''

I commented, ''And it wouldn't have done the general's career much good to pull rank on Moore and his daughter, and thereby admit there was a problem.''

Colonel Fowler replied, ''It was a very delicate situation. Mrs. Campbell . . . Ann's mother thought that the situation would improve if Ann was left to vent her irrational anger. So it was a standoff. But the general *had* decided to act, just a week ago. But then . . . well, it was too late.''

''How,'' I inquired, ''did the general decide to act?''

Colonel Fowler thought a moment and replied, ''I don't know if telling you anything further is relevant to this case.''

"Tell me and I'll decide."

"Well . . . all right, then. The general, a few days ago, gave his daughter an ultimatum. He gave her options. Option one was to resign her commission. Option two was to discontinue her duties at the school and agree to some sort of therapy of the general's choice—inpatient or out. Option three, the general informed her that if she turned down those options, he would have the staff judge advocate investigate her misconduct and draw up charges for a general court-martial."

I nodded. Somehow, I felt, this ultimatum, if it was true, precipitated what happened on rifle range six. I asked Colonel Fowler, "How did she respond to this ultimatum?"

"She told her father she'd have an answer for him within two days. But she didn't. She was murdered."

I said, "Maybe that was her answer."

Colonel Fowler looked somewhat startled. "What do you mean by that?"

"Think about it, Colonel."

"You mean she had Colonel Moore assist her in some sort of bizarre suicide?"

"Perhaps." I asked him, "And there is no single or specific incident from the past that would explain Captain Campbell's anger toward her father?"

"Such as what?"

"Such as . . . rival affections—mother, daughter, that sort of thing."

Colonel Fowler regarded me closely for a moment as if I were a step away from crossing the line between a murder investigation and an unspeakable breach of conduct and ethics. He replied coolly, "I don't know what you're getting at, Mr. Brenner, and I suggest you don't even try to explain."

"Yes, sir."

"Is that all?"

"I'm afraid not. It gets even muckier, Colonel. You say you had no sexual relationship with the deceased. Why not?"

"What do you mean, why not?"

"I mean, why did she not proposition you, or if she did, did you turn her down?"

Colonel Fowler's eyes flitted to the door for a second as if to assure himself that Mrs. Fowler was not around to hear this. He replied, "She never propositioned me."

"I see. Was that because you're black or because she knew it was a useless attempt?"

"I . . . I would rather think it was . . . She did date a few black officers . . . not here at Hadley, but in the past, so it wasn't that. So I'd have to say that she knew . . ." He smiled for the first time. ". . . she knew I was not corruptible." He added, again with a smile, "Or she thought I was ugly."

Cynthia said, "But you're not, Colonel, and even if you were, it wouldn't have mattered to Ann Campbell. I suspect she *did* proposition you, and you turned her down out of loyalty to your wife, your commanding officer, or because of your own sense of morality. At that point, you became Ann Campbell's second worst enemy."

Fowler had clearly had enough and said, "I don't think I've ever had a conversation like this in my life."

I replied, "You've probably never been involved in a homicide investigation."

"No, I haven't, and if you would make that arrest, this investigation would be over."

"Actually, it would continue right up to and through a court-martial. I don't make many mistakes, Colonel, but when I think I may have, I don't mind working hard to expose my own errors."

"I commend you, Mr. Brenner. Perhaps, though, Colonel Moore can satisfy your doubts."

"He can try, but he may have his own version of events. I like to have everyone's version so I can make a better evaluation as to the quality of the bullshit."

"As you wish."

Cynthia asked him, "Did Captain Campbell have any brothers or sisters?"

"There is a brother."

"What can you tell us about him?"

"He lives out on the West Coast. Some place with a Spanish name. Can't think of it."

"He's not military?"

"No. He's . . . he has explored many careers."

"I see. You've met him?"

"Yes. He comes home most holidays."

"Does he strike you as suffering from the same problems you suggested his sister was suffering from?"

"To some extent . . . but he chose to distance himself from the family. That's how he deals with it. During the Gulf War, for instance, when some California TV station wanted to interview him, they couldn't find him."

Cynthia asked, "Would you describe him as alienated from his parents?"

"Alienated? No . . . just distant. When he's home, they all seem quite happy to see him, and then sad that he's left."

"And how was the relationship between brother and sister?"

"Very good, from what I could see. Ann Campbell was very accepting of him."

"In regard to his . . . what? His life-style?"

"Yes. John Campbell—that's his name—is gay."

"I see. And did General Campbell accept this?"

Fowler thought a moment, then replied, "I think he did. John Campbell was always discreet—never brought male lovers home, dressed pretty much mainstream and all that. I think if the general hadn't had his hands full with his daughter and her indiscretions, he might have been more disappointed in his son. But compared to Ann, John is a solid citizen."

"I understand," Cynthia said. "Do you think that General Campbell perhaps pushed his daughter into a traditional male role—I mean West Point and the Army—to make up for his son's lack of interest in those pursuits?"

"That's what everyone says. But, as with most of life, things aren't that pat. In fact, Ann was a very enthusiastic cadet at West

Point. She *wanted* to be there and she did very well. After her four-year active-duty obligation, she stayed in. So, no, I don't think the general pushed her or coerced her, or withheld affection from her as a child, if, for instance, she showed no interest in going to the Point. That's what this psychologist suggested, but it was very much the opposite. Ann Campbell, as I remember her in high school, was a tomboy, and a good candidate for a military career. In fact, she wanted to continue the tradition. Her father's father was a career Army officer as well.''

Cynthia thought a moment, then reminded him, ''You said she hated the Army.''

''Yes . . . I said that, but, as you pointed out, it was her father she hated.''

''So you were in error when you said that?''

''Well . . .''

It's always good to highlight a lie, even a small one, during an interrogation. It puts the suspect or witness on the defensive, where he or she belongs.

Colonel Fowler sought to correct his original statement and said to Cynthia, ''She originally liked the Army. I can't say with certainty how she felt about it recently. She had too much anger, and she had other motives for staying in the service.''

''I think I have that clear now.'' She asked him, ''Can you give us some idea of the relationship between Ann Campbell and her mother?''

Colonel Fowler considered this a moment, then replied, ''They had a decent relationship. Mrs. Campbell, contrary to what some people think, is a strong woman, but she's chosen to defer to her husband in terms of his career, his various postings around the world, including ones where she could not accompany him, and in terms of entertaining people she may not personally care for, and those sorts of things. I use the term 'chosen' because that's what it is—a choice. Mrs. Campbell is from the old school, and if she makes a commitment to the marriage, she will stick with it, or leave the marriage if she changes her mind. She will not gripe and complain and sulk as so many modern wives do today who want to have their cake and eat it, too.''

He glanced at Cynthia, then continued, ''She will not embarrass her husband with breaches of conduct, she will take the good with the bad, she will recognize her own worth as a wife and partner, and will not get a job selling real estate downtown in a pathetic attempt to declare her independence. She does not wear the general's stars, but she knows that he would not be wearing them either if it weren't for her help, dedication, and loyalty over the years. You asked me about Ann's relationship with her mother, and I told you about Mrs. Campbell's relationship with her husband, but now you can figure out the answer to your question.''

I nodded. ''Yes, I can. And did Ann try to change her mother's behavior or philosophy?''

''I think she did at first, but Mrs. Campbell basically told her to mind her own business and stay out of her marriage.''

Cynthia commented, ''Good advice. But did it strain their relationship?''

''I'm not very attuned to mother-daughter relationships. I came from a family of four boys, and I have three sons of my own. I can't fathom women in general and I've never seen a mother-daughter relationship up close. But I know they never did things together, such as shopping or tennis or planning parties. But they would dine together, alone, at times. Is that good enough for you?''

Cynthia nodded, then asked, ''Did Mrs. Fowler know Ann Campbell well?''

Colonel Fowler replied, ''Fairly well. It comes with the social territory.''

''And of course Mrs. Fowler knows Mrs. Campbell well, so perhaps I can speak to Mrs. Fowler—about the mother-daughter relationship.''

Colonel Fowler hesitated for a beat, then replied, ''Mrs. Fowler is very upset, as you may have noticed. So unless you're insisting, I'd have to say wait a few days.''

Cynthia inquired, "Will Mrs. Fowler be available? Or is she so upset that she may go somewhere for a rest?"

Colonel Fowler looked at Cynthia and replied, "As a civilian, she can come and go as she pleases, if I read your subtext correctly."

"You do read me correctly, Colonel. I don't want to have to get a subpoena. I'd like to speak to her today. I don't have a few days, as it turns out."

Colonel Fowler took a deep breath. Obviously, we were more than he'd bargained for and he wasn't used to this kind of pressure from subordinates. I think the fact that we were in civilian clothes helped him put up with this crap and kept him from throwing us out, which is why the CID often chooses mufti for the dirty stuff. Fowler replied, finally, "I'll see if she's up to it this afternoon."

"Thank you," Cynthia replied. "It would probably be better if she spoke to us, rather than her having to speak to the FBI."

Colonel Fowler got the message and nodded.

I asked him, "For the record, Colonel, can you tell me your whereabouts on the night that Captain Campbell was killed?"

He smiled and said, "I thought that was the first question you were supposed to ask. Well, where was I? I worked until about 1900 hours, then attended a going-away party for an officer in the grill at the O Club. I excused myself early and was home by 2200 hours. I did some paperwork, made some calls, and Mrs. Fowler and I retired at 2300 hours."

It would be silly of me to ask him if Mrs. Fowler would verify that, so I asked instead, "And nothing unusual happened during the night?"

"No."

"And you awakened at what time?"

"At 0600 hours."

"And then?"

"Then I showered, got dressed, and was at work at about 0730 hours." He added, "Which is where I should be now."

"And you called Captain Campbell's house at about 0800 hours and left a message on her answering machine."

238

"Correct. General Campbell called me from his home and asked me to do that."

"He didn't want to call her himself?"

"He was annoyed and he knew Mrs. Campbell was disappointed, so he asked me to place the call."

"I see. As it happens, however, we were in her house before 0800, and when we got there, the message was already on the machine."

There was what you call a moment of silence, and in microseconds, Colonel Fowler was going to have to guess if I was bluffing, which I wasn't, or if he had a better story. He looked me in the eye and said, "Then my time is wrong. It must have been earlier. What time were you in her home?"

"I'll have to check my notes. Can I assume you didn't call her before 0700 hours to say she was late for a 0700-hour breakfast?"

"That would be a logical assumption, Mr. Brenner, though I've often called her prior to such an appointment to remind her."

"But on this occasion, you said, 'Ann, you were supposed to stop by the general's house this morning.' Then you said something about breakfast, followed by, 'You're probably sleeping now.' So if she got off duty at, let's say, 0700, and you called at, say, 0730 hours, she'd barely be home, let alone asleep."

"That's true . . . I suppose I wasn't thinking very clearly. I may have forgotten she was on duty, and I meant that she was probably not awake yet."

"But you mentioned duty in your message. The whole sentence was, 'You were supposed to stop by the general's house this morning after you got off duty.' "

"Did I say that?"

"Yes."

"Well, then, put it down to my error in times. I may have called as early as 0730. I know I called right after the general called me. Captain Campbell apparently agreed to meet her parents at 0700 hours, and though she would normally have been relieved at about that time by the officer designated to arrive at 0700 for work, it wouldn't have been unusual for her to leave early and leave the duty sergeant in charge until relieved.'' He added, ''Are you having a problem with this, Mr. Brenner?''

''No problem.'' Not for me; big problem for you. I asked, ''Considering that Captain Campbell and her father were not on good terms, why was she having breakfast with him?''

''Well, they did dine together now and then. I told you, she saw her mother fairly often.''

''Could this breakfast meeting have been for the purpose of Ann Campbell delivering her answer to the general's ultimatum?''

Fowler considered a moment, then replied, ''Yes, it could have been.''

''Do you find it curious that only hours before she had to reply to his ultimatum, she was found dead? Do you think there's any connection?''

''No, I think it's coincidence.''

''I don't believe in coincidence. Let me ask you this, Colonel: is there anything further that General Campbell required of his daughter as part of his ultimatum?''

''Such as what?''

''Well, such as names. Names of the men on post she'd slept with. Was General Campbell going to make a clean sweep?''

Colonel Fowler thought about that, then replied, ''That's entirely possible. But Ann Campbell didn't care who knew and would have been delighted to tell her father.''

''But the married officers who she slept with cared very much and would not have been as delighted.''

''I'm sure they did care,'' Fowler replied. ''But most, if not all, of them realized they couldn't count on her discretion.'' He said, ''You know, Mr. Brenner, most married men have ambivalent feelings about sexual indiscretions.'' He looked at Cynthia, then continued, ''On the one hand, they are terrified of being found out by their wives or families, or certain friends or superiors. On the other hand, they are proud of their exploits and actually brag about their conquests. When the conquest is the beautiful daughter of their boss, they can barely contain themselves and tend to shoot their mouths off. Believe me, we've all been there.''

I smiled. "Indeed we have, Colonel." I added, "But talk is one thing; photos, lists, and affidavits are another. What I'm suggesting is that somehow, perhaps through Ann Campbell herself, some of her lovers learned that General Campbell had had enough and was demanding from his daughter a full accounting of her seductions. Someone may have decided that it was time to get rid of the evidence. To get rid of Ann Campbell.''

Fowler nodded. "That thought crossed my mind. In fact, I never thought it was a total stranger who killed her. But can you explain to me why someone who wanted to shut her up would kill her that way and draw attention to the sexual nature of the act and of the victim?''

Good question. I replied, "It may have been a cover to *conceal* the nature of the act. The perpetrator needed to kill her but added the rape to confuse the investigation. I've had two husbands who murdered their wives that way to make it look like a stranger did it.''

Fowler commented, "This is your area of expertise, not mine. I see your point, but how many men would actually murder a woman just to shut her up? It's a lot less risky to face a court-martial for actions unbecoming an officer than to face a court-martial for murder.''

"I agree, Colonel, but then, we're rational men. In the irrational world, one of the prime motivators for homicide is to avoid disgrace and humiliation. Says so in the manual.''

"Well, again, that's your area of experience, not mine.''

"But think about who among Ann Campbell's lovers might consider committing murder to avoid disgrace, divorce, court-martial, and dismissal from the service.''

"Mr. Brenner, your prime suspect, Colonel Moore, was not involved with her sexually from what I hear. So he had no obvious reason for shutting her up. But he may have had many *other* reasons for raping her and killing her. So you ought to concentrate on *his* motivations if that's all that is keeping you from arresting him.''

"I'm certainly following that avenue as well, Colonel. I like to conduct homicide investigations like infantry and armor commanders conduct a campaign—multiple avenues of advance—a feint, a probing attack, a main thrust, then a breakthrough and encirclement." I added, "Surround 'em and pound 'em."

He smiled wryly, as I knew he would, and said, "That's a good way to squander your resources and to lose the initiative. Go right for the kill, Mr. Brenner, and leave the fancy stuff for the chalkboard in the tactics classroom."

"Well, maybe you're right, Colonel." I asked him, "Did you happen to see the duty sergeant—Sergeant St. John—when you got to work that morning?"

"No. In fact, I heard later that a corporal of the guard was actually holding down the fort, so to speak, when the first officer arrived, and that caused a big stink. The corporal said that the duty sergeant left hours before and never returned, and he had no idea where the sergeant was or where the duty officer was. But I didn't know that because no one brought it to my attention. Major Sanders, a staff officer, made the decision to call the MPs, and they informed him that the duty sergeant, St. John, was in their custody, though they wouldn't say why. I learned of all this at about 0900 hours and I reported it to General Campbell, who told me to follow up on it."

"And no one thought to ask where Captain Campbell had disappeared to?"

"No . . . In retrospect, it all ties together. But that morning it just seemed to me that Captain Campbell had left early, put the duty sergeant in charge, and he put a corporal of the guard in charge and took the opportunity to go somewhere—perhaps home to spy on his wife. That's all too common—a man on duty gets it in his head that his wife is being unfaithful, then sneaks off duty and checks out his house. It's a problem of military life."

"Yes, I've had two homicides and one maiming that began that way."

"So you understand. Well, that's one of the things that occurred to me. But what I knew is that St. John ran afoul of the MPs and never made it back to headquarters. I didn't push the inquiry because it was obviously Captain Campbell's early departure that led to St. John's dereliction of duty, and I knew that it would sort itself out. The last thing anyone thought is that St. John's apparent arrest had anything to do with what we discovered later was the actual sequence of events.''

Sounded solid to me. But of course if I squeezed it, it had some soft spots. I reminded him, "You said you worked late at headquarters the evening before.''

"Yes.''

"Did you see Captain Campbell when she reported in for duty that evening?''

"No. My office is on the first floor, next to the general's. The duty officer and sergeant use the large clerk-typist area on the second floor. They just pick up the logbook and any special orders from a designated officer, then choose any desk and make themselves comfortable for the night. I don't normally see any duty officer reporting in.'' He asked, "Is that satisfactory, Mr. Brenner?''

"It's reasonable, sir. I don't know if it's satisfactory until I can cross-check it. This is my job, Colonel, and I can't do it any other way.''

"I'm sure you have some latitude, Mr. Brenner.''

"Just a tiny bit. An inch to the left, an inch to the right. More than that and I'm free-falling into the jaws of my boss, Colonel Hellmann, who eats warrant officers who are afraid to ask questions of superior officers.''

"Is that a fact?''

"Yes, sir.''

"Well, I'll tell him you did a splendid job and showed no fear whatsoever.''

"Thank you, Colonel.''

"Do you enjoy this?''

"I used to. I'm not enjoying it today. Or yesterday.''

"Then we have something in common.''

"I hope so.''

We all sat a minute. My coffee was cold, but I didn't care. Finally, I asked him, "Colonel, could you arrange an appointment for us to speak with Mrs. Campbell today?"

"I'll do my best."

I said to him, "If she's as good a military wife as you describe, she'll understand the necessity." I added, "And we would like to see General Campbell today as well."

"I'll arrange it. Where can I contact you?"

"I'm afraid we'll be all over the post today. Just leave a message at the provost office. Where can I contact you?"

"At Post Headquarters."

"Are the funeral arrangements complete?"

"Yes. The body will be in the post chapel after retreat tonight, and also tomorrow morning, for those who wish to pay their last respects. At 1100 hours tomorrow, there will be a service in the chapel, then the body will be taken in a procession to Jordan Field for the ceremony, then placed aboard an aircraft and transported to Michigan for interment in the Campbell family plot."

"I see." Career Army officers usually have a will on file with the Army, and often there will be burial instructions included, so I asked Colonel Fowler, "Is that the wish of the deceased?"

"Does that question relate to the homicide investigation?"

"I suppose the date of the will and the date of the burial instructions would relate to this investigation."

"The will and the burial instructions were updated a week before Captain Campbell left for the Gulf, which would not be unusual. For your information, she asked to be buried in the family plot, and the only beneficiary of her will is her brother, John."

"Thank you." On that note of finality, I said, "You've been most cooperative, Colonel, and we appreciate it." Despite your trying to blow a little smoke up our asses.

Superior officers sit first and stand first, so I waited for him to realize I was finished, and stand, but instead he asked me, "Did you find anything in her house that would be damaging to her or anyone here on post?"

My turn to be coy, so I asked, "Such as?"

"Well . . . diaries, photos, letters, a list of her conquests. You know what I mean."

I replied, "My maiden aunt could have spent a week alone in Captain Campbell's house and not found anything she would have disapproved of, including the music." Which was true because Aunt Jean, snoop that she was, had no spatial perception.

Colonel Fowler stood, and we stood as well. He informed me, "Then you've missed something. Ann Campbell documented everything. It was her training as a psychologist, and undoubtedly her desire as a corrupter, not to rely on fleeting memories of her rolls in the hay out in some motel or in someone's office on post after hours. Look harder."

"Yes, sir." I must admit, I didn't like hearing these kinds of remarks about Ann Campbell from Kent or Fowler. Ann Campbell had become more than a murder victim to me, obviously. I would probably find her murderer, but someone had to find why she did what she did, and someone had to explain that to people like Fowler, Kent, and everyone else. Ann Campbell's life needed no apology, no pity; it needed a rational explanation, and maybe a vindication.

Colonel Fowler escorted us to the front door, probably wishing he hadn't been on the telephone before so he could have escorted us in without Mrs. Fowler's assistance. At the door we shook hands, and I said to him, "By the way, we never found Captain Campbell's West Point ring. Was she in the habit of wearing it?"

He thought a moment and replied, "I never noticed."

"There was a tan line where the ring had been."

"Then I suppose she wore it."

I said to him, "You know, Colonel, if I were a general, I'd want you for my adjutant."

"If you were a general, Mr. Brenner, you'd *need* me for your adjutant. Good morning." The green door closed and we walked down the path to the street.

Cynthia said, "We keep getting to the threshold of the great secret of Ann and Daddy, then we hit a wall."

"True." Despite the mixed metaphor. "But we know there *is* a secret, and we know that the stuff about imagined injustices and irrational anger toward her father is not cutting it. At least not for me."

Cynthia opened her door. "Me neither."

I slid into the passenger seat and said, "Colonel Fowler's wife had that look. You know that look?"

"Indeed I do."

"And Colonel Fowler needs a better watch."

"Indeed he does."

CHAPTER TWENTY-TWO

B reakfast or Psy-Ops School?'' Cynthia asked.

"Psy-Ops School. We'll eat Colonel Moore for breakfast.''

Each house on Bethany Hill had a regulation white sign with black lettering displayed on a post near the driveway, and, about five houses from Colonel Fowler's house, I saw a sign that said, "Colonel & Mrs. Kent.'' I pointed it out to Cynthia and commented, "I wonder where Bill Kent will be living next month?''

"I hope it's not Leavenworth, Kansas. I feel sorry for him.''

"People make their own bad luck.''

"Be a little compassionate, Paul.''

"Okay. Considering the extent of the corruption here, there will be a rash of sudden resignations, retirements, and transfers, maybe a few divorces, but, with luck, no courts-martial for actions unbecoming an officer.'' I added, "They'd need a whole cell block at Leavenworth for Ann Campbell's lovers. Can you picture that? About two dozen ex-officers sitting around in their cells—''

"I think you got off the compassionate track.''

"Right. Sorry.''

We left Bethany Hill and mingled with the early morning traffic of the main post—POVs and troop carriers, school buses and delivery trucks, humvees and staff cars, as well as soldiers marching or running in formation; thousands of men and women on the move, similar to, but profoundly different from, any small town at eight A.M. Stateside garrison duty in times of peace is, at best, boring, but in times of war a place like Fort Hadley is preferable to the front lines, but barely.

Cynthia commented, "Some people have trouble with time perception. I came close to buying Colonel Fowler's sequence of events, though it was cutting it close, timewise."

"Actually, I think he made the call much earlier."

"But think of what you're saying, Paul."

"I'm saying he knew she was dead earlier, but he had to make that call to establish that he believed she was alive and late for her appointment. What he didn't know is that we would be at the deceased's house that early."

"That's one explanation, but how did he know she was dead?"

"There are only three ways: someone told him, or he discovered the body somehow, or he killed her."

Cynthia replied, "He did not kill her."

I glanced at her. "You like the guy."

"I do. But beyond that, he is not a killer."

"Everyone is a killer, Cynthia."

"Not true."

"Well, but you can see his motive."

"Yes. His motive would be to protect the general and get rid of a source of corruption on post."

I nodded. "That's the sort of altruistic motive that, in a man like Colonel Fowler, might trigger murder. But he may also have had a more personal motive."

"Maybe." Cynthia turned onto the road that led to the Psy-Ops School.

I commented, "If we didn't have Colonel Moore by his curly hairs, I'd put Colonel Fowler near the top of the list, based on that telephone call alone, not to mention the look on Mrs. Fowler's face."

"Maybe." She asked, "How far are we going with Moore?"

248

"To the threshold."

"You don't think it's time to talk to him about his hair, finger-prints, and tire marks?"

"Not necessary. We worked hard for that and we're not sharing it with him. I want him to dig a deeper hole for himself with his mouth."

Cynthia passed a sign that said, "Authorized Personnel Only." There was no MP booth, but I could see the roving MP humvee up ahead.

We parked outside the Psy-Ops headquarters building. The sign in front of the building said, "Cadre Parking Only," and I saw the gray Ford Fairlane that presumably belonged to Colonel Moore.

We went inside the building, where a sergeant sat at a desk in the otherwise bare lobby. He stood and said, "Can I help you?"

I showed him my ID and said, "Please take us to Colonel Moore's office."

"I'll ring him, Chief," he replied, using the informal form of address for a warrant officer. I don't like "Chief," and I said to him, "I guess you didn't hear me, Sarge. Take us to his office."

"Yes, sir. Follow me."

We walked down a long corridor of concrete-block walls, painted a sort of slime-mold green. The floor wasn't even tiled, but was poured concrete, painted deck gray. Solid steel doors, all open, were spaced every twelve feet or so, and I could see into the small offices: lieutenants and captains, probably all psychologists, laboring away at gray steel desks. I said to Cynthia, "Forget Nietzsche. This is Kafka territory."

The sergeant glanced at me, but said nothing.

I asked him, "How long has the colonel been in?"

"Only about ten minutes."

"Is that his gray Ford Fairlane out front?"

"Yes, sir. Is this about the Campbell murder?"

"It's not about a parking ticket."

"Yes, sir."

"Where's Captain Campbell's office?"

249

"Just to the right of Colonel Moore's office." He added, "It's empty."

We reached the end of the hallway, which dead-ended at a closed door marked "Colonel Moore."

The sergeant asked us, "Should I announce you?"

"No. That will be all, Sergeant."

He hesitated, then said, "I . . ."

"Yes?"

"I hope to God you find the guy who did it." He turned and walked back down the long corridor.

The last door on the right was also closed and the sign on it said, "Captain Campbell." Cynthia opened the door and we went inside.

Indeed, the office was bare, except that on the floor lay a bouquet of flowers. There was no note.

We left the office and walked the few steps to Colonel Moore's door. I knocked, and Moore called out, "Come in, come in."

Cynthia and I entered. Colonel Moore was hunched over his desk and did not look up. The office was big, but as drab as the others we'd passed. There were file cabinets against the right-hand wall, a small conference table near the left-hand wall, and an open steel locker in the corner, where Colonel Moore had hung his jacket. A floor fan swept the room, rustling papers taped to the block wall. Beside Moore's desk was the ultimate government status symbol: a paper shredder.

Colonel Moore glanced up. "What is it—? Oh . . ." He sort of looked around, as if he were trying to figure out how we got there.

I said, "We're sorry to drop in like this, Colonel, but we were in the neighborhood. May we sit?"

"Yes, all right." He motioned to the two chairs opposite his desk. "I'd really appreciate it if you make an appointment next time."

"Yes, sir. The next time we'll make an appointment for you to come to the provost marshal's building."

"Just let me know."

Like many scientific and academic types, Colonel Moore seemed to miss the subtleties of the organizational world around him. I don't think he would have gotten it even if I'd said, "The next time we talk, it will be at police headquarters."

"What can I do for you?"

"Well," I said, "I'd like you to assure me again that you were home on the evening of the tragedy."

"All right. I was home from about 1900 hours until I left for work at about 0730 hours."

Which was about the time Cynthia and I had gotten to Victory Gardens. I asked him, "You live alone?"

"Yes, I do."

"Can anyone verify that you were home?"

"No."

"You placed a call to Post Headquarters at 2300 hours and spoke to Captain Campbell. Correct?"

"Correct."

"The conversation had to do with work?"

"That's right."

"You called her again at about noon at home and left a message on her answering machine."

"Yes."

"But you'd been trying to call her earlier, and her phone was out of order."

"That's right."

"What were you calling her about?"

"Just what I said on the message—the MPs came and completely emptied her office. I argued with them because there was classified material in her files, but they wouldn't listen." He added, "The Army is run like a police state. Do you realize they don't even need a search warrant to do that?"

"Colonel, if this was IBM corporate headquarters, the security guards could do the same thing on orders from a ranking officer of the company. Everything and everyone here belongs to Uncle Sam. You have certain constitutional rights regarding a criminal investigation, but I don't suggest you try to exercise any of them unless I

251

put the cuffs on you right now and take you to jail. Then everyone, myself included, will see that your rights are protected. So are you in a cooperative frame of mind this morning, Colonel?''

''No. But I'll cooperate with you under duress and protest.''

''Good.'' I looked around the office again. On the top shelf of the open steel locker was a toilet kit from which, I assumed, the hairbrush had been taken, and I wondered if Moore had noticed.

I looked in the receptacle of his paper shredder, but it was empty, which was good. Moore was not stupid and neither was he the benign absentminded professor type; he was, in fact, as I said, somewhat sinister-looking and cunning. But he had an arrogant carelessness about him so that, if I had seen a sledgehammer and tent pegs on his desk, I wouldn't have been too surprised.

''Mr. Brenner? I'm very busy this morning.''

''Right. You said you would assist us in certain psychological insights into Captain Campbell's personality.''

''What would you like to know?''

''Well, first, why did she hate her father?''

He looked at me for a long moment and observed, ''I see you've learned a few things since our last conversation.''

''Yes, sir. Ms. Sunhill and I go round and round and talk to people, and each person tells us a little something, then we go back and reinterview people, and, in a few days, we know what to ask and who to ask, and by and by we know the good guys from the bad guys, and we arrest the bad guys. It's kind of simple compared to psychological warfare.''

''You're too modest.''

''Why did she hate her father?''

He took a deep breath, sat back, and said, ''Let me begin by saying that I believe General Campbell has what is called an obsessive-compulsive personality disorder. That is to say, he is full of himself, domineering, can't tolerate criticism, is a perfectionist, has trouble showing affection, but is totally competent and functional.''

''You've described ninety percent of the generals in the Army. So what?''

252

"Well, but Ann Campbell was not much different, which is not unusual considering they are related. So, two like personalities grow up in the same house, one an older male, the father, the other a younger female, the daughter. The potential for problems was there."

"So this problem goes back to her unhappy childhood."

"Not actually. It starts off well. Ann saw herself in her father and liked what she saw, and her father saw himself in his daughter and was equally pleased. In fact, Ann described to me a happy childhood and a close relationship with her father."

"Then it went bad?"

"Yes. It has to. When the child is young, the child wants to win the father's approval. The father sees no threat to his dominance and thinks of the son or daughter as a chip off the old block, to use an expression. But by adolescence, they both begin to see traits in the other that they don't like. The irony is that these are their own worst traits, but people cannot be objective about themselves. Also, they begin to vie for dominance, and begin to voice criticisms of the other person. Since neither can tolerate criticism, and since both are in fact probably competent and high achievers, the sparks start to fly."

"Are we speaking in general terms," I asked, "or specifically about General and Captain Campbell, father and daughter?"

He hesitated a moment, probably out of a deeply ingrained habit against revealing privileged information. He said, "I may speak in generalities, but you should make your own conclusions."

"Well," I replied, "if Ms. Sunhill and I are asking specific questions, and you're giving general answers, we may be misled. We're a little dense."

"I don't think so, and you can't fool me into thinking you are."

"All right, down to cases." I said to him, "We were told that Ann felt she was in competition with her father, realized she could not compete in that world, and rather than opting out, she began a campaign of sabotage against him."

"Who told you that?"

"I got it from someone who got it from a psychologist."

"Well, the psychologist is wrong. An obsessive-compulsive personality always believes they *can* compete and will go head-to-head with a domineering figure."

"So, that wasn't the actual cause of Ann Campbell's hate of her father? They didn't mind the head-butting."

"Correct. The actual reason for her deep hate of her father was betrayal."

"Betrayal?"

"Yes. Ann Campbell would not develop an irrational hate of her father because of rivalry, jealousy, or feelings of inadequacy. Despite their growing competitiveness, which was not necessarily bad, she in fact loved her father very much right up until the point he betrayed her. And that betrayal was so great, so total, and so traumatic that it nearly destroyed her. The man she loved, admired, and trusted above all others betrayed her and broke her heart." He added, "Is that specific enough for you?"

After a few seconds of silence, Cynthia leaned forward in her seat and asked, "*How* did he betray her?"

Moore did not reply, but just looked at us.

Cynthia asked, "Did he rape her?"

Moore shook his head.

"Then what?"

Moore replied, "It really doesn't matter *what* specifically it was. It only matters to the subject that the betrayal was total and unforgivable."

I said, "Colonel, don't fuck with us. What did he do to her?"

Moore seemed a little taken aback, then recovered and said, "I don't know."

Cynthia pointed out, "But you know it wasn't rape and incest."

"Yes. I know that because she volunteered that. When we discussed her case, she only referred to this event as the betrayal."

"So," I said sarcastically, "it may be that he forgot to buy her a birthday present."

Colonel Moore looked annoyed, which was my purpose in being

sarcastic. He said, "No, Mr. Brenner, it's not usually something so trivial. But you can understand, I hope, that when you love and trust someone unconditionally, and that person betrays you in some fundamental and premeditated way—not a forgetful or thoughtless way, such as you suggested, but in a profoundly personal and self-serving way—then you can never forgive that person." He added, "A classic example is a loving wife who idolizes her husband and discovers he's having an intense affair with another woman."

Cynthia and I thought about this a moment, and I suppose a few personal thoughts ran through our minds, and neither of us spoke.

Finally, Moore said, "Here's a more relevant example for you: An adolescent or young adult female loves and worships her father. Then one day she overhears him speaking to one of his friends or professional associates, and the father says of his daughter, 'Jane is a very weird girl, she's a stay-at-home, hangs around me too much, fantasizes about boys but is never going to have a date because she's awkward and very plain. I wish she'd get out of the house once in a while, or go find her own place to live.' " He looked at us. "Would that devastate a young woman who idolized her father? Would that break her heart?"

No doubt about it. It broke my heart hearing it, and I'm not even sensitive. I said, "Do you think it was something like that?"

"Perhaps."

"But you don't know what it was. Why wouldn't she tell you?"

"Often, the subject can't bear to discuss it because to tell the therapist invites judgment or evaluation, which is not what the subject usually wants. The subject knows that the betrayal might not seem so total to an objective listener. Though sometimes the betrayal *is* enormous by any conventional standards—such as incest. It wasn't that, but I believe it was terrible by any standards."

I nodded as though I were following all of this, and I suppose I was. But the question remained, and I asked it. "Can you take a guess at what it was?"

"No, and I don't have to know what her father did to her—I had only to know that he did it, and that it was traumatic. A complete breach of trust after which nothing was ever the same between them.''

I tried to apply my own standards to this statement, but I couldn't. In my job, you *must* know who, what, where, when, how, and why. Maybe Moore knew at least when, so I asked him, "When? When did this happen?"

He replied, "About ten years ago."

"She was at West Point about ten years ago."

"That's correct. It happened to her in her second year at West Point."

"I see."

Cynthia asked, "And when did she begin to seek revenge? Not immediately."

"No, not immediately. She went through the expected stages of shock, denial, then feelings of depression, and finally anger. It wasn't until about six years ago that she decided she had to seek revenge rather than try to cope with it. She, in fact, became somewhat unstable, then obsessed with her theory that only revenge could make things right."

I asked, "And who put her on that path? You or Friedrich Nietzsche?"

"I refuse to take any responsibility for her campaign against her father, Mr. Brenner. As a professional, I did my job by listening."

Cynthia observed, "She might as well have spoken to a canary, then. Didn't you advise her that this was destructive?"

"Yes, of course. Clinically, she was doing the wrong thing, and I told her that. But I never promoted it, as Mr. Brenner just suggested."

I said, "If her campaign of revenge had been directed toward *you*, then you'd have been a little less clinically aloof."

He stared at me and said, "Understand, please, that sometimes the subject does not want to begin the healing process in a therapeutic way, but wants to hold the grudge and settle the score in his or her own way, usually in a like manner—you betrayed me, I'll betray you. You seduced my wife, I'll seduce your wife. Usually, to try to exact a revenge that is similar to the original crime is not realistic or possible. Sometimes it is. Conventional psychology will say that this is not healthy, but the average layperson knows that revenge can be cathartic and therapeutic. The problem is that revenge takes its own mental toll, and the avenger becomes the persecutor.''

I said to him, ''I understand what you're saying, Colonel Moore, though I'm wondering why you persist in speaking in clinical and general terms. Is that your way of distancing yourself from this tragedy? Your way of avoiding any personal responsibility?''

He didn't like that at all and replied, ''I resent the implication that I failed to try to help her, or that I encouraged her behavior.''

''Resent it or not,'' I informed him, ''it seems to be a strong suspicion in some quarters.''

''What do you expect from—'' He shrugged and said, ''Neither I, nor my work here, nor this school, nor my relationship with Ann Campbell, was very much appreciated or understood on this post.''

I said, ''I can relate to that. You know, I've seen some of Captain Campbell's video lectures, and I think you people are performing some vital functions. But maybe you were straying into areas that made people nervous.''

''Everything we do here is sanctioned by higher command.''

''I'm glad to hear that. But I think Ann Campbell took some of it out of the classroom and tried it on her own battlefield.''

Moore didn't respond to that.

I asked him, ''Do you know why Ann Campbell kept files of therapy sessions with criminals? Sex offenders?''

He thought a moment, then replied, ''I don't know that she did. But if she did, it was a private pursuit. There's hardly a psychologist here who doesn't have an outside project or interest. Most times it has something to do with a Ph.D. program.''

''Sounds reasonable.''

Cynthia asked him, ''How did you feel about her having sexual relations with multiple partners?''

He didn't reply at first, then said, ''Well . . . I . . . Who told you that?''

Cynthia said, ''Everybody but you.''

''You never asked.''

"I'm asking now. How did you personally feel about her having sexual relations with men she didn't care about just to get at her father?"

He coughed into his hand, then replied, "Well . . . I thought it was not wise, especially for the reasons she was doing it—"

"Were you jealous?"

"Of course not. I—"

Cynthia interrupted him again. "Did you feel betrayed?"

"Certainly not. We had a good, platonic, intellectual, and trusting relationship."

I wanted to ask him if that included staking her out naked on the ground, but I had to know *why* he did it. Actually, I thought I knew why now. And, beyond finding the killer, I could see now, based on what Moore had said so far about betrayal, that Ann Campbell's life and unhappiness needed to be understood.

I took a shot in the dark and said to him, "I understand that when you and Captain Campbell were in the Gulf, you proposed a psy-ops program called Operation Bonkers."

He replied, "I'm not at liberty to discuss that."

"Captain Campbell had great faith in the power of sex as a means to achieve apparently unrelated goals. Correct?"

"I . . . Yes, she did."

"As I said, I've seen her psy-ops lecture series on video, and I can see where she was coming from. Now, while I don't deny the power of sex, I see it as a force for good, as an expression of love and caring. But somehow, Ann Campbell got it wrong. Would you agree with that?"

He may have, but he replied, "Sex is neither good nor bad in itself. But it is true that some people—mostly women—use it as a tool, a weapon, to achieve their goals."

I turned to Cynthia. "Do you agree with that?"

She seemed a little annoyed, though I don't know whom she was annoyed at. She replied, however, "I agree that some women use sex, sometimes, as a weapon, but that is understood to be unacceptable behavior. In the case of Ann Campbell, she may have seen sex as her *only* weapon against some injustice, or against her feelings of powerlessness. I think, Colonel Moore, if you knew she was doing that, it was your ethical duty, not to mention your duty as her commanding officer, to try to stop it.''

Moore sort of stared at Cynthia with those beady little eyes and said, ''I was not in a position to stop anything.''

''Why not?'' she shot back. ''Are you an officer or a cabin boy? Were you her friend or not? And surely, since you weren't seduced by her charms, you could have reasoned with her. Or did you find her sexual experiments interesting in a clinical way? Or perhaps you were titillated by the knowledge that she had sex with multiple partners?''

Moore looked at me and said, ''I refuse to answer that or to speak to this woman.''

I informed him, ''You can't stand behind the Fifth Amendment until we read you your rights as an accused, which I have no intention of doing at this time. It's frustrating, I know. But we'll let the question pass for now, and I promise you that Ms. Sunhill will try to phrase her questions so that you don't mistake them for insubordination.''

Colonel Moore seemed to see no advantage in keeping up the moral indignation routine, so he nodded and sat back in his chair. The body language said, ''You're both beneath my contempt. Fire away.''

Cynthia got herself under control, and, in a nonadversarial tone of voice, asked him, ''When would Ann Campbell have considered the score even?''

Moore didn't look at Cynthia or at me, but replied in a toneless, professional voice, ''Unfortunately, only she knew that. Apparently, what she was doing to him was not enough to satisfy her. Part of the problem was General Campbell himself.'' Moore smiled, but it was more of a sneer, and said, ''This is a general who will not admit he's being damaged, let alone admit he's beaten and raise the white flag. To the best of my knowledge, he never asked for a cease-fire, to continue the military metaphor, nor did he ever ask for peace talks. He apparently felt that whatever he had done to her was canceled out by what she was doing to him.''

''In other words,'' Cynthia said, ''they were too stubborn to negotiate. He never apologized for his initial betrayal.''

''Well, he did, in a manner of speaking, but you can guess what sort of apology you'd get from such a man.''

Cynthia observed, ''It's too bad so many innocent people had to be hurt while these two fought it out.''

Moore replied, with some surprisingly normal insight, ''That's life, that's war. When has it been any different?''

Indeed so, I thought. Or, as Plato said, ''Only the dead have seen an end to war.''

Cynthia asked Colonel Moore, ''When you left home on the morning of the murder, did you notice that Ann Campbell's car was not in front of her house?''

He thought a moment, then said, ''I may have. Subconsciously.''

''Don't you normally take note of her car?''

''No.''

''So you don't ever know if your subordinate, neighbor, and friend is still home or on her way to the office.''

''Well, I suppose on most mornings I do.''

''Did you ever share a ride?''

''Sometimes.''

''Did you know that Captain Campbell had an appointment for breakfast with her parents that morning?''

''No . . . well, yes, now that you mention it. She did tell me that.''

''What was the purpose of this breakfast meeting?''

''Purpose?''

''Did the Campbells often get together to enjoy one another's company?''

''I suppose not.''

Cynthia said, ''It's my understanding, Colonel, that General Campbell gave his daughter an ultimatum regarding her behavior, and that Ann Campbell's reply to that ultimatum was to be given at that breakfast. Correct?''

Colonel Moore for the first time looked a bit uneasy, probably wondering how much we knew and from whom we knew it.

"Correct?"

"I . . . She did tell me that her father wanted to resolve this problem."

Cynthia was getting herself worked up again and said sharply, "Colonel, either she did or didn't tell you all about this. Either she did or didn't use words like ultimatum, court-martial, ordered therapy, and resignation from the service. Did she or didn't she confide completely in you, and did she or didn't she ask your advice?"

Colonel Moore was clearly angry again at Cynthia's tone, but he was also uneasy about this particular question, which had obviously touched on something that frightened him. He must have decided that we could not possibly know enough to hammer him on this, so he replied, "I've told you all I know. She never told me what he proposed, and she never asked my advice. I told you, as her therapist I listened, kept my questions to a minimum, and only gave advice when asked."

Cynthia replied, "I don't believe any man is capable of that amount of self-restraint with a woman he's known for six years."

"Then you don't understand therapy, Ms. Sunhill. I certainly offered advice in terms of her career, assignments, and such, and even personal advice regarding living quarters, vacations, and so forth. But the problems with her family were only discussed in therapy sessions—these were compartmentalized discussions that never spilled over into work or leisure time. This was our firm understanding and we never deviated from it. Medical doctors, for instance, don't appreciate friends asking them for a diagnosis on the golf course, and attorneys have similar rules about legal advice in bars. Mental health workers are no different."

Cynthia replied, "Thank you for that information, Colonel. I see you've thought about it. Am I to assume, then, that the deceased never had the opportunity to arrange a formal session with you to discuss this ultimatum and deadline?"

"That's correct."

"So, after all these years, when this heartache, misery, and anger are about to come to a head, one or both of you was too busy to talk about it."

"It was Ann herself who decided not to discuss it with me. We did, however, decide to meet after she'd spoken to her father. In fact, we were to meet yesterday afternoon."

Cynthia said, "I don't believe you, Colonel. I think there is a connection between the general's ultimatum and what happened to her, and you know what that connection is."

Colonel Moore stood. "I will not be called a liar."

Cynthia stood also and they glared at each other. Cynthia said, "We already know you're a liar."

Which was true. We knew that Moore had been on rifle range six with Ann Campbell, and I think Moore now realized we knew this. How else could we get away with abusing a full colonel? But we were about half a step over the threshold now, and that was far enough. I stood also. "Thank you for your time, Colonel. Don't bother to complain to Colonel Kent about us. One all-inclusive complaint is good enough for a week or so." I added, "I'm posting an MP at your door, sir, and if you attempt to shred any papers or carry anything out of here with you, you'll be placed under restraint and confined to post."

The man was shaking now, but I couldn't tell if it was from fright or rage, and I didn't care. He said, "I'm going to bring formal charges against both of you."

"I really wouldn't do that if I were you. We are your last best hope to avoid a noose—or is it a firing squad? I have to check. They just don't execute enough people for me to remember how they do it. But anyway, don't piss me off. You know what I'm talking about. Good day, Colonel."

And we left him standing there, contemplating his options, which definitely didn't include pissing me off.

CHAPTER TWENTY-THREE

Cynthia parked in the provost marshal's parking field a few spaces away from my Blazer. As we started toward the provost building, we saw three news vans and a group of people outside who were obviously journalists. They saw us coming, and we must have fit someone's description of the detectives in charge, because they moved toward us like a cloud of locusts. As I said, Hadley is an open post, so you can't keep the taxpaying citizens out, and you normally don't want to, but I didn't need this.

The first reporter to reach us, a well-dressed young man with coiffed hair, had a microphone, and the grubbier ones around him had pencils and pads. I was aware of cameras turned on us. The coiffed one asked me, "Are you Warrant Officer Brenner?" then put the microphone under my nose.

"No, sir," I replied, "I'm here to service the Coke machine." We kept walking, but this great cloud engulfed us as we continued toward the front doors.

A female reporter asked Cynthia, "Are you Warrant Officer Sunhill?"

"No, ma'am, I'm with the Coke guy."

But they weren't buying it, and the questions rained out of this cloud until we finally got to the steps of the provost building, where two huge MPs stood guard with M-16 rifles. I climbed the steps and turned to the crowd, who could go no further, and said, "Good morning."

The crowd of journalists became quiet, and I saw now three TV cameras and about a dozen photographers snapping away. I said, "The investigation into the death of Captain Ann Campbell is continuing. We have several leads, but no suspects. However, all the available resources of Fort Hadley, the Army Criminal Investigation Division, and the local civilian police have been mobilized, and we are working on the case in close cooperation. We will schedule a news conference in the near future." Bullshit.

Boom! The storm of questions broke, and I could hear a few of them: "Wasn't she raped, too?" "Was she found tied up and naked?" "Was she strangled?" "Who do you think did it?" "Isn't this the second rape here within a week?" And interestingly, "Have you questioned her boyfriend, the chief of police's son?" and so on.

I replied, "All your questions will be answered at the news conference."

Cynthia and I went inside the building, where we bumped into Colonel Kent, who looked unhappy and agitated. He said, "I can't get them to leave."

"No, you can't. That's what I love about this country."

"But they're confined to main post, but that includes Beaumont House, and I had to put a dozen MPs there. They can't go out to the rifle ranges or Jordan Field—I have MPs on the road. But they're snooping around all over the damn place."

"Maybe they'll have better luck than we did."

"I don't like this." He asked me, "Anything new?"

"We spoke to Colonel Fowler and Colonel Moore. I'd like you to send two MPs to Colonel Moore's office, ASAP, and baby-sit him. He may not use his shredder, and he may not take anything from his office."

"Okay. I'll get on that." He asked, "Are you going to arrest Moore?"

I replied, "We're still trying to get a psychological autopsy of the deceased from him."

"Who cares?"

"Well," I replied, "Ms. Sunhill and I do."

"Why? What does that have to do with Colonel Moore?"

"Well, the more I learn, the less motivation I can find for Colonel Moore to kill his subordinate. On the other hand, I see that other people could have strong motives."

Kent looked exasperated, and he said, "Paul, I understand what you're doing up to a point, and so will everyone else. But you've passed that point, and if you don't arrest Moore now and he turns out to be the killer, and the FBI arrests him, then you look really stupid."

"I know that, Bill. But if I do arrest him and he's not the killer, I look worse than stupid."

"Show some balls."

"Fuck you."

"Hey! You're speaking to a superior officer."

"Fuck you, *sir*." I turned and walked down the hall toward our office. Cynthia followed, but Kent did not.

In our office, we were greeted by a stack of white telephone messages, a pile of reports from forensic and the coroner, and other pieces of paper that appeared to be "read and initial" internal memos, half of which didn't concern me. The Army could screw up your pay records, send your furniture to Alaska and your family to Japan, and lose all track of your leave time—but if you reported into someplace on temporary duty, you immediately got on the distribution list for bullshit memos even if you were working undercover with an assumed identity in a borrowed office.

Cynthia commented, "That wasn't a smart thing to do."

"You mean him telling me to show some balls? No, it wasn't."

"Well, that wasn't smart of him, either. But I mean you telling him, quote, fuck you, unquote."

"No problem." I leafed through the stack of telephone messages.

Cynthia stayed silent a moment, then said, "Well, but he did do something wrong, didn't he?"

"You got that right. And he knows it."

"Still . . . you don't have to rub his face in it. If nothing else, we need him even if he is damaged goods."

I looked up from the phone messages and said, "I don't have a lot of compassion for an officer who breaks a trust."

"Except if her name is Ann Campbell."

I refused to respond to that.

"Anyway, how about some coffee and donuts?"

"Sounds good."

Cynthia pushed the intercom button and asked for Specialist Baker to report.

I sat down and opened Ann Campbell's medical file, which was exceedingly thin for her years in service, leading me to believe that she used civilian doctors. There was, however, a gynecological report dating back to her entrance physical at West Point, and a doctor had noted, "H. imperforatus." I showed it to Cynthia and asked, "Does that mean an intact hymen?"

"Yes, intact and without any opening. But it is not absolute evidence of virginity, though it's very likely that nothing very big ever got that far."

"So we can rule out her father raping her when she was a young girl."

"Well, pretty much. But we can't rule out other forms of sex abuse." She added, "But what Colonel Moore said seemed to have the ring of truth. Whatever her father did to her, he did it to her in her second year at West Point, and I doubt if he could rape his twenty-year-old daughter at West Point . . . but it's interesting that she was probably a virgin when she got there. Any other gynecological reports in there?"

I looked but saw none. I said, "They are strangely missing. I suspect she used private doctors whenever she could."

"Right. You don't go that long without seeing a gynecologist." She thought a moment, then said, "Why do I think that whatever happened to her at West Point was sexual?"

"Because it fits. Something to do with an eye for an eye."

"We know it had to do with her father . . . maybe he forced her on some superior officer, or maybe . . . ."

266

"Right. We're getting close. But let's wait until we know more."
I gave the medical file to Cynthia and said, "Read the psychiatrist's report in the back of the file."

Specialist Baker came in and I introduced her to Cynthia, but they'd already met. I asked Baker, "What do you think?"

"Sir?"

"Who did it?"

She shrugged.

Cynthia looked up from the file and asked Baker, "A boyfriend or a stranger?"

She thought a moment and replied, "A boyfriend." Baker added, "But she had lots of them."

"Really?" I asked her, "Did anyone here in the provost office or anyone else ask you to give them any information on this case?"

"Yes, sir."

"Who?"

"Well, I've been taking calls for both of you all yesterday and this morning, and everyone keeps asking questions. A Colonel Moore, the victim's boss, plus Colonel Fowler, the post adjutant, Major Bowes, the CID commander, Police Chief Yardley from Midland, and a whole bunch of other people, including reporters. I wrote all the calls down on the slips."

"And they were all nosy?"

"Yes, sir. But I just told them to speak to either of you."

"Okay. Tell me, did anyone here in the provost marshal's office say anything to you that we should know about?"

Specialist Baker understood the question, wrestled with it, and finally said, "There's a lot of talk going around here, a lot of rumors, gossip, and things that may or may not be true."

"Right. I figured that out already, Baker. This is privileged information, and I'll guarantee you not only anonymity but a transfer to anyplace in the universe you want to go. Hawaii, Japan, Germany, California. You name it. Okay?"

"Yes, sir . . ."

"Tell me first about Colonel Kent. What's the news around the office?"

267

She cleared her throat and said, "Well . . . there were always rumors that Colonel Kent and Captain Campbell were . . ."

"Fucking. We know that. What else?"

"Well . . . that's about it."

"How long have you been stationed here?"

"Only a few months."

"Do you think he was in love with her?"

She shrugged. "Nobody said that. I mean, you couldn't tell because they'd be real cool when they were together. But you could sort of tell something was going on."

"She'd come here to his office?"

"Sometimes, usually during the day. At night, he'd go to her office. The MP patrols would see his car heading to the Psy-Ops School, and they'd radio a niner-niner—you know, all points—and say something like 'Randy Six is inbound to Honey One.' It was sort of a joke, you know, but Colonel Kent monitored his own car radio, for sure, and he figured out that these made-up call signs referred to him and Captain Campbell, but the callers never ID'ed themselves and always disguised their voice, so he couldn't do anything about it. I don't think he would have done anything anyway, because that would just make the rumors worse." She added, "You can't get away with much on a small base, and with the MPs, they see a lot of what's going on like that, but if it's not against the law, or against regulations, they don't make too much of it, especially if it has to do with ranking officers." She added, "Especially if it's the boss."

Well, I was glad I asked. I had another question. "Baker, Captain Campbell was the post duty officer on the night she was murdered. You know that?"

"Yes."

"Was it Colonel Kent's habit to work late on those nights when Captain Campbell had night duty?"

"Well . . . that's what I hear."

"Do you know if Colonel Kent was here on the night she was murdered?"

"He was. I wasn't here, but the word going around is that he left the office about 1800 hours and returned about 2100 hours, then worked until about midnight, then left. The personnel who were on duty said he was spotted in his staff car cruising past the Post Headquarters, then he went up to Bethany Hill where he lives."

"I see. And was it common knowledge that Mrs. Kent was out of town?"

"Yes, sir, it was."

"And I assume at least one MP patrol cruises Bethany Hill each evening."

"Yes, sir. At least one each night."

"And what was the word on Randy Six that night?"

She suppressed a smile. "Well . . . no visitors, and no one saw his staff car leave the driveway all night. But he could have left in his POV and no one noticed."

Or he could have used his wife's car, though I didn't see any car in his driveway when I drove past this morning. But there was a garage out to the rear of the property. I said to Baker, "You understand the nature of these questions?"

"Oh, yes."

"This will not become part of the office conversations."

"No, sir."

"Okay, thanks. Have someone send in coffee and donuts or something."

"Yes, sir." She turned and left.

Cynthia and I sat in silence a moment, then she said, "That was a good idea."

"Thanks, but I can't place a lot of confidence in office scuttlebutt."

"But this is MP Headquarters."

"True." I said, "You see why I'm annoyed at Kent. The stupid bastard has become a laughingstock in his own command."

"I see that."

"I mean, forget morality if you want. You never, never diddle where you work. People *laugh*."

"I'll bet they laughed at us in Brussels and Falls Church."

"I'm certain they did."

"How embarrassing."

"Right. I hope you learned your lesson."

She smiled, then looked at me. "What were you trying to establish with Baker? That Kent is the butt of office jokes?"

I shrugged.

She said, "The distance from Bethany Hill to rifle range six is about five or six miles. You could drive there in under ten minutes, even if you did the last few miles without lights, because there was bright moonlight that night."

"The thought had occurred to me. And you could drive from Beaumont House to range six in a little over ten minutes, if you pushed it."

She nodded. "Facts to keep in mind." She looked at the medical file in front of her and said, "What do you make of this psychiatrist's report?"

I replied, "Ann Campbell had suffered some sort of trauma and wasn't sharing it with anyone. What do *you* think?"

"Same. There's not much to go on in this report, but I'd guess that the problem was not stress or fatigue, but a single event that traumatized her and led somehow to her betrayal by her father. In other words, Daddy was not there for her when whatever happened, happened. Does that all fit?"

"Seems to." I thought a moment, then said, "I keep thinking that it's sexual, and that it's something to do with a guy who had one or two more stars than Daddy, and that Daddy backed off and convinced his daughter to do the same."

"Something like that."

I added, "We have to get her service academy file, but I would not be at all surprised if we found it contained nothing relevant to what Moore said."

The coffee came in a big stainless-steel galley pitcher, with a plastic tray of donuts, cold, stale, and greasy. Cynthia and I dug in and talked awhile.

The phone had been ringing almost constantly, but Specialist Baker or someone else had been picking up. This time, however, when the phone rang, the intercom buzzed, and Specialist Baker said, "Colonel Hellmann."

"I'll take it." I put the phone on two-way speaker so Cynthia could hear and speak, and said into the microphone, "Brenner and Sunhill, sir."

"Ah, we speak of little else here."

Karl actually sounded light this morning, which throws me off a bit. I replied, "Is that so?"

"It is. Are you both well?"

Cynthia replied, "Very well, Colonel."

"Good. I've received some complaints about your behavior."

I replied, "Then you know we're doing our job."

He replied, "I know you're starting to annoy people, which is sometimes an indication that you're doing a good job. But I called to see if you know that the case is being taken out of your hands."

"Yes, sir, we know."

"I did what I could to keep it a CID matter, but the FBI has more influence than I do."

"We may have this case completed soon, anyway," I assured him.

"Really? Well, I hope you can wrap it up within the next fifteen minutes, because the FBI has jumped the gun and the task force has already arrived at Fort Hadley."

"They should stay out of our way until 1200 hours tomorrow."

"They should, but you'll trip over a few of them."

I said, "I get the impression you're relieved to be out of this."

"What gives you that impression, Mr. Brenner?"

"Your tone of voice, sir. You sound happy."

There was a pause, then he said, "You should be happy, too. Nothing good could come of this case for you or for the CID."

"That's not how I decide what cases to take." Actually, it was, sometimes. But sometimes you took a case because you felt it was your duty to do so, or because you felt a personal attachment to it,

271

or simply because you wanted to be the person to catch a particularly nasty bad guy. I informed Karl, "I'm going to solve the case and bring credit and glory on all of us."

"Well, I respect that, Paul. I do. On the other hand, the potential for discredit and disaster is great." He added, "The FBI has given us an out. The idiots want the case."

"So do the two idiots here."

Karl changed the subject and said, "Forensic tells me you have a suspect. A Colonel Moore."

"We have an individual who was at the scene of the crime. He is a suspect, yes."

"But you haven't arrested him."

"No, sir."

"They want you to."

"Who are *they*?"

"You know. Well, do what you think best. I never interfere."

"Hardly ever."

"Any more suspects?"

"No, sir, but I was just about to dial 1-800-SUSPECT when you called."

Silence, then, "Ms. Sunhill, in your report you said the rape may have in fact been a consensual act."

"Yes, sir."

"So that might indicate that the perpetrator was a friend. Wouldn't it?"

"Yes, sir."

"But not her superior officer, Colonel Moore, who was apparently at the scene?"

Cynthia glanced at me, then replied, "It's become very complex, Colonel." She added, "Captain Campbell had many boyfriends."

"Yes, I'm hearing that." He added, in a rare moment of comprehension, "It's a mess out there, isn't it?"

"Yes, sir."

Hellmann said, "Paul, you haven't made contact with Major Bowes yet."

272

"No, Colonel. Major Bowes may be part of the problem here. That's only hearsay, but you might think about calling him back to Falls Church for a chat."

"I see." He stayed silent a moment, then said, "The CID doesn't need that."

"No."

"Are you engaging in damage control?"

"No," I replied, "that's not my job." I added with some satisfaction, "I think I mentioned to you that this was going to be a sensitive case."

Silence, then, "I only care about the reputation of my officers."

"Then get Bowes out of here."

"All right. Can you fax me a report before 1800 hours?"

"No, Colonel, there will be no further reports. We're extremely busy trying to find a murderer. We'll report to you in person as soon as they boot us out of here."

"Understood. Is there anything here we can do for you?"

Cynthia replied, "Yes, sir. We have some information that Captain Campbell and her father had a serious falling-out while she was in her second year at West Point. Whatever happened then is possibly related to this case. It's possible that what happened may have been public, or at least well known at the academy, or perhaps in the civilian community around West Point."

"All right, I'll put some people on it immediately. Academy records, local newspapers, people who were there at the time, and I'll contact the Criminal Investigation Records Depository in Baltimore. Correct?"

"Yes, sir. And speed is very important," Cynthia reminded him.

I said to him, "We're sort of circling around some sensitive issues, Karl, but eventually we have to go right to the heart of the problem. I'm talking about the general."

"Understood. Do what you have to do. I'm behind you."

"Right. Do you want to stand in front of me?"

Silence again, then, "I'll fly down if you wish."

Cynthia and I glanced at each other, then I said, "We appreciate that, Karl, but if you just hang tough with the boys in the Pentagon, we'd like that.''

''I'll do what I can.''

''Thanks.''

He asked, ''Are you two working well together?''

Neither Cynthia nor I responded immediately, but then she said, ''Very well.''

''Good. There's nothing like intense heat to forge a strong working team.''

I said to Cynthia so that Karl could hear, ''Tell him you apologized to me for Brussels, and that it was all your fault.''

She smiled, then said into the speaker, ''That's correct, Colonel.''

''Noted. I'll get back to you ASAP with the West Point information if I have any luck.''

''Fine.''

''On another subject, I'm not pleased with your handling of the arms deal case.''

''Then turn it over to the FBI.''

Silence, then, ''I have your personnel file in front of me, Paul. You have over twenty years in.''

''I can't live on full pay. How am I going to live on half pay?''

''I'm concerned for you. I don't like to lose good men, but I can sense that you're tired. Do you want a staff job here in Falls Church?''

''You mean in the same building with you?''

''Consider your options.'' He added, ''I'm here if you just want to talk. Good luck.'' He hung up and I shut off the speaker and said to Cynthia, ''He sounded almost human.''

''He's worried, Paul.''

''Well, he should be.''

CHAPTER TWENTY-FOUR

We spent the next hour going through the paperwork on the desk, returning and making phone calls, including trying to pin down Colonel Fowler regarding the appointments with his wife, Mrs. Campbell, and General Campbell.

I called Grace Dixon, our computer expert, who had flown in from Falls Church and was at Jordan Field trying to get Ann Campbell's PC to give up its files. "How's it going, Grace?"

"Going fine now. Some of the computer files were encrypted. We finally found a list of passwords in her home study—inside a cookbook—and I'm pulling up all sorts of things."

I motioned to Cynthia to pick up the other receiver and said to Grace, "What kinds of things?"

"Some personal letters, a list of people and phone numbers, but the major entry is a diary. Pretty steamy stuff, Paul. Names, dates, places, sexual practices and preferences. I guess that's what you're looking for."

"I guess so. Give me some names, Grace."

"Okay . . . hold on . . . Lieutenant Peter Elby . . . Colonel William Kent . . . Major Ted Bowes . . ." And on she went, reading off about two dozen names, some of which I knew, such as Colonel Michael Weems, the staff judge advocate, Captain Frank Swick, the medical officer, and Major Arnold Eames, the head chaplain, of all people, and some of whom I didn't know, but they were all military and probably all in some way in the general's immediate or extended retinue. But then Grace read, "Wes Yardley, Burt Yardley—"

"Burt?"

"Yes. I guess she liked the family."

Cynthia and I glanced at each other. I said to Grace, "Right . . . and you didn't come across the name of Fowler?"

"Not yet."

"Charles Moore?"

"Yes . . . but he appears only as someone she has sessions with. I guess he's a shrink. This diary goes back about two years and begins, 'Report for duty at Daddy's fort. Operation Trojan Horse begins.' " She added, "This is really crazy stuff, Paul."

"Give me an example of crazy."

"Well, I'll read this . . . It's the last entry . . . Okay, I'm reading from the monitor. It says, '14 August—invited Daddy's new operations officer, Colonel Sam Davis, to stop by my house for a get-acquainted drink. Sam is about fifty, a little heavy but not too bad-looking, married with grown children, one of whom still lives with him on Bethany Hill. He seems to be a devoted family man, and his wife, Sarah, whom I met at the new officer reception, is quite attractive. Sam got to my house at 1900 hours, we had a few stiff drinks in my living room, then I put on some slow music and asked him to help me practice a new dance step. He was nervous, but he'd had enough drinks to give him courage. He was wearing summer greens, but I'd put on a white cotton shift, sans bra, and I was barefoot, and, within a few minutes, we were nuzzling, and the guy had . . . the guy had . . .' "

"Grace?"

" 'Had an erection . . .' "

"Ah-ha, one of those." Grace Dixon is a middle-aged, matronly woman, a civilian employee with a happy home life, and most of her work is done for the CID's Contracts Fraud Unit, so it's usually numbers and double entries that she's after. This was a real treat for her. But maybe not. "Go on."

"Okay . . . where was I?"

"Erection."

"Yes . . . 'and I made sure I brushed it with my fingers, then he finally took the initiative and slipped my shoulder straps off, and I wiggled out of the shift and we danced, with me in my panties. Sam was somewhere between ecstasy and fainting out of fear, but I took him by the hand and led him into the basement. Drinks included, the whole seduction took less than twenty minutes. I showed him into my room in the basement and slipped off my panties . . .' "

"You still there, Grace?"

"Yes . . . my goodness . . . is this real or fantasy?"

I replied, "For Sam Davis, it started as adventureland and went right to fantasyland."

"She takes all these men into the basement. She has some sort of room down there with sexual devices . . ."

"Really? Go on."

"Oh . . . let's see . . ." She continued reading from the monitor, " 'I put on some music in the room, then knelt down and unzipped his fly. The guy was hard as a rock, and I was afraid he was going to come if I just touched it. I told him he could do anything he wanted to me and told him to look around the room to see what interested him. He was so hot he was just trying to pull his pants off, but I told him I wanted him to stay dressed, to make me his slave, to order me around, to use the strap on me or whatever, but it was his first time and he wasn't very cooperative about my needs. Finally, he just bent me over the bed, and, with his pants down, he entered me vaginally from behind and came in about two seconds.' " Grace said, "Do I hear heavy breathing on the line?"

"That's Cynthia," I assured her. "Is that the end of the entry?"

"No, she goes on to say, 'I took his clothes off, and we showered together. He was anxious to get going and kept apologizing for coming so fast. I made him lie down on the bed naked and put a silly pig mask on his face, then took two shots with a Polaroid and gave one to him, and we joked about it, and he was too polite to ask for the other photo, but you could tell he was nervous about the whole thing. I told him I'd like to see him again and assured him

277

that this was our little secret. He got dressed, and I showed him upstairs to the front door. I was still naked. He looked panicky, like he was afraid to even go outside and be seen leaving my place, and he definitely wasn't going straight home with his heart still pounding and his knees shaking. Finally, he said that he didn't want to see me again, and would I mind getting that photo, so I went into my crying routine, and he hugged and kissed me, and I had to wipe lipstick off his face. He left and I watched him from the window, racing to his car and glancing over his shoulder. The next time, I'll ask him to bring me a case of wine and see how fast he can run up the walk with that in his hands.' "

Grace said, "This has got to be made up."

"Grace, you will not breathe a word of this to anyone, you will not print out a word of anything, and you will guard those computer passwords with your life. Understand?"

"Understand."

I thought a moment, then said, "Correction. Print out a few Burt Yardley meetings, put them in a sealed envelope, and have them sent to me here, ASAP."

"Understood." She said, "There are over thirty different men mentioned here over a two-year period. Do single women sleep with thirty different men in twenty-four months?"

"How would I know?"

"And the way she describes these encounters . . . my Lord, she's got a problem—had a problem—with men. I mean, she makes them abuse her, but she's controlling them and thinking they're complete fools."

"She was right about that." I said to her, "Pull up recent entries for Colonel Weems and Major Bowes and tell me if it's hot stuff."

"Okay . . . hold on . . ." She said, "Here's Weems, 31 July, this year . . . Yes, very steamy stuff. You want me to read it?"

"No, I can't handle much more. How about Bowes?"

"Right . . . 4 August, this year . . . wow! This guy is weird. Who is this?"

"Our local CID man."

278

"Oh . . . no!"

"Yes. Mum's the word. Speak to you later, Grace." I hung up.

Cynthia and I sat silently for a moment, then I said, "Well . . . if I was a married colonel, the general's new operations officer, and the general's beautiful daughter invited me over for a drink . . ."

"Yes?"

"I'd run."

"Which way?"

I smiled, then said, "Couldn't he have held out for more than twenty minutes?"

Cynthia commented, "You know, Paul, I understand from my experience in rape cases that some men have difficulty controlling their urges. But you guys should try to think with the big head, not the little head."

"A rising cock has no conscience, Cynthia." I added, "In the case of Sam Davis, don't blame the victim."

"You're right. But I think she was a victim, too. This is not about sex."

"No, it's not. It's about Operation Trojan Horse." I thought a moment, then said, "Well, we can assume that Burt Yardley knows where the basement playroom is."

"Probably," Cynthia agreed. "But I doubt that she brought Wes Yardley down there."

"That's true. He was the boyfriend. He had no real power, on or off post, and he isn't married, so he couldn't be compromised or blackmailed. But I wonder if Wes knew about his old papa dipping into the same honeypot."

"You have a way with words, Paul."

Specialist Baker came in and informed us, "Police Chief Yardley and Police Officer Yardley are here to see you."

I replied, "I'll let you know when I want to see them."

"Yes, sir."

"Someone from the CID detachment at Jordan Field will be here shortly with an envelope. Bring it in as soon as it arrives."

"Yes, sir." She left.

I said to Cynthia, "We're going to have to separate Burt and Wes at some point."

"Right."

I stood. "I have to go see a buddy of mine in the lockup." I left the office and followed a maze of intersecting corridors to the holding cells. I found Dalbert Elkins in the same corner cell where I'd put him. He was lying on the cot, reading a hunting and fishing magazine. They hadn't given him a uniform, and he was still in his shorts, T-shirt, and sandals. I said, "Hello, Dalbert."

He looked up, then sat up, then stood up. "Oh . . . hi . . ."

"They treating you okay, buddy?"

"Yeah."

"You mean, yes, sir."

"Yes, sir."

"Did you write a good confession?"

He nodded. He looked less frightened now, and more sulky. It is my policy, shared by most CID criminal investigators, to visit the people you've locked up in jail. You make sure the MPs or the stockade guards are not abusing them, which unfortunately happens in military confinement from time to time. You make sure their families are okay, they have some money for sundries, have writing materials and stamps, and you give them a friendly ear. I asked Elkins about all these things, and he assured me he was not being mistreated, and he had everything he needed. I asked him, "You want to stay here, or do you want to go to the stockade?"

"Here."

"You can play baseball in the stockade."

"Here."

"Are you being cooperative with the CID guys?"

"Yes, sir."

"Do you want a lawyer?"

"Well . . ."

"You have a right to be represented by counsel. You may have a JAG lawyer at no expense to you, or you may hire a civilian attorney."

"Well . . . what do you think?"

"I think if you get a lawyer, you'll make me very angry."

"Yes, sir."

"Do you feel like the dumbest, sorriest son-of-a-bitch who ever lived?"

"Yes, sir."

"You're going to make it right."

"Yes, sir."

"My name is Warrant Officer Brenner, by the way. I was just kidding about that Sergeant White stuff. If you need anything, or your family wants to contact anyone, you ask for Brenner. If anyone messes you around, you tell them you're being watched over by Brenner. Okay?"

"Yes, sir . . . thanks."

"I won't be around too much longer, but I'll get you 'another CID guy to watch after you. I'll try to get you out of jail and confined to barracks, but I'm going to tell you, Dalbert, if you run away, I'll come and find you, and kill you. Understood?"

"Yes, sir. If you get me out of here, I'll stay put. Promise."

"And if you don't, I'll kill you. Promise."

"Yes, sir."

I went back to my office, where Cynthia was reading Ann Campbell's personnel file. I called the local CID and got hold of a Captain Anders. We discussed Dalbert Elkins awhile, and I recommended confinement to barracks. Anders seemed hesitant, but agreed if I would sign a recommendation for release. I said I would and asked to speak to Major Bowes. While I waited, I wondered, *Why do I stick my neck out for people I put in jail?* I have to find a new line of work, something not so exciting.

As I scribbled out a recommendation for release from confinement, Major Bowes came on the line. "Bowes here."

"Good morning, Major."

"What is it, Brenner?"

I'd never worked with or met this guy, and I didn't know anything about him except that he was commander of the Fort Hadley CID detachment, and that he was a steamy entry in Ann Campbell's diary.

"Brenner?"

"Yes, sir. I just wanted to touch base with you."

"This is not a baseball game. What can I do for you?"

"I assume you're annoyed because I've asked that you be kept off this case."

"You assume right, Mister."

"Yes, sir. Actually, it was Colonel Kent who decided to use an outside investigator." And he was probably sorry he'd asked.

"Colonel Kent does not make those kinds of decisions. And you should have paid a courtesy call on me."

"Yes, sir. I've been busy. The phone works both ways."

"Watch yourself, Chief."

"How is Mrs. Bowes?"

"What?"

"Are you married, Major?"

Silence, then, "What kind of question is that?"

"That is an official question, pertaining to the murder investigation. That's what kind of question it is. Please answer it."

Silence again, then, "Yes, I'm married."

"Does Mrs. Bowes know about Captain Campbell?"

"What the hell—?"

Cynthia looked up from what she was doing.

I said to Bowes, "Major, I have proof of your sexual involvement with Ann Campbell, proof that you visited her at her home and had sexual relations with her of an illicit nature in the basement bedroom of her home, and that you engaged in and performed sexual acts that are a violation of the Uniform Code of Military Justice, as well as being against the law in the state of Georgia." Actually, I didn't know what was against the law in Georgia, and I didn't know yet what Bowes and Ann Campbell engaged in, but who cares? Throw enough bullshit and some of it's going to stick.

Cynthia picked up the phone and listened, but Bowes was not talking.

I waited through the silence, then Bowes said, "I think we should meet."

"I'm kind of overbooked, Major. Someone from Falls Church will be calling you if they haven't already. Have a bag packed. Good day."

"Wait! We should talk about this. Who knows about this? I think I can explain this—"

"Explain the photos I found in her basement."

"I . . . I can't be linked to those photos . . ."

"The mask didn't hide your dick or your ass, Major. Maybe I'll have your wife pick you out of the photos."

"Don't threaten me."

"You're a cop, for Christ's sake. And an officer. What the hell's wrong with you?"

After about five seconds, he replied, "I fucked up."

"You sure did."

"Can you cover me?"

"I suggest you make a full confession and throw yourself on the mercy of the bosses in Falls Church. Bluff a little, and threaten to go public. Cut a deal, take half pay, and get out."

"Right. Thanks for nothing."

"Hey, I didn't fuck the general's daughter."

"You would have."

"Major, regarding on-the-job sex, the thing to remember is you never get your meat where you get your bread."

"Depends on the meat."

"Was it worth it?"

He laughed. "Hell, yeah. I'll tell you about it someday."

"I'll read about it in her diary. Have a good day, Major." I hung up.

Cynthia put down the phone and said, "Why were you being so hard on him? These men didn't commit a real crime, Paul."

"No, but they're stupid. I'm sick of stupid men."

"I think you're jealous."

"Keep your opinions to yourself."

"Yes, sir."

I rubbed my temples. "Sorry. Just tired."

"Do you want to see the Yardley boys now?"

"No. Fuck 'em. Let them cool their heels." I picked up the telephone and called the staff judge advocate's office and asked to speak to Colonel Weems, the commanding officer. I got his clerk-typist, a man who wanted to know my business. I said, "Tell Colonel Weems this has to do with the murder case."

"Yes, sir."

Cynthia picked up her extension and said to me, "Be nice."

Colonel Weems got on the line and inquired, "Are you the investigating officer in charge?"

"Yes, sir."

"Good. I've been instructed to draw up a charge sheet against Colonel Charles Moore, and I need some information."

"Well, here's your first piece of information, Colonel. Colonel Moore is not to be charged until I say so."

"Excuse me, Mr. Brenner, but I've received these instructions from the Pentagon."

"I don't care if you received them from Douglas MacArthur's ghost." Army lawyers, even colonels, can be pushed around a little because, like Army doctors, psychologists, and such, their rank is basically a pay grade, and they know they shouldn't take it too seriously. In fact, they should all be warrant officers, like I am, and they'd be much happier, and so would everyone else. I said to him, "Your name has come up in connection with that of the victim."

"Excuse me?"

"You married, Colonel?"

"Yes . . ."

"You want to stay married?"

"What the hell are you talking about?"

"I have information that you were sexually involved with the victim, that you committed offenses under the Uniform Code of Military Justice, to wit: Article 125, unnatural carnal copulation, plus Article 133, conduct unbecoming an officer and a gentleman, and Article 134, disorders and neglects to the prejudice of good order and discipline, and conduct of a nature to bring discredit upon the armed forces." I asked him, "How's that, Counselor?"

"That's not true."

"Do you know how you can tell when a lawyer is lying? No? His lips move."

He didn't appreciate the joke, and said, "You'd better have damn good evidence to back that up."

Spoken like a true lawyer. I said, "Do you know what three hundred lawyers at the bottom of the ocean are called? No? A good start."

"Mr. Brenner—"

"Have you lost any sleep over that basement playroom? I found it, and you're in a videotape." Maybe.

"I was never . . . I . . ."

"Polaroid photos."

"I . . ."

"And in her diary."

"Oh . . ."

"Look, Colonel, I don't care, but you really can't be involved with this case. Don't compound your problem. Call the judge advocate general, or better yet, fly to Washington and ask to be relieved of your command. Draw up a charge sheet on yourself or something. Meanwhile, turn this over to someone who kept his dick in his pants. No, better yet, who's the ranking woman on your staff?"

"Uh . . . Major Goodwin . . ."

"She's in charge of the Campbell case."

"You can't give me orders—"

"Colonel, if they could bust officers, you'd be a PFC tomorrow. In any case, by next month you'll be looking for a job in a small firm, or you'll be the attorney-in-residence at Leavenworth. Don't stonewall this. Cut a deal while you can. You may be called as a witness."

"To what?"

"I'll think about it. Have a good day." I hung up.

Cynthia put down the phone and inquired, "Have you caused enough misery for one day?"

"I told them to have a good day."

"Paul, you're going a little overboard. I realize you hold most of the cards—"

"I have this post by its collective balls."

"Right. But you're exceeding your authority."

"But not my power."

"Take it easy. It's not personal."

"Okay . . . I'm just angry. I mean, what the hell is the officer code about? We've sworn to do our duty, to uphold high standards of morality, integrity, and ethics, and we've agreed that our word is our bond. So now we find out that about thirty guys threw it all away, for what?"

"Pussy."

I couldn't help but laugh. "Right. Pussy. But it was pussy from hell."

"We're not so pure, either."

"We never compromised our duty."

"This is a murder case, not an ethics inquiry. One thing at a time."

"Right. Send in the clowns."

Cynthia called Baker on the intercom and said, "Send in the . . . civilian gentlemen."

"Yes, ma'am."

Cynthia said to me, "Now calm down."

"I'm not angry at those bozos. They're civilians."

The door opened, and Specialist Baker announced, "Chief Yardley and Officer Yardley."

Cynthia and I stood as the Yardleys, dressed in tan uniforms, came into the office. Burt Yardley said, "Don't appreciate bein' kept waitin'. But we'll let that slide." He looked around the small room and commented, "Hell, I got holdin' cells bigger an' nicer than this."

"So do we," I informed him. "I'll show you one."

He laughed and said, "This here's my son Wes. Wes, meet Miss Sunhill and Mr. Brenner."

Wes Yardley was a tall, extremely lean man of about twenty-five, with long swept-back hair that would have gotten him in trouble on most police forces, except the one he was on. We didn't shake hands, but he did touch his cowboy hat and nod to Cynthia.

The southern male doesn't usually remove his hat indoors when he's calling on inferiors or peers, because to arrive with his hat literally in his hand is to admit he's in the presence of social superiors. It all goes back to plantation houses, gentlemen, sharecroppers, slaves, white trash, good families and bad families, and so on. I don't quite get it, but the Army is heavy on hat rules, too, so I respect the local customs.

Lacking enough chairs, we all remained standing. Burt Yardley said to me, "Hey, I got all your stuff packed nice and neat in my office. You come on down and pick it up any ol' time."

"That's very good of you."

Wes sort of smirked, and I wanted to bury my fist in his bony face. The guy looked hyperactive, sort of jiggling around, like he was born with two thyroids.

I said to Burt, "Did you bring the government property with you?"

"Sure did. Don't need no trouble with the government. I gave it all to your little girl out there. That's sort of a peace offering, Paul. Can I call you Paul?"

"Sure thing, Burt."

"Good. And I'm thinkin' about lettin' you into the deceased's house."

"I'm real pleased, Burt."

"Now, you want to talk to my son about this business?" He looked at Wes and said, "Tell these people everything you know about that girl."

Cynthia said, "She was a woman, an officer in the United States Army. Specialist Baker is also a woman, a soldier in the United States Army."

287

Burt did a little bow and touched his hat. "I'm sorry, ma'am."

I really felt like pulling my Glock on these two yahoos, and I would have painted them red in a heartbeat, except that I had a short deadline on this case.

Anyway, Wes started his spiel. "Yeah, I was seein' Ann now and then, but I seen other women, too, and she was seein' other men, and neither of us took it real personal. The night she was killed, I was ridin' patrol in North Midland, midnight-to-eight shift, and I got about a dozen people who seen me, includin' my partner and gas station guys, 7-Eleven guys, and like that. So that's all you got to know."

"Thank you, Officer Yardley."

No one spoke for a few seconds, then Cynthia asked Wes, "Are you upset over Ann Campbell's death?"

He seemed to think that over, then replied, "Yes, ma'am."

I asked him, "Can I get you a sedative or something?"

Burt laughed and said to his son, "Forgot to tell you, boy, this here guy's real funny."

I said to Burt, "I'd like to speak to you alone."

"Anything you got to say, you can say in front of my boy."

"Not everything, Chief."

He looked at me a moment. "Well . . ." He said to his son, "I'm gonna leave you alone with this young lady, Wes, and you behave now." He laughed. "She don't know what a mover you are. Probably thinks you just fell off the turnip truck."

On that note, Burt and I left the office, and I found an empty interview room. We sat across a long table, and Burt said, "Damned reporters out there are gettin' too damn nosy. Startin' to ask about these rumors that the general's daughter got around. Understand?"

I didn't recall a single question of that nature from the press, but I said, "Law officers don't engage in speculation in front of the press."

"Hell, no. Me and the general get along fine, and I wouldn't want to see his girl talked about after she's dead."

"If you're leading up to something, Chief, spit it out."

"Well, it occurs to me that maybe people think the Army CID

288

pulled a fast one on me, and when y'all catch this guy, my organization won't get no credit.''

Double negatives annoy me, but Burt Yardley annoyed me more. I said, "Rest assured, Chief, your department will get all the credit it deserves.''

He laughed. "Yeah, that's what I'm afraid of, son. We need to get involved in this here case.''

"Take it up with the FBI. They're in charge as of tomorrow.''

"Is that a fact?''

"Sure is.''

"Okay. Meantime, you write a nice report sayin' how the Midland police helped you.''

"Why?''

"Why? Because you're runnin' around talkin' about subpoena'n' my records, because the goddamn reporters are askin' questions about my boy's involvement with the deceased, because you're startin' to make me look like a damn fool 'cause I don't know shit, and because you goddamn well need me.'' He added, "You're goin' to make things right.''

The man was obviously annoyed, and I really couldn't blame him. There is a strange symbiotic relationship between an Army post and the local community, especially in the South. At its worst, the relationship seems like one of an army of occupation ensconced in the defeated old Dixieland. At its best, the locals realize that most of the officers and enlisted personnel are southerners themselves, and the post is no more intrusive than a big auto factory. But big auto factories don't have their own laws and customs, so the reality is somewhere in between. Anyway, in the spirit of cooperation, I said to Burt Yardley, "I'll introduce you to the FBI man in charge when I know who it is and give him a glowing report of your assistance and accomplishments.''

"That's real decent of you, Paul. You write somethin' out, too. Bill Kent's doin' that right now. Why don't we call him in here, and we'll have that big sit-down your little assistant there talked about.''

"I don't have a lot of time for big sit-downs, Chief. You'll be involved in the continuing investigation to the fullest extent possible. Don't worry about it."

"Why do I think you're bullshittin' me, Paul?"

"I don't know."

"I'll tell you why. 'Cause you don't think I got one goddamn thing you want, and you don't give nothin' for nothin'. Fact is, I think I got what you need to wrap up this here case."

"Is that a fact?"

"Sure is. I found some evidence in the deceased's house that you overlooked, son. But it's goin' to take a lot of work between us to sort it out."

"Right. You mean the stuff in the basement bedroom."

His eyes got wide, and he didn't speak for a second, which was a treat, but then he said, "Why'd you leave all that shit there?"

"I thought you were too stupid to find it."

He laughed. "Now who's stupid?"

"But I didn't leave it all. We carried some bags of photos and videotapes out of there." I didn't, but I should have.

He regarded me closely for a moment, and I could tell he was not real happy with that possibility. He said, "Well, ain't you a smart boy."

"Yes, I am."

"Where's that stuff?"

"In my trailer. You missed it."

"Don't mess with me, son. There ain't nothin' in that trailer."

"Why do you care where the stuff is?"

" 'Cause it's my stuff."

"Wrong."

He cleared his throat and said, "There's some dumb-ass guys who got a shitload of explainin' to do when I do fingerprints in that there room, and when we match those pictures and those movie tapes to their buck-naked bodies."

"Right. Including you."

He stared at me, and I stared back. Finally, he said, "I don't bluff real easy."

"You see, Chief, I think that Wes and Ann had more going for

290

them than Wes is letting on. They weren't the happiest couple who ever came down the pike, but they did go out for almost two years, and my information says they were hot and heavy. Now the question I have for you is this—did your son know you were fucking his girlfriend?''

Chief Yardley seemed to be mulling over his answer, so, to fill the silence, I asked, "And did Mrs. Yardley know you were fucking the general's daughter? Hey, I wouldn't want to have dinner at your house tonight, Burt.''

The chief was still mulling, so I said, "You didn't find that room by accident, but that's what you told Wes. Maybe Wes knew that his girlfriend dated on the side now and then, but when he screwed her, he did it in her bedroom, because if he'd seen that room downstairs, he'd have beat the shit out of her and left her like any good gentleman of the South. You, on the other hand, knew all about her but never told your son, because Ann Campbell told you you'd better not. She liked Wes. You were just someone she screwed because you had influence over Wes, and because you could fix things for her in town if she ever needed anything fixed. You were kind of an afterthought, extra insurance, and maybe you came through for her a few times. So, anyway, you and Wes have more in common than blood, and Ann Campbell made your life exciting and damned scary. She told you at some point that if you broke into her place and took that stuff, it didn't matter, because she had copies of the photos and videotapes someplace else. It wouldn't be too hard to identify your fat ass in those pictures. So you get to thinking about your wife, your son, your other sons, your standing in the community, your pastor and Sunday church socials, your thirty years on the force to get to the top, and one day, you decide to get rid of this time bomb.'' I looked at him and said, "Correct?''

Yardley's ruddy face had not gone pale, but it had gone redder. Finally, he said, "I wasn't dumb enough to have my picture taken.''

"Are you sure about that? Are you sure your voice isn't on an audiotape?''

"That ain't good enough.''

291

"It's good enough to smear your name like shit on the mayor's new carpet."

We both sat awhile, like two checker players trying to see three moves down the road. Yardley nodded to himself, then looked me in the eye. "I thought about killing her once or twice."

"No kidding?"

"But I couldn't bring myself to kill a woman for somethin' stupid that I did."

"Chivalry is not dead."

"Yeah . . . anyway, I was in Atlanta overnight on business when it happened. Got lots of witnesses."

"Good. I'll talk to them."

"You go right ahead and make a fool out of yourself."

"I'm not the one with a motive for murder." Actually, I didn't think Burt Yardley was the murderer, but people get nervous when you tell them you have to check out their alibis. It's embarrassing and causes all sorts of awkwardness. That's why cops do it to people that are holding back, and who piss them off.

Yardley said, "You can take your motives, put a light coat of oil on them, and shove 'em up your butt. But I might be interested in what you got regardin' me and the deceased."

"Might you? Well, I might have a photo of you when you were sleeping in her bed."

"Then again, you might not."

"Then again, how did I connect your fat ass to that room?"

"Well, that's the question, ain't it, son?" He slid back his chair as though to leave and said, "You're blowin' smoke up my ass. I ain't got no time for this."

There was a knock on the door and it opened. Specialist Baker handed me a sealed transmittal envelope and left. I opened the envelope, which contained about a dozen sheets of typed paper. Without a preamble to cushion the blow, I took a page at random and read aloud, " '22 April—Burt Yardley stopped by about 2100 hours. I was busy with reports, but he wanted to go downstairs. Thank God this guy needs it only about once a month. We went down into the basement, and he ordered me to strip for a search. I think he strip-searches every female he has half a reason to. So I stripped in front of him while he stood there with his hands on his hips and watched, then he ordered me to turn around, bend over, and spread my cheeks, which I did. He put his finger in my anus and told me he was looking for drugs or poison or secret messages. Then he made me lie on the gurney for a vaginal search, and—' ''

"Okay, son."

I looked up from the page. "Does that ring a bell, Chief?"

"Uh . . . not right off." He asked, "Where'd you get that?"

"Her computer."

"Don't sound like admissible evidence to me."

"Well, in test cases, it's been ruled admissible."

"Could be all female craziness. You know, like some dumb make-believe."

"Could be. I'll turn it over to the JAG and to the Georgia attorney general for evaluation by legal and mental health professionals. Maybe you'll be cleared."

"Cleared of what? Even if every goddamn word is true, I didn't break no laws."

"I'm not an expert on Georgia sodomy laws. But I think you may have broken your marriage vows."

"Oh, can that shit, son. You're a man. Act like a goddamn man. Think like a goddamn man. You some kind of queer or what? You married?"

I ignored him and flipped through the pages. "My goodness, Burt . . . you used your flashlight to look up her . . . and here you use your nightstick to . . . and your *pistol*? This is really gross. You've got this fetish about long, hard objects, I see. But I don't seem to see where your own object gets long or hard . . . ."

Burt stood. "You keep a close eye on your ass, boy, because it's mine if you stick it anyplace off this post." He went to the door, but I knew he wasn't going anywhere, so I paid no attention. He came back to the table, took the chair beside me, and spun it around, then sat on it and leaned toward me. I'm not sure what the reversed chair symbolizes beyond the obvious fact that it's the opposite of sitting down and relaxing. Maybe it's protective, maybe aggressive, but whatever it is, it's annoying. I stood, and sat on the table. "Okay, Burt, what I want from you is every damned piece of evidence you took out of that room."

"No way."

"Then I'll send copies of these diary pages to everyone in the Midland phone book."

"Then I'll kill you."

We were getting somewhere now, so I said, "We'll swap evidence."

"Hell, no. I got enough stuff to fuck up most of the top boys on this here post. You want that to happen?"

"You've only got masked photos. I have the diary."

"I got goddamned fingerprints all over the place down there. We're gonna run those through the FBI and the Army."

"Are the contents still in the room?"

"My business."

"Okay, how about a bonfire? We'll use these pages of your sexual perversions to start it. Probably won't even need a match."

He thought a minute. "Can I trust you?"

"My word as an officer."

"Yeah?"

"Can I trust *you*?"

"No, but I don't want you shooting off your wiseass mouth to my wife and boy."

I stood and looked out the window. The reporters were still there, but a cordon of MPs had now moved them back about fifty meters to the road in front of the building so that people could come and go without being harassed. I thought about what I was about to enter into with Chief Yardley. Destroying evidence could get me a few years in Kansas. On the other hand, destroying lives is not part of my job. I turned and walked toward Yardley. "Done deal."

He stood and we shook. I said, "You throw everything in a dump truck, including the furniture, sheets, carpet, videotapes, photos, whips and chains, and all that stuff, and bring everything to the town incinerator.''

''When?''

''After I make an arrest.''

''When's that gonna be?''

''Soon.''

''Yeah? You want to tell me about that?''

''No.''

''You know, dealin' with you is like jerkin' off with sandpaper.''

''Thank you.'' I handed him the computer printouts and said, ''When we burn the stuff, I'll have this deleted from the computer. You can watch.''

''Yeah. Now you're blowin' sunshine up my ass. Well, I'm gonna trust you, son, 'cause you're an officer and a gentleman. But if you fuck me, I'll kill you as God is my witness.''

''I think I understand that. And I make you the same promise. Have your first good night's sleep tonight. It's almost finished.''

We walked out into the corridor and back toward the office. On the way, I said to him, ''Have my personal luggage delivered to the visiting officers' quarters, okay, Burt?''

''Sure thing, son.''

Cynthia and Wes Yardley were sitting at the desks and stopped talking as we entered.

Burt said, ''Hey, we interruptin' somethin'?'' He laughed.

Cynthia gave Burt a look that seemed to say, ''You're a jackass.''

Wes stood and ambled to the door. He looked at the papers in his father's hand and asked, ''What's that?''

''Uh . . . just some Army crap I got to read.'' He looked at Cynthia and touched his hat. ''A pleasure as always, ma'am.'' He said to me, ''Keep me informed.'' He and his son left.

Cynthia asked, ''Did Baker find you?''

''Yes.''

''Hot stuff?''

''Burt found it a little embarrassing.'' I told her most of what transpired and said to her, ''The incriminating photos and other evidence in Ann Campbell's fun room will be disposed of, but the less you know about it, the better.''

"Don't be protective, Paul. I don't like that."

"I'd do the same for any officer. You're going to be questioned under oath someday, and you don't have to lie."

"We'll discuss this another time. Meanwhile, Wes Yardley turns out to be a little less macho than he appears."

"They all are."

"Right. He's quite upset over Ann Campbell's death, and has been turning Midland upside down trying to find who did it."

"Good. Did you get the feeling that he thought Ann Campbell was his personal property?"

"Sort of. I asked him if she was allowed to date other men, and he said he only allowed her to have dinner, drinks, and such, on official occasions on post. He never wanted to escort her to any of those things, so he was good enough to permit her to do what she had to do with the asshole officers. Quote, unquote."

"There's a man after my own heart."

"Right. But people can't be watched all the time, and where there's a will, there's a way."

"Correct. So he had no idea, obviously, that she was furthering her career in nontraditional ways."

"I very much doubt it."

"And if he found out that his father was sharing the honey, he'd be annoyed."

"To say the very least."

"Good. I've never had my hands around so many balls."

"Don't let it go to your head."

"Not me. I'm just doing my job."

"Do you want a sandwich?"

"You buying?"

"Sure." She stood. "I need some air. I'll run over to the O Club."

"Cheeseburger, fries, and a Coke."

"Tidy up this place while I'm gone." She left.

I called Baker on the intercom, and she reported. I gave her my handwritten note regarding Dalbert Elkins and asked her to type it.

She said to me, "Would you recommend me for CID School?"

"It's not as much fun as it looks, Baker."

"I really want to be a criminal investigator."

"Why?"

"It's exciting."

"Why don't you talk to Ms. Sunhill about it?"

"I did, when she was here yesterday. She said it was fun and exciting, lots of travel, and you meet interesting people."

"Right, and you arrest them."

"She said she met you in Brussels. That sounds romantic."

I didn't reply.

"She said she's got orders for a permanent duty station in Panama when she's finished here."

"Would you get me some fresh coffee?"

"Yes, sir."

"That will be all."

She left.

Panama.

CHAPTER TWENTY-FIVE

Colonel Fowler called at 1645 hours and I took the call, telling Cynthia to pick up the other line and listen.

Colonel Fowler said, "My wife is available at 1730 hours, at home, Mrs. Campbell at 1800 hours, at Beaumont House, and the general will see you at his office at Post Headquarters at 1830 hours, sharp."

I commented, "That's cutting the interviews close."

"Actually," he replied, "it's cutting them short."

"That's what I meant."

"The three parties you wish to speak to are under a great deal of stress, Mr. Brenner."

"So am I, but I thank you."

"Mr. Brenner, has it occurred to you that you may be upsetting people?"

"It has occurred to me."

"The funeral, as I said, is tomorrow morning. Why don't you and Ms. Sunhill brief the FBI people, attend the funeral if you wish, then leave. The investigation will proceed nicely without you, and the murderer will be brought to justice in good time. This is not a timed exercise."

"Well, it wasn't, but the idiots in Washington made it one."

"Mr. Brenner, from the very beginning, you chose to charge

through here like Grant took Richmond, with no regard to protocol or other people's sensibilities.''

''That's how Grant took Richmond, Colonel.''

''And they are still pissed-off at Grant in Richmond.''

''Right. Colonel, I knew from the beginning that this case would be pulled away from me, from the CID. The Pentagon and the White House did the politically correct thing, and God bless civilian control of the military. But if I have about twenty hours left, I'll use it my way.''

''As you wish.''

''Trust me to conclude this case in a way that will not bring discredit on the Army. Don't trust the FBI or the Attorney General's Office to do that.''

''I won't comment on that.''

''Best that you don't.''

''On another topic, Mr. Brenner, your request to seize the contents of Colonel Moore's office has gone all the way to the Pentagon, and they turned it down for national security reasons.''

''That's the very best of reasons, sir. But it's odd that the people in Washington want me to arrest Colonel Moore for murder, but I can't get permission to examine his files.''

''That's what happens when you ask. You know that.''

''Indeed I do. That's the last time I go through channels.''

''That's your call. But the Pentagon did say that if you arrest Colonel Moore at this time, they will fly someone down here with the necessary clearance and authority to assist you in going through the files on a selective basis. But it can't be a fishing expedition. You must know what you're looking for.''

''Right. I've been that route before. If I knew what the hell I was looking for, I probably wouldn't need it.''

''Well, that's the best I could do. What clearance do you have?''

''Oh, about five foot eleven.'' He didn't laugh, so I said, ''Secret clearance.''

''All right, I'll pass that on. Meantime, the Psy-Ops School is sending people down to Jordan Field to collect the contents of

Captain Campbell's office and return everything to the school. You and Colonel Kent will not be charged with a crime for removing the contents, but letters of reprimand have been put in your files.'' He added, ''You must obey the law like the rest of us.''

''Well, I usually do when I know what it is.''

''You don't confiscate classified material without proper authorization.''

''Someone's trying to sandbag me, Colonel.''

''Not only that, someone's trying to screw you. Why?''

''I don't know.''

''You've made inquiries about Captain Campbell's time at West Point. Correct?''

''That's correct. Did I ask the wrong question?''

''Apparently.''

I glanced at Cynthia and inquired of Colonel Fowler, ''Can you tell me anything about that, Colonel?''

''I know nothing about it, except that they're asking me why you're asking.''

''Who are *they*?''

''I can't say. But you hit a nerve, Mr. Brenner.''

''It sounds like you're trying to help me, Colonel.''

''Upon consideration, you and Ms. Sunhill may be the best people for this job. But you won't conclude this case in time, so I'm advising you to protect yourselves.'' He added, ''Lay low.''

''Ms. Sunhill and I are not criminals. We are criminal investigators.''

''The letter of reprimand was a warning shot. The next shot is aimed for the heart.''

''Right, but I'm firing it.''

''You're a damned fool. We need more people like you.'' He added, ''Be sure your partner understands what she's getting into.''

''I'm not sure *I* understand.''

''Neither do I, but you definitely asked the wrong question about West Point. Good day.'' He hung up.

I looked at Cynthia. ''My goodness.''

She said, "We definitely asked the right question about West Point."

"Apparently." I called Jordan Field and got Grace Dixon on the line. "Grace, I just got a tip that there are people en route to your location from the Psy-Ops School to reclaim Captain Campbell's files, and I'm sure that includes her computer."

"I know. They're already here."

"Damn it!"

"No problem. After I spoke to you, I copied everything onto a floppy disk." She added, "They're taking the computer now, but I don't think anyone could come up with the passwords to access those files."

"Nice going, Grace." I asked, "What are the passwords?"

"There are three: one for the personal letters, one for the list of boyfriends' names, addresses, and telephone numbers, and one for the diary." She continued, "The password for the letters is 'Naughty Notes,' for the boyfriends' names, addresses, and telephone numbers, she used the words 'Daddy's Friends,' and the password for the diary is 'Trojan Horse.' "

"Okay . . . hold on to that disk."

"It's close to my heart."

"Good. Sleep with it tonight. Talk to you later." I hung up, called Falls Church, and got through to Karl. I said to him, "I'm hearing that my inquiry about West Point got some people angry, upset, or scared."

"Who told you that?"

"The question is, What did you find?"

"Nothing."

I said to him, "This is important."

"I'm doing my best."

"Tell me what you've done."

"Mister Brenner, I don't report to you."

"Right. But I've asked you to use your resources to get me a piece of information."

"I'll call you when I have something."

Cynthia pushed a note toward me that read: *Tapped?* I nodded. Karl definitely sounded weird. I asked him, "Did they get to you, Karl?"

After a few seconds, he said, "All the doors slammed in my face. Proceed with the case without this information. I've been assured you don't need it."

"All right. Thanks very much for trying."

"I'll see you here tomorrow or the next day."

"Fine. Since you're not busy with my request, perhaps you can arrange a thirty-day administrative leave for me and Ms. Sunhill, and a confirmed MAC flight to a place of my choice."

"The Pentagon would like nothing better."

"And get that fucking letter of reprimand out of my file." I hung up.

Cynthia said, "What the hell is going on here?"

"I think we opened a Pandora's box, took out a can of worms, and threw it at a hornet's nest."

"You can say that again."

But I didn't. I said, "We've been cut loose." I thought a moment, then added, "But I think we can go it alone."

"I guess we have no choice. But I still want to know about West Point."

"Karl has assured us it's not important to the case."

Cynthia stayed silent a moment, then said, "Karl disappoints me. I never thought he'd back off from a criminal investigation like that."

"Me neither."

We spoke for a few minutes trying to figure out where to go regarding the West Point inquiry. I looked at my watch. "Well, let's get to Bethany Hill." We got up to leave, but there was a knock on the door, and Specialist Baker came in with a sheet of paper in her hand. She sat at my desk and glanced at the paper.

I said to her, sarcastically, "Have a seat, Baker."

She looked up at us and said in an assured tone of voice, "Actually, I'm Warrant Officer Kiefer from the CID. I've been here about two months on undercover assignment for Colonel Hellmann. I've

302

been investigating charges of improper conduct in the traffic enforcement section—petty stuff, nothing to do with Colonel Kent or any of that. Colonel Hellmann told me to get myself assigned as your clerk-typist.'' She looked at us. ''So I did.''

Cynthia said, ''Are you serious? You've been spying on us for Colonel Hellmann?''

''Not spying, just helping. It's done all the time.''

I replied, ''It is, but I'm still pissed-off.''

Specialist Baker, a.k.a. Warrant Officer Kiefer, said, ''I don't blame you, but this case is explosive, and Colonel Hellmann was concerned.''

I said, ''Colonel Hellmann just took a dive on us.''

She didn't respond to that, but said, ''In the two months I've been here, I've heard those rumors about Colonel Kent and Captain Campbell that I told you about. That's all true, but I never wrote him up because I don't like doing that to people. I couldn't see one incident where he compromised his duties, and all I had was office gossip anyway. But now I suppose that's all relevant.''

Cynthia replied, ''Relevant, but maybe not evidence of anything except stupidity.''

Ms. Kiefer shrugged. She handed me a sheet of paper and said, ''I got a call from Falls Church a few minutes ago telling me to identify myself to you, and instructing me to stand by the fax machine. That's what came across.''

I looked at the fax sheet, which was addressed to me and Sunhill, via Kiefer, eyes only. I read aloud, '' 'Regarding the West Point inquiry, as indicated on the phone, all files sealed or nonexistent, all verbal inquiries met with silence. However, I phoned a retired CID person who was stationed at the Point during the period in question. That person spoke on condition of anonymity, and briefed me as follows: During the summer between Cadet Campbell's first and second year at West Point, she was hospitalized in a private clinic for a few weeks. Officially, she'd had a training accident at Camp Buckner Military Reservation during night exercises. My source says that General Campbell flew in from Germany the day after the 'accident.' Here is the story as my source pieced it together from rumors: In August, during recondo training, the cadets were engaged in night patrols in the woods, and by accident or design, Cadet Campbell was separated from a larger group and found herself with five or six males—either cadets or men from the Eighty-second Airborne Division who were assisting with the training. They wore camouflage paint, and it was dark and so forth. These male personnel grabbed Cadet Campbell, stripped her, and staked her out with pegs from their pup tents, then took turns raping her. What happened next is unclear, but presumably the men threatened her if she reported the rape, then untied her and ran off. She was reported missing until dawn, when she appeared at the bivouac area, disheveled and hysterical. She was taken first to Keller Army Hospital and treated for minor cuts and bruises, exhaustion, and so forth. Medical records do not indicate sexual assault. General Campbell arrived, and she was removed to a private clinic. No one was charged, no action taken, incident hushed for the good of the academy, and Cadet Campbell reported for classes in September. Rumor was that the general put pressure on his daughter not to pursue the matter— the general was probably pressured himself from higher-ups. So that's it. Shred this message and destroy fax activity report. Good luck. (Signed) Hellmann.' ''

I passed the fax to Cynthia, and she said, ''It all makes sense now, doesn't it?''

I nodded.

Kiefer asked us, ''You know who killed her?''

I replied, ''No, but I think we know now why she was out there on the range.''

Cynthia put Karl's message through the shredder and said to Kiefer, ''So you wanted to be a detective?''

Kiefer looked a little embarrassed but replied, ''Specialist Baker wanted to be a detective.''

Cynthia said, ''Specialist Baker can stay a clerk-typist for a while. We don't need another detective.''

''Yes, ma'am,'' replied Kiefer, slipping back into her assumed rank and role. ''But I'll keep my eyes and ears open.''

"You do that."

I said to Baker, "Tell Colonel Kent that Mr. Brenner wants Colonel Moore restricted to post and available until further notice."

"Yes, sir."

Cynthia and I left the office, went out the back way, and made it to the parking lot without getting waylaid by reporters. I said, "My turn to drive." I found my keys and we got into my Blazer.

As I drove toward Bethany Hill, I said, "Karl is okay for a bastard."

She smiled. "Even if he did pull a fast one on us. Do you believe that?"

"It comes with the territory, Cynthia." I added, "I thought she looked familiar. There was something not right about her."

"Oh, cut the crap, Paul. You were as fooled as I was. God, I have to get out of this job."

"What about Panama?" I glanced at her, and our eyes met.

Cynthia said, "I put in for a permanent duty station out of the continental United States because I wanted to get away from my about-to-be ex."

"Good thinking." I changed the subject. "So this West Point thing is high explosives."

"Yes. I can't believe a father would participate in a cover-up . . . well, if you think about it . . . I mean, there's so much tension at West Point since it went co-ed. It's unbelievable what's happening there. Plus, the general had his own career to think about, and maybe he was thinking of his daughter's career and reputation as well. But he wasn't doing her any favors."

"No, he was not."

"Women who suppress a sexual assault, or who are made to suppress it, usually pay for it later."

"Or make other people pay for it," I pointed out.

"That's right. Sometimes both." She added, "What happened on rifle range six was a reenactment of the rape at West Point, wasn't it?"

"I'm afraid it was."

305

"Except this time someone killed her."

"Right."

"Her father?"

"Let's get the last piece of information we need to reenact the entire crime, from beginning to end."

She stayed silent a moment, then asked me, "Do you know who killed her?"

"I know who didn't kill her."

"Don't be enigmatic, Paul."

"Do you have a suspect?"

"I have a few."

"Build a case against them and we'll put them on trial tonight in the VOQ."

"Sounds good. I hope we can hang someone in the morning."

CHAPTER TWENTY-SIX

We arrived at the Fowler residence on Bethany Hill and rang the bell.

Mrs. Fowler greeted us, looking only slightly less distressed than she'd looked that morning. She showed us into the living room and offered us coffee or whatever, but we declined. She sat on a couch, and we sat in club chairs.

Cynthia and I had discussed a line of questioning, and we decided that Cynthia would lead off. She chatted with Mrs. Fowler about life, the Army, Fort Hadley, and so forth, then, when Mrs. Fowler was relaxed, Cynthia said to her, "Please be assured that we only want to see justice done. We are not here to ruin reputations. We are here to find a murderer, but we are also here to make certain that innocent men and women are not falsely accused."

Mrs. Fowler nodded.

Cynthia continued, "You know that Ann Campbell was sexually involved with many men on this post. I want first to assure you that in all the evidence that we've gathered, your husband's name has not been linked with Ann Campbell."

Again she nodded, a little more vigorously, I thought.

Cynthia continued, "We understand Colonel Fowler's position as General Campbell's adjutant and, I assume, his friend. We appreciate your husband's honesty and his willingness to let us speak to you. I'm sure he's told you to be as honest with us as he's been with us, and as we've been with you."

Tentative nod.

Cynthia went on, circling around any direct question, saying positive things, showing compassion, empathy, and so on. You have to do this with civilian witnesses who are not under subpoena, and Cynthia was doing a much better job than I could have done.

But the time had come, and Cynthia asked her, "You were home on the evening of the murder?"

"Yes, I was."

"Your husband came home from the O Club at about ten P.M."

"That's right."

"You retired about eleven P.M.?"

"I believe so."

"And sometime between 0245 and 0300 hours, three A.M. or so, you were awakened by someone ringing your doorbell."

No reply.

"Your husband went downstairs and answered the door. He came back to the bedroom and told you it was the general, and that he had to go off on urgent business. Your husband got dressed and asked you to do the same. Correct?"

No reply.

Cynthia said, "And you went with him." Cynthia added, "You wear a size seven shoe, I believe."

Mrs. Fowler replied, "Yes, we both got dressed and left."

No one spoke for a few seconds, then Cynthia said, "You both got dressed and left. And did General Campbell remain in your house?"

"Yes."

"And was Mrs. Campbell with him?"

"No, she was not."

"So General Campbell stayed behind, and you accompanied your husband to rifle range six. Correct?"

"Yes. My husband said that the general told him Ann Campbell was naked, and he told me to bring a robe with me. He said that

308

Ann Campbell was tied up, so he took a knife for me to cut the rope.''

''All right. You drove along Rifle Range Road, and for the last mile or so, you drove without headlights.''

''Yes. My husband did not want to attract the attention of the guard. He said there was a guard up the road.''

''Yes. And you stopped at the parked humvee, as General Campbell instructed. It was now what time?''

''It was . . . about three-thirty.''

''It was about three-thirty. You got out of your car and . . .''

''And I could see something out on the rifle range, and my husband told me to go out there and cut her loose and make her put the robe on. He said to call him if I needed help.'' Mrs. Fowler paused, then added, ''He said to slap her around if she didn't cooperate. He was very angry.''

''Understandably so,'' Cynthia agreed. ''So you walked out on the range.''

''Yes. My husband decided to follow about halfway. I think he was concerned about how Ann would react. He thought she might become violent.''

''And you approached Ann Campbell. Did you say anything?''

''Yes, I called her name, but she didn't . . . she didn't reply. I got right up to her, and . . . I knelt beside her, and her eyes were open, but . . . I screamed . . . and my husband ran to me . . .'' Mrs. Fowler put her hands over her face and began crying. Cynthia seemed prepared for this and sprang out of her seat and sat beside Mrs. Fowler on the couch, putting her arm around her and giving her a handkerchief.

After about a minute, Cynthia said, ''Thank you. You don't have to say any more. We'll see ourselves out.'' And we did.

We got into my Blazer and drove off. I said, ''Sometimes a shot in the dark hits its mark.''

Cynthia replied, ''But it wasn't a shot in the dark. I mean, it all makes sense now, it's all logical, based on what we know of the facts, and what we know of the personalities.''

"Right. You did a nice job."

"Thank you. But you set it up."

Which was true, so I said, "Yes, I did."

"I suppose I don't like false modesty or humility in a man."

"Good. You're in the right car." I said, "Do you think Colonel Fowler told her to tell the truth, or did she decide on her own?"

Cynthia thought a moment, then replied, "I think Colonel Fowler knows that we know a, b, and c. He told his wife that if we asked about x, then she should answer about x, and go on about y and z and get it off her chest, and get it finished with."

"Right. And Mrs. Fowler is her husband's witness that Ann Campbell was dead when they got there, and that Colonel Fowler did not kill her."

"Correct. And I believe her, and I don't believe he killed Ann Campbell."

We drove in silence back toward the main post, both of us deep in thought.

We arrived at Beaumont House a little early, but decided that protocol had to take a backseat to reality for a change, and we went to the front door, where an MP checked our IDs, then rang the bell for us.

As luck would have it, young and handsome Lieutenant Elby opened the door. He said, "You're ten minutes early."

Young Elby wore the crossed-rifles insignia of an infantry officer, and though there was no indication on this uniform that he'd seen combat anywhere, I deferred to his infantry status and his rank as a commissioned officer. I said to him, "We can leave and come back, or we can speak to you for a few minutes."

Lieutenant Elby seemed an amicable sort and showed us in. We went into the waiting room where we'd been before, and, still standing, I said to Cynthia, "Didn't you want to use the facilities?"

"What? Oh . . . yes."

Lieutenant Elby pointed and said, "There's a powder room to the left of the foyer."

"Thank you." She left.

I said to Elby, "Lieutenant, it has come to my attention that you and Captain Campbell dated."

Elby looked at me closely, then replied, "That's correct."

"Did you know she was also dating Wes Yardley?"

He nodded, and I could tell by his expression that this was still a painful memory for him. I could certainly understand this—a clean-cut young officer having to share his boss's daughter with a less-than-clean-cut townie, a sort of bad-boy cop. I said to Elby, "Did you love her?"

"I'm not answering that."

"You already have. And were your intentions honorable?"

"Why are you asking me these questions? You're here to speak to Mrs. Campbell."

"We're early. So you knew about Wes Yardley. Did you hear other rumors that Ann Campbell dated married officers on post?"

"What the hell are you talking about?"

I guess he didn't hear those rumors. And I guess he didn't know about the room in the basement, either. I said to him, "Did the general approve of your relationship with his daughter?"

"Yes, he did. Do I have to answer these questions?"

"Well, three days ago you didn't, and you could have told me to go to hell. And a few days from now, you could probably tell me the same thing. But right now, yes, you have to answer these questions. Next question—did Mrs. Campbell approve?"

"Yes."

"Did you and Ann Campbell ever discuss marriage?"

"Yes, we did."

"Talk to me, Lieutenant."

"Well . . . I knew she was involved with this Yardley guy, and I was . . . annoyed . . . but it wasn't just that . . . I mean, she told me that . . . that she had to be sure her parents approved, and when the general gave his blessings, we would announce our engagement."

"I see. And you discussed this with the general, man-to-man?"

"Yes, I did, a few weeks ago. He seemed happy, but he told me

311

to take a month to think it over. He said that his daughter was a very headstrong young woman.''

"I see. And then recently you received orders to go to someplace on the other side of the world.''

He looked at me, sort of surprised. "Yes . . . Guam.''

I almost laughed, but didn't. Though he was my superior, he was young enough to be my son, and I put my hand on his shoulder. I said to him, "Lieutenant, you could have been the best thing to happen to Ann Campbell, but it wasn't going to happen. You got caught in a power struggle between General and Captain Campbell, and they moved you up and down the board. Somewhere in the back of your mind you understand this. Get on with your life and your career, Lieutenant, and the next time you think about marriage, take two aspirin, lie down in a dark room, and wait for the feeling to pass.''

Unfortunately, Cynthia returned at that very moment and gave me a nasty look.

Lieutenant Elby seemed confused and irritated, but something was clicking in his brain. He looked at his watch and said, "Mrs. Campbell will see you now.''

We followed Elby into the hallway, and he showed us into a large, sort of Victorian parlor at the front of the house.

Mrs. Campbell rose from her chair and we went to her. She was wearing a simple black dress, and as I got closer I could see the resemblance to her daughter. At about sixty years old, Mrs. Campbell had made that transition from beautiful to attractive, but it would be another ten years at least before people would begin using the neutral and sexless expression "a handsome woman.''

Cynthia took her hand first and went through the condolences. I also took her hand and did the same. She said, "Won't you be seated?'' She indicated a love seat near the front window. We sat, and she took the love seat opposite. Between us was a small round table on which sat a few decanters of cordials and glasses. Mrs. Campbell was drinking tea, but asked us, "Would you like some sherry or port?''

Actually, I wanted the alcohol, but not if I had to drink sherry or port to get at it. I declined, but Cynthia said yes to sherry, and Mrs. Campbell poured one for her.

Mrs. Campbell, I was surprised to discover, had a southern accent, but then I remembered seeing her on television once during the Gulf War, and I recalled thinking what a politically perfect pair they were: a rock-hard general from the Midwest and a cultured lady from the South.

Cynthia made some light chatter, and Mrs. Campbell, for all her grief, kept up her end of the conversation. Mrs. Campbell, it turned out, was from South Carolina, herself the daughter of an Army officer. June Campbell—that was her name—was, I thought, the embodiment of everything that was good about the South. She was polite, charming, and gracious, and I recalled what Colonel Fowler had said about her, and I added loyal and ladylike but tough.

I was aware that the clock was ticking, but Cynthia seemed in no hurry to get to the nasty stuff, and I assumed she had decided it wasn't appropriate and/or had lost her nerve. I didn't blame her at all. But then Cynthia said, "I assume Mrs. Fowler, or perhaps Colonel Fowler, called you before we arrived."

Good shot, Cynthia.

Mrs. Campbell put her teacup down and replied in the same quiet tone of voice she'd been conversing in, "Yes, it was Mrs. Fowler. I'm so glad she had the opportunity to speak to you. She's been very upset and feels so much better now."

"Yes," Cynthia replied, "it's often that way. You know, Mrs. Campbell, I'm assigned mostly to cases of sexual assault, and I can tell you that when I begin questioning people who I know can tell me something, I can almost feel the tension. It's sort of like everybody is wound up, but once the first person speaks up, it begins to unwind, as it has here."

This was Cynthia's way of saying that once the code of silence is broken, everyone falls all over one another to go on the record as a government witness. Beats the hell out of being a suspect.

Cynthia said to Mrs. Campbell, "So from what Mrs. Fowler tells me, and from what Mr. Brenner and I have discovered from other sources, it appears that the general received a call from Ann in the early morning hours, asking him to meet her on the rifle range, presumably to discuss something. Is that correct?''

Another shot in the dark or, to give Cynthia some credit, a very good guess.

Mrs. Campbell replied, ''The red telephone beside the bed rang at about one forty-five A.M. The general immediately answered it, and I woke up as well. I watched him as he listened. He never spoke, but hung up and got out of bed and began getting dressed. I never ask him what these calls are about, but he always tells me where he's going and when he expects to be back.'' She smiled and said, ''Since we've been at Fort Hadley, he doesn't get many calls in the middle of the night, but in Europe, when the phone rang, he'd fly out of bed, grab a packed bag, and be off to Washington or to the East German border, or who knows where. But he'd always tell me . . . This time he just said he'd be back in an hour or so. He put on civilian clothes and left. I watched him pull away and noticed that he used my car.''

''What kind of car is that, ma'am?''

''A Buick.''

Cynthia nodded and said, ''Then at about four or four-thirty in the morning, the general returned home and told you what had happened.''

She stared off into space, and for the first time I could see the face of a tired and heartsick mother, and I could only imagine what toll these years had taken. Surely, a wife and mother could not have countenanced what a father and husband had done to their daughter in the name of the greater good, in the name of career advancement and positive public images. But on some level, she must have come to terms with it.

Cynthia prompted, ''Your husband came home about four-thirty A.M.''

''Yes . . . I was waiting up for him . . . here in the front room. When he walked in the door, I knew my daughter was dead.'' She stood. "And that's all I know. Now that my husband's career is ended, all we have left is the hope that you can find who did this. Then we can all go on and make our peace."

We stood also, and Cynthia said, "We're doing our best, and we thank you for putting aside your grief to speak to us."

I said that we could find our way out, and we made our departure.

Outside, on the way to my vehicle, I said, "The general's career ended ten years ago in Keller Army Hospital at West Point. It just took some time for it to catch up with him."

"Yes, he not only betrayed his daughter, but he betrayed himself and his wife."

We got into the Blazer and I pulled away from Beaumont House.

CHAPTER TWENTY-SEVEN

What did you speak to Lieutenant Elby about?'' Cynthia asked as I drove.

"Love and marriage."

"Yes, I heard that piece of enduring wisdom."

"Well . . . you know, he's too young to settle down. He had proposed marriage to Ann Campbell."

"Marrying Ann Campbell is not what I'd call settling down."

"True." I briefed Cynthia on my short conversation with Elby, and added, "Now the poor bastard is being shipped to Guam. That's what happens—like in those old Greek plays when a mortal has carnal knowledge of a goddess. They wind up insane, turned into an animal or some inanimate object, or get banished to Guam or its Aegean equivalent."

"Sexist nonsense."

"Right. Anyway, I get the feeling that the family dynamics among the Campbells was so pathological that love and happiness could never flourish, and God help anyone who got caught in their misery and pain."

She nodded. "Do you think they were all right before she was raped at West Point?"

"Well . . . according to Colonel Moore, yes. I think that's an accurate picture. And speaking of pictures, I'm thinking back to

that photo album we found in Ann's house . . . If you think about
the pictures as before and after—before and after the rape in the
summer between her first and second year at West Point—you can
see a difference.''

"Yes. You can almost pinpoint any family tragedy that way if
you know what you're looking for.'' She added, ''Those men who
gang-raped her had a little fun and went on with their lives, and
they never thought about the human wreckage they left behind.''

"I know. We both see that if we stay around long enough after
an act of violence. But usually we can get some justice. In this case,
nobody called the cops.''

"No, not then. But we're here now.'' She asked me, ''How do
you want to handle General Campbell?''

"I'd like to rough him up. But I think he's already paid the
supreme price for his great mistake. I don't know . . . tough call.
Play it by ear. He's a general.''

"Right.''

The Post Headquarters parking lot was nearly empty, but there
were a few cars left, including the general's olive-drab staff car.
There was also a humvee, a few of which are usually authorized for
Post Headquarters, and I assumed that the one sitting in the hangar
at Jordan Field had been replaced.

Cynthia and I stood in the parking lot to the right of the headquarters building, and I said, ''She walked out that side door at about
0100 hours, got into one of the humvees, and drove off to confront
the ghosts of the past.''

"And the ghosts won.''

We walked around to the front of the headquarters building. The
two-story, dark brick structure vaguely resembled a public school
built in the 1930s, except that the walk was lined with spent 155mm
howitzer shell casings, each one sprouting flowers, which was unin-
tentionally ironic. Also on the lawn were old field artillery pieces
from different eras, a graphic display of the progression of the boom
factor.

We entered the front doors, and a young PFC at the information

317

desk stood. I told him we had an appointment with General Campbell. He checked his appointment sheet and directed us down a long corridor toward the rear of the building.

Cynthia and I walked down the deserted, echoing corridor with the spit-shined linoleum floor. I said to her, "I've never arrested a general before. I'm probably more nervous than he is."

She glanced at me and replied, "He didn't do it, Paul."

"How do you know?"

"I can't picture it, and if I can't picture it, it didn't happen."

"I don't remember that in the manual."

"Well, in any case, I don't think you're allowed to arrest a general officer. Check the manual."

We came to a sort of second lobby, which was deserted, and straight ahead was a closed door with a brass plate that said, "Lt. General Joseph I. Campbell."

I knocked on the door, and it was opened by a female captain whose nametag read Bollinger. She said, "Good evening. I'm General Campbell's senior aide."

We shook hands all around, and she showed us into a small secretarial area. Captain Bollinger was about thirty-five, chunky, but friendly-looking and animated. I said to her, "I don't think I've ever heard of a female aide to a male general since Ike's lady friend."

She smiled and replied, "There are a few. The general's other aide is a male, Lieutenant Elby."

"Yes, we've met him." It occurred to me that if Lieutenant Elby was a pawn in the game between father and daughter, then Captain Bollinger was certainly not; she was not seducible by Ann, and she was also homely enough for Mrs. Campbell's requirements. It really sucks at the top.

Captain Bollinger escorted us into an empty outer office and said, "The general has allocated all the time you want. But please understand that he's . . . well, he's just plain grief-stricken."

Cynthia replied, "We understand."

I also understood that this interview was scheduled for after-duty

318

hours so that if it got messy, the troops wouldn't be around to see or hear it.

Captain Bollinger knocked on a nice oak door, opened it, and announced us as Warrant Officers Brenner and Sunhill. She stepped aside and we entered.

The general was standing and came forward to greet us. We exchanged quick salutes, then shook hands.

General Campbell indicated a grouping of upholstered chairs, and we all sat. Generals, like CEOs, have varying degrees of seating in the office, but generals also have the option of letting you stand at attention or, if they're being nice, at parade rest or at ease. But Cynthia and I were being shown far more courtesy than our rank required. It must have had something to do with the fact that we'd just heard two confessions of criminal conduct from two wives, to wit: accessory after the fact, and conspiracy. But perhaps he just liked us.

He asked, "Would either of you like a drink?"

"No, thank you, sir." But in truth, the cannon had sounded and the flag was down, and in the Army that is the equivalent of Pavlov's starving dogs hearing the dinner bell.

No one spoke for a minute or so, and I looked around the office. The walls were white plaster, and the trim and moldings were natural oak, as were the desks, tables, and so forth. The area rug over the oak floor was a red Oriental, probably picked up overseas. There was not much in the way of war trophies, souvenirs, framed certificates, or any of that, but on a small round table in the corner was a blue cape laid out like a tablecloth on which lay a sheathed saber, an old long-barreled pistol, a blue dress hat, and other odds and ends.

The general saw me looking and said, "Those are my father's things. He was a colonel in the old horse cavalry back in the 1920s."

I replied, "I was in the First Battalion of the Eighth Cavalry in Vietnam, minus horses."

"Really? That was my father's regiment. Old Indian fighters, though that was before his time."

319

So, we had something in common after all. Almost. Cynthia was probably immediately bored by the old boola-boola routine, but a little male bonding is a good thing before you go for the balls.

General Campbell asked me, "So you weren't always a detective?"

"No, sir. I used to do honest work."

He smiled. "Awards? Decorations?"

I told him and he nodded. I think he was better able to accept what I had to do to him if I was a combat vet. Even if I hadn't been, I'd have told him I was. I'm allowed to lie in the pursuit of truth, and an unsworn witness may also lie, while a sworn witness better not, and a suspect can exercise his or her right against self-incrimination anytime. Often, however, the problem is deciding who's who.

The general looked at Cynthia, not wanting to exclude her, and asked her about her military background, civilian roots, and so forth. She told him, and I learned a few things myself, though she may have been lying. Generals, and sometimes colonels, I've noticed, always ask enlisted personnel and lower-ranking officers about their hometowns, civilian schools, military training, and all that. I don't know if they care, or if it's some kind of imported Japanese management tool they learned at the War College, or what the hell this is all about, but you have to play the game, even if you're about to broach the subject of criminal activity.

So, with all the time allotted that we needed, we chewed the fat for about fifteen minutes, then finally the general said, "I understand that you've spoken to Mrs. Fowler and Mrs. Campbell, so you know something of what went on that evening."

I replied, "Yes, sir, but to be perfectly frank, we had figured out a lot of what went on prior to our speaking to Mrs. Fowler and Mrs. Campbell."

"Had you? That's very impressive. We do a good job training our CID people."

"Yes, sir, and we've had a lot of on-the-job experience, though this case presented unique problems."

"I'm sure it did. Do you know who killed my daughter?"

"No, sir."

He looked at me closely and asked, "It wasn't Colonel Moore?"

"It may have been."

"I see you're not here to answer questions."

"No, sir, we're not."

"Then how would you like to conduct this interview?"

"I think it may be easier on everyone, sir, if you just start by telling us what happened on the evening in question. Beginning with the phone call at 0145 hours. I may interrupt when I need a point clarified."

He nodded. "Yes, all right. I was sleeping, and the red phone rang on my nightstand. I answered it, but there was no reply to my saying, 'Campbell here.' Then there was a sort of click, then . . . then my daughter's voice came on the line, and I could tell it was recorded."

I nodded. There were telephones in the fire control towers on the ranges, but they were secured at night. Ann Campbell and Charles Moore obviously had a mobile phone with them and a tape player.

He continued, "The message—the recorded message said, 'Dad, this is Ann. I want to discuss something extremely urgent with you. You must meet me at rifle range six no later than 0215 hours.' " The general added, "She said if I didn't come, she'd kill herself."

Again I nodded. I said to him, "Did she tell you to bring Mrs. Campbell with you?"

He glanced at me and Cynthia, wondering how much we actually knew, thinking perhaps we'd somehow found that tape. He replied, "Yes, she did say that, but I had no intention of doing that."

"Yes, sir. Did you have any idea of what she wanted to speak to you about that was so urgent that she wanted you to get out of bed and drive out to the rifle range?"

"No . . . I . . . Ann, as you may have learned, was emotionally distressed."

"Yes, sir. I think, though, that someone mentioned to me that you had given her an ultimatum and a deadline. She was to give you her answer at breakfast that morning."

"That's correct. Her behavior had become unacceptable, and I told her to shape up or ship out."

321

"So when you heard her voice at that hour, you realized that this was not just a random emotional outburst, but was in fact connected to your ultimatum and her response."

"Well, yes, I suppose I did realize that."

"Why do you think she communicated with you by recorded message?"

"I suppose so there would be no argument. I was very firm with her, but since I couldn't reason or argue with a recorded voice, I did what any father would do and went to the designated meeting."

"Yes, sir. And as it turned out, your daughter was already out on the rifle range, and she called you from there with a mobile phone. She'd actually left Post Headquarters at about 0100 hours. Did you wonder why she picked a remote training area for this meeting? Why didn't she just show up at breakfast and give you her answer to your ultimatum?"

He shook his head. "I don't know."

Well, perhaps he didn't know at first, but when he saw her, he knew. I could see that he was genuinely grieved and was barely holding it together. But he *would* hold it together no matter how hard I pushed, and he'd tell the obvious truths relating to fact and hard evidence. But he would not voluntarily reveal the central truth of *why* his daughter presented herself to him staked out and naked.

I said to him, "She mentioned killing herself if you didn't come. Did you think that she might be contemplating killing *you* if you *did* come?"

He didn't reply.

I asked him, "Did you take a weapon with you?"

He nodded, then said, "I had no idea what I was going to find out there at night."

No, I'll bet you didn't. And that's why you didn't take Mrs. Campbell along. I said, "So you dressed in civilian clothes, took a weapon, took your wife's car, and drove out to rifle range six with your headlights on. What time did you reach your destination?"

"Well . . . about 0215 hours. At the time she designated."

"Yes. And you put your lights out, and . . ."

There was a long silence while General Campbell considered my hanging conjunction. Finally, he said, "I got out of the car and went to the humvee, but she wasn't there. I became concerned and called her name, but there was no reply. I called again, then heard her call to me, and I turned in the direction of the rifle range and saw . . . I saw her on the ground, or I saw this figure on the ground, and I thought it was her and that she was hurt. I moved quickly toward the figure . . . she was naked, and I was . . . I suppose I was shocked, confused . . . I didn't know what to make of this, but she was alive, and that's all I cared about. I called out and asked if she was all right, and she replied that she was . . . I got up to her . . . you know, it's difficult to talk about this."

"Yes, sir. It's difficult for us, too. That's not to try to compare your loss with our feelings, but I think I speak for Ms. Sunhill, too, when I say that during the course of this investigation, we've come to . . . well, to like your daughter." Well, maybe I wasn't speaking for Ms. Sunhill. I continued, "Homicide detectives often have feelings for the deceased even though they've never met them. This is an unusual case in that we've viewed hours of videotapes of your daughter's lectures, and I felt that your daughter was someone I'd like to have known . . . but I should let you tell us what happened next."

General Campbell was starting to lose it again, and we all sat there awkwardly for a minute or so while he took a lot of deep breaths, then he cleared his throat and said, "Well, then I tried to untie her . . . it was very embarrassing, I mean to her and to me . . . but I couldn't get the rope untied, and I couldn't get the stakes out of the ground . . . I tried . . . I mean, whoever did it drove those stakes very deep, and tied those knots . . . so I said to her I'd be right back . . . and I went to the car and to the humvee, but I couldn't find anything to cut the ropes . . . so I went back to her and told her . . . I told her . . . I said that I'd drive up to Bethany Hill and get a knife from Colonel Fowler . . . Bethany Hill is less than ten minutes from range six . . . In retrospect, I should have . . . well, I don't know what I should have done."

Again I nodded. I asked him, "And while you were trying to untie the ropes, you spoke, of course."

323

"Just a few words."

"But surely you asked her who had done that to her?"

"No . . ."

"General, surely you said something like, 'Ann, who did this?' "

"Oh . . . yes, of course. But she didn't know."

"Actually," I informed him, "she wouldn't say."

The general looked me in the eye. "That's correct. She wouldn't say. Perhaps you know."

"So you drove back along Rifle Range Road toward Bethany Hill."

"That's right. And I called on Colonel Fowler for assistance."

"Did you know that there was a guard posted at the ammo shed about another kilometer in the opposite direction?"

"I don't know the location of every guard post at this fort." He added, "I doubt I would have gone there anyway. I certainly didn't need a young man to see my daughter like that."

"Actually, it was a woman. But that's irrelevant. What I'm wondering is why you made the U-turn with your headlights off, sir, and why you proceeded for at least a few hundred meters with them off."

He must have wondered how I knew this, then he probably realized I'd interviewed the guard. Finally, he replied, "To be honest with you, I didn't want to attract attention at that point."

"Why not?"

"Well, would you? If you just left your daughter tied naked to the ground, would you want anyone else involved? I had it clear in my mind that I had to go to Colonel and Mrs. Fowler for help. Obviously, I didn't want this incident to become public."

"But the incident, sir, was a crime, was it not? I mean, didn't you think she'd been molested by some madman or several madmen? Why would you wish to keep that private?"

"I suppose I didn't want to embarrass her."

Cynthia spoke up. "Rape should not be embarrassing to the victim."

General Campbell replied, "But it is."

Cynthia asked, "Did she indicate to you in any way that she was willing to lie there while you went and got Colonel and Mrs. Fowler?"

"No, but I thought it was the best thing."

Cynthia inquired, "Wasn't she frightened out of her mind that the rapist or rapists would return while you were gone?"

"No . . . well, yes, she did say to hurry back. Look, Ms. Sunhill, Mr. Brenner, if you're suggesting that I did not take the best course of action, then you're probably correct. Perhaps I should have tried harder to get her loose, perhaps I should have put my pistol in her hand so she could try to protect herself while I was gone, perhaps I should have fired the pistol to attract the attention of MPs, perhaps I should have just sat there with her until a vehicle came along. Don't you think I've thought about this a thousand times? If you're questioning my judgment, you have a valid point. But do not question my degree of concern."

Cynthia replied, "General, I'm not questioning either. I'm questioning what actually went on out there."

He started to reply, then decided to say nothing.

I said to him, "So you drove to the Fowlers, explained the situation, and they went back to assist Captain Campbell."

"That's correct. Mrs. Fowler had a robe and a knife to cut the ropes."

"And you didn't see your daughter's clothes anywhere at the scene?"

"No, I didn't."

"Did you think to cover her with your shirt?"

"No . . . I wasn't thinking very clearly."

This was the man who, as a lieutenant colonel, led a mechanized infantry battalion into the besieged city of Quang Tri and rescued an American rifle company who were trapped in the old French citadel. But he couldn't figure out how to aid his daughter. Obviously, he had no intention of offering her aid and comfort. He was royally pissed-off.

I asked him, "Why didn't you accompany the Fowlers, General?"

325

"I wasn't needed, obviously. Only Mrs. Fowler was needed, but Colonel Fowler went along, of course, in case there was trouble."

"What sort of trouble?"

"Well, in case the person who did that was still around."

"But why would you leave your daughter alone, tied, naked, and exposed if you thought there might be any chance of that?"

"It didn't occur to me until after I was back on the road. Until I was nearly at the Fowlers' house. I should point out that the drive to the Fowlers took under ten minutes."

"Yes, sir. But the round trip, including your waking them and them getting dressed and driving back, would take close to thirty minutes. After waking them and asking for their assistance, the natural response of any person—a father, a military commander— would be to race back to the scene and to secure the situation until the alerted cavalry arrived, to use a military analogy."

"Are you questioning my judgment or my motives, Mr. Brenner?"

"Not your judgment, sir. Your judgment would have been excellent if your motives were pure. So I guess I'm questioning your motives." Normally, you don't question a general about anything. But this was different.

He nodded and said, "I suppose you both know more than you're letting on. You're very clever. I could see that from the beginning. So why don't you tell me what my motives were?"

Cynthia responded to that and said, "You wanted to make her squirm a little."

The fortifications had been breached, to continue the military metaphor, and Cynthia charged right through. She said, "In fact, General, you knew that your daughter was not the victim of some rapist, that she hadn't been attacked while waiting out there for you. But, in fact, she and an accomplice called you, played her message, and got you out there for the sole purpose of you and Mrs. Campbell finding her in that position. That, sir, is the only logical explanation for that sequence of events, for you leaving her there alone, for you going to the Fowlers and telling them to take care of it, for you staying behind in their house and waiting for them to return with your daughter and with her humvee, and for you not reporting a word of this until this moment. You were very angry with her for what she did."

General Campbell sat there, deep in thought, contemplating, perhaps, his options, his life, his mistake a few nights ago, his mistake ten years ago. Finally, he said, "My career is ended, and I've drafted a resignation that I will submit tomorrow after my daughter's funeral. I suppose what I'm thinking about now is how much you have to know to find the murderer, how much I want to confess to you and to the world, and what good it would do anyone to further dishonor my daughter's memory. This is all self-serving, I know, but I do have to consider my wife and my son, and also the Army." He added, "I'm not a private citizen, and my conduct is a reflection on my profession, and my disgrace can only serve to lower the morale of the officer corps."

I wanted to tell him that the morale of the senior officers at Fort Hadley was already low as they all waited for the ax to fall, and that, indeed, he wasn't a private citizen and had no reasonable expectation to be treated like one, and that, yes, he sounded a little self-serving and that his daughter's reputation was not the issue at hand, and to let me worry about how much I had to know to find the murderer, and, last but not least, his career was, indeed, over. But instead, I told him, "I understand why you did not notify the MPs that your daughter was staked out naked on the rifle range— indeed, General, it was a private matter up until that point, and I confess to you I would have done the same thing. I understand, too, why and how the Fowlers got involved. Again, I confess, I would probably have done the same thing. But when the Fowlers returned and told you that your daughter was dead, you had no right to involve them in a conspiracy to conceal the true nature of the crime, and no right to involve your wife in the conspiracy as well. And no right, sir, to make my job and Ms. Sunhill's job more difficult by sending us up false trails."

He nodded. "You're absolutely correct. I take full responsibility."

I took a deep breath and informed him, "I must tell you, sir, that your actions are offenses that are punishable under the Uniform Code of Military Justice.''

He nodded again, slowly. ''Yes, I'm aware of that.'' He looked at me, then at Cynthia. ''I would ask one favor of you.''

''Yes, sir?''

''I would ask that you do everything you can to keep the Fowlers' name out of this.''

I was prepared for that request, and I'd wrestled with the answer long before General Campbell asked. I looked at Cynthia, then at the general, and replied, ''I can't compound this crime with a crime of my own.'' In fact, I'd already done that by striking a deal with Burt Yardley. But that was off-post stuff. This was not. I said, ''The Fowlers found the body, General. They did not report it.''

''They did. To me.''

Cynthia said, ''General, my position is somewhat different from Mr. Brenner's, and though detectives are never to disagree in public, I think we can keep the Fowlers out of this. In fact, Colonel Fowler *did* report the crime to you, and you told him you would call Colonel Kent. But in your shock and grief, and Mrs. Campbell's grief, the body was discovered before you could call the provost marshal. There are more details to work out, but I don't think justice would be served any better by dragging the Fowlers into this.''

General Campbell looked at Cynthia for a long time, then nodded.

I was not happy, but I was relieved. Colonel Fowler, after all, was perhaps the only officer who'd shown some degree of honor and integrity throughout, including not screwing the general's daughter. In truth, I did not possess that kind of willpower myself, and I was in awe of a man who did. Still, you don't give something for nothing, and Cynthia understood that, because she said to the general, ''But I would like you, sir, to tell us what actually happened out there, and why it happened.''

General Campbell sat back in his chair and nodded. He said, ''All right, then. The story actually begins ten years ago . . . ten years ago this month at West Point.''

CHAPTER TWENTY-EIGHT

General Campbell related to us what had happened at Camp Buckner, West Point's field training area. In regard to the actual rape, he knew not much more than we did, or, probably, the authorities did. What he did know was that, when he saw his daughter at Keller Army Hospital, she was traumatized, hysterical, and humiliated by what had happened to her. He told us that Ann clung to him, cried, and begged him to take her home.

He offered the information that his daughter told him she was a virgin, and that the men who raped her made fun of this. She told him that the men had pulled off her clothes and staked her on the ground with tent pegs. One of the men had choked her with a rope while he was raping her, and told her he'd strangle her to death if she reported the assault.

Neither I nor Cynthia, I'm sure, expected the general to provide these small, intimate details. He knew that this incident was only related to the murder in a peripheral way, and there was no clue there regarding her murderer. Yet, he wanted to talk, and we let him talk.

I got the impression, though he didn't address the issue directly, that his daughter expected him to see to it that justice was done, that there was no question that she'd been brutally raped, and that the men who'd done it were to be expelled from the military academy and prosecuted.

These, of course, were reasonable expectations for a young woman who'd been trying her damnedest to live up to Daddy's expectations, who had put up with all the hardships that were part of life at West Point, and who had been criminally assaulted.

But there were some problems, it seemed. First, there was the question of Cadet Campbell being alone with five men in the woods at night. How did she get separated from the forty-person patrol? By accident? On purpose? Second, Cadet Campbell could not identify the men. They not only wore camouflage paint, but they had mosquito nets over their faces. It was so dark, she couldn't even identify the uniforms and could not say for certain if the men were other cadets, West Point cadre, or soldiers from the 82nd Airborne Division. In all, there were close to a thousand men and women on training exercises that night, and the chance of her identifying her five attackers was almost nil, according to what General Campbell had been told.

But this was not precisely true, as Cynthia and I knew. By process of elimination, you could begin to narrow the field. And as you got closer to the perpetrators, it was inevitable that one of them would crack to save himself from long jail time. And also you had semen tests, saliva tests, hair tests, fingerprints, and all the other magic of forensic science. In fact, gang rapes were easier to solve than solitary rapes, and I knew that, Cynthia certainly knew it, and I strongly suspected that General Campbell knew it.

The real problem was not identifying who did it; the problem was that the rapists were either cadets, cadre, or soldiers. The problem was not in the area of police science, but in the area of public relations.

Basically, it came down to the fact that five erect penises penetrated one vagina, and the entire United States Army Military Academy at West Point could be torn apart in the same act that had torn Ann Campbell's hymen imperforatus. These were the times that we lived in; rape was not an act of sex—consensual sex is easily available. Rape was an act of violence, a breach of military order and discipline, an affront to the West Point code of honor, a definitive no vote against a co-ed academy, against women in the Army, against female officers, and against the notion that women could coexist with men in the dark woods of Camp Buckner, or the hostile environment of the battlefield.

The exclusive male domain of West Point had been infiltrated by people who squatted to piss in the woods, as that colonel at the O Club bar would put it. During the academic year, in the classroom, it wasn't intolerable. But out in the woods, in the hot summer night, in the dark, men will revert to ancient modes of behavior.

The entire field training experience, as I remember too well, was a call to arms, a call to war, a call to bravery, and an intentional imitation of a primitive rite of passage for young men. There were no women in the woods when I took my training, and if there had been, I would have felt sorry for them and been frightened for them.

But the people in Washington and the Pentagon had heard and heeded the call to equality. It was a good call, a necessary call, a long-overdue call. And certainly attitudes and perceptions had changed since I was a young man training for Vietnam. But not everyone's attitudes changed, and the move to equality proceeded at different paces in different sections of the national life. There are glitches in the system, little pockets of resistance, situational behavior, primitive stirrings in the loins. This is what happened on a night in August ten years before. The commandant of West Point did not announce that a hundred women in the woods with a thousand men did not get raped during recondo training. And he wasn't about to announce that one did.

So the people in Washington, in the Pentagon, at the Academy, had reasoned with General Joseph Campbell. And, as he related it to Cynthia and me, it certainly sounded reasonable. Better to have one unreported and unvindicated rape than to rock the very foundations of West Point, to cause doubts about a co-ed academy, to cast suspicion on a thousand innocent men who did not gang-rape a woman that night. All the general had to do was to convince his daughter that she—as well as the Academy, the Army, the nation, and the cause of equality—would best be served if she just forgot about the whole thing.

Ann Campbell was given a drug to prevent pregnancy, she was

tested and retested for sexually communicated diseases, her mother flew in from Germany and brought her a favorite childhood doll, her cuts and bruises healed, and everyone held their breath.

Daddy was convincing, Mommy was not as convinced. Ann trusted Daddy, and, at twenty years old, for all her world travel as a military brat, she was still Daddy's girl and she wanted to please him, so she forgot she was raped. But later, she remembered, which was why we were all sitting in the general's office that evening.

So that was the sad story, and the general's voice cracked now and then, got husky, got quiet. I heard Cynthia sniffle a few times, too, and I'd be a liar if I said I didn't feel a lump in my throat.

The general stood but motioned us to remain seated. He said, "Excuse me a moment." He disappeared through a door, and we could hear water running. As melodramatic as it sounds now, I almost expected to hear a gunshot.

Cynthia kept her eye on the door and said softly, "I understand why he did what he did, but as a woman, I'm outraged."

"As a man, I'm outraged, too, Cynthia. Five men have a memory of a fun night, and here we are dealing with the mess. Five men, if they were all cadets, went on to graduate and become officers and gentlemen. They were classmates of hers and probably saw her every day. Indirectly, or perhaps directly, they were responsible for her death. Certainly they were responsible for her mental condition."

Cynthia nodded. "And if they were soldiers, they went back to their post and bragged about how they all fucked this little West Point bitch cadet."

"Right. And they got away with it."

General Campbell returned and sat again. After a while, he said, "So you see, I got what I deserved, but Ann was the one who paid for my betrayal. Within months of the incident, she went from a warm, outgoing, and friendly girl to a distrustful, quiet, and withdrawn woman. She did well at the Point, graduated in the top of her class, and went on to postgraduate school. But things were never the same between us, and I should have thought of that consequence of my behavior." He added, "I lost my daughter when she lost her faith in me.'' He took a deep breath. ''You know, it feels good to talk it out.''

''Yes, sir.''

''You know about her promiscuousness, and professionals have explained to me what that was all about. It wasn't just that she was trying to corrupt the people around me or to embarrass me. She was saying to me, 'You thought nothing of my chastity, my decision to remain a virgin until I was ready, so what I'm giving to every man who wants it is nothing you care about. So don't lecture me.' ''

I nodded but could not and would not comment.

The general said, ''So the years pass, and she arrives here. Not by accident, but by design. A person in the Pentagon, a person who was closely involved with the West Point decision, strongly suggested that I consider two options. One, that I leave the service so that Ann might decide to leave also or might decide that her misbehavior was no longer profitable.'' He added, ''They were quite honestly afraid to ask for her resignation, because she obviously had something on the Army, though she never had a name. My second option was to take this uncoveted command at Fort Hadley, where the Psy-Ops School has its subcommand. They said they would have Ann transferred here, which would be a natural career assignment for her, and I could solve the problem in close quarters. I chose the second option, though my resignation would not have been unusual after the success in the Gulf and my years of service.'' He added, ''However, she told me once that if I ever accepted a White House appointment, or ever accepted a political nomination, she would go public with this story. In effect, I was being held hostage in the Army by my daughter, and my only options were to stay or to retire into private life.''

So, I thought, that explained General Campbell's coyness regarding political office or a presidential appointment. Like everything else about this case, this Army post, and the people here, what you saw, and what you heard, were not what was actually happening.

He looked around his office as though seeing it for the first time, or the last time. He said, ''So I chose to come here to try to make amends, to try to rectify not only my mistake but the mistake of my superiors, many of whom are still in the service or in public life, and most of whose names you would know.'' He paused and said, ''I'm not blaming my superiors for putting pressure on me. It was wrong what they did, but the ultimate decision to cooperate in the cover-up was mine. I thought I was doing what I did for good and valid reasons—for Ann and for the Army—but in the final analysis, they were not good reasons, and I was selling out my daughter for myself.'' He added, ''Within a year of the incident, I had my second star.''

At the risk of sounding too empathetic, I said, ''General, you are responsible for everything your subordinates do or fail to do. But in this case, your superiors betrayed you. They had no right to ask that of you.''

''I know. They know. All that talent, experience, and brain-power, and there we were meeting in a motel room in upstate New York in the middle of the night, like criminals talking ourselves into a completely dishonorable and stupid decision. But we're human, and we make bad decisions. However, had we truly been men of honor and integrity, as we said we were, we'd have reversed that bad decision no matter what the cost.''

I couldn't have agreed more, and he knew it, so I didn't say it. I said instead, ''So for two years, you and your daughter engaged in close-quarter hand-to-hand combat.''

He smiled grimly. ''Yes. It turned out to be not a healing process at all. It was war, and she was better prepared for it than I was. She had right on her side, and that made for might. She beat me at every turn, while I offered to make peace. I thought, if she won, she'd accept my apology and sincere regrets. It tore me apart, as a father, to see what she was doing to herself and her mother. I didn't care about myself any longer. But I was also concerned for the men she was using . . .'' He added, ''Though in some odd way, I was happy just to have her around on any terms. I missed her, and I miss her now.''

Cynthia and I sat quietly and listened to him breathe. Clearly, the man had aged ten years in the last few days, and probably another ten in the last two years. It struck me that this was not the same man who had returned in triumph and glory from the Gulf not so long ago. It was amazing, I thought, how even kings and emperors and generals could be brought down by domestic discord, by the wrath and fury of a wronged woman. Somehow, amid all the sophistication and diversions of this world, we forgot the basics: take care of business at home first, and never betray your blood.

I said to him, "Tell us about rifle range six, and then we'll leave you, General."

He nodded. "Yes . . . well, I saw her there on the ground, and . . . and I . . . I honestly thought at first that she'd been assaulted . . . but then she called out to me . . . she said, 'Here's the answer to your damned ultimatum.'

"I didn't understand at first what she was talking about, but then, of course, I remembered what they'd done to her at West Point. She asked me where her mother was, and I told her that her mother didn't know anything about this. She called me a damned coward, then she said, 'Do you see what they *did* to me? Do you *see* what they did to me?' And I . . . I did see . . . I mean, if her purpose was to make me *see*, then she achieved her purpose."

"And what did you say to her, General?"

"I . . . just called out to her . . . 'Ann, you didn't have to do this.' But she was . . . she was wild with anger, as though she'd completely lost her sanity. She yelled out for me to come closer, to see what they did to her, to see what she'd suffered. She went on like that for some time, then she said since I'd given her some choices, she was going to give me some choices." General Campbell paused a moment, then continued. "She said she had a rope around her neck . . . and I could strangle her if I wanted to . . . or I could cover this up like I did once before . . . I could come and untie her and take her away . . . take her to Beaumont House . . . to her mother. She also said I could leave her there, and the MPs or the guards or someone would find her, and she'd tell the MPs everything. Those were my choices."

335

Cynthia asked, "And did you go to her and try to untie her, as you told us you did?"

"No . . . I couldn't. I didn't go near her . . . I didn't try to untie her . . . I just stood near the car, then . . . I completely snapped. My anger and rage at all those years of trying to make things right got the best of me . . . I shouted back at her that I didn't give a damn what they'd done to her ten years ago . . . I told her I was going to leave her there and let the guards or the MPs find her, or the first platoon who came out to fire on the range or whoever, and that the whole world could see her naked for all I cared, and—" He stopped in midsentence and looked down at the floor, then continued. "I told her she couldn't hurt me anymore, and then she started shouting this Nietzsche junk—'whatever hurts you makes me stronger, what does not destroy me makes me stronger,' and so on. I said that the only hold she had over me was my rank and my position, and that I was resigning from the service, and that she had destroyed any feelings I had for her and that she had more than equaled the score."

The general poured himself some water from a carafe and drank it, then continued, "She said that was fine, that was good . . .'Let someone else find me—you never helped me . . .' Then she started to cry, and she couldn't stop crying, but I thought I heard her say . . . she said, 'Daddy' . . ." He stood. "Please . . . I can't . . ."

We stood also. I said, "Thank you, General." We turned and made toward the door before he began crying, but a thought came into my head, and I turned back to him and said, "Another death in the family won't solve anything. It's not the manly thing to do. It's very cowardly." But his back was toward us, and I don't know if he even heard me.

CHAPTER TWENTY-NINE

I drove out of the Post Headquarters parking lot, went a few hundred meters, then pulled off to the side of the road. A sort of delayed reaction to the interview came over me, and I actually felt shaky. I said, "Well, we know now why the lab people found dried tears on her cheeks."

Cynthia said, "I feel sick."

"I need a drink."

She took a deep breath. "No. We have to finish this. Where's Moore?"

"He'd damned well better be someplace on post." I put the Blazer into gear and headed toward the Psy-Ops School.

On the way, Cynthia said, as if to herself, "But in the end, the general did not abandon his daughter this time the way he did at West Point. He left her on the rifle range in a fit of rage, but somewhere on the road, he realized that this was the last chance for both of them."

She thought a moment, then continued, "He probably considered turning around, but then he thought about what he would need—a knife if the rope needed to be cut, clothing, a woman's presence. Those attentions to detail that are drummed into us overcame his shock and confusion, and he drove to Bethany Hill, to the one man on this post that he could trust." Cynthia paused, then asked,

"When the Fowlers got there, I wonder if they thought that the general strangled her?"

I replied, "It may have crossed their minds. But when they got back to the house and told him she was dead . . . they must have seen the shock and disbelief on his face."

Cynthia nodded. "Would they . . . should they have cut her loose and taken the body away?"

"No. Colonel Fowler knew that moving the body would only make matters worse. And I'm sure that Colonel Fowler, with his military experience, could determine that she was definitely dead. And as to any suspicion that he himself killed her, I'm sure he blessed the moment when he, the general, or Mrs. Fowler herself suggested that she go along."

"Yes, if it were Colonel Fowler alone, he'd be in a bad position."

I considered a moment, then said, "So we know that, aside from the victim, four other people were out there—Colonel Moore, the general, and Colonel and Mrs. Fowler. And we don't think any of them was the murderer. So we have to place a fifth person out there during that critical half-hour window of opportunity." I added, "That person, of course, is the killer."

Cynthia nodded. "Maybe we should have asked General Campbell if he had any idea who it was who arrived during that half hour."

"I think he believes it was Colonel Moore. If he thought it was anyone else, he'd have told us. I don't think it has occurred to him that Moore was the accomplice, not the killer. Bottom line, I just couldn't push the guy any further."

"I know. I hate to interview a victim's family. I get all emotional . . ."

"You did fine. I did fine. The general did fine."

I pulled into the Psy-Ops School, but Moore's car was not in its reserved spot. I drove around, past the school's dining facility, but we didn't see the gray Ford. I said, "If that SOB left post, I'll put his ass in a meat grinder."

An MP jeep pulled up alongside me, and our old friend, Corporal

Stroud, was in the passenger seat. "You looking for Colonel Moore, Chief?"

"None other."

Stroud smiled. "He went to see the provost marshal to get his restriction lifted."

"Thanks." I turned around and headed toward main post. I said to Cynthia, "I'm going to nail his ass to the wall."

"What happened to the meat grinder?"

"That, too."

I drove to main post, and, as I approached the provost marshal's building, I noticed that the news media were still there. I parked on the road directly in front of the main doors, and Cynthia and I got out and climbed the steps. We entered the building and went directly to Kent's office. His clerk said he was in conference.

"With Colonel Moore?"

"Yes, sir."

I opened his door, and there in Kent's office was Colonel Moore, Kent, and another man in uniform, a captain. Kent said to us, "Well, I guess I'm glad you're here."

The third man stood, and I saw by his branch insignia that he was a JAG officer—a lawyer. The man, whose name tag said Collins, asked me, "Are you Warrant Officer Brenner?"

"I'll ask the questions, Captain."

"I guess you are," he said. "Colonel Moore has requested that he be represented by counsel, so anything you have to say to him—"

"I'll say to him."

Moore was still sitting in front of Kent's desk and was pointedly not looking up. I said to Moore, "I'm placing you under arrest. Come with me."

Captain Collins motioned for his client to remain seated and said to me, "What is the charge?"

"Conduct unbecoming an officer and a gentleman."

"Oh, really, Mr. Brenner, that's a silly, catch-all—"

"Plus, Article 134, disorders and neglects, and so forth. Plus, accessory after the fact, conspiracy, and making false statements.

Plus, Captain, you are on the verge of Article 98, noncompliance with procedural rules.''

''How dare you?''

I asked Kent, ''Do you have two sets of cuffs handy?''

Colonel Kent looked worried now. He said, ''Paul, we have some questions of law and fact here. You can't arrest—well, you can, but I'm in the middle of a conversation with a suspect and his lawyer—''

''Colonel Moore is not a suspect in the murder, so there's no reason for a conversation, and if there were a reason, I'd be having the conversation, not you, Colonel.''

''Damn it, Brenner, you've gone too far—''

''Colonel, I'm taking my prisoner out of here.'' I said to Moore, ''Stand up.''

Without a glance toward his lawyer, he stood.

''Come with me.''

Cynthia and I left Kent's office with poor Colonel Moore in tow.

We escorted him down the corridors and into the holding cells. Most of the cells were empty, and I found an open door right next to Dalbert Elkins. I gave Moore a little nudge into the cell and slammed the door shut.

Dalbert Elkins looked at Moore, then at me, and said in a surprised tone, ''Hey, Chief, that's a full colonel.''

I ignored Elkins and said to Moore, ''You're charged with what I said before. You have the right to remain silent, you have the right to counsel of your choice.''

Moore spoke for the first time, reminding me, ''I *have* counsel. You just threatened to arrest him.''

''Right. And anything you say may be held against you in a court-martial.''

''I don't know who did it.''

''Did I say you did?''

''No . . . but . . .''

Dalbert Elkins was following all this closely. He said to Moore through the bars, ''Colonel, you shouldn't get a lawyer. It makes him mad.''

Moore glanced at Elkins, then turned his attention back to me. "Colonel Kent informed me that I was restricted to post, so I had no choice but to seek counsel—"

"Now you're worse than restricted. You're confined."

Dalbert said, "They're letting me out. Restricted to barracks. Thanks, Chief."

I ignored Elkins and said to Moore, "I have hard evidence that puts you at the scene of the crime, Colonel. There are enough charges against you to put you in jail for ten or twenty years."

Moore reeled backward as if I'd hit him, and he sat heavily on the cot. "No . . . I didn't do anything wrong. I just did what she asked me to do . . ."

"*You* suggested it."

"No! *She* suggested it. It was *her* idea."

"You knew fucking well what her father did to her at West Point."

"I only knew about a week ago—when he gave her his ultimatum."

Elkins looked at Cynthia and asked her, "What did he do to you?"

I said to Elkins, "Pipe down."

"Yes, sir."

I said to Moore, "I want you out of this Army. I may let you resign for the good of the service. That depends on how cooperative you are."

"I'm willing to cooperate—"

"I don't care if you're willing or not, Colonel. You *will* cooperate. You *will* fire your attorney."

Elkins began to second that, but thought better of it and sat down on his cot.

Moore nodded.

"What were you wearing out on rifle range six?"

"My uniform. We thought it would be best, in case I ran into any MPs—"

"Those shoes?"

"Yes."

341

"Take them off."

He hesitated, then took them off.

"Give them to me."

He handed them through the bars.

I said to him, "I'll see you later, Colonel." I said to Elkins, "How's my buddy?"

He stood. "Fine, sir. They're letting me out tomorrow morning."

"Good. If you run, you die."

"Yes, sir."

I walked away from the cells, and Cynthia followed. She asked, "Who was that other guy?"

"My buddy. The reason I'm here at Hadley." I explained briefly, then went into the office of the lockup sergeant. I identified myself and said to him, "I have a Colonel Moore in lockup. Have him strip-searched and give him only water tonight. No reading material allowed."

The sergeant looked at me wide-eyed. "You have an officer in lockup? A colonel?"

"He may not have access to counsel until sometime tomorrow. I'll let you know."

"Yes, sir."

I put Moore's shoes on his desk. "Have these tagged and delivered to hangar three at Jordan Field."

"Yes, sir."

We left and headed toward our office. Cynthia said, "I didn't know you were going to lock him up."

"Neither did I until I saw the lawyer. Well, everyone wanted me to arrest him."

"Yes, but for murder. And you don't put a commissioned officer in a common lockup."

"Silly custom. If he goes to Leavenworth, this is good training." I added, "Besides, people talk better when they've tasted jail."

"Right. Not to mention a strip-search and no rations. The regulations say he has to have at least bread and water."

"In each twenty-four-hour period. Meanwhile, I haven't had a decent meal myself in forty-eight hours."

"You're going to be officially criticized for the way you've handled this."

"That's the least of my problems at the moment."

We entered our office, and I flipped through the phone messages. Aside from the news media, there weren't many calls. No one wanted to speak to me anymore. There was, however, a message from the worried Major Bowes of the CID, the worried Colonel Weems of the staff judge advocate's office, and the anxious Colonel Hellmann. I called Hellmann at his home in Falls Church, where his wife assured me that I was interrupting his dinner. "Hello, Karl."

"Hello, Paul," he said in his jovial manner.

"Thanks for the fax," I said.

"Don't mention it. Don't *ever* mention it."

"Right. We've spoken to General and Mrs. Campbell, as well as to Mrs. Fowler. Cynthia and I can reconstruct nearly everything that happened that evening from about the time Captain Campbell had chicken for dinner at the O Club, to the time she reported for duty officer, to the time she took the humvee out ostensibly to check the guard posts, right up to and including the murder and beyond the murder, to dawn and to me becoming involved in the case."

"Very good. Who killed her?"

"Well, we don't actually know."

"I see. Will you know by noon tomorrow?"

"That's the program."

"It would be good if the CID could solve this case."

"Yes, sir. I'm looking forward to a promotion and a raise."

"Well, you'll get neither. But I will get that letter of reprimand out of your file as you politely requested."

"Terrific. Really good. You may get another to take its place. I arrested Colonel Moore, had him thrown in the lockup here, strip-searched, and put on water."

"Perhaps you could have just restricted him to post, Mr. Brenner."

"I did, but then he ran off and got a JAG lawyer."

"That's his right."

343

"Absolutely. In fact, I arrested him in front of his lawyer, and almost arrested the lawyer for interfering."

"I see. What is the charge, if not murder?"

"Conspiracy to conceal a crime, actions unbecoming, being an asshole, and so forth. You don't want to discuss this on the phone, do you?"

"No. Why don't you fax me a report?"

"No reports. Maybe Warrant Officer Kiefer can fax you a report."

"Oh, yes. I hope she's being helpful."

"We didn't know we had a third partner."

"Now you know. I actually called you because the CID commander there called Falls Church, and he's rather upset."

I didn't reply.

"Major Bowes. You remember him?"

"We've never met."

"Nevertheless, he's making all sorts of threats."

"Karl, there are about thirty officers on this post, almost all of them married, who were sexually involved with the deceased. They're all going to threaten, beg, plead, cajole, and—"

"*Thirty?*"

"At least. But who's counting?"

"*Thirty?* What is going on out there?"

"I think it's something in the water. I'm not drinking it."

Cynthia stifled a laugh, but too late, and Karl said, "Ms. Sunhill? Are you there?"

"Yes, sir. Just picked up."

"How do you know that thirty married officers were sexually involved with the deceased?"

Cynthia answered, "We found a diary, sir. Actually, a computer file. Grace got into the deceased's computer." She added, "The officers include most of the general's personal staff."

There was no reply, so I said, "I think we can control this if that's what they want in the Pentagon. I'd suggest transfers to thirty different duty stations, followed by individual resignations at varying intervals. That wouldn't draw any attention. But it's not my problem.''

Again, no response.

Cynthia said, ''General Campbell intends to resign tomorrow after his daughter's funeral.''

Karl spoke. ''I'm flying down tonight.''

I replied, ''Why don't you wait until tomorrow? There's an electrical storm here, tornado warnings, wind shear—''

''All right, tomorrow. Anything further?''

''No, sir.''

''We'll speak tomorrow.''

''Looking forward to it. Enjoy your dinner, sir.''

He hung up and we did the same.

Cynthia commented, ''I think he likes you.''

''That's what I'm afraid of. Well, how about a drink?''

''Not yet.'' She pushed the intercom and asked Ms. Kiefer to come in.

Kiefer entered with her own chair, now that we were all equals, and sat down. She inquired, ''How's it going, guys?''

''Fine,'' Cynthia replied. ''Thanks for sticking around.''

''This is where the action is.''

''Right. I'd like you to go through all your MP patrol reports for the night of the murder. Listen to the tapes of the radio transmissions, check the desk sergeant's log, see if any traffic or parking tickets were issued that night, and talk to the MPs who had duty that night, but be discreet. You know what we're looking for.''

Kiefer nodded. ''Yes. Cars and people where they're not supposed to be after about 2400 hours. Good idea.''

''Actually, you gave me the idea when you told us about Randy Six. That's the sort of thing that could be significant. See you later.''

We left Ms. Kiefer in our office. In the hallway, I said to Cynthia, ''You may have something there.''

''I hope so. We don't have much else.''

''Drink?''

''I think you should go talk to Colonel Kent. You've been very rough with him. I'll wait for you out front. Ask him to join us for a drink. Okay, Paul?''

I looked at Cynthia a moment, and our eyes met. It seemed from her tone of voice and her demeanor that she wanted more from Kent than his goodwill. I nodded. ''Okay.'' I went toward his office, and Cynthia continued on toward the front lobby.

I walked slowly toward Kent's office, my mind going faster than my legs. *Colonel William Kent*—motive, opportunity, the will to act, a strong presumption of innocence, but a weak alibi.

Position determines perspective. Or, to put it more simply, what you see depends on where you're standing. I'd been standing in the wrong place. I'd been standing too close to William Kent. I had to step back and see Kent from a different angle.

It had been gnawing at me for the last two days, but I couldn't bring myself to say it, or even think it. Kent had invited me to take the case, and that had put me in a certain mind-set. Kent was my only on-post ally at Fort Hadley. Everyone else was a suspect, a witness, a compromised officer, or a victim of sorts. Kent had belatedly confessed to being compromised, too, but only because he thought I'd eventually discover something regarding him and Ann Campbell, and he may also have suspected that Cynthia and I had found the room. In fact, if I thought about it, Burt Yardley probably told Kent that the door of the room had been glued shut, and they suspected that it had to be me who did that. The contents of the room appeared to be intact when Yardley came upon the room, but neither he nor Kent could be sure of what I had found there or taken away.

Burt Yardley, cunning bastard that he was, had feigned surprise that I knew about the room, but he knew that Ann Campbell wouldn't have glued it shut—therefore, he suspected that Brenner did. Burt Yardley took that information to Kent, and Kent decided to confess to sexual misconduct, but hedged his bet and never mentioned the room. Now the contents of the room were in Yardley's possession, and I didn't know who had whom by the balls, and what the relationship was of those two men, but if either of them killed her, the other didn't know about it.

346

I recalled how Kent resisted my decision to go directly to the victim's off-post house. That was understandable on the face of it— it was an irregular procedure—but I thought now that Kent had intended to call Yardley early that morning, or may have tried to call him before or after he called me, and intended to say something like, "Chief, Ann Campbell has been murdered on post. You should probably get a court order and go through her house, ASAP. Collect evidence." And Yardley would know what evidence had to be collected and disposed of, ASAP. But Yardley, according to his own statement, had been inconveniently or conveniently in Atlanta, and Kent found himself in a bind.

Right. So I got there first, and Kent had to make a different kind of call to Yardley in Atlanta, explaining what had happened. Then Kent and Yardley crossed their fingers, hoping that the hidden room would stay that way. Just as Cynthia and I had hoped for the same thing, not knowing that the Midland police chief and the Fort Hadley provost marshal had both been guests in that room.

Kent, too, had dragged his feet about notifying General and Mrs. Campbell. That could be an understandable human reaction, a natural aversion to being the bearer of bad news, though it was uncharacteristically unprofessional of Kent. But if Kent had killed the general's daughter, then I could see why he couldn't get up the courage to do his duty.

And Kent would not call Major Bowes, because Kent knew that Bowes knew about the room, the major having been entertained there as well. And Kent did not want Bowes to go there and collect evidence on Kent. And Kent could not get to that room in Ann Campbell's house himself, because, if he was the one who killed her, the place where he had to be was at home, and damned quick, to wait for the call from the MPs when she was found.

I could almost picture it . . . almost. Kent, for some reason that I still didn't know, was out there on or near rifle range six. I didn't know how or if he knew what was going to go on there, but I could sort of picture him after General Campbell left: big, tall Bill Kent, probably in his uniform, walking that fifty meters from the road, toward the naked and bound Ann Campbell. He stops and they look

347

at each other, and he realizes that fate has dropped this in his lap. His problem was Ann Campbell and her willingness to take everyone down with her. The answer to his problem was the rope that was already around her neck.

He may or may not have known what this scenario was all about, he may or may not have heard the exchange with her father. If he hadn't, then perhaps he mistook what he saw for a sexual rendezvous with another man, and he was jealous, enraged. In any event, they certainly spoke, and it was very possible that Ann Campbell said the wrong thing at the wrong time.

Or perhaps it didn't matter what she said—Kent had had enough. He knew that there was trace evidence from other people at the scene, and he knew he'd be back in an official capacity within hours, and any evidence of his presence was explainable and expected. He's a cop, and he computes all of it very quickly. Not only would this be the perfect crime, but it was the necessary crime. All he has to do is kneel down and tighten the rope. But did he have the will to act? Didn't she plead with him? Could he have been that cold and callous? Or was it heat and rage that drove him?

What did I know about this man whom I'd seen maybe a dozen times in the last ten years? I searched my memory, but all I could say for sure about him was that he was always more concerned about the appearance of propriety than with propriety itself. He was very aware of his reputation as Mr. Clean Cop. He never made sexual comments or jokes, and he was tough on the men in his command who did not live up to his high standards of conduct and appearance. But then he was seduced by the general's daughter. He knew he was the butt of jokes, according to Ms. Kiefer, he knew he was losing respect, and he knew you don't get to be a general by fucking one of their daughters.

And was it possible, somewhere in the dark recesses of his mind, that he *knew* that certain people on post, certainly people under his command, would wonder in awe if it was Colonel Kent who had done it, if the top cop at Hadley had solved not only his problem but the problems of thirty senior officers and their wives? The average person might feel revulsion against a killer, but a killer can also command fear and respect, especially if there's a sense that the killer was doing something not quite all bad.

But given all that, given the fact that these speculations and deductions made sense and fit the facts, did that make Colonel William Kent, provost marshal of Fort Hadley, a suspect in the murder of Captain Ann Campbell? With all the other possible men, and perhaps women, on post who had a motive—revenge, jealousy, concealment of a crime, to avoid humiliation or disgrace, or even homicidal mania—why Kent? And, if Kent, how would I go about proving it? In the rare cases when a cop at the scene of a crime may be the perpetrator of the crime, the investigating officer has a real problem.

I stood in front of Kent's door a moment, then knocked.

CHAPTER THIRTY

I pointed the Blazer toward the Officers' Club, and we drove in silence, then I asked Cynthia, "Why do you think it was Kent?"

"Instinct."

"Instinct is what put Kent between Ann Campbell's thighs. Why do you think he murdered her?"

"I don't know that he did, Paul. But we've eliminated other suspects. The Yardley boys have tight alibis, we know what Colonel Moore did, and the Fowlers are each other's witnesses, and the general, and, for that matter, Mrs. Campbell, are clean as far as I'm concerned. Sergeant St. John and MP Casey, who found the body, are not likely suspects, and neither is anyone else we've spoken to or heard about."

"But there's Major Bowes, Colonel Weems, Lieutenant Elby, the head chaplain, the medical officer, and about thirty other officers who had a motive. Plus, there are the wives of those officers, if you think about that. That's a possibility."

"True. And there could very well be someone else out there whom we haven't even heard of. But you have to consider opportunity and the will to commit murder."

"Right. Unfortunately, we don't have the time to interview all the men in her diary. And I'd hate to think of the FBI doing that,

350

because they'll write a two-hundred-page report on every one of them. Kent is a possible suspect, but I don't want him to be a convenient suspect like he—and some others here—tried to make of Colonel Moore.''

''I understand that. But it just struck me at some point that Kent fits.''

''When did it strike you?''

''I don't know. In the shower.''

''I'll pass on that.''

''Do you think he'll join us for a drink?''

''He was vague. But if he's the murderer, he'll be there. I've never seen it fail yet. They want to be close, to see, to hear, to try to manipulate the investigation. And the bright ones are not obvious about it. I certainly wouldn't say that if Kent joined us for a drink he is the murderer. But if he doesn't show up, I'd bet money that he isn't.''

''I understand.''

In my years in the CID, I had managed to avoid every Department of the Army mandated personnel management class, sensitivity session, race and gender relations course, and so on, which was obviously why I was having problems in the new Army. But I did take lots of leadership classes, and within those classes was everything you needed to know about human relations, such as: respect subordinates and superiors, don't ask your people to do anything you wouldn't do, earn respect, don't demand it, give praise when it's due. So, in that spirit, I said to Cynthia, ''You're doing a fine job, you've shown good initiative, good judgment, and poise under pressure. You're very professional, very knowledgeable, and very hardworking. It's a pleasure to be working with you.''

''Is this a recorded message?''

''No, I—''

''No feeling, Paul. Completely atonal. Speak from your heart, if you have one.''

''I resent that.'' I pulled into the Officers' Club parking lot and nosed into a space. ''That's judgmental, very—''

"I love you. Say it."

"I said it last year. How many times—?"

"Say it!"

"I love you."

"Good." She jumped out of the Blazer, slammed the door, and began walking across the parking lot. I followed and caught up. We didn't exchange another word until we got into the main lounge. I found an empty table in the corner and checked my watch, which gave me the civilian time of eight-fifteen P.M. The dining room was full, but the lounge was half-empty now that half-price Happy Hour was over. The new Army officially frowns on half-price Happy Hour, but the clubs are quasi-independent, and some of them still honor the ancient and honorable tradition of cheap whisky for an hour or two, a minor reward for putting up with bullshit that no civilian—except a recent immigrant from a military dictatorship—would put up with. But the Army has its moments. Unfortunately, there are fewer of them these days. A waitress came around, and Cynthia ordered her bourbon and Coke, and I ordered a Scotch with a beer chaser. I said, "I'm dehydrated. God, it's hot out there."

"You've been sweating like a pig all day," she agreed. She smiled. "You need a shower."

"Do we have time?"

"We might have to share it again."

"This is a demanding job."

The drinks came and we toasted. She said, "To Ann Campbell. We'll do our best for you, Captain."

We drank.

I said, "This case is getting to me. Is that because of the case, or because I'm tired and old?"

"It's because of the case, Paul. Because you care. Because it's not just a case. It's a human tragedy."

"What other kind of tragedies are there? We're all a heartbeat away from tragedy."

"Right. When we find the killer, it won't be a time to celebrate. It will be another tragedy. It will be someone who knew her. Maybe loved her."

"Like Kent."

"Yes. I keep thinking of something I read once . . . something I think about when I'm interviewing a woman who's been raped. It goes like this—'Compared to shame, death is nothing.' I think that's what happened here, starting with Ann Campbell's shame and humiliation at West Point. I mean, think of it, Paul. They teach officers to be proud, to be assertive, to stand tall. People like Ann Campbell are already predisposed to this type of personality, so they gravitate toward someplace like West Point. Then, when something like that happens, a rape, a humiliation, they can't handle it. They don't bend like most people. They stand tall, then snap."

I nodded. "I see that."

"Right. They pick up the pieces and go on, but they're never the same again. I mean, no woman is after a brutal rape, but someone like Ann Campbell can't even begin to heal inside."

"I understand that some people think that the only cure for shame and humiliation is revenge."

"Correct. So take that a step further and think of the average male officer. He's been seduced by Ann Campbell in about twenty minutes, including drinks, he's been led into a sex room and encouraged or coerced into engaging in kinky acts, then at some point he's either discarded or asked by Ann to bend a few rules for her. He has a mix of emotions—starting with a little male vanity at his conquest, but eventually, if he's married and if he takes any of this officer stuff seriously, he feels shame. Most men would not feel a great deal of shame for a consensual sex act, but some men— officers, clergy, pillars of the community—will feel shame. So we get back to 'Compared to shame, death is nothing.' Or call it dishonor, to put it in a military context. This could apply to Ann Campbell, General Campbell, and to any number of men who either wished themselves or Ann Campbell dead. That's why I think it was someone she knew, someone who felt that the act of murder was a way to end the shame and dishonor of the victim as well as of the murderer. Kent, as a ramrod kind of cop, an officer, might well fit that theory."

I nodded again. I'd thought something similar, though with a

353

different slant. But it was interesting that we both had a psychological profile of the killer that could fit Kent. Then again, there's nothing like hindsight. "Kent," I said, "Kent."

"Speaking of whom . . ."

In walked Colonel Kent, and a few heads turned. Any post's top cop usually gets a few heads to turn, a few side glances. But now, at Hadley, with a sensational murder still hot news, Kent was the man of the hour. He saw us and walked over.

Cynthia and I stood, as was customary. I might shove it up his butt in private, but in public I gave him the respect he was supposed to deserve.

He sat and we sat. A waitress came over and Kent ordered drinks for us and a gin and tonic for himself. "On me," he said.

We chatted awhile, everyone agreeing what a strain this had been and how tempers were getting short, sleepless nights, hot days, and all that crap. As casual and chatty as Cynthia and I were, Kent was a pro and he smelled the rat, or perhaps felt like the rat being maneuvered into the corner.

He said to us, "Will you stay on awhile after the funeral, and brief the FBI?"

"I think that's what we're supposed to do," I replied. "But I'd like to be gone by nightfall tomorrow."

He nodded, then smiled at us. "You two getting along? Or is that a leading question?"

Cynthia returned the smile. "We're renewing our friendship."

"Right. Where'd you meet?"

"Brussels."

"Great city."

And so on. But every once in a while, he would nonchalantly ask something like, "So Moore's definitely not the murderer?"

"Nothing is definite," Cynthia replied, "but we don't think so." She added, "It's scary how close we came to accusing the wrong man."

"If he *is* the wrong man. You're saying he tied her up and left?"

"Right," I replied. "I can't reveal why, but we know why."

"Then he's an accessory to murder."

"Not legally," I said. "It was something completely different."

"Weird. Did your computer lady get what she needed?"

"I think so. Unfortunately for some guys, Ann Campbell left a sort of sexual diary in the computer."

"Oh, Jesus . . . am I in there?"

"I think so, Bill." I added, "With about thirty other officers."

"My God . . . I knew she had lots of . . . but not that many . . . God, I feel like a fool. Hey, can we get the diary classified?"

I smiled. "You mean like top secret? Come up with a national security angle and I'll see what I can do. Meanwhile, the decision rests with the judge advocate general, or the attorney general, or both. I think you have enough company not to be too concerned with being singled out."

"Well, but I'm a cop."

"There were guys in that diary with more power and prestige than you."

"That's good. How about Fowler?"

"Can't say. Hey, did you know that Burt Yardley was also in the honey?"

"No kidding . . . ? Jesus . . ."

"You see, you had more in common with Burt than you realized." *But seriously, Bill.* "Do you know him well?"

"Only professionally. We attend the monthly G-5 meetings."

That's civilian affairs, and if I'd thought about it, I'd have realized that they were thrown together often enough, chief and provost, top cop and top cop, to work out a mutual ass-covering arrangement.

Kent asked, "Have either of you gone over to the chapel yet?"

"No," Cynthia replied. "I think we'll wait until the service tomorrow. Are you going to the chapel tonight?"

He glanced at his watch. "Yes, of course. I was a lover."

I asked, "How big is that chapel?"

We both shared a little laugh, but it was definitely a crude remark, and Cynthia gave me a really mean look.

I asked him, "Is Mrs. Kent still in Ohio?"

"Yes."

"Until when?"

"Oh . . . another few days."

"That's a long drive. Or did she fly?"

He glanced at me, then replied, "Flew." He forced a smile. "On her broom."

I returned the phony smile and said, "Can I ask if her departure is related to ugly rumors about you and Captain Campbell?"

"Well . . . there was a little of that, I guess. We're trying to work it out. But she really doesn't *know*. She just *thinks*. You're not married, but maybe you understand."

"I *was* married. Cynthia is married."

He looked at her. "Are you? Military?"

"Yes. He's at Benning."

"Tough life."

And so forth. Perfectly pleasant. Two warrant officers, CID types, and a senior commissioned officer, the MP commander, drinking and talking about life, love, the job, and, every once in a while, sandwiching in the subject of murder. This is an interesting interrogation technique, and it's quite effective in appropriate situations, like this one. In fact, I call it the murder sandwich—a little bread, meat, lettuce, blood, cheese, tomato, blood, and so forth.

But Bill Kent wasn't your average suspect, and I had the distinct impression that he knew what this was about, and that he knew that we knew that he knew, and so on. So it became a little dance, a charade, and at one point our eyes met, and then he knew for sure, and I knew for sure.

At this point, when a guy realizes you're on to him, it's kind of awkward for everyone, and the suspect goes into an exaggerated nonchalance, trying to show how completely at ease he is. Sometimes, too, a perverse or reverse sort of logic takes over, and the suspect gets ballsy. In fact, Kent said to us, "I'm glad I asked you two to take this case. I was pretty sure Bowes was involved with her, but I didn't want to say that in case it wasn't true. He has no special homicide investigators on his team here anyway, and they'd have just sent somebody like you two from Falls Church eventually. Or they'd have called the FBI right away. So I was glad you were here." He looked at me and said, "We've worked together before, and I knew you'd be right for this case." He added, "You've only got until noon tomorrow, right? But you know what? I think you're going to wrap it up before noon."

And so we sat there a minute, playing with cocktail stirrers and napkins, Cynthia and I wondering if there was a murderer at the table, and Bill Kent contemplating the end of his career at the very least, and perhaps wrestling with the notion of telling us something that would get us out of here by noon tomorrow.

Sometimes people need encouragement, so I said to him in a tone he'd understand, "Bill, do you want to take a walk? Or we can go back to your office. We can talk."

He shook his head. "I have to go." He stood. "Well . . . I hope those butchers at the morgue left enough of her for an open casket. I'd like to see her again . . . I don't have a photo . . ." He forced another smile. "There aren't too many souvenirs of an extramarital affair."

Actually, there had been a room full of them. Cynthia and I stood also, and I said, "Get one of those recruiting posters before everyone else thinks the same thing. Collector's item."

"Right."

"Thanks for the drinks," I said.

He turned and left.

We sat. Cynthia watched him walking away, then said, as if to herself, "He could be upset over the end of his career, his soon-to-be-public disgrace, his troubled marriage, and the death of someone he cared for. Maybe that's what we're seeing. Or . . . he did it."

I nodded. "Hard to evaluate his behavior given all he's going through. Yet, there is something about a person's eyes . . . they speak their own language, from the heart and soul. They speak love, grief, hate, innocence, and guilt. They speak the truth even as the person is lying."

Cynthia nodded. "They sure do."

We both sat in silence awhile, then Cynthia asked, "So?"

I looked at her, and she looked back into my eyes, a sort of experiment, I guess, and we both agreed without speaking that Bill Kent was our man.

CHAPTER THIRTY-ONE

We skipped dinner and drove out on Rifle Range Road toward Jordan Field. As Kent had indicated earlier, there was an MP checkpoint on the road, and we had to stop and identify ourselves. When we got to the MP booth at the entrance to Jordan Field, we went through another identification procedure, then yet another at the door of hangar three. The Army liked to keep reporters in the press conference room, where the Army thought they belonged. Reporters liked to roam. These differences of opinion have been going on for a few hundred years. The Army citing security considerations, the press invoking their traditional and lawful privileges. The Army has gotten the upper hand in recent decades, having learned at least one lesson in Vietnam.

My own experiences with the press began in Vietnam when a reporter stuck a microphone under my nose while we were both pinned down by machine-gun fire. The news camera rolled, and the reporter asked me, "What's happening?" I thought the situation spoke for itself, but young idiot that I was, I replied, "An enemy machine gun's got our range." The guy asked, "What are you going to do now?" I said to him, "Leave you and the camera guy here." And I made a hasty withdrawal, hoping the enemy gunner would concentrate his fire on the gentlemen of the press. Somewhere, that news footage was in an archive, preserved for posterity. I never saw the two guys again.

The hangar was nearly deserted, most of the forensic people having gone back to Fort Gillem, or on to other assignments, with their equipment. But about half a dozen people had stayed behind to type reports and complete a few more tests.

Ann Campbell's home was still there, as well as the humvee and her BMW, but her office was gone. Nevertheless, Grace Dixon sat at a camp desk, yawning, in front of an IBM personal computer.

She looked up at us as we approached and said, "I requisitioned another PC. I'm sorting files, reading letters and diaries, but not printing out, as you said. You got that stuff on Yardley that I sent you?"

"Yes," I replied. "Thanks."

Grace said, "This is very hot stuff here. I love it."

"Take a cold shower tonight, Grace."

She laughed and wiggled her ample rear end in the seat. "I'm sticking to the chair."

Cynthia asked, "Where are you staying tonight?"

"Guest house on post. I'll sleep with the disk. No men. Promise." She added, "The post chaplain is in this diary. Is nothing sacred?"

I wanted to point out that sleeping with a goddess was itself a sacrament, but I didn't think either of the two ladies would appreciate it. I asked Grace, "Can you print out all entries that mention the name of Colonel William Kent?"

"Sure. I've seen him in here. I can scan for that. What's his job or title in case it's under that?"

"He's the provost marshal. Known to friends as Bill."

"Right. I saw him in here. You want printouts every time his name appears, right?"

"Correct. Also, the FBI may be around tonight or early tomorrow. The MPs outside will not stop them from coming through that door. But if you see the type walking across the hangar, you take the disk out and make believe you're typing a report. Okay?"

"Sure. But what if they have a court order or a search warrant or something?"

It's easier to deal with military types because they follow orders. Civilians want explanations and ask too many questions. I replied to her, "Grace, you're just typing reports. Put the disk on your person, and if they want to look under your dress, slap them."

She laughed. "What if they're cute?"

Obviously, something had fired up this woman's libido.

Cynthia said to her, "It's really important, Grace, that no one but us three sees that stuff."

"Okay."

I asked her, "Is Cal Seiver still here?"

"Yes. He's grabbing some cot time over there." Grace was playing with the keys again. I don't know much about computers, and I want to know less. But people like Grace, who are into them, are a little weird. They can't seem to break away from the screen, and they sit there, talk, type, mumble, curse, squeal with delight, and probably go without sex, sleep, and food for extended periods. Actually, I guess that goes for me, too. Cynthia and I left Grace without bothering her with a farewell.

I rolled a chalkboard in front of her so that anyone coming in the door wouldn't see her, then we found Cal Seiver in a deep sleep on a cot, and I woke him. He stood unsteadily and seemed confused by his surroundings.

I gave him a few seconds, then asked him, "Did you find anything new and interesting?"

"No, we're just putting it all in order now."

"You have disqualifying footprints and fingerprints from Colonel Kent?"

"Sure."

"Did you find any of his prints out at the scene? On the humvee, on her handbag, the latrines?"

He thought a moment, then said, "No. But his bootprints are all over. I took boot impressions from him to disqualify those."

"Did you get Colonel Moore's shoes?"

"Sure did. I compared them to unidentified plaster casts. They lead right to the body, then back to the road."

"Do you have a diagram yet?"

"Sure." He walked over to a rolling bulletin board and snapped on a portable light. Tacked to the board was a four-foot-by-eight-foot diagram of the murder scene. The scene took in a stretch of road, the victim's parked humvee, the beginning of the bleachers, and, on the other side of the road, a small section of the firing range that included a few pop-up targets and a sketch of a spread-eagled figure that the artist had rendered sexless.

Footprints were marked by colored pins, and there was a legend at the bottom of the board identifying the known owners of the boot- and shoeprints, with black pins indicating unknown owners or un-clear footprints. Little arrows showed directions, and notes indicated whether the prints were fresh, old, rained on, and so forth. In cases where a print was superimposed on another print, the most recent print had a longer pin. There were other notes and explanations to try to add some clarity to the chaos. Eventually, this whole board would be fed into a computer, and you would see a more graphic display, including, if you wished, the prints appearing one after an-other, as if a ghost were walking. Also, you could eliminate or call up any set of prints you wanted. But for now, I had to make do with my own experience, and that of Cynthia and Cal Seiver.

Seiver said, "We really haven't analyzed this. That's sort of your job."

"Right. I remember that from the manual."

He added, "We've got to spiffy this up a little for the FBI. There's too many variables and unknowns here, including the fact we don't have the footwear that you wore."

"That might be in the VOQ now."

"When people hold off on providing footprints, I get suspi-cious."

"Fuck off, Cal."

"Right." He looked at the legend and said, "Colonel Moore is yellow."

361

I replied, "Colonel Kent is who we want."

Pause. *"Kent?"*

"Kent." I looked at the legend. Kent was blue.

We all studied the diagram, and, in the quiet hangar, you could hear the computer printer spewing out paper.

I said to Cal Seiver, "Talk to me."

"Right." Seiver began, and, from what he was saying, it appeared that Colonel William Kent had visited the body no fewer than three times. Cal explained, "See, here he walks from the road to the body. Stops very near the body, probably kneels or squats because, when he turns, his prints rotate, then he probably stands and goes back to the road. This was probably the first time, when he went out there with his MP who found the body . . . See, here's her print . . . Casey. She's green. Then the next time may have been here where he accompanied you and Cynthia with her running shoes. Cynthia is white." He managed to remind me again, "You're black. Lots of black. I'll give you pink pins when I get your boots. But for now, I can't tell you from—"

"Okay. I get it. How about the third time he walked out to the body?"

Cal shrugged. "He walked there when I was there, but we had tarps down by then. I guess he went out to the body more than once before you two got there, because it seems that we've got three trails of his prints from the road to the body. But even that's hard to say for sure because no trail is complete. We got prints over prints, and we got soft ground and hard ground, and grass."

"Right." We all studied the pins, the arrows, and the notations.

I said, "There was a man and woman out there also, wearing civilian shoes. I could get you the shoes, but what I'm interested in is Colonel Kent. I think he visited the scene earlier, probably in uniform, with the same boots he wore later, somewhere between, say, 0245 and 0330 hours."

Cal Seiver thought a moment, then replied, "But the body wasn't found until . . . what time? . . . 0400, by the duty sergeant, St. John."

I didn't reply.

Seiver scratched his bald head and stared at the diagram. "Well
. . . could be . . . I mean, here's something that doesn't make sense
. . . here's St. John's bootprint. Orange. That's a definite. The guy
had a wad of gum on his sole and it printed. Okay . . . so here we
have St. John's bootprint, and it *seems* to be superimposed on a
bootprint that we *think* is Colonel Kent's. Kent had very new boots
with clear tread. So . . . I mean, if St. John was there at 0400 hours,
and Colonel Kent didn't arrive until the MPs called him at what
. . . after 0500 hours, then St. John's bootprint *on top of* Kent's
bootprint wouldn't make sense. But you have to understand that
while we can ID the impressions of most footwear if the medium
is good—snow, mud, soft soil, and such—it's not as precise as
fingerprints. And in this case, where we have two good prints, we
can't say for certain which was superimposed on which."

"But you have St. John's noted as being superimposed on
Kent's."

"Well, that's a judgment call by the tech. Could be a mistake.
Probably was, now that I see it. St. John was there first, so he
couldn't have walked over Kent's . . . but you're saying you think
Kent was there before St. John found the body."

"I'm saying it," I replied, "but you will not say it to anyone."

"I only give information to you two and to a court-martial
board."

"Correct."

Cynthia said to Cal, "Let's see the plaster impression of this
spot."

"Right." Cal looked at some sheets of typed paper on the bulletin
board and matched something to something, then led us to a distant
corner of the hangar where about a hundred white plaster casts of
footprints sat on the floor, looking like the evidence of Pompeii's
populace heading out of town.

The casts were numbered with black grease pencil, and he found
the one he wanted, hefted it up, and carried it over to a table. There
was a fluorescent lamp clamped to the table, and I turned it on.

We all stared at the cast a few seconds, then Cal said, "Okay, this bootprint is St. John's, heading toward the body. This little mark at the edge is the direction of the body. Okay, also heading toward the body is this bootprint, which is Colonel Kent's."

I looked at the two bootprints. They were superimposed side by side, the left side of Kent's left boot overlapping the right side of St. John's right boot—or St. John's overlapping Kent's. That was the question. I didn't say anything, and neither did Cynthia. Finally, Cal said, "Well . . . if you . . . do you see that indent there? That's the wad of gum on St. John's boot, but it wasn't touched by Kent's boot or vice versa. You see, we have two military boots of the same make, same tread, and the prints were made within hours of each other . . . and we have intersecting and interlocking tread marks . . ."

"Do you need a deerstalker cap for this?"

"A what?"

"Why did someone put the shorter pin on Kent's print on the diagram?"

"Well, I'm not an expert on this."

"Where is the expert?"

"He's gone. But let me give it a try." He changed the position of the lighting, then shut it off and looked at the cast in the shadowy overhead light of the hangar, then got a flashlight and tried different angles and distances. Cynthia and I looked as well, this not being an exact science but more a matter of common sense. In truth, it was nearly impossible to say with any certainty which bootprint had been made first.

Cynthia ran her finger over the places where the two bootprints intersected. With a smooth sole, you could easily tell which was deeper, but even that was not proof that the deeper one was made first, given the fact that people walk differently and are of different weights. But the deeper print is usually first because it compresses the earth or the snow or the mud, and the next footstep is walking on compressed earth and will not sink in as far, unless the person is a real lard-ass. Cynthia said, "St. John's print is a hair higher than Kent's."

Cal said, "I've seen Kent, and he weighs about two hundred pounds. How about St. John?"

I replied, "About the same."

"Well," said Seiver, "it really depends on how hard they came down. Relative to their other prints on the diagram, and considering the flat impressions of both prints, neither was running. In fact, I'd guess that both were walking slowly. So if Kent's print is a hair deeper, you'd have to guess that Kent's print was made first, and St. John walked over Kent's print later. But that's just a guess." He added, "I wouldn't send anybody to the gallows on that."

"No, but we can scare the shit out of him."

"Right."

"Can you get the latent-footprint guy back here tonight?"

Cal shook his head. "He's off to Oakland Army Base on assignment. I can get someone else flown in by chopper."

"I want the original guy. Get this cast on a flight to Oakland and have him analyze it again. Don't tell him what he thought the first time. Right? He's not going to remember this one out of a few hundred."

"Right. We'll see if we get the same analysis. I'll get on it. We may have to put it on a commercial flight out of Atlanta to San Francisco. I may go myself."

"No way, pal. You're stuck at Hadley with me."

"Shit."

"Right. Okay, I do want a latent-footprint team from Gillem. I want them out at the rifle range at first light. They're looking for more of Colonel Kent's bootprints. Have them look alongside the road, out further on the range, around the body again, and near the latrines and so on. I want a clear diagram showing only Kent's prints. Better yet, feed everything into a computer program, and be prepared to show it by noon tomorrow. Okay?"

"We'll do our best." He hesitated, then asked, "Are you sure about this?"

I gave him a slight nod, which was all the encouragement he needed to roust people out of bed and get them back to Hadley at dawn. I said, "Cal, the FBI might come around tonight or early

365

tomorrow. They have jurisdiction over this case as of noon tomorrow. But not until then."

"I hear you."

"Work out some kind of early warning signal with the MPs outside, and alert Grace so she can stuff the disk she's working on."

"No problem."

"Thanks. You've done a good job."

Cynthia and I went back to Grace Dixon, who was making a neat pile of printouts on her desk. She said, "Here's the last one. That's all the diary entries that mention Bill Kent, William Kent, Kent, and so on."

"Good." I took the stack and leafed through it. There were about forty sheets of paper, some with more than one dated entry, the first going back to June of two years ago, and the most recent was just last week.

Cynthia commented, "They saw a lot of each other."

I nodded. "Okay, thanks again, Grace. Why don't you put the disk in your secret place and go get some sleep?"

"I'm okay. You look like hell."

"See you tomorrow."

I took the printouts with me, and we made the long walk across the hangar and exited through the small door. It was one of those still nights where the humidity hung in the air, and you couldn't even smell the pines unless you were on top of them. "Shower?" I asked.

"No," Cynthia replied. "Provost office. Colonel Moore and Ms. Baker-Kiefer. Remember them?"

We got into my Blazer, and the clock on the dashboard said ten thirty-five. That gave us less than fourteen hours to tie it up.

Cynthia saw me looking at the clock and said, "The FBI guys are probably yawning and thinking about turning in. But they'll be all over the place tomorrow morning."

"Right." I put the Blazer in gear, and we headed away from Jordan Field. I said, "I don't care if they get credit for solving this case. I'm not into the petty crap. I'll turn this all over to them at

366

noon tomorrow, and they can run with it. But the closer we get to the perpetrator, the less dirt they have to dig up. I'll point them in Kent's direction and hope that's as far as it goes.''

''Well, that's very big of you to let them wind it up. Your career is sort of winding up, too. But I could use the credit.''

I glanced at her. ''We're military. We just take orders. In fact, you take orders from me.''

''Yes, sir.'' She sulked for a minute, then said, ''The FBI are masters at the public relations game, Paul. Their PR people make the Army Public Information Office look like an information booth at a bus station. We've got to finish this ourselves, even if it means putting a gun to Kent's head and threatening to blow his brains out unless he signs a confession.''

''My, my, aren't we assertive tonight.''

''Paul, this is important. And you're right about the FBI digging up unnecessary dirt. They'll leak the contents of that diary to every paper in the country, and to add insult to injury, they'll say they found the disk and cracked it. These guys are good, but they're ruthless. They're almost as ruthless as you.''

''Thank you.''

''And they don't care about the Army. Talk about Nietzsche— the FBI philosophy is, 'Whatever makes any other law enforcement agency or institution look bad makes us look better.' So we have to wrap it up by noon.''

''Okay. Who's the murderer?''

''Kent.''

''Positive?''

''No. Are you?''

I shrugged. ''I like the guy.''

She nodded. ''I don't dislike him, but I'm not overly fond of him.''

It was funny, I thought, how men and women often had a different opinion of the same person. The last time I can remember when a woman and I both agreed that we really liked a guy, the woman was my wife, and she ran off with the guy. I asked, as a matter of information, ''What is it about Kent that you don't like?''

"He cheated on his wife."

Makes sense to me. I added to that, "He may also be a killer. Minor point, but I thought I'd mention it."

"Can the sarcasm. If he murdered Ann Campbell, he did it on the spur of the moment. Cheating on his wife was a two-year, premeditated infidelity. It shows weakness of character."

"I'll say." I headed up the long, dark road through the pine forest. In the distance, I could see the lights of Bethany Hill, and I wondered what was going on at the Fowler house and the Kent house. I said, "I wouldn't want to be up there for dinner tonight."

Cynthia looked out the windshield. "What a mess. I came here to Hadley to investigate a rape, and I wind up involved with the aftershock of a ten-year-old rape."

"Crime breeds crime breeds crime," I pointed out.

"Right. Did you know that a rape victim is statistically more likely to get raped again than a female who has never been raped?"

"I didn't know that."

"But no one seems to know why. There's no common denominator like job, age, neighborhood, or anything like that. It's just that if it happened once, it's more likely to happen again. Makes no sense. It's scary, like there's some sort of evil out there that knows . . . ."

"Spooky," I agreed. I didn't have that experience in homicide cases. You only get killed once.

Cynthia began talking about her job, about how the job got her down sometimes, and how it had probably affected her marriage.

Cynthia obviously needed to talk, to start healing herself before the next case. But there's always a residue of each case, and it's like a soul toxin that makes you spiritually sicker each year. But it's a job that needed to be done, and some people decided to do it, and some people decided they needed another job. You form a callus around your heart, I think, but it's only as thick as you want it to be, and sometimes a particularly vicious crime cuts right through the callus, and you're wounded again.

Cynthia kept talking, and I supposed I realized that this talk was not just about her, or her marriage, or the job, but about me, and about us.

She said, "I think I might apply for a transfer to . . . something else."

"Like what?"

"The Army band." She laughed. "I used to play the flute. Do you play anything?"

"Just the radio. How about Panama?"

She shrugged. "You go where they send you. I don't know . . . Everything's up in the air."

I guess I was supposed to say something, to offer an alternative. But in truth, I wasn't as confident and decisive in my personal life as I was in my professional life. When a woman says "commitment," I ask for an aspirin. When she says "love," I immediately lace up my running shoes.

Yet, this thing with Cynthia was real, because it had withstood some test of time, and because I'd missed her and thought about her for a year. But now that she was here, right beside me, I was starting to panic. But I wasn't going to blow it again, so I said to her, "I still have that farmhouse outside of Falls Church. Maybe you'd like to see it."

"I'd love to."

"Good."

"When?"

"I guess . . . day after tomorrow. When we go back to headquarters. Stay the weekend. Longer if you want."

"I have to be at Benning on Monday."

"Why?"

"Lawyers. Papers. I'm getting divorced in Georgia. I was married in Virginia. You'd think there'd be a national divorce law for people like us."

"Good idea."

"I have to be in Panama by the end of this month. I'd like to finalize the divorce before then or it'll take another six months if I'm out of the country."

"Right. I got my divorce papers delivered in the mail call by chopper while I was under fire."

"Really?"

369

"Really. Plus a dunning letter for my car loan, and antiwar literature from a peace group in San Francisco. Some days it doesn't pay to get out of bed. Actually, I had no bed. Goes to show you. Things could be worse."

"Things could be better. We'll have a good weekend."

"Looking forward to it."

CHAPTER THIRTY-TWO

We arrived back at the provost marshal's building. The media had decamped, and I parked in a no-parking zone on the road. Carrying the printouts of Ann Campbell's diary, we went inside the building.

I said to Cynthia, "We'll speak with Colonel Moore first, then see what Ms. Kiefer has found."

As we walked toward the holding cells, Cynthia observed, "It's hard to comprehend that the man who runs this whole place could be a criminal."

"Right. It kind of messes up the protocols and the standard operating procedures."

"Sure does. How do you feel about that bootprint?"

"It's about all we've got," I replied.

She thought a moment, then said, "But we've got motive and opportunity. Though I'm not certain about our psychological profile of the killer or Kent's will to act. Also, we have almost no circumstantial evidence." She added, "But after having drinks with him, I think our intuition is correct."

"Good. Tell it to the FBI."

I asked the lockup sergeant to accompany us, and we went to Colonel Moore's cell. Moore was sitting up in his cot, fully dressed except for his shoes. Dalbert Elkins had pulled his chair up to the

371

common bars and was talking to Moore, who was either listening very intently or had gone into a catatonic trance.

They both saw us approaching and both stood. Elkins seemed glad to see me, but Moore looked apprehensive, not to mention disheveled.

Elkins said to me, "Still set for tomorrow, Chief? No problem?"

"No problem."

"My wife says to say thanks to you."

"She does? She told me to keep you here."

Elkins laughed.

I said to the MP sergeant, "Will you unlock Colonel Moore, please?"

"Yes, sir." He unlocked Moore's cell and asked me, "Cuffs?"

"Yes, please, Sergeant."

The MP sergeant barked at Moore, "Wrists, front!"

Moore thrust his clenched hands to his front, and the sergeant snapped the cuffs on him.

Without a word, we walked down the long, echoing corridor, past the mostly empty cells. Moore, in his stockinged feet, made no echoes. There are few places on this earth more dismal than a cell block, and few scenes more melancholy than a prisoner in handcuffs. Moore, for all his intellectualizing, was not handling this well, which was the purpose.

We went into an interrogation room, and the sergeant left us. I said to Moore, "Sit."

He sat.

Cynthia and I sat at a table opposite him.

I said to him, "I told you that the next time we spoke, it would be here."

He didn't reply. He looked a little frightened, a little dejected, and a little angry, though he was trying to suppress that, since he realized it wouldn't do him any good. I said to him, "If you'd told us everything you knew the first time, you might not be here."

No reply.

"Do you know what makes a detective really, really angry?

When the detective has to waste valuable time and energy on a witness who's being cute.''

I verbally poked him around awhile, assuring him that he made me sick, that he was a disgrace to his uniform, his rank, his profession, his country, and to God, the human race, and the universe.

All the while, Moore stayed silent, though I don't think this was an expression of his Fifth Amendment right to do so as much as it was his accurate estimate that I wanted him to shut his mouth.

Cynthia, meanwhile, had taken the printouts of the diary and had gotten up and left for most of the verbal abuse. After about five minutes, she came back without the printouts, but she was carrying a plastic tray on which was a Styrofoam cup of milk and a donut.

Moore's eyes flashed to the food, and he stopped paying attention to me.

Cynthia said to him, ''I brought you this.'' She set the tray down out of his reach and said to him, ''I've asked the MP to unlock your cuffs so you can eat. He'll be here when he gets a moment.''

Moore assured her, ''I can eat with my cuffs on.''

Cynthia informed him, ''It's against regulations to make a prisoner eat with wrist manacles, chains, cuffs, and such.''

''You're not *making* me. I'm perfectly willing to—''

''Sorry. Wait for the sergeant.''

Moore kept looking at the donut, which, I suspected, was the first mess hall donut he'd ever shown any interest in. I said to him, ''Let's get on with this. And don't jerk us around like you did the last few times. Okay, to show you how much shit you're in, I'm going to tell you what we already know from the forensic evidence. Then you're going to fill in the details. First, you and Ann Campbell planned this for at least a week—from the time her father gave her the ultimatum. Okay, I don't know whose idea it was to re-create the West Point rape''—I stared at him and saw his reaction to this, then went on—''but it was a sick idea. Okay, you called her at Post Headquarters, coordinated the times, and drove out to rifle range five, where you pulled across the gravel lot and behind the bleachers there. You got out of your car, carrying the tent pegs, rope, a hammer, and so forth, and also a mobile phone, and maybe the tape player. You walked along the corduroy trail to the latrines at rifle range six, and perhaps called her again from there to confirm that she'd left Post Headquarters.''

I spent the next ten minutes re-creating the crime for him, basing my narrative on forensic evidence, conjecture, and supposition. Colonel Moore looked duly impressed, very surprised, and increasingly unhappy.

I continued, ''You called the general's red phone, and when he answered, Ann played the taped message. It was then, knowing you had about twenty minutes or so, that you both began to set the stage. She undressed in or near the jeep in case someone came along unexpectedly. You put her things in a plastic bag which you left at the humvee. Correct?''

''Yes.''

''She kept her watch on.''

''Yes. She wanted to keep track of the time. She could see the watch face, and she thought that would be reassuring somehow as she waited for her parents.''

Odd, I thought, but a lot less odd than the scene that presented itself to me the first time I saw her naked and staked out, wearing a watch and nothing else. In fact, I had come a long way since that morning, when I thought I was looking at the work of a homicidal rapist. In truth, the crime had taken place in phases, in stages, and the genesis of the crime was a decade old, and what I saw was not what it seemed to all the world to be. What I saw was the end product of a bizarre night that could have ended differently.

I said to Moore, ''By the way, did you notice if she had her West Point ring on?''

He replied without hesitation, ''Yes, she did. It was a symbolic link to the original rape. It was engraved with her name on the inside, of course, and she intended to give it to her father as a token of some sort—as a way of saying that the bad memories that it symbolized were in his possession, and she did not want to be reminded of them again.''

''I see . . .'' My goodness, this was a unique, if somewhat

troubled, woman. And it occurred to me that there was some sort of psychosexual thing between father and daughter that was buried deep down there, and probably Moore understood it, and maybe all the Campbells understood it, but I damned sure didn't want to know about it.

I exchanged glances with Cynthia, and I think she had the same thought that I did. But back to the crime in question. I said to Moore, "Then you both walked out on the range, picked a spot at the base of the closest pop-up target about fifty meters from the road, and she lay down and spread her arms and legs." I looked at him and asked, "How does it feel to be thought of as a handy eunuch?"

He showed a flash of anger, then controlled it and said, "I have never taken sexual advantage of a patient. No matter how bizarre you may think this therapy was, it was designed to help, to act as a catharsis for both parties. The therapy did not include me having sex with, or raping, my patient when she was tied up."

"You're one hell of a guy, an absolute paragon of professional standards. But let me not get myself all pissed-off again. What I want to know from you is what happened after you tied the last knot. Talk to me."

"All right . . . Well, we spoke a moment, and she thanked me for risking so much to assist her in her plan—"

"Colonel, cut the self-serving crap. Continue."

He took a deep breath and went on. "I walked back to the humvee, collected the plastic bag of clothes, and also my briefcase, which I had used to carry the tent stakes and rope, and which now held only the hammer, then I went to the latrine sheds behind the bleacher seats and waited."

"Waited for what? For whom?"

"Well, for her parents, of course. Also, she was concerned that someone else might come by first and see her humvee, so she asked me to stay until her parents got there."

"And what were you supposed to do if anyone else showed up first? Hide your head in the toilet bowl?"

I felt Cynthia kick me under the table, and she took over the interview. She asked Moore, nicely, "What were you supposed to do, Colonel?"

He looked at her, then at the donut, then at her again and replied, "Well, I had her pistol in the plastic bag. But . . . I don't know exactly what I was supposed to do, but if anyone else came along and saw her before her parents did, I was prepared to see that no harm came to her."

"I see. And it was at this point that you used the latrine?"

Moore seemed a little surprised, then nodded. "Yes . . . I had to use the latrine."

I said to him, "You were so scared, you had to piss. Right? Then you washed your hands like a good soldier, then what?"

He stared at me, then directed his reply to Cynthia. "I stood behind the latrine shed, then I saw the headlights on the road. The vehicle stopped, and when the driver's side door opened, I could see it was the general. In any case, it was full moonlight, and I recognized Mrs. Campbell's car, though I didn't see her." He added, "I was afraid that General Campbell might not take his wife along."

"Why?"

"Well . . . without Mrs. Campbell, the situation had the potential to get out of hand. I never thought that the general would be able to approach his own daughter, naked . . . I was fairly certain that, if it were only those two, the sparks would fly."

Cynthia looked at him a long moment, then asked, "Did you stay around for the exchange between General Campbell and his daughter?"

"No."

"Why not?"

"We decided that I should not. As soon as I was sure it was the general, I threw the plastic bag with her clothing onto the latrine roof, then I hurried back along that log trail. It was about a five-minute walk back to my car, and I couldn't be certain how long this exchange between the two was going to last. I wanted to get my car on the road and head back toward post as soon as possible, which I did."

Cynthia asked, "And did you see any other vehicle on the road as you were driving back to post?"

"No, I did not."

Cynthia and I glanced at each other, and I looked at Moore. I said to him, "Colonel, think. Did you see any other headlights going in either direction?"

"No. Absolutely not. That's what I was concerned about . . . ." He added, "I was certain I wasn't seen."

"And you saw no one on foot?"

"No."

"Did you see or hear anything when you were at rifle range five or six? How about at the latrine, the humvee, on the trail?"

He shook his head. "No."

"So after you left, someone killed her."

"Yes. I left her alive."

"Who do you think killed her?"

He looked at me, sort of surprised. "Well, the general, of course. I thought you knew that."

"Why do you say that?"

"Why? You know what happened. You know that my part was only to help her re-create the rape scene for her parents to see. He got there—I saw him with my own eyes—and later that morning she was found strangled. Who else could have done it?"

Cynthia asked him, "What did she expect her parents to do? What did she say to you about that?"

Moore thought a moment, then replied, "Well . . . I think she expected them to . . . She didn't know quite how they were going to deal with what they saw, but she fully expected them to get her out of there no matter how difficult it was for them." He added, "She knew they wouldn't leave her there, so they would be forced to confront her, confront her nakedness, her shame and humiliation, and to physically undo her bonds, and thereby psychologically free not only her but themselves." He looked at us. "Do you understand?"

Cynthia nodded. "Yes, I understand the theory."

I put in my opinion. "Sounds screwy to me."

Moore said to me, "If Mrs. Campbell had been there, it might have worked. Certainly, it would not have ended in tragedy."

"Well, the best-laid plans of shrinks usually go astray."

He ignored me and said to Cynthia, "Could you at least pass that cup of milk here? I'm very dry."

"Sure." Cynthia put the milk near his manacled hands, and he took the cup with both hands and drained it in one long gulp. He put the cup down, and we all stayed silent for a minute or so while Moore savored the milk as if it were a glass of that cream sherry he liked.

Cynthia said to him, "Did she ever indicate to you that she thought her father might come alone, might become enraged, and actually kill her?"

Moore answered quickly, "No! If she had, I would never have agreed to her—to the plan."

I nodded to myself. I didn't know if that was true or not, and only two people did. One of them was dead, the other, sitting here, was going to lie about it to mitigate what he'd done. The general himself knew, of course, how he'd felt in that moment when his daughter had hurled the challenge at him. But he couldn't even tell himself what he felt, and he wasn't going to tell me. In a way, it didn't matter anymore.

Cynthia asked the prisoner, "Did it occur to you or Ann Campbell that the general did not come prepared to free his daughter—I don't mean psychologically—I'm referring to a knife or stake puller."

Moore replied, "Yes, she considered that. In fact, I stuck a bayonet in the ground . . . you found that, didn't you?"

Cynthia asked, "Where was the bayonet?"

"Well . . . sort of between her legs . . . The men who raped her at West Point took her bayonet and jammed it in the ground, close to her . . . her vagina, then warned her about not reporting what happened, then she was cut loose."

Cynthia nodded. "I see . . ."

Moore continued, "She was trying to shock him, of course, shock both of them, and they were going to have to retrieve the bayonet and cut her loose. Then she thought he would offer her his shirt or jacket. I'd left her bra there, and her panties were around her neck, as I'm sure you found them. That's how they had left her in the woods at West Point. They'd thrown her clothes around, and she'd had to retrieve them in the dark. In this case, however, she intended for her parents to help her back to the humvee, then she intended to tell her father where her clothes were—on top of the latrine—and make him go get them. She'd left her handbag in the humvee with her keys, and it was her intention to get dressed and drive off as if nothing had happened, then return to duty at Post Headquarters. Then she was going to show up at the breakfast meeting she had with her parents, and, at that point, they would all confront the issues.''

Again Cynthia nodded. She asked, "Did she have much hope for this breakfast meeting?"

He considered a moment, then replied, "Yes, I think she did. Depending, of course, on how her father and mother had reacted to the rape scene. Well, as it turned out, Mrs. Campbell had not come along. But I think that Ann realized that whatever forces she unleashed that night, no matter how her father reacted, things could not get any worse. There is a high risk with shock therapy, but when you've nothing left to lose, when you've hit bottom, then you're ready to gamble everything and hope for the best."

Cynthia nodded again, the way they tell you to do in the interrogation manual. Be positive, affirming. Don't appear stone-faced, or judgmental, or skeptical when a suspect is rolling. Just keep nodding, like a shrink during a therapy session. Perhaps Moore recognized the technique, which was ironic, but in his present mental and physical state, all he wanted was a smile, a nod, and the stupid donut. Cynthia asked him, "Did she tell you why she had hope for this meeting? I mean, why this time, after all those years?"

"Well . . . she was finally ready to forgive. She was prepared to say anything that morning, to promise anything that would make things right again. She was tired of the war, and she felt the catharsis even before she'd gone out to the rifle range. She was hopeful, almost giddy, and to tell you the truth, she was happy and close to peace for the first time since I'd known her.'' He took a long breath and looked at us, then said, ''I know what you think of me, and I don't blame you, but I had only her best interests at heart. She had seduced me, too, in another way, and I went along with what I knew was . . . unorthodox. But if you could have seen how optimistic she was, how almost girlish she was acting—nervous, frightened, but filled with hope that this was the end of the long nightmare . . . In fact, however, I knew that the damage she had done to herself and others was not going to disappear just like that, just because she was going to say to her parents, 'I love you, and I forgive you if you forgive me' . . . but she believed this, and she had me believing it too . . . But she miscalculated . . . I miscalculated her father's rage . . . and the irony is, she thought she was so close to being happy again . . . and she kept rehearsing what she was going to say to them that night . . . and at breakfast . . .''

Then the oddest thing happened. Two tears rolled down Moore's cheeks, and he put his face in his hands.

Cynthia stood and put her hand on his shoulder and motioned me to come with her. We went out into the corridor, and she said to me, ''Let him go, Paul.''

''Hell, no.''

''You got your jailhouse interview. Let him go sleep in his office, attend the funeral tomorrow. We'll deal with him tomorrow or the next day. He's not going anywhere.''

I shrugged. ''All right. God, I'm getting soft.'' I went to the guard office and spoke to the sergeant. I filled out a confinement release form and signed it—I hate confinement release forms—then I walked out to the corridor where Cynthia was waiting for me.

I said, ''He's free, but restricted to post.''

''Good. It was the right thing.''

''We don't know that.''

''Paul . . . anger is not going to change anything that happened, and vindictiveness is not going to bring justice. That's the lesson you should learn from this. Ann Campbell never did. But what happened to her should at least be a useful example of that.''

"Thank you."

We walked to our office, and I sat at the desk, dividing the diary printouts between Cynthia and myself. Before we began to read, I said to her, "What happened to the bayonet?"

She replied, "I don't know. If General Campbell never approached his daughter, then he never saw it, and never knew that he could have cut her loose. He told us two versions of that story— one was that he tried to get her free by pulling at the stakes, the other that he couldn't bring himself to get that close." She added, "He actually never got that close."

"Right. So the next person on the scene—let's say it was Kent— saw the bayonet, and Kent had the same choice—if it was Kent. Then came the Fowlers, who had their own knife . . . but she was already dead. Then came Sergeant St. John, then MP Casey . . . I don't know, but it's interesting that whoever pulled the bayonet out of the ground kept it . . ." I noodled this awhile, then said, "If we accept the general's second version, that he never went near her, then it wasn't him. The killer had no reason to take the bayonet. Neither did St. John or MP Casey."

"Are you saying the Fowlers took it?"

"I'm saying that when the Fowlers found her dead, and saw that the means of freeing her was right there between her legs, if you will, they realized that the general had lied to them, that the general had not tried to free her, as I'm sure he told them he did. That, in fact, as General Campbell told us truthfully in the second version, he had kept his distance from her, and they had shouted to each other. So when the Fowlers saw the bayonet, they realized that the general *could* have freed her, but did not, and as a result, she was dead. Not wanting to tell him this, or have him find out through the official report, they took the bayonet and discarded it. This was another favor they were doing for him, but they weren't doing us any favors."

Cynthia thought a moment, then said, "Yes, that's probably what happened." She looked at me. "And her West Point ring?"

"Beats the hell out of me."

"The Fowlers again?"

381

"Possible. Another favor, though I don't get it. Maybe the killer took it as a sentimental remembrance. I don't think MP Casey or St. John would do something so ghoulish, but you just never know what people are going to do in the presence of a dead body. Then again, maybe the gencral got a little closer to his daughter than he said. He took the bayonet, considered cutting her loose, then changed his mind, took her ring off, and told her she was dishonoring her uniform, or lack of same, and left—then had a change of heart and drove to the Fowlers. Who knows? Who cares at this point?''

"I do. I have to know how people act, what goes on in their hearts. It's important, Paul, because it's what makes this job more than what's in the manual. Do you want to become like Karl Hellmann?''

I forced a smile. "Sometimes, yes.''

"Then you'll never again be able to determine a motive or understand who is good and who is evil.''

"Sounds okay to me.''

"Don't be contrary.''

"Speaking of motives, of good and evil, of passion, jealousy, and hate, let's give this stuff a quick read.''

We read for a while and discovered what William Kent's sexual preferences were, but more important, I discovered that Ann Campbell considered him a growing problem. I said to Cynthia, "Here's an entry from last month.'' I read aloud, " 'Bill is becoming possessive again. I thought we solved that problem. He showed up here tonight when Ted Bowes was here. Ted and I hadn't gone downstairs yet, and Bill and he had a drink in the living room, and Bill was nasty to him and pulled rank on him. Finally, Ted left, and Bill and I had words. He says he's prepared to leave his wife and resign his commission if I promise to live with him or marry him or something. He knows why I do what I do with him and the other men, but he's starting to think there's more to it with us. He's pressing me, and I tell him to stop. Tonight, he doesn't even want sex. He just wants to talk. I let him talk, but I don't like what he's saying. Why do

382

some men think they have to be knights in shining armor? I don't need a knight. I am my own knight, I am my own dragon, and I live in my own castle. Everyone else are props and bit players. Bill is not very cognitive. He doesn't understand, so I don't try to explain. I did tell him I'd consider his offer, but in the meantime, would he only come here with an appointment? This put him into a rage, and he actually slapped me, then ripped off my clothes and raped me on the living room floor. When he was done, he seemed to feel better, then left in a sulk. I realize he could be dangerous, but I don't care, and, in fact, of all of them, he's the only one except for Wes who has actually threatened me or hit me, and it's the only thing that makes Bill Kent interesting.' "

I looked up from the paper, and Cynthia and I exchanged glances. Clearly, Colonel Kent was dangerous. There's nothing more dangerous than a prim and proper stuffed shirt who falls in lust and gets obsessed. I was about to read another printout aloud when there was a knock on the door, and it opened. I expected to see Warrant Officer Kiefer, but it was Colonel Kent, and I wondered how long he'd been standing there.

CHAPTER THIRTY-THREE

I gathered up the printouts and slipped them in a folder.
Kent stood there and watched but said nothing.

Kent had his helmet on, what we call cover in the military. You're usually uncovered indoors, unless you're armed, then you must be covered. Interesting regulation probably having to do with keeping your hands free if you're armed, or letting people know at a distance that you're armed. Kent, in fact, was wearing his sidearm.

So was I, and so was Cynthia, but ours were hidden, and we didn't have to wear hats to give us away.

The office was dark, lit only by two desk lamps, and I could hardly see Kent's features from where I was sitting, but I thought he looked sort of grim, perhaps subdued, and I remembered that he'd gone to the chapel to view the body.

He spoke in a quiet, almost toneless voice. He said, ''Why was Specialist Baker snooping around?''

I stood and replied, ''She's not snooping around. She's gathering some items that I asked for.''

''This is my command. Anything you need, you ask me.''

Quite right, actually. Except, in this case, the items had to do with the commander. I said, ''It was just a minor administrative thing, Colonel.''

''Nothing in this building is minor.''

"Well, parking and traffic tickets are minor."

"Why do you need those?"

"It's a standard procedure. You must know that it's to establish if any vehicles were anyplace that—"

"I know that. And you wanted MP patrol reports, the desk sergeant's log, and tapes of the radio transmissions for that night. Are you looking for any vehicle in particular?"

Actually, yes. Your vehicle. But I replied, "No. Where is Baker?"

"I relieved her of her duties and ordered her out of the building."

"I see. Well, I'm going to ask you, officially, to rescind that order."

"I've assigned you another clerk. I will not tolerate any breach of internal security by anyone, for any reason. You have broken the rules, and perhaps the law. I'll take this up with the staff judge advocate tomorrow."

"That's certainly your right, Colonel. Though I think Colonel Weems has other things on his mind at the moment."

Kent seemed to know what I was talking about and replied, "The Uniform Code of Military Justice is not dependent on any single individual, and everyone here is subject to that law, including both of you."

"That's very true. I take full responsibility for what Baker did."

Cynthia stood now and said, "It's actually my responsibility, Colonel. I ordered Baker to do that."

Kent looked at her and replied, "All you had to do was ask me first."

"Yes, sir."

Having taken the offensive, Kent continued his attack, though he seemed to have no enthusiasm for it. He said to me, "I didn't say anything when you had Colonel Moore confined to jail, but I will make an official report regarding your treatment of him. You don't treat officers that way." Obviously, Kent was thinking into the future, and his complaint had nothing to do with Colonel Moore.

I replied, "Officers don't usually act that way. He abused his rank, his profession, and his office."

"Nevertheless, he could have been restricted to post and given suitable quarters until an official inquiry was completed, and charges recommended or not recommended."

"You know, Colonel, I personally think that the higher you are, the harder you should fall. Young enlisted personnel who screw up because of ignorance, immaturity, or high spirits get the book thrown at them. I think that mature officers who screw up should be made an example of."

"But rank still has its privilege, and one of those privileges is that an officer should not be subject to pretrial confinement, Mister Brenner."

"But when you break the law, your punishment should be in direct proportion to your rank, your job, and your knowledge of the law. An officer's rights and privileges carry a heavy responsibility, and any breach of duty and discipline should carry a proportionately heavy punitive burden." *I'm talking about you, Bill, and you know it.*

He replied, "A soldier's past performance has to be factored into that. If a person has performed honorably for twenty years—as Colonel Moore has—then he should be treated with honor and respect. A court-martial will decide his punishment, if any."

I looked at Kent for a long moment, then responded, "An officer, I believe, having been given special privileges and having taken an oath of office, has an obligation to fully confess his crimes and to relieve a court-martial board of the unpleasant duty of convening for a public trial. In fact, I sort of like the ancient tradition of an officer falling on his sword. But since no one has the balls for that anymore, I think that an officer who has committed a capital crime or has dishonored himself and his uniform should at least consider blowing his brains out."

Kent replied, "I think you're crazy."

"Probably. Maybe I should talk to a shrink. Charlie Moore could square me away. You'll be happy to know that I've signed a release order for him, and he should be gone by now, probably riding around looking for a place to sleep tonight. You should try the Psy-

Ops School officers' quarters if you want to find him. He thinks, by the way, that the general murdered his own daughter. I know the general didn't. So whoever did murder her will have to decide if he is going to let Moore tell the FBI what he suspects, and allow that suspicion to hang over the head of a basically honorable man. Or will this person who committed the crime redeem his honor and confess?''

Kent and I looked at each other, then Kent said, ''I think whoever killed her didn't think it was a crime. You like to talk about honor, ancient customs, and the rights and duties of an officer. Well, I'll bet that the murderer feels no reason to bother the military justice system with this act of . . . of personal justice and honor. There's your philosophy looked at from the other point of view.''

''True enough. Unfortunately, these are the legalistic times we live in, and my personal feelings are as unacceptable as yours. I've investigated homicides for over ten years, Colonel, and you've seen enough of them, too. In almost all cases, the murderer thinks he or she was justified. Civilian juries are starting to buy it, too. Bottom line on that, though, is if you felt it was justified, then let's hear it.'' Somehow, we had gotten from the general to the almost specific, depending on how one interpreted the personal pronoun ''you.''

Kent looked at me, then at Cynthia, then said, ''I went to the chapel earlier. I'm not a religious man, but I said a prayer for her. She looked very peaceful, by the way. I guess that's the undertaker's art, but I'd like to think that her soul is free and her spirit is happy again . . .'' He turned and left.

Cynthia and I sat in the silence of the dark office for a few seconds, then Cynthia spoke. ''Well, we know where Ann Campbell's anguish and torment are residing at the moment.''

''Yes.''

''Do you think he'll confess?''

''I don't know. Depends on who wins the battle he's going to fight between now and dawn.''

''I don't believe in suicide, Paul, and you had no right to even mention it to him.''

I shrugged. "The thought of suicide is a great consolation, and it's gotten people through many a bad night."

"Nonsense."

"No, Nietzsche."

"Sick." She stood. "Let's find Baker."

"Kiefer." I stood also, took the folder with the printouts, and we left the office and the building and went out into the night.

Outside, on the steps of the provost marshal's building, I could see heat lightning in the distance, and a wind was picking up. "Storm coming."

"Typical Georgia," Cynthia replied. She said, "If it had stormed two nights ago . . ."

"Right. But more to the point, if men didn't rape, and if institutions didn't try to cover their institutional asses, and if parents and children could communicate, and if revenge wasn't so sweet, and if monogamy was a biological imperative, and if everyone treated everyone else the way they would like to be treated, then we'd be out of a job, and they could use the cell blocks to breed bird dogs."

Cynthia put her arm through mine, and we walked down the steps to the Blazer.

We got into the vehicle as the first few drops of rain fell, and she asked, "How will we find Kiefer?"

"Kiefer will find us."

"Where will she find us?"

"Where she knows we will be. The VOQ." I started the car, put it into gear, and turned on the headlights.

The rain got heavier, and I put on the wipers. We drove in silence through the nearly deserted streets of the main post. My civilian clock said ten to midnight, but, despite the hour and the short sleep the night before, I felt fine. Within a few minutes, I pulled into the VOQ lot, which was when the sky burst open, and the rain was so heavy I could hardly hear myself say to Cynthia, "Do you want me to drive you to the door?"

She called back over the beating rain, "No. Do you want me to drive *you* to the door?"

There's an upside to modern women; they don't melt in the rain. Actually, my suit looked far more expensive than her outfit, and I nearly took her up on it, but after a minute of waiting for the rain to slacken, we dashed for it.

The lot was flooded, compliments of the Army Corps of Engineers, and by the time we got to the door, less than fifty meters away, we were soaked. Actually, it felt good.

In the small lobby, the CQ, a young corporal, informed me, "Some Midland cop came by and left some luggage here for you, sir."

I shook myself off. "Right." My buddy Burt was showing me he was true to his word. "Where is it?" I asked. "In my room, all unpacked for me, pressed and hung?"

"No, sir, it's over there on the floor."

"How many stars does this place have, Corporal?"

"Well, if we got one more, we'd be up to zero."

"Right. Any messages?"

"Two." He handed me two message slips. Kiefer and Seiver. I went over to my luggage, which consisted of two civilian suitcases, an Army duffel bag, and an overnight bag. Cynthia offered to help and took a suitcase and the overnight bag. Together we climbed the interior staircase, and, within a few minutes, we were in my room and dumping the luggage on the floor.

Cynthia caught her breath and said, "I'm going to change. Are you going to return those calls?"

"Yes." I threw my wet jacket over a chair, sat on the bed, and slipped my shoes off as I dialed the number Kiefer had left. A woman answered, "Five-four-five MP Company, CQ speaking."

"This is Colonel Hellmann," I said, as much for kicks as for identification, "may I speak to Specialist Baker, please."

"Yes, sir, hold on."

Cynthia had left, and as I waited with the phone cradled between my ear and shoulder, I peeled off my wet shirt and tie and got out of my socks and trousers. Baker-Kiefer had chosen to live in the barracks, which was good for cover, but inconvenient for life. I knew that the CQ runner had gone off to get her, which was the Army's answer to private telephones in each room.

The line clicked, and I heard her voice, "Specialist Baker here, sir."

"Can you talk?"

"No, sir, but I'll call you back from a pay phone here as soon as one opens up. VOQ?"

"Right." I hung up and sat on the floor, opening my suitcases and looking for my robe. That bastard Yardley had stuffed everything together, including dirty laundry, shoes, and shaving gear. "Bastard."

"Who?"

I looked over my shoulder and saw that Cynthia was back in the room, wearing a silk kimono and drying her hair with a towel. I said, "I'm looking for my robe."

"Here, let's get you organized." And she began sorting and hanging things in the closet, and folding things, and so on.

Women have this incredible knack with fabrics, and they make it look easy, but I can't even get a pair of pants to hang straight on a hanger.

I felt a little silly in my undershorts, rooting around on the floor, but I finally found my robe jammed into the duffel bag, and I slipped it on as the phone rang. I said to Cynthia, "Kiefer calling back."

I picked up the phone and said, "Brenner here."

But it was not Kiefer, it was Cal Seiver. He said to me, "Paul, I studied that footprint chart until I went blind, and I studied plaster casts until I got a hernia. I can't find any further evidence that Colonel Kent was at the scene earlier than he says he was. I figured, since we know what we're looking for now, I could have the footprint team do it again tomorrow, but this rain is a washout."

"Did you leave the tarps and pavilion there?"

"No. Maybe I should have, but Colonel Kent said he'd take care of scene security and cover the whole area with rolled canvas. But I was out there a little while ago, and there's no canvas down, and not even an MP to secure the scene. The crime scene is ruined, polluted."

390

"Yup. Sure is."

"Sorry."

"No problem. Did you get the cast off to Oakland?"

"Yeah. Chopper to Gillem, and they'll find a military flight to the left coast. I'll hear something by morning."

"Fine."

"You still want the latent-footprint team?"

"What do you think?"

"I think it's all muck out there."

"Okay, forget it. We got lucky enough for one case. Where's Grace?"

"Glued to her screen. She wanted me to tell you that she pulled up a recent letter from the deceased to Mrs. William Kent—you were interested in Kent."

"Still am. What did the letter say?"

"Basically, it said that Colonel Kent was making more of a platonic friendship than he should, and would Mrs. Kent be so kind as to speak to her husband before she—Captain Campbell—had to make an official complaint. Captain Campbell suggested counseling for the Kents." He added, "Wouldn't want one of those to go to my wife."

"What was the date of the letter?"

"Hold on."

I watched Cynthia separating underwear from toilet articles. That bastard Yardley.

Cal came back on the line. "Ten August."

That would be eleven days ago, and I assumed that Mrs. Kent had decamped Bethany Hill upon receipt of that letter. Obviously, too, the letter was written as a result of Kent's unscheduled visit to Ann Campbell's house, not to mention his bad manners in throwing her boyfriend of the evening out, and raping his hostess. My goodness. So Ann Campbell had decided to do something about Kent, but she was handling unstable explosives, and that letter was the detonator. I said to Cal, "Need a printout of that. Hold it for me."

"Right. Also, three gentlemen of the Federal Bureau of Investigation arrived about a half hour after you left."

391

"Were they charming?"

"Couldn't have been nicer. Complimenting me on the setup here, congratulating me on every fucking fingerprint I took. They poked around and grilled me for about an hour. Grace played possum on a cot. One of the guys was messing with the computer, but the disk was in the cot with Grace." He added, "They said they'd be back in the morning with their own forensic people."

"Okay. Turn it all over to them at noon. Anything else?"

"Nope. It's late, raining, too wet to plow, and I'm too tired to dance."

"Right. Get on the footprint guy in Oakland. This case is hanging on the question of who stepped on whose bootprint. Talk to you tomorrow." I hung up and briefed Cynthia while I helped her get me straightened out.

I've had live-in friends on occasion, and I enjoy the presence of a woman in the house for brief periods of time. They fall into two categories: the organizers and the slobs. There's probably a third category—the naggers, who try to get you to do things, but I've never run into one of those. Oddly, I have no preference regarding organizers or slobs, as long as they don't try to pick my clothes for me. Basically, all women are nurturers and healers, and all men are mental patients to varying degrees. It works fine if people stick to their fated roles. But nobody does, so you have six or seven good months, then you discover exactly what it is you hate about each other, then you run the moving-in and unpacking tape in reverse and watch the door slam.

Cynthia folded the last pair of socks and said to me, "Who does your laundry and ironing?"

"Oh, I have a sort of housekeeper. Farm woman, keeps an eye on things when I'm gone."

"Are you the helpless type?"

"Well, yes, with fabrics and stuff, and needles and thread, but I can field-strip an M-16 rifle blindfolded and have it together again within three minutes."

"So can I."

"Good. I have one at home you can clean for me."

The phone rang, and I motioned to Cynthia to answer it. It was Kiefer, and I went into the bathroom and dried my hair with a towel. Cynthia had laid out my toilet articles, and I combed my hair, brushed my teeth, and slipped my shorts off under my robe. Second greatest feeling in the world.

I ditched the shorts in the trash can and went back into the bedroom. Cynthia was sitting at the edge of the bed, listening on the phone, her legs crossed, rubbing her foot with her free hand. Cynthia, I noted in passing, had good legs.

She looked up and smiled at me, then said into the phone, "Okay, thanks. Good work." She hung up and stood. "Well, Kiefer turned up one interesting tidbit. Seems that Mrs. Kent drives a black Jeep Cherokee, and that Mrs. Kent is known in MP radio circles as the Bat Lady, and the Jeep is called the Batmobile. Kiefer heard one reference on the master radio tape to the Batmobile. An unidentified MP on mobile patrol said, 'Niner-niner, Batmobile with Randy Six parked in library lot. Heads up.' " Cynthia added, "That's a typical officer-in-the-area kind of warning to the troops. Also, in case you never noticed, the library is across the road from Post Headquarters."

"Right. What time was that?"

"At 0032. And at about 0100, Ann Campbell left Post Headquarters, got into the humvee, and drove out to rifle range six." Cynthia asked me, "What was Kent doing in his wife's car across the street?"

"What every lovesick jerk does. Just sitting there watching the light in the window."

"Maybe he had something more malevolent in mind."

"Maybe. Could be, though, that he was just trying to decide if he should go into the building and say hello. Or he was waiting for St. John to leave on some business. Or he was waiting for the object of his desire to do the same, which she in fact did."

Cynthia tucked her feet under her, sort of like the lotus position. I don't know how people can sit like that. I sat in the only chair, which faced the bed, and noticed that she'd kept her panties on. She modestly adjusted her kimono. I said, "If my wife had gotten a letter like that from my girlfriend, I'd be damned angry, and I'd keep my distance from the girlfriend. On the other hand, if my wife had left town because of the letter, and my girlfriend was working late, I might not be able to resist the temptation to try to make contact."

"Sounds like you've been there."

"Hey, we've all been there."

"Not I," said Cynthia, "except there was this guy once in Brussels, and I would make sure I bumped into him wherever he went, and the jerk finally figured it out."

"The jerk probably figured it out sooner than you think, but you looked like trouble."

"No comment." She thought a moment—I guess the lotus position lends itself to contemplation—then said, "He followed her, obviously."

"Right. But he may also have confronted her in the headquarters parking lot first. We don't know."

"But how could he follow her without her seeing his vehicle on the range road?"

"It was his wife's vehicle."

"Would Ann know Mrs. Kent's vehicle?"

I replied, "Every girlfriend knows every wife's car. But there're enough Jeep Cherokees on this post to transport a battalion, so it wouldn't stand out. Fact is, the Fowlers own a Cherokee, though it's red."

"Still, Paul, how far down Rifle Range Road could Kent follow her without her becoming concerned about the headlights behind her?"

"Not too far. But far enough." I stood and rummaged around in a side pocket of my overnight bag, coming up with a marking pen. There was a blank expanse of white wall between the windows, and I began drawing. "Okay, the road goes south from main post and dead-ends at the last rifle range, a distance of about ten miles. There are only two turnoffs—the first, here, is General Pershing Road, coming off to the left; the second, a mile farther down to the right, is Jordan Field Road, here.'' I drew a road on the wall. ''Okay, he follows her at a normal distance with his headlights on, sees that she doesn't turn left on General Pershing Road, and he keeps following. She also doesn't turn off on Jordan Field Road, but he knows that *he* has to turn off there, or she will realize she's being followed. Right?''

''So far.''

''So he turns toward Jordan Field, and she sees this in her rear-view mirror and breathes easy. But Kent now knows that she's bottled up on the range road and can't go anywhere except to the end and back. Correct?''

She looked at my scribbles on the wall and nodded. ''Sounds right. What does he do then? Follow without lights? Walk? Wait?''

''Well . . . what would I do? It's a moonlit night, and, even without headlights, the vehicle can be seen at a few hundred meters. Also, there's the noise of the engine, and the interior lights when you open the door, and even the brake lights could be seen at certain angles. So for maximum stealth, you have to walk—or jog. So he puts the Cherokee in four-wheel drive and pulls into the pines where Jordan Field Road and Rifle Range Road intersect. He gets out and heads south on Rifle Range Road on foot.''

''This is supposition.''

''Partly. Partly it's intuition and detection, and partly it's just the logical solution to a standard field problem. We've all been to the same schools, and we've all been through these night exercises. You have to consider your mission, the weather, distances, time, security, and all that, and you have to know, for instance, when to stay with your motor transportation, and when to dismount and hump the bush.''

''Okay, he dismounts, and walks or jogs.''

''Right. By this time, it's somewhere between 0115 and 0130 hours. Colonel Moore has already traveled the road and is waiting for Ann Campbell. That much we know for sure. General Campbell has not yet received the phone call. Kent is double-timing along the road, looking for the headlights of the humvee up ahead. But, at some point, Ann turned her lights off and has now reached rifle range six and has met Colonel Moore." I put an "X" to mark rifle range six.

Cynthia, still sitting on the bed, seemed unimpressed with my cartography. She asked, "What is Bill Kent thinking about now? What is his purpose?"

"Well . . . he's very curious about why she's out there alone, though he knows she could be just checking the last guard post. If this is the case, he will meet her coming back, stand in the road, and confront her. He had a taste of rape a few weeks ago, and he might be thinking of doing it again."

"She's armed."

"So is he." I added, "Even in modern relationships, you should never pull a gun on your date. Especially if she's armed, too. However, he thinks he can handle it. Maybe he just wants to talk."

"Maybe. But I wouldn't want to meet an ex-lover on a lonely road. I'd run him over."

"I'll keep that in mind. But he doesn't know how women think. He can't relate to how she might feel about him following her and his waylaying her. All he knows is that they're lovers, and this is special to him. His wife's out of town, and he's a horny, lovesick jerk. He wants to talk. Really he wants to have sex with her, one way or the other. He is what we call sexually obsessed."

"So he walks down the lonely, dark road, looking for her humvee."

"Right. The other thing that he gets into his mind is that she's out there for a sexual rendezvous with someone else. This would not be out of character for Ann Campbell, and Bill Kent's heart is pounding at the thought of surprising her with a lover, and he's nuts with jealousy. Sound right to you?"

"If you say so."

"Okay, by now it's around 0215 hours, and Colonel Moore has made the recorded call to General Campbell, has tied up Ann

Campbell, and is waiting near the latrines for the general to show up. Bill Kent is on his own mission, and he's following the manual. He knows that he can see the headlights of a car at least a half mile away on the dark, straight road, so a car traveling at, say, forty-five miles an hour could be on him in less than a minute unless he sees its headlights first. So every thirty seconds or so, he looks back over his shoulder. At about 0215, he in fact sees headlights behind him, and he drops into the drainage ditch on the side of the road and waits for the car to pass.''

"He thinks this is her lover.''

"Probably. In some perverse way, he would like to catch her *in flagrante delicto*. He got a charge out of kicking Major Bowes out of Ann's house, then raping her. This is a very troubled and irrational man who thinks that Ann Campbell will respond well to his aggressive virility, to his shining armor, and to his slaying dragons for her. Correct?''

She nodded. "There is that type. Half the rapists I interview claim the women enjoyed it. None of the women ever seconded that.''

"Right. But to be a little fair to Bill Kent, Ann Campbell never disabused him of that notion.''

"True. But the letter to his wife should have told him that she was finished with him. But, okay, he's as crazy as she was. So he sees the car pass him.''

"Right. Coming up the road at about 0215 with its headlights on. *These* are the headlights that PFC Robbins saw. Moore had traveled the last mile or so without lights, and so had Ann Campbell. The general did not. The general's car passes, and Kent gets up on one knee. He may or may not recognize Mrs. Campbell's Buick.''

Cynthia commented, "So here we have two high-profile guys— Colonel Kent and General Campbell—sneaking around at night in their wives' cars.''

"Right. If everyone on post knew your staff car, and you had the unofficial radio call sign of Randy Six, you might choose alternate transportation as well.''

397

"I might just stay home. Okay, so at this point, Kent speeds up his pace. Meanwhile, Moore is running back along the log trail, gets into his car at range five, and heads north on Rifle Range Road, back toward post. But he didn't see Kent walking toward him."

"No," I replied. "Kent was either past rifle range five by now, or Kent spotted the headlights as Moore came across the gravel field, and Kent dropped into the ditch again. By this time, Kent figures that his girlfriend is entertaining a procession of lovers, one every fifteen or twenty minutes, or, more likely, he's confused."

"Confused or not," Cynthia replied, "he's thinking the worst. He's not thinking that she may just be doing her job, or that maybe she's in danger, or that perhaps the two vehicles were unrelated to her. He's sure she's out there fucking. Is that what you would think?"

"Absolutely. I'm all man. I think too much with the little head, and not enough with the big head."

Cynthia laughed despite herself. "Okay, enough. Go on."

I sat back in the chair and thought a moment. "All right . . . it's at this point that we can't know exactly what happened. Kent rounds the bend where rifle range five and six connect, and up ahead in the moonlight he sees two vehicles parked on the road—the humvee and the Buick that passed him from behind. We know that by this time the scene between father and daughter is unfolding, or maybe it's finished."

Cynthia said, "In either case, Kent stayed where he was."

"Yes, we know for sure that Kent did not dash up on this scene and discover that the Buick on the road had brought General Campbell to rifle range six. Kent watched from a distance—say, two or three hundred meters—and he may have heard something, because the wind was blowing from the south. But he decided not to make a complete fool of himself, not to get into a possible armed confrontation with another man."

"Or," Cynthia said, "the exchange between father and daughter *was* finished, and the general was back in his car by now."

"Quite possible. At this point, the general's car comes toward him, without headlights, and Kent again drops into the drainage ditch. This is the only way it could have happened—with Kent on foot—because neither Moore nor the general saw any other vehicle.''

"And when the general's car passes, Bill Kent stands and walks toward Ann Campbell's humvee.''

"Right. He's moving very quickly, maybe with his sidearm drawn, ready for anything—rape, romance, reconciliation, or murder.''

We sat a moment, she on the bed, me in the chair, listening to the rain outside. I was wondering, and I'm sure Cynthia was, too, if we'd just fashioned a noose for an innocent man in the privacy of our own room. But even if we didn't have the details just right, the man himself had as much as told us, or signaled to us, that he'd done it. There was no mistaking his tone, his manner, and his eyes. But what he was also saying is that she deserved it, and we'd never prove he did it. He was wrong on both counts.

Cynthia got out of the lotus position and let her legs dangle over the foot of the bed. She said, "And Kent finds Ann Campbell staked out on the range, probably still crying, and he can't figure out if she's been raped, or just waiting for the next friend to keep his appointment.''

"Well . . . who knows at that point? But he definitely walked out to her, slowly, as Cal Seiver said, and he definitely kneeled beside her, and she was not happy to see him.''

"She was frightened out of her mind.''

"Well . . . she's not the type. But she's at a disadvantage. He says something, she says something. She, thinking her father has abandoned her, may have settled in for a long wait, knowing that the guard truck would be by at about 0700 hours, and she's considered this possibility, and she thinks this would be a good payback for Daddy's second betrayal. General's daughter found naked by twenty guards.''

Cynthia nodded. She said, "But she knows that her father will eventually realize the same thing, and will *have* to come back in order to avoid that disgraceful occurrence. So in either case, she wants Kent gone.''

''Probably. He's interfering with her script. He sees the bayonet stuck in the ground—assuming the general didn't take it—and offers to cut her loose. Or he figures that she can't walk away from a conversation with him under the circumstances, and he asks her what's going on, or asks her to marry him, or whatever, and the dialogue develops, and Ann, who's been tied to the bedposts many times in her basement, is not so much frightened or embarrassed as she is annoyed and impatient. We just don't know what was said, what went on.''

''No, we don't, but we know how the conversation ended.''

''Right. He may have twisted the rope to get her undivided attention, he may even have sexually stimulated her while he was causing sexual asphyxia, a trick he may have learned from her . . . but at some point, he twisted the rope and didn't stop twisting.''

We sat there a full minute, playing it over again in our minds, then Cynthia stood and said, ''That's about what happened. Then he walked back to the road, realized what he'd done, and ran all the way back to his Jeep. He may have reached the Jeep before the Fowlers even started out, and he sped out of there and reached Bethany Hill as the Fowlers were leaving their house. He may even have passed them on one of the streets. He went home, parked his wife's Jeep in the garage, went inside, probably cleaned up, and waited for the phone call from his MPs.'' She added, ''I wonder if he slept.''

''I don't know, but when I saw him a few hours later, he looked composed, though now that I think about it, he was a little distracted.'' I added, ''He disassociated himself from the crime, as criminals usually do after the first few hours, but it's coming back to him now.''

''Can we prove any of this?''

''No.''

''So what do we do?''

''Confront him. The time has come.''

400

"He'll deny it all, and we'll be looking for work in the civilian sector."

"Probably. And you know what? We may be wrong."

Cynthia was pacing now, having a debate with herself. She stopped and said, "How about finding the place where he pulled the Jeep off the road?"

"Yes, first light is at 0536. Should I call you or nudge you?"

She ignored this and said, "The tire tracks will be washed out. But if he broke brush, we can see where the vehicle left the road."

"Right. This will remove some of our doubts. But it still leaves reasonable doubt, and we need beyond a reasonable doubt."

She said, "There might be brush or pine needles stuck on his vehicle that can be matched to the vegetation that was broken."

"There might be if the guy was an idiot, but he's not. That Jeep is as clean as a humvee waiting for an IG inspection."

"Damn it."

"We have to confront him, and we have to do it at the right psychological moment . . . tomorrow, after the funeral service. That's our first, last, and only chance to get a confession."

Cynthia nodded. "If he's going to talk, he'll do it then. If he wants to get it off his chest, he'll do it with us, not the FBI."

"Correct."

"Time for bed." She picked up the phone and asked the CQ to ring us at 0400 hours, which would give me three hours sleep if I passed out in the next ten seconds. But I had another idea. I said, "Let's shower now and save time."

"Well . . ."

Bad response. As my father once said, "Women control seventy percent of the wealth in this country, and a hundred percent of the pussy." Cynthia and I were a little shy, I think, the way ex-lovers are when they try it again. And all the rape talk didn't help set the mood. I mean, there was no music here, no candles, no champagne. The only thing here was the ghost of Ann Campbell, the thought of her murderer sleeping in his bed on Bethany Hill, and two exhausted people far from home. I said, "Maybe it wouldn't be appropriate."

"No, it wouldn't be. Let's wait until we can make it special. This weekend at your place. We'll be glad we waited."

Right, I'm absolutely fucking thrilled to wait. But I wasn't in the mood to argue, and not clever enough to seduce. So I yawned and threw back the covers of my bed. "*Bon soir*, as we say in Brussels."

"Good night . . ." She moved toward the bathroom door, then, as she did last time, she turned back. She said, "Something to look forward to."

"Right." I turned off the lamp, shucked my robe, and crawled, naked, into bed.

I heard the shower running in the bathroom, heard the rain outside, heard a couple giggling in the hallway.

I never heard the phone ring at 0400.

CHAPTER THIRTY-FOUR

Cynthia was dressed, the sun was coming in the window, and I smelled coffee.

She sat on the side of my bed, I sat up, and she handed me a plastic mug. "They have a coffee bar downstairs."

I asked, "What time is it?"

"A little after seven."

"*Seven?*" I started to get out of bed, but remembered I was buck naked. "Why didn't you wake me?"

"How many people does it take to look at broken bush?"

"You were out there? Did you find anything?"

"Yes. A vehicle definitely went off Jordan Field Road, fifty meters from Rifle Range Road. Left ruts, though the tread marks are washed out, but there's broken bush, including a freshly skinned pine tree."

I sipped on the coffee as I tried to clear my head. Cynthia was dressed in blue jeans and a white tennis shirt, and looked good. I asked, "Skinned a tree?"

"Yes. So I went over to Jordan Field and woke up poor Cal. He and another guy went back with me to the place, and cut off the damaged section of the tree."

"And?"

"Well, we went back to the hangar, and under magnification we could see flecks of paint. Cal is sending the wood sample to Fort Gillem. I told him we suspected a black Jeep Cherokee, and he says that they can confirm that with the manufacturer, or through their on-file samples of car paint.''

''Right. And we'll find the scrape on Mrs. Kent's Jeep.''

''I hope so. Then we'll have the evidence we need to support your reconstruction of Kent's movements.''

''Right.'' I yawned and cleared my throat. ''Unfortunately, if the paint is from a black Jeep Cherokee, it only proves that a black Jeep Cherokee scraped that tree. Still, it settles it in my mind.''

''Me, too.''

I finished the coffee and put the mug on the nightstand. ''I wanted to be woken. Did you try to wake me?''

''No. You looked dead.''

''Well . . . okay. Good job.''

''Thanks. I also took your boots to Cal Seiver, and he matched your prints to unidentified plaster casts and was able to post your prints on his chart.''

''Thank you. Am I a suspect?''

''Not yet. But Cal did need to disqualify your prints.''

''Did you polish my boots?''

She ignored this and said, ''Cal's got a computer program from Fort Gillem, and he's programming the computer in the hangar to show the footsteps of each identified and unidentified person. I gave Cal a complete briefing on what we think happened that night.'' She stood and went to the window. ''Rain stopped. Sun's out. Good for the crops. Good for the funeral.''

I noticed a sheet of paper on the bed and picked it up. It was the computer printout of Ann Campbell's letter to Mrs. Kent. It began: *''My dear Mrs. Kent, I'm writing you regarding a situation that has developed between your husband and me.''* The letter ended: *While I respect your husband professionally, I have no personal interest in him. I would suggest that he seek counseling, alone or with you, and that perhaps he should seek a transfer, or ask for a leave of absence. My concern is for his career, his reputation, my reputation, and the avoidance of any appearance of impropriety within my father's command. Yours very truly, Ann Campbell.* I said aloud, "Impropriety within my father's command." I almost laughed, and Cynthia turned around and commented, "She had balls. I'll give her that."

I threw the letter on the nightstand. "I'm sure Kent saw the original of this, and it freaked him out. Anyway, did Cal hear from the footprint guy in Oakland?"

"Not yet."

"Okay, I'm going to rise and shine, and I'm naked."

Cynthia threw me my robe and turned back to the window. I got out of bed and into the robe and went into the bathroom. I washed my face and lathered up. .

The phone rang in my room, and Cynthia took it. I couldn't hear much over the running water, but a minute later, Cynthia stuck her head in the door while I was shaving and said, "That was Karl."

"What did he want?"

"He wanted to know if he'd rung the wrong room."

"Oh . . ."

"He's in Atlanta. He'll be here by 1000 hours."

"Call him back and tell him we're having tornados."

"He's on his way."

"Great." I finished shaving and began brushing my teeth. Cynthia went back to my room. As I turned on the shower, I heard the phone ringing in her room. I didn't think she could hear it, so I looked into my room, but she was on my phone. So, thinking it was official and important, I went into her room and picked it up. "Hello?"

A male voice inquired, "Who's this?"

I replied, "Who are *you*?"

"This is Major Sholte. What are you doing in my wife's room?"

Good question. I could have said the clerk rang the wrong room, I could have said a lot of things, but I said, "Basically, I'm doing what I did in Brussels."

"What? Who the hell . . . Brenner? Is this *Brenner*?"

405

"At your service, Major."

"You bastard. You're dead meat. You know that, Brenner? You're dead meat."

"You had your chance in Brussels. You only get one chance."

"You son-of-a-bitch—"

"Ms. Sunhill is not here. May I take a message?"

"Where is she?"

"In the shower."

"You *bastard*."

Why was this guy getting so bent up if they were getting a divorce and he had a girlfriend? Well, men are funny, and they still feel proprietary toward their wives, even when they're finalizing a divorce. Right? No, something was not right, and I had the distinct feeling I'd made a big boo-boo.

Major Sholte said to me, "Your ass is grass, Brenner, and I'm the fucking Grim Reaper."

Interesting metaphor. I asked him, "Are you and Cynthia in the process of a divorce?"

"Divorce? Who the fuck told you that? You put that bitch on the phone."

"Trial separation?"

"Put her on the goddamned phone. Now!"

"Hold on." I laid the phone on the bed and thought about things. Life really sucks sometimes, then it gets better and you get optimistic again, and your heart lightens up a little and you get a little spring back in your step, then somebody pulls the rug out and you're on your ass once more. I picked up the phone and said, "I'll have her call you back."

"You fucking well better, you rat-fucking, mother-fucking—"

I hung up and went back into the common bathroom. I slipped off my robe and got into the shower.

Cynthia stood in the doorway and called out over the water, "I phoned the Psy-Ops School and confirmed that Colonel Moore spent the night there. I left a message for him to meet us at the provost office in an hour. Okay?"

"Okay."

"I laid out your uniform. We should wear our uniforms to the service."

"Thanks."

"I'm going to change into uniform."

"Okay."

I could see her through the glass, walking across the bathroom into her own room. Her door closed, and I shut off the shower and got out.

By 0800 hours, we were dressed in the A uniform, and we were in my Chevy Blazer, pulling up to the provost building. Cynthia asked, "Is something bothering you?"

"No."

I had another cup of coffee in our office and went through phone messages and memos. Colonel Moore showed up looking a bit ragged, but dressed in his A uniform for the funeral. He had acquired a pair of dress shoes somewhere. Cynthia offered him a seat. Without preliminaries, I said to him, "Colonel, we have reason to suspect that Colonel Kent murdered Ann Campbell."

He seemed surprised, almost stunned, and didn't reply.

I asked him, "Does it fit?"

He thought about that for a long moment, then replied, "He was becoming a problem, but . . ."

"What did Ann say to you about him?"

"Well . . . that he was calling her at all hours, that he wrote her letters, dropped in on her unexpectedly at home and in the office."

And so on. I asked him, "On the night she was murdered, when you called her at Post Headquarters, did she say he'd been around to see her or that he'd called her?"

He thought a moment, then answered, "As a matter of fact, she did tell me that she wouldn't be using her BMW that night, which was the original plan. She told me to look for a humvee instead. She said that Bill Kent was annoying her again and that she'd be less conspicuous in a humvee, and that she wanted him to see her

407

car in the headquarters lot all night. This presented a problem because her car had a wired-in phone, and I had a portable phone, and we intended to stay in touch as she drove out to the range. But it wasn't a major problem, and she drove out with the humvee and we rendezvoused on schedule.''

Cynthia asked him, ''Did she mention Kent when you met?''

''No . . .''

''Did she mention that she'd been followed?''

''No . . . Well, she said she saw one vehicle behind her, but it turned off toward Jordan Field.'' He added, ''She felt that everything was all right, and I placed the call to her father on my portable phone.''

Cynthia said, ''Then you went out on the rifle range?''

''Yes.''

''After you were done, you waited by the latrine shed to be sure it went as planned.''

''Yes.''

''Did it occur to you,'' Cynthia asked, ''that Colonel Kent might be a likely person to come on the scene?''

He pondered that a moment, then replied, ''I suppose it crossed my mind. He seemed to be hounding her.''

''And it never occurred to you that he *did* follow her and possibly murdered her?''

''Well . . . now that I think about it—''

I said, ''You're some sharp detective, Colonel.''

He seemed put off by that and replied, ''I thought it was the general who . . . Well, I didn't know what to think. My first thought when I heard she'd been murdered was that her father had done it . . . but it also occurred to me that her father had simply left her there, and some other person . . . some maniac . . . happened along . . . I just never thought in terms of Kent . . .''

''Why not?'' I asked.

''He . . . he's the provost . . . a married man . . . he loved her . . . but, yes, now that you mention it, it does fit. I mean, from a psychological point of view, he had become obsessed and irrational. Ann could no longer control him.''

408

"Ann," I pointed out, "had created a monster."

"Yes."

"Did she understand that?"

"On one level. But she wasn't used to dealing with men she couldn't control. Except her father, and perhaps Wes Yardley. In retrospect, she didn't pay enough attention to Bill Kent. She misjudged."

"She failed Abnormal Psych 101."

He didn't respond.

"Okay, what I want you to do is go back to your office and write it out."

"Write what?"

"Everything. A full account of your involvement in this matter. Deliver it to me at the chapel after the service. You have almost two hours. Type fast. Don't mention a word of this to anyone."

Colonel Moore got up and left, looking, I thought, like a faint shadow of the man I'd met just the other day.

Cynthia commented, "This case looked hard, and we all worked hard, but the answer was literally under our nose the whole time."

"That's why it was hard to see it."

Cynthia made small talk for a few minutes, and I made big silences. She kept looking at me.

To avoid any unpleasantness, I picked up the phone and called Colonel Fowler at Post Headquarters. He took my call immediately, and I said to him, "Colonel, I'd like you to take the shoes that you and Mrs. Fowler wore out to rifle range six and destroy them. Secondly, get your story straight with General Campbell. You never went out to the range. Third, get Mrs. Fowler in a car or on a plane immediately after the funeral."

He replied, "I appreciate what you're saying, but I feel I have to reveal my involvement in this."

"Your commanding officer's wish is that you don't do that. A general's wish is his command."

"It's an illegal command."

"Do everyone a favor—yourself, your wife, your family, the Army, me, the Campbells—forget it. Think about it."

409

"I'll think about it."

"Question—did you take her West Point ring?"

"No."

"Was there a bayonet stuck in the ground when you got there?"

"Not in the ground. The handle was stuck in her vagina."

"I see."

"I removed it and disposed of it."

"Where?"

"I threw it off the Chickasaw River Bridge." He added, "I suppose you'd have liked to check it for fingerprints."

"I would have, yes." But in fact, Kent would not leave a print behind.

"I apologize. It was a gut reaction."

"Lot of that going around."

"This is a mess, Brenner. We've all made a mess of things."

"Shit happens."

"Not to me it doesn't. Not until she got here two years ago. But you know what? It was our fault, not hers."

"I tend to agree." I added, "I may make an arrest this afternoon."

"Who?"

"Can't say. I'll see you at the service."

"Fine."

I hung up. Just when you think you've got your ration of shit-happens for the day, someone heaps on another helping. In this case, an MP major named Doyle was the bearer of the shit. He came into the office and glanced at Cynthia, then addressed me. "Mister Brenner, you signed a release order for a Staff Sergeant Dalbert Elkins. Correct?"

"Yes, sir."

"We found him quarters at the MP company barracks."

"Fine." *Who gives a shit?*

"Under the terms of his restriction, he was to sign into the company dayroom every three hours."

"Sounds reasonable."

410

"He missed his first sign-in at 0800 hours."

Jesus H. Christ. "What?"

"And no one has seen him since."

Cynthia looked at me, then looked away.

Major Doyle informed me, "We've put out an all-points bulletin for his arrest, and notified the Midland police, the county police, and the Georgia state police." He added, "The CID commander, Major Bowes, demands a full report from you on this matter." Major Doyle smiled unpleasantly and said, "You blew it." He turned and left.

I stared at nothing in particular for a while. Cynthia finally spoke. "That happened to me once."

I didn't reply.

"But it happened to me *only* once. So you can't get cynical about human nature."

Wanna bet? Timing being everything, this was the time to mention her husband's phone call, but Karl Hellmann's timing was not good, and he picked that moment to show up.

Cynthia and I stood as the big man walked into the little office. He nodded perfunctorily, glanced around, then we all shook hands. Cynthia, being the lowest-ranking person in the room, offered him her desk chair, which he took, while Cynthia took the spare chair, and I sat at my desk.

Karl was wearing his green dress uniform, as we were, and he threw his hat on the desk.

Like me, Karl was once an infantryman, and we both served in Vietnam at about the same time. Our uniforms sported basically the same awards and decorations, including the Bronze Star for valor and the coveted Combat Infantryman's Badge. Being products of the same crucible, and both being middle-aged, we usually dispense with some of the formalities. But I wasn't in a Karl mood that morning, so I intended to stick to courtesies and protocols. I said, "Coffee, sir?"

"No, thank you."

Karl is a good-looking man with a full head of grayish-black hair,

411

firm jaw, and blue eyes. Women, however, don't find him sexy. It may be his manner, which is stiff and formal. In fact, he's rather tight-assed, and if you put a lump of coal up his butt, he'd produce a diamond within a week. That aside, he's a pro.

We exchanged pleasantries for three seconds, then Karl said to me in his slight accent, "I understand our star witness in the arms sale case has become a fugitive."

"Yes, sir."

"Can you recall your line of reasoning in releasing him?"

"Not at the moment, no, sir."

"One wonders why a man who has been offered immunity would decide to commit yet another felony and flee."

"One does wonder."

"Did you explain to him that he had immunity?"

"Yes, sir, but apparently not very well."

"It's a problem, you know, Paul, dealing with stupid people. You project your own intelligence and rationality onto a person who is a complete idiot, and he lets you down. He's ignorant and frightened, and he is a slave to his instincts. The jail door opens, and he runs. Quite understandable."

I cleared my throat. "I thought I had reassured him and won his trust and confidence."

"Of course you did. That's what he wanted you to think when he was on the other side of the bars. They're cunning."

"Yes, sir."

"Perhaps you'll consult me the next time, before you release a prisoner in a major felony case."

"He was actually a witness, sir."

Karl leaned toward me and said, "He had not one fucking iota of understanding regarding the difference. You put him in jail, you let him out, he ran."

"Yes, sir."

"Article 96 of the Uniform Code of Military Justice deals with the improper releasing of a prisoner through neglect or design. You're in trouble."

"Yes, sir."

He leaned back in his chair. "Now, tell me, what are the most recent developments here?"

Well, to begin with, I never got the chance to sleep with Cynthia, she lied to me about her husband, I'm crushed and pissed, I still can't get Ann Campbell out of my mind, the provost marshal down the hall is probably a murderer, dopey Dalbert beat feet, and I'm not having a good day.

Hellmann turned to Cynthia. "Perhaps you'll speak to me."

"Yes, sir." Cynthia began by discussing forensic evidence, Grace Dixon's computer discoveries, the Yardley boys, and the unfortunate involvements of Major Bowes, Colonel Weems, and other staff officers.

Karl listened.

Cynthia then reported an edited version of our conversations with General Campbell, Mrs. Campbell, Colonel Fowler, Mrs. Fowler, and Colonel Moore. I was barely listening, but I did note that she did not mention Colonel and Mrs. Fowler's precise role in the case, or Ann Campbell's basement room, and neither did she mention Bill Kent at all. This is exactly the way I would have handled it, and I was impressed with how much she'd learned in the last two days. Cynthia said to Karl, "So you see, it all had to do with revenge, retribution, a perverted experiment in psychological operations, and what happened at West Point a decade ago."

Karl nodded.

As an afterthought, Cynthia did mention Friedrich Nietzsche, in the context of Ann Campbell's personal philosophy. Karl seemed interested in that, and I realized that Cynthia was playing to her audience.

Karl sat back and pondered, his fingers pressed together like some great sage about to provide the answer to Life. Cynthia concluded, "Paul has done an outstanding job, and it's been an education working with him."

Barf.

Karl sat motionless for a full minute, and it occurred to me that

413

the great sage didn't have a fucking clue. Cynthia was trying to catch my eye, but I refused to look at her.

Finally, Colonel Hellmann spoke. "Nietzsche. Yes. In revenge and in love, woman is more barbarous than man."

I asked, "Is that Nietzsche, sir, or your personal opinion?"

He looked at me in a way that suggested the ice under me was getting thinner. He said to Cynthia, "Very good. You've exposed motives, massive corruption, and great secrets here."

"Thank you."

He looked at me, then at his watch. "Should we be going to the chapel?"

"Yes, sir."

He stood and we stood. We took our hats and headed out.

We all got into my Blazer, with Karl in the honorary position in the rear. As I drove toward the post chapel, Karl finally asked, "Do you know who did it?"

I replied, "I think so."

"Would you care to share that with me?"

What's it worth to you? I replied, "We have some circumstantial evidence, some testimony, and some forensic evidence that points to Colonel Kent." I looked into my rearview mirror and got my first thrill of the day when I saw Karl's eyes widen. The rock jaw did not drop, however. "The provost marshal," I prompted.

Karl recovered and asked, "Are you both prepared to make a formal charge?"

Thank you for the ace, Karl. I replied, "No. I'm turning over our evidence to the FBI."

"Why?"

"It needs some research and development."

"Tell me what you know."

I pulled into the parking field of the post chapel, a big Georgian brick structure, suitable for military weddings, funerals, Sunday worship, and solitary prayer before shipping out to a combat zone. We got out of the Blazer and stood in the hot sun. The lot was nearly full, and people were parking on the road and on the grass.

414

Cynthia took a piece of paper out of her handbag and handed it to Karl. She said, ''That was in Ann Campbell's computer. It's a letter to Mrs. Kent.''

Karl read the letter, nodded, and handed it back to Cynthia. ''Yes, I can understand Colonel Kent's anger and humiliation at having his wife receive such a letter. But would that make him kill?'' Just then, Colonel William Kent himself walked by with a wave of the hand. Cynthia informed Karl, ''That is Colonel Kent.''

Karl watched him walk to the chapel. Karl observed, ''He doesn't look haunted.''

''He vacillates,'' Cynthia replied. ''I think he's on the verge of convincing himself that what he did was right, then telling us the same thing.''

Karl nodded. ''Yes, that's the great secret of this job—not confronting a criminal with the moral question of right or wrong, but giving him the opportunity to explain his reasons.'' He asked Cynthia, ''What other evidence do you have?''

Cynthia gave him a quick rundown of the diary entries, the critical bootprint, the Jeep in the pine brush, and our conversations with the suspect. She concluded, ''He had motive, opportunity, and probably the will to act, at least at that moment. He's not a killer, but he's a cop, and therefore no stranger to homicide. He also had good cover, being on the inside of the investigation, and was able to manipulate it and control the evidence—he let the crime scene become polluted, for instance—but his alibi for the time of the murder is weak or nonexistent, as is often the case with crimes of opportunity.''

Hellmann nodded as Cynthia spoke. Then the great one delivered his opinion. ''If you're right, and you can prove it, then you've ended this case before it engulfs everyone. If you're wrong, this case will eat you both, and destroy many more lives while the investigation continues.''

Cynthia replied, ''Yes, sir, that's why we worked day and night. But it's really out of our hands now.'' She looked at me, then continued, ''Paul is correct in that we don't want to recommend formal charges. There's nothing in that for us, for you, for the CID, or the Army.''

Karl contemplated the chess board in his head, then turned to me. ''You're uncharacteristically quiet.''

''I have nothing to say, Colonel,'' I replied, using his rank to remind him that the buck stopped at his silver eagle.

''Are you upset over your prisoner fleeing?''

''He was a witness, and, no, I'm not.''

Cynthia chimed in, ''He's been sulky all morning. Even before you got here.'' She smiled at me, but I stone-faced it, and her smile faded. I really wanted to be out of here, out of Hadley, out of the hot sun, out of Georgia, and out of touch. I said, ''We won't get a seat.'' I turned toward the chapel and walked.

Karl and Cynthia followed. Karl spoke to Cynthia. ''You should give him a last opportunity to confess.''

''You mean Paul?'' she said playfully.

''No, Ms. Sunhill. Colonel Kent.''

''Right. We've considered that.''

''People confess to the most heinous crimes, you know, if you put them in the right mood. Murderers who have killed a loved one carry an enormous burden, and they want to share the weight with someone. Unlike professional criminals, they have no partners in crime, no confidants, and they are isolated, without a living soul to tell of the greatest secret of their life.''

''Yes, sir,'' Cynthia replied.

Karl said, ''Do you think it was simple expediency that made Colonel Kent call you and Paul regarding this crime? No. It was an unconscious desire to be found out.''

And on he went, saying things I already knew, and making the pitch for us to confront the suspect, who, though professionally damaged, was a high-ranking and powerful man with a lot of resources left to him. I sort of pictured myself in front of a board of inquiry, trying to make a case for Colonel William Kent as murderer, while seven steely-eyed officers sat there waiting to eat my ass for lunch. But sucker that I was, I was willing to give it a shot.

However, I was going to keep Karl hanging until he ordered me to confront Kent.

I looked toward the chapel and noticed that the ceremonies relating to the receiving of the casket were completed; the honorary pallbearers were not on the steps, and, in fact, the old caisson, taken from the museum, did not have the casket on it.

The news media, according to a memo I'd seen on my desk, were limited to a pool of selected print journalists, and the only photographers present were two from the Army Public Information Office. The memo, signed by Colonel Fowler, had suggested not giving direct quotes to the journalists.

We climbed the steps and went into the narthex, where a dozen men and women stood conversing in hushed funereal tones. We all signed the guest book, and I walked into the dark chapel, which was no cooler than outside, and noted that the pews were nearly all full. The funeral of the commanding officer's daughter was not a command-attendance situation, but only a moron would fail to show up here, or at least at the ceremonies later.

In fact, not all of Fort Hadley's officers and spouses, or Midland's civilian dignitaries, could fit into the chapel, which held about five or six hundred people, but I was certain that there were people already assembling at Jordan Field for the final send-off.

The organ was playing softly in the choir loft above us, and we stood in the center aisle a moment, each of us, I think, trying to decide if we should walk to the casket, which sat on a catafalque at the foot of the altar steps. Finally, I began the long walk, and Cynthia and Karl followed.

I approached the flag-draped and half-opened casket on the left, stopped, and looked down at the deceased.

Ann Campbell looked peaceful, as Kent had indicated, her head resting on a pink satin pillow, and her long hair sort of fanned out around her head and face. I noted that she had more makeup on in death than she'd probably ever worn in life.

They had dressed her in the evening white uniform that a female officer would wear to formal functions, and it was an appropriate choice, I thought, the white waistcoat with gold braid and the white ruffled blouse, making her appear gossamery, if not virginal. She wore her medals on her left breast, and her sheathed West Point saber was laid on her body so that her clasped hands, which might hold a cross or rosary beads depending on one's religion, held, instead, the hilt of her sword at her midriff. The sheathed blade disappeared beneath the half-lid of the casket.

It was quite a striking sight, to be honest: the beautiful face, the golden hair, the gold braid, the glittering brass and steel of the saber, and the snow-white uniform against the pink satin lining of the casket.

I took all this in very quickly, of course, no more than five seconds, then, good Catholic that I am, I made the sign of the cross and moved around the casket and started down the center aisle.

I saw the Campbells in the first two rows on the right: the general, Mrs. Campbell, a young man whom I recognized from the family album in Ann Campbell's house as their son, and various other family members, old and young, all wearing black outfits and black mourning bands, which are still customary in the military.

I avoided eye contact with any of them and proceeded up the aisle slowly until my coterie caught up with me.

We found three seats together in the same pew that held Major Bowes, whom I knew only from his name tag, and a woman I presumed to be Mrs. Bowes. Bowes nodded to Colonel Hellmann, who failed to acknowledge the presence of an adulterer and jackass. Mrs. Bowes, incidentally, was rather attractive, proving once again that men are basically pigs.

Despite having just viewed the mortal remains of a young woman, I was feeling slightly better, as people do who consider their position relative to less fortunate souls, such as people with big career problems, like Bowes, murder suspects, like Kent, or married people in general, and the sick, dying, and dead.

The chaplain, Major Eames, wearing only the green dress uniform with no ecclesiastic vestments, came to the pulpit, and a hush fell over the crowd. Major Eames began, "Dearly beloved, we are gathered here in the presence of God to bid farewell to our sister, Ann Campbell.''

A lot of people sobbed.

I whispered to Karl, "The chaplain fucked her, too."

Karl's jaw dropped this time. The day still had possibilities.

CHAPTER THIRTY-FIVE

The simple service proceeded with prayers, organ music, and a few hymns. Senior military officers are great churchgoers, of course; it comes with the territory of God and Country. But they tend to be nondenominational, which is safe, gray, and nondescript, like most of their careers.

The upside of this at military weddings and funerals is that you get to pick and choose the best aspects of each denomination's liturgy, hymns, and prayers, and you can make it short. I can tell you from experience that a Catholic funeral mass can be long and arduous enough to kill off a few of the old folks.

Anyway, at the designated time, Colonel Fowler mounted the lectern to deliver the eulogy.

Colonel Fowler acknowledged the presence of family, friends, fellow officers, coworkers, and Midland dignitaries. He said, "In our chosen profession, more than in any other profession, we see and hear of the untimely deaths of young men and women. We do not grow accustomed to death, and we do not become hardened to death, but rather we cherish life more because we know and accept the fact that Army life puts us in harm's way. When we took the oath, we fully understood that we could be called upon to risk our lives in the defense of our country. Captain Ann Campbell understood that when she accepted her commission from the Military

Academy, she understood that when she went to the Gulf, and she understood that when, at an hour when most people are safe in their homes, she volunteered to go out and see that all was secure at Fort Hadley. This was a completely voluntary act, not specifically related to her duties, but the sort of thing that Ann Campbell did without being told.''

I listened, and it occurred to me that, if I didn't know better, I'd buy it. Here was a gung-ho young female officer volunteering for night duty officer, then taking the initiative to go out to check the guard and being murdered while she was doing a good deed. How sad. That's not the way it happened, but the truth was even sadder.

Colonel Fowler went on, ''I'm reminded of a line from Isaiah 21:11—'Watchman, what of the night?' '' He repeated it, '' 'Watchman, what of the night?' and the watchman replied, 'Morning is coming.' And aren't we all watchmen? This is our calling in life, as soldiers, to stand the watch, each day, each night, eternally vigilant so that others may sleep peacefully until morning, until the day when it pleases God to call us into His Kingdom, and we need not stand the watch, nor fear the night.''

Fowler had a good, deep speaking-voice, and his delivery was flawless. Clearly, the man could have been a preacher, or a politician, if he weren't so obsessed with right and wrong.

I'm not a good public listener, and I tend to drift. So I drifted to Ann Campbell's open casket, her face, the sword, and her folded hands around the hilt, and I realized what was wrong with that picture: someone had slipped a West Point ring on her finger. But was it *her* ring? And if it was, who had put it there? Fowler? General Campbell? Colonel Moore? Colonel Kent? Where did it come from? But did it make any difference at this point?

Colonel Fowler was still speaking, and I tuned back in.

He said, ''I knew Ann as a child—a very precocious, high-spirited, and bratty child.'' He smiled, and there was subdued laughter. He became serious again and continued, ''A beautiful child, not only physically but spiritually beautiful, a special and gifted child of God. And all of us here who knew her and loved her . . .''

421

Fowler, smooth as he was, couldn't slide over that double entendre, but it was only a momentary breath pause, noticed solely by those who *had* known her intimately and loved her well.

''. . . all of us will miss her deeply.''

Colonel Fowler had a lot of people sobbing now, and I could see one reason why the Campbells had asked him to deliver the eulogy. The other reason, of course, was that Colonel Fowler had not slept with the deceased, putting him on the short list of potential eulogizers. But I'm being cynical again. Fowler's eulogy was moving, the deceased had suffered a great wrong, a wrongful and untimely death had occurred, and I was feeling like crap again.

Colonel Fowler did not mention specifically how she died, but did say, ''The battlefield, in modern military jargon, is described as a hostile environment, which it most certainly is. And if you expand the meaning of battlefield to include any place where any soldier is standing and serving, then we can truthfully say that Ann died in battle.'' He looked out over the crowd and concluded, ''And it is only proper and fitting that we remember her not as a victim, but as a good soldier who died doing her duty.'' He looked at the casket and said, ''Ann, that's how we'll remember you.'' Colonel Fowler came down from the lectern, stopped at the casket, saluted, then took his seat.

The organ began playing, and the service continued for a few more minutes. Chaplain Eames led the mourners in the Twenty-third Psalm, everyone's favorite, and concluded with a benediction that ended with ''Go in peace.''

The organist played ''Rock of Ages,'' and everyone stood.

All in all a good service, as funeral services go.

The eight honorary pallbearers stood in the front left pew and filed into the aisle at the foot of the casket, while the six casket bearers took up their positions on either side of the casket. I noted that the six casket bearers were all young male lieutenants, picked, perhaps, for their youth and strength, or perhaps for their lack of involvement with the deceased. Even Lieutenant Elby, I noticed, whose intentions had been honorable, had been barred from carrying the casket.

Likewise, the honorary pallbearers, who would normally be high-ranking associates of the general or close personal friends of the deceased, were obviously chosen for their clean hands; they were, in fact, all female officers, including the general's other aide, Captain Bollinger. An all-female contingent of honorary pallbearers seemed appropriate on the surface of it, but for those who understood why senior male officers had been excluded, it seemed that the general had finally gotten his way in keeping his daughter's intimates away from her.

The eight female officers proceeded toward the chapel entrance, and the six casket bearers closed the top half of the lid, covered it with the American flag, grasped the side handles of the casket, and hefted it off the catafalque.

Chaplain Eames walked in front of the casket, and the Campbells in the rear. As is customary when the casket is in motion, everyone in the pews who was in uniform faced the body and saluted.

The chaplain led the procession to the entrance, where the eight honorary pallbearers stood at attention and saluted as the casket passed between them. At this point, the mourners began filing out.

Outside, in the hot sun, I watched as the casket bearers secured the flag-draped casket to the old wooden caisson, which was, in turn, hitched to a humvee.

Assembled on a large stretch of grass across from the chapel were the escort vehicles—staff cars and buses to transport the family, the band, the pallbearers, the firing party, and the color guard. Every veteran has the right to be buried in a national cemetery with full honors, but you only get all this hoopla if you die on active duty. If there's a war on, however, they may bury the numerous dead overseas, or, as in Vietnam, they send them back by the planeload for reshipment to various hometowns. In any case, whether you're a general or a private, you get the twenty-one-gun salute.

People mingled awhile, as people do, speaking to one another, to the chaplain, comforting the Campbells.

I spotted a few of the journalists, who were trying to figure out whom to interview, and I saw the Army PIO photographers discreetly taking pictures from a distance. The news stories to date had been guarded and vague, but hinted at things that I thought were best left alone.

I noticed a young man standing near the Campbells who, as I said, I recognized from the family album as the son, John. But I would have recognized him anyway. He was tall, good-looking, and had the Campbell eyes, hair, and chin.

He looked a bit lost, standing off to the side of the clan, so I went up to him and introduced myself as Warrant Officer Brenner, and said to him, "I'm investigating the circumstances of your sister's death."

He nodded.

We spoke a moment, I passed on my condolences, and we chatted about nothing in particular. He seemed a likable guy, well-spoken, clean-cut, and alert. In many ways, he was what we called officer material; but he had not opted for that role, either because he didn't want to follow in his father's footsteps or because he felt his free spirit might be a hindrance. He may have been right in both cases, but, like many sons of the high and the mighty, he had not found his place in the world.

John strongly resembled his sister in appearance, and my purpose in speaking to him was not solely to express my sympathy. I said to him, "Do you know Colonel William Kent?"

He thought a moment, then replied, "Name sounds familiar. I think I met him at some parties."

"He was a great friend of Ann's, and I'd like you to meet him."

"Sure."

I led him to where Kent was standing on the sidewalk, speaking to a few of his officers, including my recent acquaintance, Major Doyle. I interrupted the conversation and said to Kent, "Colonel Kent, may I introduce Ann's brother, John?"

They shook hands, and John said, "Yes, we did meet a few times. Thank you for coming."

Kent seemed not able to find the words for a reply, but he glanced at me.

I said to John, "Colonel Kent, aside from being a friend of Ann's, has been a great help in the investigation."

John Campbell said to Kent, ''Thank you. I know you're doing all you can.''

Kent nodded.

I excused myself and left them to chat.

One could criticize the appropriateness of introducing the suspected murderer to the brother of the victim at the victim's funeral. But if all's fair in love and war, let me tell you, anything goes in a homicide investigation.

I felt, of course, that Bill Kent was on the edge, and anything I could do to nudge him into taking that last step into the great abyss was right and honorable.

The crowd was thinning as people made their way to their vehicles. I noticed the Yardley boys, father and son, with a woman who looked enough like them to be a blood relative of both, but who was probably Burt's wife—*and* his not-too-distant relative. I suspected that there weren't many branches on the Yardley family tree.

There were a number of other civilians present, including the town mayor and his family, but it was mostly male officers and their wives, though I'm sure some wives chose not to attend. There were no enlisted personnel present except the post's command sergeant major, who, by tradition, represented all the enlisted men and women at certain functions such as these, where privates and sergeants could not be specifically excluded, but where their numbers might present logistical problems. Basically, there is no fraternization between officers and enlisted personnel, in life or in death.

I spotted Karl talking to Major Bowes, the about-to-be-fired CID commander, and Bowes had his heels together, nodding vigorously like a malfunctioning wind-up toy. Karl is not the kind of guy who would fire somebody on Christmas Eve, or at the person's birthday party, or wedding, or anything like that. But he might consider it at a funeral.

Cynthia was speaking to Colonel and Mrs. Fowler and General and Mrs. Campbell, and I gave her credit for that. I always try to avoid that sort of situation, which I find awkward.

Taking stock of the known lovers, I also spotted Colonel Weems, the staff judge advocate, sans wife, and young Lieutenant Elby, who was clearly out of his depth in this situation, trying to look both sad and brave while keeping an eye on the mass of brass around him.

At the edge of the thinning crowd, I saw Warrant Officer Kiefer, dressed in her officer's uniform now, which was the ticket of admission to this event. I went over to her, and I filled her in on the Batmobile. Despite the occasion, she seemed perky as usual, and I suspected that she was always perky. Jerk that I am, and needing some ego reinforcement, I shamelessly flirted with her.

She found this amusing and interesting, and we made indefinite plans to have drinks here, or back at Falls Church.

Cynthia tapped me on the shoulder and said, "We should be going."

"Okay." I said good-bye to Kiefer and walked toward the parking field.

Colonel Hellmann fell in with us, and we ran into Colonel Moore, who was obviously looking for me, a sheaf of typed papers in his hand. I introduced Moore to Hellmann, who did not acknowledge Moore's extended hand and regarded him with a look that I never want to see directed at me.

Colonel Moore, however, was too dense to be flustered, and he said to me, "Here is the report you asked for."

I took it, and following my commanding officer's lead, I didn't thank Moore, but said to him, "Please remain available today, do not speak to the FBI, and do not speak to Colonel Kent."

I got into my Blazer and started it up. Cynthia and Karl got in after the air-conditioning got cranking. We fell in with a long line of vehicles all moving south on Chapel Road, toward Jordan Field. I said to Karl, "I promised Colonel Moore immunity if he cooperated."

Karl, in the rear, said, "You've given more immunity this week than a doctor."

Fuck you, Karl.

Cynthia said, "That was a beautiful service."

Karl asked me, "Are you certain about the chaplain?"

"Yes, sir."

"Does everyone here know about everyone else?"

I replied, "To some extent. She was not discreet."

Cynthia commented, "Do we have to talk about that at this time?"

I said to her, "Our commanding officer is entitled to any information he wants or needs at this time, or any other time."

She looked out the side window and didn't respond.

I glanced at Karl in the rearview mirror and saw that he was a bit taken aback at my curtness. I said to him, "The deceased's West Point ring had been missing throughout the investigation, but I noticed it on her finger."

"Really? Perhaps it's a substitute."

"Could be."

Cynthia glanced at me, but didn't say anything.

We passed Beaumont House, then, later, the Psy-Ops School, then skirted around Bethany Hill and found ourselves on Rifle Range Road.

It was noon, and the sun was so hot I could see heat ripples rising from the blacktop. I said to Colonel Hellmann, "The CID is officially relieved of this case as of now."

"I've gotten us another hour as a result of my presence here, and I can get us another hour more."

Lucky us. "That's good," I replied with zero enthusiasm.

I followed the long line of vehicles onto Jordan Field Road, and we passed the MP booth, where two unfortunate MP corporals were standing in the sun, saluting every car that went by.

More MPs were directing the vehicles to wide expanses of ample parking on the concrete in front of the hangars. I drove around awhile until I saw Kent's staff car parked near hangar three. I parked close to it, and we all got out and followed the crowd to a designated assembly area. The body is usually interred at this point, of course, but in this case, the body was to be flown to Michigan for burial, and the Air Force had generously provided air transportation, a big, olive-drab C-130 that sat on the concrete apron nearby.

As I suspected, people who had not attended the chapel service had come to Jordan Field, including a hundred or so enlisted personnel in uniform, some of the curious from Midland and the surrounding area, plus veterans groups from town, and the remainder of Fort Hadley's four hundred or so officers and spouses.

Everyone was assembled, including the band, the color guard, the firing party, and the honorary pallbearers. The drummer began beating a slow, muffled march, and the six casket bearers appeared from between two hangars wheeling the caisson to a spot near the open tailgate of the C-130. Those in uniform saluted, and those in civilian attire put their right hands over their hearts. The caisson was positioned in the patch of shade under the tail of the C-130. The drumming ceased, and everyone lowered their arms.

It was not only brutally hot, it was windless, and the flags never stirred unless one of the color guard moved the staff. The short ceremony proceeded.

The honorary pallbearers took the edges of the flag that was draped over the casket and held it waist-high over the casket as Chaplain Eames said, "Let us pray." At the conclusion of the committal service, the chaplain intoned, "Grant her eternal rest, O Lord, and let Your perpetual light shine upon her. Amen."

The seven-member firing party raised their rifles and fired three volleys into the air, and as the final volley trailed away, the bugler, stationed near the casket, sounded taps into the quiet air. I like this bugle call, and it is appropriate, I think, that the last call that a soldier hears at night has been chosen to be played over his or her grave to mark the beginning of the last, long sleep, and to remind those assembled that as day follows night, so will the final taps be followed by the great reveille to come.

The pallbearers folded the flag and gave it to Chaplain Eames, who presented it to Mrs. Campbell, who looked very dignified. They spoke a moment as everyone stood motionless.

It must have been the sun, I suppose, as well as the rifle volleys, the bugler, the associations with Fort Hadley and Jordan Field— but whatever it was, my mind went back to the summer of 1971, to the White Camellia Motel, of all places, a swinging spot on the highway outside of Midland, and I recalled a midnight pool party there at which no bathing suits were required. My God, I thought, how young we were, and how we stood that town on its ear— thousands of us full of hormones and alcohol. But we were not your typical carefree, callous youths with no thought of the future. Quite the opposite—the future hung over every thought, every word, every frenzied sexual encounter. Eat, drink, and be merry, we said, because the body bags were piling up at Jordan Field.

I recalled two infantry-school buddies who had been detailed to unload body bags here for a month or so. And one day, they got orders—not to Vietnam, but to Germany—and they kept reading the orders and made everyone else in the barracks read them, as if they had gotten a lawyer's letter telling them they were heirs or titled nobility.

There appeared to be some cause-and-effect relationship between unloading bodies from Vietnam and not becoming one yourself, so, all of a sudden, hundreds of infantrymen were volunteering for the ghoul detail, hoping to get their tickets punched for Germany or some other good place. And so I unloaded bodies at Jordan Field, too, but the assumption that the Army was sensitive to the feelings of body handlers turned out to be untrue; I got my orders saying, "You are hereby ordered to report to Oakland Army Base for further assignment to Southeast Asia." Even the Army didn't use the "V" word.

I came back to the present, which was no less burdensome than the past. I saw the general and Mrs. Campbell speaking to a few people who had come forward, including family, the Fowlers, and the general's aide, Captain Bollinger. The casket, I noted, was gone, and had been carried up the tailgate of the transport plane during my mental absence.

Suddenly, the four turboprops fired and exploded into action, giving off a deafening roar. Then the general saluted those around him, took Mrs. Campbell by the arm as John Campbell took her other arm, and they walked up the inclined tailgate of the aircraft.

For a moment, I thought they were entering the aircraft to say a final good-bye, but then it occurred to me that they had picked this time to leave Fort Hadley for good, and to leave the Army forever. In fact, the tailgate rose up and locked into place. A ground controller signaled the pilots, and the big aircraft moved off the apron onto the taxiway.

Most everyone was surprised, I think, by this sudden departure of the Campbells on the same aircraft that was bearing their daughter's body to Michigan. But on second thought—and it seemed as if everyone had that second thought simultaneously—it was the best thing for the Campbells, for the fort, and for the Army.

Everyone watched as the C-130 lumbered down the runway, picked up speed, then, about four thousand feet from where everyone stood, it rose off the ground, silhouetted first by the tall line of green pines, then by the blue sky. As if that were the signal everyone needed, the crowd broke up, and the color guard, firing party, band, pallbearers, and others marched in formation to the waiting buses.

Vehicles began starting up behind me, and I turned and walked toward them, Cynthia and Karl on either side of me. Cynthia was dabbing at her eyes with a handkerchief. She said to me, "I'm not feeling very well."

I gave her my car keys. "Sit in the air-conditioning awhile. I'll meet you in hangar three when you're up to it."

"No, I'll be all right." She took my arm.

As the three of us walked to the vehicle, Karl said to me, "Paul, I ask that you go in for the kill now. We don't have any time left, and we have no choice."

"It's true that we have no time, but I do have a choice."

"Do I have to make this a direct order?"

"You can't order me to do something that I think is tactically incorrect and may jeopardize the case for the FBI."

"No, I cannot. Do you believe it's incorrect for you to confront Kent at this time?"

"No."

"Then?"

Cynthia said to Karl, "*I'll* confront him." She looked at me. "In the hangar, right?"

I didn't reply.

Karl said to her, "Fine. Mr. Brenner and I will wait in the vehicle for you."

Having shown enough petulance, I grunted, "All right, I'll do it. I'm up to my ass in trouble anyway."

Cynthia motioned up ahead, and I saw Kent, with two junior officers, walking toward his staff car. I said to Cynthia, "Wait ten minutes, then join me."

I came up behind Kent and tapped him on the shoulder.

Kent turned around, and we stood there a second looking at each other. Finally, I said, "Colonel, may I see you alone?"

He hesitated, then replied, "Sure." He dismissed his two subordinates, and we stood there on the hot concrete in front of the hangar as cars began pulling out around us.

I said, "It's hot in the sun. Let's go into this hangar."

We walked side by side, as though we were colleagues, cops on the same mission, and I suppose, when all was said and done, that's what we were.

CHAPTER THIRTY-SIX

Hangar three was slightly cooler than outside and much quieter.

Kent and I walked past Ann Campbell's BMW and continued on toward the area where her home was laid out. I indicated an upholstered chair in her study, and Kent sat.

Cal Seiver, dressed in his class A uniform, had apparently just come from the ceremonies himself. I separated from Kent and took Seiver off to the side, and said to him, "Cal, please clear everyone out of here except Grace. I want her to print out the relevant entries in Captain Campbell's diary." I cocked my head toward Kent. "Then she can leave. Have her leave the disk here."

"Okay."

"Did you hear from the footprint guy in Oakland?"

"Yes. What it comes down to is that he can't say for sure now. But if he *had* to say, he'd say that Colonel Kent's print was made *before* St. John's print."

"Okay. And the paint flecks from the damaged tree?"

"I had the tree section helicoptered to Gillem a few hours ago. They tell me the paint is black in color and tentatively matches the type used by Chrysler for the Jeep model. Where's the Jeep, by the way?"

"It's probably in Colonel Kent's garage. He lives on Bethany

Hill. So why don't you send someone there, photograph the scrape on the Jeep, and scrape off some paint for comparison."

"Can I do that?"

"Why not?"

"I need something in writing from his immediate commander to do that."

"His immediate commander has resigned and just flew off to Michigan. But he told me it's okay to do whatever we have to do. Don't get civilian on me, Cal. This is the Army."

"Right."

"Can you demonstrate to Colonel Kent and me your footprint graphics on the monitor screen?"

"Sure can."

"Good. Kent's print definitely came first."

"Understood." He glanced at Kent sitting in Ann Campbell's study, then said to me, "Is this it? The bust?"

"Could be."

"If you think it's him, go for it."

"Right. And if he slaps the cuffs on *me* and takes me to the lockup, will you visit me?"

"No, I've got to get back to Gillem. But I'll write."

"Thanks. Also, tell the MPs outside to keep the FBI out while I'm in here."

"Done. Good luck." He slapped me on the shoulder and walked off.

I rejoined Kent and sat on the couch. I said to Kent, "We're tying up some loose ends before the FBI gets here."

He nodded, then commented, "I understand that your witness in the arms sales case beat feet."

"You win some, you lose some."

"How about this one?"

"This one's a squeaker. Clock ticking, FBI massing, only one suspect."

"Who's that?"

I stood and took off my jacket, exposing my shoulder holster with the Glock 9mm. Kent did the same, exposing *his* shoulder holster with a .38 Police Special, sort of like show me yours, and I'll show you mine. That out of the way, we sat, loosened our ties, and he asked again, "Who's the suspect?"

"Well, that's what I want to speak to you about. We're waiting for Cynthia."

"Okay."

I looked around the hangar. The remainder of the forensic team were leaving, and I saw Grace at the PC, printing out.

I glanced across the hangar toward the personnel door but did not see Cynthia yet. Despite my current mood regarding her, she deserved to be in on the end, whatever the end was to be. I knew that Karl would distance himself from this—not out of a normal instinct to cover his ass if it went badly, but out of a respect for me and my work. Karl never micro-managed, and he never took credit from the investigators in the field. On the other hand, he didn't deal very well with failure, especially if it was someone else's failure.

Kent said, "I'm glad that's over."

"We all are."

He asked me, "Why did you want me to meet John Campbell?"

"I thought you might like to say something comforting to him."

Kent did not respond to that.

I noticed that the refrigerator in Ann Campbell's kitchen had been plugged into an extension cord, and I walked through the invisible walls, opened the refrigerator, and saw that it was filled with beer and soft drinks. I took three cans of Coors and carried them back into the study, giving one to Kent.

We popped them and drank. Kent said, "You're off the case now. Right?"

"I've been handed a few more hours."

"Lucky you. Do they pay overtime in the CID?"

"Yes, they do. Double time after the first twenty-four hours of each day, triple that on Sundays."

He smiled, then informed me, "I have a pile of work back in my office."

"This won't take long."

He shrugged and finished his beer. I gave him the extra one, and he opened it. He said, "I didn't know that the Campbells were leaving on the aircraft."

"Took me by surprise, too. But it was a smart move."

"He's finished. He could have been the next vice-president, maybe president one day. We were ready for a general again."

"I don't know much about civilian politics." I saw Grace put the printouts and floppy disk on the table beside her. She got up, waved to me, then headed out. Cal went over to the PC and put his footprint graphic program in and began fooling around with it.

Kent asked me, "What are they doing?"

"Trying to figure out who did it."

"Where's the FBI?"

"Probably crowded around the door outside waiting for my clock to run out."

"I don't enjoy working with the FBI," Kent commented. "They don't understand us."

"No, they don't. But none of them slept with the deceased."

The door opened, and Cynthia appeared. She came into the study and exchanged greetings with Kent. I got her an RC Cola from the refrigerator and another beer for Kent. We all sat. Kent, at this point, began to look uneasy.

Cynthia said, "It was very sad. She was young . . . I felt awful for her parents and her brother."

Kent did not respond.

I said to him, "Bill, Cynthia and I have turned up some things that are disturbing us and that we think need some explaining."

He drank more of his beer.

Cynthia said, "First of all, there's this letter." She took the letter from her bag and handed it to Kent.

He read it, or actually didn't read it, since he probably knew it by heart, and handed it back to Cynthia.

She said, "I could see how you'd be disturbed by that. I mean, here was a woman who was giving it out all over post, and the one person who cared for her is the person who she causes trouble for."

435

He seemed a bit more uncomfortable and took a long hit on his beer. Finally he asked, "What makes you think I cared for her?"

Cynthia replied, "Just intuition. I think you cared for her, but she was too self-absorbed and disturbed to respond to your concern and honest feelings for her."

A homicide cop has to speak badly of the dead in front of the suspect, of course. The murderer doesn't want to hear that he killed a paragon of virtue, a child of God, as Colonel Fowler had described Ann Campbell. You don't completely remove the moral question of right and wrong, as Karl suggested; you just cast the question in a different light and suggest to the suspect that what he did was understandable.

But Bill Kent was no idiot, and he saw where this was going, so he said nothing.

Cynthia continued, "We also have her diary entries regarding each and every sexual encounter she had with you."

I added, "They're over there near the computer."

Cynthia went to the computer desk and came back with the printouts. She sat in front of Kent on the coffee table and began reading. The descriptions were, of course, explicit, but not really erotic. They were the sort of thing you'd read in a clinical study; there was no mention of love or emotion, as you'd expect in a diary, just a cataloging of the sex that transpired. Certainly, this was embarrassing to Bill Kent, but it was also an affirmation that Ann Campbell thought no more of him than she did of her vibrator. I could see in his face that he was getting angry, which is the least controllable of human emotions, and the one that invariably leads to self-destruction.

Kent stood and said, "I don't have to listen to this."

I stood also. "I think you should. Please sit down. We really need you here."

He seemed to be deciding whether to stay or go, but it was an act. The most important thing in his life was happening here and now, and, if he left, it would happen without him.

With feigned reluctance, he sat, and I sat.

Cynthia continued reading as if nothing had happened. She found a particularly kinky entry and read, " 'Bill has really gotten into sexual asphyxia now after resisting it for so long. His favorite is putting a noose around his neck and hanging from a spike on the wall while I give him a blow job. But he also likes to tie me to the bed, which he did tonight, and tightening the rope around my neck while he uses the big vibrator on me. He's become good at it, and I have intense and multiple orgasms.' " Cynthia looked up at Kent for a moment, then flipped through the pages.

Kent seemed no longer angry, nor embarrassed, nor uncomfortable. He seemed, in fact, sort of far away, as if he were remembering those better days, or looking into a bad future.

Cynthia read the last entry, the one that Grace had read to us over the phone. " 'Bill is becoming possessive again. I thought we solved that problem. He showed up here tonight when Ted Bowes was here. Ted and I hadn't gone downstairs yet, and Bill and he had a drink in the living room, and Bill was nasty to him and pulled rank on him. Finally, Ted left, and Bill and I had words. He says he's prepared to leave his wife and resign his commission if I promise to live with him or marry him or something. He knows why I do what I do with him and the other men, but he's starting to think there's more to it with us. He's pressing me, and I tell him to stop. Tonight, he doesn't even want sex. He just wants to talk. I let him talk, but I don't like what he's saying. Why do some men think they have to be knights in shining armor? I don't need a knight. I am my own knight, I am my own dragon, and I live in my own castle. Everyone else are props and bit players. Bill is not very cognitive. He doesn't understand, so I don't try to explain. I did tell him I'd consider his offer, but in the meantime, would he only come here with an appointment? This put him into a rage, and he actually slapped me, then ripped off my clothes and raped me on the living room floor. When he was done, he seemed to feel better, then left in a sulk. I realize he could be dangerous, but I don't care, and, in fact, of all of them, he's the only one except for Wes who has actually threatened me or hit me, and it's the only thing that makes Bill Kent interesting.' "

Cynthia put the papers down, and we all sat there. I asked Kent, "You raped her right over there on the living room floor?" I nodded toward the next room.

Kent wasn't answering questions. But he did say, "If your purpose is to humiliate me, you're doing a fine job of it."

I replied, "My purpose, Colonel, is to find out who murdered Ann Campbell, and, not least of all, to find out why."

"Do you think I . . . that I know something I'm not telling?"

"Yes, we think so." I picked up the remote control and turned on the TV and the VCR. Ann Campbell's face came into focus, in the middle of a lecture. I said to Kent, "Do you mind? This woman fascinates me, as I'm sure she fascinated you and others. I need to see her every once in a while. It helps."

Captain Ann Campbell was speaking. "The moral question arises concerning the use of psychology, which is usually a healing science, as a weapon of war." Ann Campbell took the microphone from the lectern and walked toward the camera. She sat on the floor with her legs dangling over the edge of the stage and said, "I can see you guys better now."

I glanced at Kent, who was watching closely, and, if I could judge his feelings by my own, I guessed that he wished she were alive and in this very room so that he could speak to her and touch her.

Ann Campbell continued her talk about the morality of psychological operations, and about the wants, needs, and fears of human beings in general. She said, "Psychology is a soft weapon—it's not a 155mm artillery round, but you can take out more enemy battalions with leaflets and radio broadcasts than with high explosives. You don't have to kill people if you can get them to surrender to your will. It's a lot more satisfying to see an enemy soldier running toward you with his hands on his head, dropping to his knees at your feet, than it is killing him."

I turned off the TV and commented, "She had a certain presence, didn't she, Bill? One of those people who keep your attention visually, verbally, and mentally. I wish I'd known her."

Kent replied, "No, you don't."

"Why not?"

He took a deep breath and replied, "She was . . . evil."

"Evil?"

"Yes . . . she was . . . she was one of those women . . . you don't see many like that . . . a woman whom everyone loves, a woman who seems clean and wholesome and sweet . . . but who has everyone fooled. She really didn't care about anyone or anything. I mean, she seemed like the girl next door on one level—the kind of girl most men want, but her mind was completely sick."

I replied, "We're starting to find that out. Can you fill us in?"

And he did, for the next ten minutes, giving us his impressions of Ann Campbell, which sometimes touched on reality, but often did not. Cynthia got him another beer.

Basically, Bill Kent was drawing up a moral indictment, the way the witch-hunters did three hundred years ago. She was evil, she possessed men's minds, bodies, and souls, she cast spells, she pretended to worship God and tend to her labors by day, but consorted with dark forces at night. He said, "You can see by those videotapes how charming and nice she could be around men, but just read those diary pages—just read that stuff, and you can see what she was really like. I told you she was into Nietzsche—Man and Superman, the Antichrist, and all that sick crap." He took a breath and went on. "I mean, she would go into men's offices at night and perform sexual acts with them, then the next day barely acknowledge they were alive."

And on he went.

Cynthia and I sat and listened and nodded. When a murder suspect speaks badly of the deceased, he's either not the murderer, or he's telling you why he did it.

Kent realized he was going on a bit and toned it down. But I think, sitting there in Ann Campbell's house, so to speak, he was speaking as much to her as to us. Also, I think her image, reinforced by the videotape, was very much on his mind. Cynthia and I were setting the mood for him, and obviously on some level, he knew it.

The four beers helped a bit, which is my answer to the ban on truth drugs. Works almost every time.

I stood and said, "Take a look at this."

We all walked to the far side of the hangar where Cal Seiver sat at the computer. I said to Cal, "Colonel Kent would like to see this display."

"Right." Cal called up a fairly good graphic of the crime scene, including the road, the rifle range, the bleachers, and the pop-up target, but without the spread-eagled body. "Okay," he said, "it's about 0130 hours now, and the victim's humvee pulls up . . ." A top view of a vehicle entered the screen traveling from left to right. "It stops, the victim dismounts." Instead of a profile or top view of a woman, the screen showed only two footprints beside the humvee. "Okay, from the latrines comes Colonel Moore . . ." Yellow footprints appeared on the screen walking from the top, toward the humvee, then stopping. "They talk, she takes off her clothes, including her shoes and socks—we don't see that, of course, but we see now where they leave the road and begin walking out onto the rifle range . . . She's red, he's still yellow . . . side by side . . . We picked up her bare footprints there and there, and we're extrapolating the rest, which are blinking to show the extrapolation. Same with his. Okay?"

I glanced at Kent. "Okay?"

He stared at the screen.

Seiver continued. "Okay, they stop at that pop-up target, and she lies down . . ." A spread-eagled stick figure, in red, appeared on the screen at the base of the target. "We see no more of her footprints, of course, but after Moore ties her up, he leaves, and we can see where he turned and walked back to the road." Seiver added, "Colonel, your dogs picked up his scent in the grass between the road and the latrines."

I commented, "This is the sort of visual display that impresses a court-martial board."

Kent said nothing.

Seiver continued, "Okay, at about 0217 hours, General Campbell shows up in his wife's car."

I looked at Kent, who seemed no more surprised by this revelation than by the revelation that Colonel Moore had met Ann Campbell, staked her out on the ground, and left her.

Seiver continued, "It's a problem getting a general to give you his boots or shoes that he wore to the scene of the crime, but I suspect that he never got more than a few yards from the road and did not approach the body. Okay, they talk, and he leaves in the car."

I said to Colonel Kent, "Are you following this?"

He looked at me, but again said nothing.

Cynthia prodded him. "Colonel, what we're saying is that neither Colonel Moore nor General Campbell killed Ann. This was an elaborate setup, planned with military precision, sort of a psychological trap for the general. She was not meeting a lover out there, as some of us suspected, nor was she jumped by a maniac. She was getting back at her father."

Kent did not ask for an explanation of that, but just stared ahead at the screen.

Cynthia explained, "She had been gang-raped when she was a cadet at West Point, and her father had forced her to remain silent and had conspired with high-ranking men to cover it up. Did you know any of that?"

He looked at Cynthia, but gave no indication that he understood a word of what she was saying.

Cynthia said, "She was re-creating what had happened to her at West Point to shock and humiliate her father."

I didn't think I wanted Kent to know all of that, but in Kent's present state of mind, perhaps it was just as well that he did.

I said to Kent, "Did you think she was out there to act out a sexual fantasy?"

He didn't reply.

I added, "Such as having a series of men come along to rape her?"

Finally, he replied, "Knowing her, a lot of people thought that."

"Yes. We thought that, too, after we found that room in her

441

basement. I guess you thought that, too, when you first saw her out there on the ground. It looked to you like an Ann Campbell script, and it was. But you weren't reading it right.''

No response.

I said to Cal, "Go on."

"Right. So the general leaves, then here we see this set of prints . . . these are your prints, Colonel . . . the blue—''

"No," Kent said, "mine came later. After St. John and my MP, Casey, got there."

"No, sir," Cal replied, "yours came *before* St. John's. See here, we have your print and St. John's print superimposed . . . The plaster cast verifies that St. John stepped on your footprint. So you got there before he did. No doubt about that.''

I added, "In fact, Bill, when you got there, after the general left, Ann was alive. The general went off and got Colonel and Mrs. Fowler, and when they returned to the scene, Ann Campbell was dead.''

Kent stood absolutely motionless.

I said, "Your wife's Jeep Cherokee, with you in it, was spotted by one of your MPs at about 0030 hours, parked in the library lot across from Post Headquarters. You were again spotted," I lied, "driving in the direction of Rifle Range Road. We found where you turned off onto Jordan Field Road and hid the Cherokee in the bush. You left tire marks and hit a tree. We have matched the paint on the tree to your wife's Jeep, and have seen the scrape on the Jeep. Also, we found your footprints,'' I lied again, "in the drainage ditch along Rifle Range Road, heading south, toward the scene of the crime." I added, "Do you want me to reconstruct the entire thing for you?''

He shook his head.

I said, "Given the amount of evidence—including the evidence for motive, which is the diary entries, the letter to your wife, and other evidence of your sexual involvement and obsession with the deceased—given all that, plus this forensic evidence and other evidence, I have to ask you to take a polygraph test, which we are prepared to administer now.''

Actually, we weren't, but now or later it didn't really matter. I said to him, "If you refuse to take the test now, I have no choice but to place you under arrest, and I will get someone in the Pentagon to order you to take the polygraph."

Kent turned away and began walking back toward the layout of Ann Campbell's house. I exchanged glances with Cynthia and Cal, then Cynthia and I followed.

Kent sat on an arm of an upholstered chair in the living room and looked down at the carpet for a while, staring, I suppose, at the spot where he'd raped her on the floor.

I stood in front of him and said, "You know your rights as an accused, of course, and I won't insult you by reading them. But I'm afraid I have to take your weapon and put the cuffs on you."

He glanced up at me, but didn't respond.

I said, "I won't take you to the provost building lockup, because that would be gratuitously humiliating to you. But I am going to take you to the post stockade for processing." I added, "May I have your weapon?"

He knew it was over, of course, but like any trapped animal, he had to have a last growl. He said to me and to Cynthia, "You'll never prove any of this. And when I'm vindicated by a court-martial board of my peers, I'll see to it that you're both brought up on charges of misconduct."

"Yes, sir," I replied. "That is your right. A trial by your peers. And if you are found not guilty, you may well decide to bring charges against us. But the evidence of your sexual misconduct is fairly conclusive. You may beat the murder charge, but you should plan on at least fifteen years in Leavenworth for gross dereliction of duty, misconduct, concealing the facts of a crime, sodomy, rape, and other violations of the punitive articles contained in the Uniform Code of Military Justice."

Kent seemed to process this, then said, "You're not playing very fair, are you?"

"How so?"

"I mean, I voluntarily told you about my involvement with her in order to help find her killer, and here you are charging me with

443

misconduct and sexual crimes and then twisting the other evidence around to try to show that I killed her. You're desperate.''

"Bill, cut the crap.''

"No, *you* cut the crap. For your information, I *was* out there before St. John, and when I got there, she was already dead. If you want to know what I think, I think Fowler and the general did it.''

"Bill, this is not good. Not at all.'' I put my hand on his shoulder and said to him, "Be a man, be an officer and a gentleman—be a cop, for Christ's sake. I shouldn't even be asking you to take a lie-detector test. I should just be asking you to tell me the truth, without me having to use a lie detector, without me having to show you evidence, without me having to spend days in an interrogation room with you. Don't make this embarrassing for any of us.''

He glanced at me, and I could see he was on the verge of crying. He looked at Cynthia to see if she noticed, which was important to him, I think.

I continued, "Bill, we know you did it, you know you did it, and we all know why. There's a lot of extenuating and mitigating circumstances, and we know that. Hell, I can't even stand here and look you in the eye and say to you, 'She didn't deserve that.' '' Actually, I could, because she didn't deserve it, but just as you give a condemned man any last meal he wants, so, too, you give him anything he wants to hear.

Kent fought back the tears and tried to sound angry. He shouted, "She *did* deserve it! She was a bitch, a fucking whore, she ruined my life and my marriage . . .''

"I know. But now you have to make it right. Make it right for the Army, for your family, for the Campbells, and for yourself.''

The tears were running down his cheeks now, and I knew he would rather be dead than be crying in front of me, Cynthia, and Cal Seiver, who was watching from the other side of the hangar. Kent managed to get a few words out and said, "I can't make it right. I can't make it right anymore.''

"Yes, you can. You know you can. You know how you can. Don't fight this. Don't disgrace yourself and everyone else. That's all that's left in your power to do. Just do your duty. Do what an officer and a gentleman would do.''

Kent stood slowly and wiped his eyes and nose with his hands.

I said, ''Please hand me your weapon.''

He looked me in the eye. ''No cuffs, Paul.''

''I'm sorry. I have to. Regulations.''

''I'm an officer, for Christ's sake! You want me to act like an officer, treat me like one!''

''Start acting like one first.'' I called out to Cal, ''Get me a pair of handcuffs.''

Kent pulled the .38 Police Special out of his shoulder holster and shouted, ''Okay! Okay! Watch this!'' He put the revolver to his right temple and pulled the trigger.

CHAPTER THIRTY-SEVEN

The human eye can distinguish fifteen or sixteen shades of gray. A computer image processor, analyzing a fingerprint, can distinguish two hundred fifty-six shades of gray, which is impressive. More impressive, however, is the human heart, mind, and soul, which can distinguish an infinite number of emotional, psychological, and moral shadings, from the blackest of black to the whitest of white. I've never seen either end of that spectrum, but I've seen a lot in between.

In truth, people are no more constant or absolute in their personalities than a chameleon is in terms of color.

The people here at Fort Hadley were no different from, no better or worse than, people I'd seen at a hundred other posts and installations around the world. But Ann Campbell was most certainly different, and I try to imagine myself in conversations with her if I'd met her when she was alive, if, for instance, I'd been assigned to investigate what was going on here at Fort Hadley. I think I would have recognized that I was not in the presence of a simple seductress, but in the presence of a unique, forceful, and driven personality. I think, too, that I could have shown her that whatever hurts other people does not make her stronger, it only increases the misery quotient for everyone.

I don't think I would have wound up like Bill Kent, but I don't discount the possibility, and, therefore, I'm not judging Kent. Kent judged himself, looked at what he had become, was frightened to discover that another personality lurked inside his neat, orderly mind, and he blew it out.

The hangar was filled with MPs now, and FBI men, medical personnel, plus the forensic people who had remained behind at Fort Hadley and who had thought they were almost finished with this place.

I said to Cal Seiver, "After you're done with the body, get the carpet and furniture cleaned up and have all the household goods packed and shipped to the Campbells in Michigan. They'll want their daughter's things."

"Right." He added, "I hate to say this, but he saved everybody but me a lot of trouble."

"He was a good soldier."

I turned and walked the length of the hangar, past an FBI guy who was trying to get my attention, and out the door into the hot sun.

Karl and Cynthia were standing beside an ambulance, talking. I walked past them toward my Blazer. Karl came up to me and said, "I can't say I'm satisfied with this outcome."

I didn't reply.

He said, "Cynthia seems to believe that you knew he was going to do that."

"Karl, all that goes wrong is not my fault."

"No one's blaming you."

"Sounds like it."

"Well, you might have anticipated it and gotten his gun—"

"Colonel, to be perfectly honest with you, not only did I anticipate it, but I encouraged it. I did a fucking head number on him. She knows that and you know that."

He didn't acknowledge this because it was not what he wanted to hear or know. It wasn't in the manual, but, in fact, giving a disgraced officer the opportunity and encouragement to kill himself was historically a time-honored military tradition in many armies of the world but never caught on in this Army and has fallen out of favor nearly everywhere. Yet, the idea, the possibility, permeates the subconscious of every officer corps who are linked by common attitudes and overblown feelings of honor. Given my choice of a court-martial for rape, murder, and sexual misconduct that I knew I couldn't beat, or taking the .38-caliber easy way out, I might just consider the easy way. But I couldn't picture myself in Bill Kent's situation. Then again, neither could Bill Kent a few months ago.

Karl was saying something, but I wasn't listening. Finally, I heard him say, "Cynthia's very upset. She's still shaking."

"Comes with the job." In fact, it's not every day that someone blows his brains out right in front of you. Kent should have excused himself and gone into the men's room to do it. Instead, he splattered his brains, skull, and blood all over the place, and Cynthia caught a little of it on her face. I said to Karl, "I've been splattered in 'Nam." In fact, once I'd gotten hit in the head by a head. I added, helpfully, "It washes off with soap."

Karl looked angry. He snapped, "Mister Brenner, you're not funny."

"May I go?"

"Please do."

I turned and opened my car door, then said to Karl, "Please tell Ms. Sunhill that her husband called this morning, and he wants her to call him back." I got into the Blazer, started it, and drove off.

Within fifteen minutes, I was back at the VOQ. I got out of my uniform, noticing a spot of gore on my shirt. I undressed, washed my face and hands, and changed into a sports coat and slacks, then gathered up my things, which Cynthia had laid out. I gave the room a last look and carried my luggage downstairs.

I checked out, paying a modest charge for maid and linen service, but I had to sign an acknowledgment-of-damage slip regarding my writing on the wall. I'd be billed later. I love the Army. The CQ helped me put the bags in my Blazer. He asked me, "Did you solve the case?"

"Yes."

"Who did it?"

"Everybody." I threw the last bag in the back, closed the hatch, and got in the driver's seat. The CQ asked me, "Is Ms. Sunhill checking out?"

"Don't know."

"Do you want to leave a forwarding address for mail?"

"Nope. No one knows I'm here. Just visiting." I put the Blazer in gear and headed out through main post, north to the MP gate, and out onto Victory Drive.

I drove past Ann Campbell's town-house complex, then reached the interstate and got on the northbound entrance. I put a Willie Nelson tape in the deck, sat back, and drove. I would be in Virginia before dawn, and I could catch a morning military flight out of Andrews Air Force Base. It didn't matter where the flight was going, as long as it was out of the continental United States.

My time in the Army had come to an end, and that was okay. I knew that before I'd even gotten to Fort Hadley. I had no regrets, no hesitation, and no bitterness. We serve to the best of our ability, and if we become incapable of serving, or become redundant, then we leave, or, if we're dense, we're asked to leave. No hard feelings. The mission comes first, and everyone and everything are subordinate to the mission. Says so in the manual.

I suppose I should have said something to Cynthia before I left, but no one was going to benefit from that. Military life is transient, people come and go, and relationships of all kinds, no matter how close and intense, are understood to be temporary. Rather than good-bye, people tend to say, "See you down the road," or "Catch you later."

This time, however, I was leaving for good. In a way, I felt that it was appropriate for me to leave now, to put away my sword and armor, which were getting a little rusty anyway, not to mention heavy. I had entered the service at the height of the cold war, at a time when the Army was engaged in a massive land war in Asia. I had done my duty, and gone beyond my two years of required national service, and had seen two tumultuous decades pass. The

449

nation had changed, the world had changed. The Army was engaged now in a drawdown, which means, "Thanks for everything, good job, we won, please turn out the lights when you leave."

Fine. This was what it was all about, anyway. It was not meant to be a war without end, though it seemed so at times. It was not meant to give employment to men and women who had few career prospects, though it did.

The American flag was being lowered on military installations all over the world, and all over the nation. Combat units were being dissolved, and their battle flags and streamers were being put into storage. Maybe someday they'd close up NATO Headquarters in Brussels. Truly, a new era was dawning, and, truly, I was happy to see it, and happier that I didn't have to deal with it.

My generation, I think, was shaped and molded by events that are no longer relevant, and perhaps, too, our values and opinions are no longer relevant. So, even if we do have a lot of fight left in us, we've become, as Cynthia sort of suggested to me, anachronisms, like old horse cavalry. Good job, thanks, half pay, good luck.

But twenty years is a lot of learning, and a lot of good times. On balance, I wouldn't have done it any differently. It was kind of interesting.

Willie was singing "Georgia on My Mind," and I changed the tape to Buddy Holly.

I like driving, especially away from places, though I suppose if you're driving away from a place, you have to be driving to a place. But I never see it like that. It's always away.

A police car appeared in my rearview mirror, and I checked my speed, but I was only doing ten mph over the limit, which in Georgia means you're obstructing the flow of traffic.

The jerk put his red flasher on and motioned me over. I pulled over to the shoulder and sat in the Blazer.

The officer got out of the police car and came over to my window, which I lowered. I saw that he was a Midland cop, and I remarked, "You're a little far from home, aren't you?"

"License and registration, sir."

I showed him both, and he said, "Sir, we're going to get off at the next exit, come around, and you're going to follow me back to Midland.''

"Why?"

"Don't know. Got it over the radio.''

"From Chief Yardley?''

"His orders, yes, sir.''

"And if I say no?''

"Then I have to take you in cuffs. You pick.''

"Is there a third choice?''

"No, sir.''

"All right.'' I pulled back onto the highway. The cop car stayed behind, we went around the cloverleaf, and I found myself heading south toward Midland.

We got off at an exit near the west edge of town, and I followed him to the town recycling center, which used to be called the dump.

The car stopped at the incinerator, and I stopped behind him and got out.

Burt Yardley was standing near a big conveyor belt, watching a truck being unloaded onto the moving belt.

I stood and watched, too, as Ann Campbell's basement bedroom headed into the flames.

Yardley was flipping through a stack of Polaroid photos and barely gave me a glance, but he said, "Hey, look at this, son. You see that fat ass? That's me. Now look at that teeny weenie. Who you suppose that is?'' He threw a handful of the photos onto the conveyor, then picked up a stack of videotapes at his feet and also threw them onto the belt. "I thought we had an appointment. You gonna make me do all this here work myself? Grab some of that shit, son.''

So I helped him throw furniture, sexual paraphernalia, linens, and such onto the belt. He said, "I'm as good as my word, boy. Didn't trust me, did you?''

"Sure I do. You're a cop.''

"Right. What a fucked-up week. Hey, you know what? I cried all through that funeral.''

"I didn't notice.''

451

"Cryin' on the inside. Lots of fellas there cryin' on the inside. Hey, did you get rid of that computer stuff?"

"I burned the disk myself."

"Yeah? None of that shit floatin' around, is there?"

"No. Everyone is clean again."

"Until next time." He laughed and pitched a black leather mask onto the conveyor. "God bless us, we're all gonna sleep better now. Includin' her."

I didn't reply.

He said, "Hey, sorry to hear about Bill."

"Me, too."

"Maybe them two are talkin' it out now, up there at the pearly gates." He looked into the incinerator. "Or someplace."

"Is that it, Chief?"

He looked around. "Pretty much." He took a photo out of his pocket and looked at it, then handed it to me. "Souvenir."

It was a full frontal nude of Ann Campbell standing, or actually jumping, on the bed in the basement room, her hair billowing, her legs parted, her arms outstretched, and a big smile on her face.

Yardley said, "She was a lot of woman. But I never understood a goddamned thing about her head. You figure her out?"

"No. But I think she told us more about ourselves than we wanted to know." I threw the photo onto the conveyor belt and headed back toward my Blazer.

Yardley called out, "You take care, now."

"You, too, Chief. Regards to your kinfolk."

I opened the car door and Yardley called out again, "Almost forgot. Your lady friend—she told me you'd be headin' north on the interstate."

I looked at him over the roof of my car.

He said, "She asked me to tell you good-bye. Said she'd see you down the road."

"Thanks." I got into the Blazer and drove out of the dump. I turned right and retraced my route to the interstate, along the road lined with warehouses and light industry, a perfectly squalid area to match my mood.

Down the road, a red Mustang fell in behind me. We got onto the interstate together, and she stayed with me past the exit that would have taken her west to Fort Benning.

I pulled off onto the shoulder and she did the same. We got out of our vehicles and stood near them, about ten feet apart. She was wearing blue jeans, a white T-shirt, and running shoes, and it occurred to me that we weren't in the same generation. I said to her, "You missed your exit."

"Better than missing my chance."

"You lied to me."

"Well . . . yes. But what would you have said if I told you I was still living with him, but that I was seriously thinking about ending it?"

"I'd have told you to call me when you got your act together."

"See? You're too passive."

"I don't take other people's wives."

A big semi rolled by, and I couldn't hear what she said. "What?"

"You did the same thing in Brussels!"

"Never heard of the place."

"Capital of Belgium."

"What about Panama?"

"I told Kiefer to tell you that to get you to *do* something."

"You lied again."

"Right. Why do I bother?"

A state trooper pulled over and got out of his car. He touched his hat to Cynthia and asked, "Everything okay, ma'am?"

"No. This man is an idiot."

He looked at me. "What's your problem, fella?"

"She's following me."

He looked back at Cynthia.

Cynthia said to him, "What do you think of a man who spends three days with a woman and doesn't even say good-bye?"

"Well . . . that's mighty low . . ."

"I never touched her. We only shared a bathroom."

"Oh . . . well . . ."

"He invited me to his house in Virginia for the weekend and never bothered to give me his phone number or address."

The state trooper looked at me. "That true?"

I said to him, "I just found out she's still married."

The trooper nodded. "Don't need that kind of trouble."

Cynthia asked him, "Don't you think a man should fight for what he wants?"

"Sure do."

I said, "So does her husband. He tried to kill me."

"Gotta watch that."

"*I'm* not afraid of him," Cynthia said. "I'm going to Benning to tell him it's over."

The trooper said to her, "You be careful, now."

"Make him give me his phone number."

"Well . . . I don't . . ." He turned to me. "Why don't you just give her your phone number and we can all get out of the sun, here."

"Oh, all right. Do you have a pencil?"

He took a pad and pencil out of his pocket, and I told him my phone number and address. He ripped off the page and handed it to Cynthia. "There you are, ma'am. Now, let's everybody get in their cars and go off to where they got to be. Okay?"

I walked back to my Blazer, and Cynthia went to her Mustang. She called out to me, "Saturday."

I waved, got into my Blazer, and headed north. I watched her in my rearview mirror making an illegal U-turn across the center divide, then heading for the exit that would take her to Fort Benning.

Passive? Paul Brenner, the tiger of Falls Church, passive? I crossed into the outside lane, cut the wheel hard left, and drove across the center divide through a line of bushes, then spun the Blazer around into the southbound lanes. "We'll see who's passive."

I caught up with her on the highway to Fort Benning and stayed with her all the way.